Relative Values

Phil Whitney

Completely Novel Edition

Copyright 2015 Phil Whitney

Author's Note

This book is a work of fiction. Although I have tried to stick as closely as possible to historical facts, it is important to note that the Campolargo and Caddick families are products solely of my imagination. Any resemblance they may bear to persons living or dead is completely coincidental.

Acknowledgements

I would like to thank Lucia without whose support bringing this novel to completion would have been much more difficult. I would like to thank my former colleagues and experts on English Language and Literature, Anji Marples and Lynda Taylor for taking the time to read drafts and for making helpful suggestions and comments. Thanks also to my many friends in Italy who have answered many questions and shared their memories with me whilst I was planning and writing the novel particularly to my neighbour in Italy, Alessio di Bene.

~ 2 ~

viciously bullied for not wearing the fascist uniform, and wondered how many of those who were wearing it were doing so because they feared the repercussions if they didn't. While he had been in Turin, where he had picked up some work in a factory during a flu epidemic, he had been told by his fellow workers that people who didn't belong to the party didn't get permanent jobs. The majority of the workers had been sympathetic to the exiled Communist leader, Palmiro Togliatti, but had been careful never to express this when within earshot of the factory owners or managers. Until they had been sure that he was not there as a spy for the management, they had been very wary of discussing anything political with him, and it was only when they were convinced that his then limited Italian was genuine that they had become less guarded with him.

His time in the factory, and the other casual jobs he had picked up since then, had done wonders for his command of the language and, when the cart that had been the cause of the angry horn blowing a few minutes earlier rounded the bend behind him, he had no problem in replying to the cheery salutation of the driver.

'Do you like walking or could you do with a lift?'

'A lift would be wonderful. Thanks.'

The driver, who seemed to be in his late twenties or early thirties, shuffled over to the left of the driver's seat to make room alongside him and he gratefully slung his bag into the back and climbed onto the wooden bench.

'Vai!' he called as he flicked the reins on the back of the strongly built grey horse that was pulling the cart. Then, as the grey slowly recommenced its steady plod, he held out a hand.

'Giorgio,' he said with a smile.

'Max. Pleased to meet you, and many thanks for the lift.'

'I'm not going too far, I'm afraid, but at least I'll get you over this hill.'

Max smiled his thanks and took stock of the driver. He was well built with black hair which, despite being fairly short, still managed to give the impression of being difficult to keep in order. This overlay a broad face where a pair of warm brown eyes flecked with yellow formed the focal point of a series of lines, probably caused by the constant screwing up his eyes to avoid the glare of the sun while working outside, but which, if they had been on the face of an Englishman, would suggest that he spent much of his time smiling.

'You're not from round here,' the Italian said, just the slightest touch of curiosity in his voice as he glanced at the fair-haired, green-eyed young man who sat beside him looking with interest at the landscape around them, clearly full of youthful curiosity and *joie de vivre*.

'No. I'm English,' Max replied, and then continued, 'I want to be an artist one day and, as there is no work in England to keep me there, Italy seemed to be the obvious place to be, to study the work and techniques of most of the best.'

'There have always been plenty of English who have come to Florence,' said Giorgio, 'but there aren't many wandering around the countryside with a pack on their back. They are usually staying in the best hotels in Florence or buying old villas on the hillside below Fiesole.'

Max wasn't sure, but he thought he could detect a trace of bitterness in Giorgio's words and hastened to reassure him; 'I'm not that sort of Englishman, although I must admit that I can understand the attraction of a villa below Fiesole. There's a big difference between the type of Englishman who travels round the great cities of Europe because they've been told that they must see classical culture, and someone like me.'

'And what would someone like you be like?' the Italian asked.

'Not rich, for a start,' said Max, 'and interested in finding out about people and how they live, instead of just learning to value people and objects by how much they cost.' There was a pause after this as Giorgio seemed to reflect on what Max had said, and he was just beginning to wonder if his Italian had been clear enough when his new acquaintance spoke again.

'We'll be at the top in a minute and the horse needs a rest – We'll have a glass of wine before we go on.'

Soon after, Giorgio pulled the cart up in front of a small tavern at the junction of the Via Cassia with a smaller road leading towards the centre of the village. Jumping down from the seat, he led the horse forwards to a drinking trough where he loosened the harness to allow it to dip its head gratefully towards the water which was constantly replenished by a steady flow running out of a spout in the wall behind. Not until the horse's thirst appeared to be quenched did he begin to think about his own needs. Max who was half watching out of the corner of his eye, while he looked at the olive groves that fell down the hillside towards the dense woods on the other side of the road, felt strangely comforted by the clear signs of affection that the man showed his animal. When, finally, the Italian moved the horse and cart forwards into a patch of shade where he hitched a rope to a large iron ring set into the wall, Max said, 'She's lucky to be looked after so well, I've seen lots of humans treated worse, especially in some of the factories.'

'She does well for me and I try to look after her,' said the Italian, patting the horse on its shoulder. 'Come on, let's get that drink,' and he moved towards the open door of the tavern.

'*Sera,*' he said as he entered: a greeting aimed vaguely at four men sitting at the roughly made wooden table, each intent on a hand of cards. One of them, who must have been thirty years younger than the others, looked up briefly and nodded before turning back to the table and throwing a dog-eared jack of spades onto the central pile. As he then shifted in his seat as if he were about to rise, Giorgio put a hand on his shoulder and said, 'Don't get up, I know where the bottle is. If you take your eyes off this lot for a second they'll take every *soldo* you've got!' He then pulled two glasses towards him from a shelf behind the bar and topped them almost to the brim with ruby red wine from a straw covered flask.

He passed one to Max and raising his own glass towards him said, 'Your health,' before putting the glass to his lips and taking a big enough first pull on it to allow himself to swill the wine around the inside of his mouth, enjoying the flavours before swallowing. 'That's better,' he said, 'I needed that,' and he wiped his mouth contentedly with the back of his hand.

Max smiled, half raised his own glass and took a more measured drink from it. Although he'd never tasted wine in England, and hadn't been completely convinced when he'd had his first taste on his way down through France, he was a quick learner and over the past few months he had come to appreciate the subtle flavours imparted by different grapes and was now able to tell a good wine from a poor one. The faintly acidic, fruity nature of the red liquid in his glass reminded him of ripe cherries on rare sunny days in England, and he gave a grunt of approval. 'Hey, Cecco,' said Giorgio to the man he had spoken to before and who had now thrown down his cards in apparent disgust, 'I think my English friend likes your wine; you'll have to put your prices up for the tourists.'

'*Salve,* Giorgio,' said the other man, apparently ignoring his comment, 'Good day's work?'

'Sold everything,' replied Giorgio, but nobody's prepared to pay very much. Most people don't seem to have any money to spare - even though Mussolini and Pavolini keep telling us how wonderfully we're doing.'

'What do you expect?' said Franco, 'People are doing well if they're friends with the right people, and you've always gone out of your way to avoid making friends with the right people.'

Giorgio shrugged and turned back to Max as Franco was dealt another hand by the taciturn elderly card-players who seemed to have run out of arguments for conversation several years before. 'Let's sit outside,' he said, and without waiting for a response, led Max through the open door and sat on a stone bench which seemed to be set into the wall outside.

'How far are you going?'

'I'm hoping to get to Siena today, then I need to find a way of earning a bit of money to get me down to Rome.'

'You'll struggle to get to Siena tonight. We can put you up for the night, if you'll give me a hand loading the cart again in the morning. And, if you need a bit of money and don't mind what sort of person you work for, there's a large farm nearby that's desperate to take someone on at the moment.'

'Why's that, I thought work was scarce here as well?'

'It is, but they'll be picking the grapes very soon and, at the place I'm thinking of, one of the regular workers had a bad accident yesterday. He may lose his leg and, even if he doesn't, he won't be working anytime soon. When the news gets round, there will be people coming out from Florence hoping for a job, but you've got the chance to get in first.'

'Would they take on a foreigner?' asked Max, doubtfully.

'A foreigner has got more of a chance than an Italian who doesn't have the right coloured shirt,' said Giorgio bitterly, 'and there are plenty of us who don't wear the uniform who wouldn't want to work there if there were any alternative.'

Max, looked at Giorgio, whose eyes seemed to be fixed on the horizon but who seemed to be thinking of other things. It was clear from what Giorgio had said that the business was clearly owned by Fascists – but then, most businesses in Italy now were. He wondered what there was that he wasn't being told and decided he needed to find out more before committing himself. 'You don't make it sound very attractive; what do you mean by, "if I don't mind who I work for"?'

Giorgio paused for a second before replying, then shook his head and turned his hands palm upwards in a gesture of resignation. 'Forget it, I've got my reasons for disliking them, and both the owner and his sons are full blown fascists, but it won't really affect you at all if you're just working around the farm for them. If you were Italian, you would need to regularly demonstrate your enthusiasm for the cause but, as you're not, they won't expect that of you.' He smiled again and said, 'Just make sure you don't let them know if you disagree with them.'

'I've seen what happens when the fascists decide to persuade people back in England. Luckily we don't have as many as you and they haven't managed to make much political progress yet but, in some of the big cities, especially London, they turn out in force and use violence whenever there are any demonstrations or protests by the workers. The police pretty much turn a blind-eye to it as the blackshirts do their work for them.' He paused and thought of the horrifying scenes in London that had been described to him, with the police pinning demonstrators back and then standing by as black shirted thugs waded in with crowbars and pieces of wood that his friend had described as cudgels. Most of the newspapers tell people what wonderful things Mussolini is achieving in Italy and want our government to join up with Oswald Mosley, who's taken over from Arnold Leese as the leader of our fascists, so that order can be assured in Britain.'

The way he spat out the word 'order' revealed a depth of bitterness that was clearly at odds with his general open cheery nature, and Giorgio waited a few seconds before clapping a hand on Max's shoulder and squeezing, 'Come on. Let's be on our way. This isn't the best place to discuss these things. We'll talk about them later.'

Chapter 2

Twenty minutes later, Max was unloading the empty crates from the back of the cart, and stacking them neatly at the back of a small but well maintained barn beside a small house at the edge of the hamlet of Bargino. The hamlet was four miles further along the Via Cassia, where the valley broadened out and the road was relatively flat after the descent from San Casciano and before it began to climb again towards Tavarnelle. Having stacked the last of the crates, he stepped outside to where Giorgio was vigorously rubbing down the horse's flanks while it contentedly ate some kind of bran, from a nosebag. He leaned against the wall while he watched Giorgio work, and again admired the care which the Italian showed for the animal.

When Giorgio had finished and the horse appeared to be satiated, he removed the bag, hung it on a nail by the door of the barn and led the horse through a gate into a paddock by the side of the barn where another horse, which seemed heavier and older to Max, was already grazing. The mare whinnied to the older horse and then trotted over to a large stone trough at the far side of the paddock. Only then did Giorgio turn away from the gate he had just carefully closed and face Max.

'Thanks for that,' he said, looking momentarily behind Max into the barn, 'You've saved me a bit of time there. You'd better come and meet my wife.' He walked past Max towards the house, putting a hand on Max's upper arm as he did so, gently propelling him in the same direction.

The door of the house was of heavy chestnut and clearly handmade to snugly fit the rough stone doorway. It was split into two parts with the bottom closed and the top half open, revealing a white-washed corridor leading towards the other side of the house.

'*Amore!*' shouted Giorgio as he reached inside to unlatch the bottom section of the door, 'I'm home... And we've got a guest.'

A toddler appeared and ran towards Giorgio, calling *'Babbo'*.

'Cecco!' said Giorgio, with a playful but proud voice, sweeping the toddler up into his arms and giving it a big kiss, as a woman appeared at the other end of corridor holding a baby in one arm and a wooden spoon in the other. As the light was behind her, Max could not at first distinguish her features until she came closer. She wore a simple light house-dress and a pair of rough, apparently homemade slippers. Her hair, which was evidently long and black, was pulled up in a kind of casual bun behind her, revealing a fairly plain, but homely face which was enlivened by the broad smile that radiated from her as she looked at her husband, who kissed her on the lips and then licked the side of the baby's face. The baby giggled and produced what seemed to Max's ears to be inarticulate sounds.

'I'm Laura,' she said, holding out a hand towards Max, and then withdrawing it quickly, with the start of a blush, as she realised she was still holding the mixing-spoon. I wish he'd tell me when he's bringing someone home, then maybe for once in my life I'll be able to welcome someone properly,' she said, and gave her husband a look that was meant to be reproachful, but which did not manage to hide the affection and pride she felt.

'Max... Pleased to meet you, and I'm sorry for the disturbance,' he said, and she smiled and gave a quick interrogatory glance at her husband.

'It's an English name,' said Giorgio. Max isn't from here; he's a travelling artist.'

Max laughed, 'Your husband flatters me. I love to draw and, very occasionally, I manage to sell something I've done, but I'm not sure that makes me an artist. There are so many beautiful things in Italy that it seemed better to try and scrape a living and travel around here than back in England.'

'Come through,' she said, and turned back and into the room at the other end of the corridor. 'Giorgio, before you take your boots off, go and get me two eggs, a couple of carrots and some beans.'

He found himself in a reasonably large kitchen which clearly also served as the family's living room. One corner of the room appeared to have been fenced off with wooden slats that were carefully wrapped in cloth, and Laura placed the baby inside on to a mat where several simple toys lay waiting to be played with. The toddler sat down just outside the baby's play area and began to pile up some wooden blocks, although Max could feel that he was being closely observed at the same time.

'He's shy, at first. But it won't last long,' said Laura looking at the toddler.

'I really am sorry to put you out,' said Max, 'only Giorgio wouldn't take no for an answer and....' she waved away his protest with a smile.

'I really don't mind,' she said, 'Giorgio loves to talk to people, especially people who've seen other places and done other things... and I love to see him happy … it just does him good to be teased occasionally.'

'She knows how to keep me in my place,' said Giorgio, who was just coming through the door and who had obviously heard the end of the exchange. 'I'm lucky to have her and she likes to remind me of it.'

'I do not,' she said in mock indignation, as she took the vegetables from him and turned towards the wooden chopping board by the stove.

Giorgio gave a pleasant burbling chuckle and dropped down to the floor by the side of the toddler. 'We'll carry on with our discussion later,' he said to Max, at the moment there are two little people here who get bored very quickly with discussions about grown-up matters, especially,' he said, turning to the toddler, 'if they haven't seen their *babbo* all day! Now, Cecco, what are we going to build today?'

'I want *babbo's* friend to build me something,' said the toddler, pointing at Max, who got up from the chair he had been ushered to at one end of the well-worn oak table and, dropped to his knees by the side of the other two.

'Max is from a long way away, from a country called *Inghilterra*,' said Giorgio, 'and I don't know if they have any big buildings there.'

He understood that he was being offered either an escape route, if he didn't want to play with the toddler, or, if he wanted, an opportunity to teach the toddler through play; he was happy to take the second option. 'Oh, we do,' he said, 'not as many beautiful buildings as there are in Italy, but we've got lots of castles, and churches and big factories where people spend all day working hard to make clothes.'

'A castle, please,' Cecco said. And the next hour passed by quickly with first Max trying to make the most realistic castle he could out of the different sized blocks and then Cecco building his own somewhat rougher approximation of a castle. Giorgio divided his time between encouraging Cecco, amusing the baby, which was a girl, and helping Laura in the kitchen. Laura was mainly focussed on using her skills on the ingredients in the pot and made only the occasional comment of encouragement to the others, or of instruction to Giorgio, while she carefully added herbs and seasoning.

'Mmmm,' said Max, when they were finally seated at the table, each of the adults with a steaming bowl of stew before them, 'This is good – *complimenti!*'

'She's a witch really,' said Giorgio, 'she does all sorts of magic in that cauldron over there. There's no other woman can cook like Laura can.'

'Don't you dare let me find out you've been trying out other women's cooking,' said Laura, pointing her knife at him with mock severity.

Max relaxed, he felt good. It had been a long time since he'd been surrounded by a real family, made up of genuine friendly people. It took him back to when he'd been a child, before his parents had both been taken by influenza in the space of a month when he'd been fourteen. His mind went back to that time when it seemed as if nothing could go wrong, and although he'd been aware of poverty, his family hadn't been desperate and he'd even been allowed to stay on at school, instead of looking for labouring jobs or queueing outside the mill each morning to see if they needed anyone that day, as had been the fate of most of the other boys he'd played with as a child.

His father, who had come through the Great War relatively unscathed, having been lucky enough to break both legs in an accident early in his flying training, had always pushed himself to study, insisting that, in the end, brains and knowledge would turn out to be more valuable than money. The desk job that his father had been given after his accident had helped him develop the administrative skills that had ensured he had always been able to find employment, despite the worsening economic situation in the twenties. He had been been pleased as punch when Max had passed his scholarship exam and been able to move from the Board School to the Central School. That same year, 1923, had also been the year when Max's older sister, Ethel, had married Stan Sykes, who had a fairly dull but very secure job in the local branch of the London, City and Midland Bank.

After a difficult start at the Central School when Max had felt that the other boys, who had mainly come from better off families, and had often had extra tuition before starting at the school, were way ahead of him and looked down on him, he had begun to enjoy the work. He soon revealed himself to have a flair for writing and history, and found that he was able to make headway in the Classics much quicker than most of the other boys. Despite his initial unhappiness and feelings of inferiority in the face of his, so-called 'betters', he had come to realise that, given a level playing field, he could more than hold his own with almost all of them, and that money was no way to measure the true value of a person; this realisation had led him to join the Communist Party of Great Britain while still at school. His one regret about his Central School education was that virtually no time was allocated to Arts and Crafts which he had always excelled at, but he spent a lot of his free time sketching and trying to copy any 'real' pictures he was able to get to see, to try and see how the artists had organised their compositions and created subtle effects with their colours. Drawing and painting, attending political meetings, reading voraciously and playing football in the streets with his old Elementary School friends took almost every free hour he had.

His parents' deaths, had left him feeling numb and, although he was lucky enough to be allowed to continue at school by Stan and Ethel, with whom he went to live, the lethargy that he felt meant that he made little progress in the following year at school, and it was only Ethel reminding him of how disappointed their parents would have been if he had given up, that persuaded him to go back again the following September and begin to put in more effort again. Despite the sacrifices that he knew Ethel and Stan made to make sure that he completed school, there was never any possibility of continuing any further with his education after eighteen and, even if it had been possible, he had the uneasy feeling that Ethel and Stan had put off starting a family while he was living with them and, much as his sister obviously loved him, would be relieved to see him start to make his own way in the world.

Despite their protestations that they wanted him to stay, he managed to secure a post as a junior clerk at a mill on the outskirts of Manchester, and lodged with a railway worker and his family in the Ancoats district, where he paid a small amount each week to share a room with their three sons. Like many families living in Ancoats at that time, Rudi and Maria were of Italian origin and, with his flair for languages, it wasn't long before Max was able to join in the family's conversations, although he quickly lost the thread when more than one person was talking at the same time. While Max got on well with the sons, and would often have a beer with the eldest, who was close to his own age, he most enjoyed listening to Rudi talk about Italy, in particular when he described the decorations inside the churches in his native city of Naples. Rudi's father had been a painter and decorator who had also often been persuaded to carry out minor restoration work on some of the paintings in the lesser known Neapolitan churches. This had not earned him any money, but he was regularly assured that he was stocking up credit for his immortal soul. The young Rudi had often accompanied his father as he carried out these restorations and listened in awe as his father had told him the stories of the paintings and talked about how they were made and how to restore them. Although Rudi had had the skills to take over from his father, he had decided that his stomach needed more urgent attention than his immortal soul and had made his way to England where he had found work on the railways and met and married Maria, whose parents had moved over fifteen years earlier. Max had lapped up all that Rudi told him and determined that one day he would go to Italy. After he'd been reported to his bosses for not just attending a meeting at which mill workers were trying to set up a union, but speaking at the meeting and calling on the workers to rise up and rebel against the bosses and the government, it had been made clear to him that, not only was he out of a job, but that no other employer in Lancashire would be prepared to take him on. At that point he'd realised that "one day" may as well be now. He'd said a tearful goodbye to Rudi and his family, sold most of his possessions, sent a letter to Ethel and Stan telling them not to worry, and made his way to the South coast, mainly by hiding on freight trains at night. From there, it had not proved difficult to find a fisherman who, for half the money he had available, was happy to slip him over the Channel.

For most of the meal, Max said little, apart from a few complimentary remarks about the cooking, and was happy just to let the family's friendly conversation and interaction with Cecco and the baby wash over him. At the end of the meal he insisted on doing the washing-up while Laura and Giorgio settled the children down for the night.

'Finally!' said Giorgio, dropping onto the chair next to Max, 'It seems like a lifetime ago that we were talking about the people who control this country and want to control yours.' Max nodded his head, leaving it to the Italian to determine the direction of the conversation. Giorgio seemed happy to have a receptive audience and explained how the fascists had managed to gain control in the years after the Great War, how with Italy at that time being less than a hundred years old, the people had no real loyalty to any of the existing institutions, and how what they wanted most was stability. Mussolini had promised them that stability and had offered them a mirage of national pride. 'In many ways, they control people in the same way as the Church has done for centuries, promising them a glorious future if they are prepared to put up with hardship now. The inner circle, of course, are already living their glorious future and this is seen as a reward for the fervour with which they support the cause. Those who aren't part of the inner circle are made to believe that it's their own fault because they haven't been dedicated enough and only renewed vigour and obedience can give them their rightful place in the new order. Of course, it's all nonsense; regimes like Mussolini's can only exist when there is inequality, and they maintain this by persecuting the only people who really want change and fairness – we communists. Anything which can't be made to look as if it's working well in the country is attributed to communist influences. Big, fancy parades and ceremonies are put on to dazzle the people and large numbers of them believe what they're told and accept what they think they see as reality.' He paused at the end of his bitter description of the way the country was run, and Laura closed her hand over his and leaned against his shoulder.

'You said, "we communists", ' said Max after a while, prompting his host to go on.

'I don't know how much you know about recent Italian history but, before the fascists seized control, Florence was one of the areas with the highest number of people who supported the communists – probably more because it hurt our pride when the capital moved to Rome than for any better reason -but anyway, because of that, the fascist thugs were more violent and out of control in the city than in many other places. They say that even Mussolini was concerned that the Florentine fascists were out of control and endangering the positive image he wanted to construct. If you were known to have spoken against the fascists and didn't have powerful protectors, you were likely to be found lying by the side of the road in the morning, lucky if all you had was a few broken bones. There were a few of the fascists who met similar ends, but our side avoided violence if they could because they knew that the reprisals would be more ferocious. On the fifteenth of May, in twenty-two my father took me along to a big event in the *Casa del Popolo* in Rifredi, just outside the centre of Florence. There was some political talk but mainly eating, singing and dancing as people tried to escape from the hardships of everyday life. All of a sudden, stones came through the windows, the doors burst open and what seemed like hundreds of hooded men with clubs burst through the doors and started laying into everyone they could reach. Some tried to fight back, but they were unarmed and taken by surprise, and most of those who did try to resist were soon on the floor – it was carnage! Most people rushed for the rear doors but found them blocked from the outside then, as fire-brands came crashing through what was left of the windows, the fascist thugs withdrew. There was no sign of the police until half an hour after the last thug had left.

'My father was one of those who tried to fight back; I was at the far end of the room when they came in and, because of the people panicking and rushing the other way, I couldn't get through to help until it was too late to do anything useful. My father had a broken arm, several broken ribs and a skull fracture.

He was never the same again after that: when he spoke, it was only in very short sentences and only about basic everyday things. He hardly left the house for the next three years until he died. Then it turned out that he had fallen behind with the rent over the last few months, so I had to move back out here where my grandparents used to live.'

Max was shocked, he'd known that the fascists used violence to crush any opposition but he hadn't realised that it had been so widespread. After a moment's heavy silence, he tried to relieve the tension by saying, 'I suppose the fact that it's such a beautiful place here is a small compensation.'

Giorgio looked at him for a moment then, disengaging his hand from Laura's stood up and, moving over to the still unshuttered window, beckoned Max to follow him.

He indicated an imposing house that stood about a kilometre up the hillside, surrounded by outbuildings. 'Domenico Campolargo,' he said, 'intimate friend of everyone who matters in and around Florence and stalwart of the Florentine fascists. He and his family live there, own more than half the land you can see, and make life as difficult as they can for everyone else. Remember that red car that went by just before I caught up with you this afternoon?' Max nodded. 'That was his eldest son, Aristide, great friend of Pavolini and a complete bastard. The Campolargos were the landlords who turned us out of the house in Florence, and now, not only do they try and make life difficult for us here, but I have to put up with seeing their house and land every day of my life.' He pulled the shutters together with a bang and moved back to the table.

To Max's surprise, after a while Giorgio gave a little laugh. 'When I said that there was a job going if you didn't mind who you worked for, the job is on the Campolargo estate.'

'I can't work for them,' said Max, 'How could I possibly work for them?'

Giorgio shrugged, 'If you don't take the job, it'll go to some fascist supporter from San Casciano. The job will still get done and fascist money will stay with fascists; you don't need to like someone to work for them.'

'Hmm, I'm not sure; I'll need to sleep on it. Tell me a bit more about the Campolargos.'

'You won't see much of Campolargo himself. He spends a lot of time in Rome, hobnobbing with the people who matter and, where rumour has it, he has at least one mistress. His wife, who everyone refers to as the *contessa*, is a sickly thing and spends most of her time at the thermal baths in Montecatini looking for a miracle cure. She was very ill a few years ago, and the two youngest kids, both girls, were sent away to school and spent most of their holidays with some distant relatives in the Alps.'

Laura, broke in here, 'A friend of mine, Gianna, who does some cleaning up at the house, says that the girls are very different to their older brothers and sister; the elder of the two is a sweet natured thing, who is always pleasant and slipped Gianna a bag of food and clothes for her parents when she heard that her father had lost his job; from what I hear of the younger one, she's fairly wild and argues with the others, unless Aristide is there. She's terrified of Aristide.'

'Aristide and his wife really run the place, although Aristide is backwards and forwards between here and Florence where he's very close to Pavolini, and makes sure that a lot of his dirty work gets done without Pavolini himself having to get his hands dirty. There's a rumour that Pavolini will be moved down to Rome and, hopefully, he'll take Aristide with him. The second son, Filippo, is a fairly brainless oaf who would be nowhere without his father and brother's influence; he lives in a smaller farm that the family owns just beyond Barberino, with his wife and kids. Margarita is married to a lawyer in Siena, who deals with the all the legal affairs of the family and a lot of the other leading local fascists as well; you're unlikely to come across them. Umberto, is a bit brighter than Filippo, but not clever enough to come near to justifying the arrogant way he has of strutting around and giving orders. There's a bit of a gap before the two younger girls as I'm fairly sure there was a child who died. Domenico's wife had some sort of problem after the birth of Maddalena, the youngest, and was sent away to a private hospital in the mountains for a couple of years, until she was relatively normal again.'

'Quite a family,' said Max, 'I thought it was mainly the poorer families who had lots of children these days.'

'The *Contessa's* brother is a Bishop,' said Laura, 'I think she must have taken his sermons about the object of marriage being procreation, a bit too seriously.'

'Or more likely, Domenico is a randy old goat,' added Giorgio.

The conversation became more general over the next hour or so. Max told Giorgio and Laura about his own background. He spoke little of his own experiences of involvement in politics and industrial activities, as he felt it paled into insignificance beside the traumatic experiences of Giorgio, but he spoke with warmth and enthusiasm about Rudi, and how his conversations with Rudi had helped him make the decision to come to Italy, and about the type of drawing and painting he himself wanted to do. He learnt more about the couple, and more about life in Florence and, by the time each went to bed, he had decided that he would try for the job with the Campolargos in the morning, as staying in the area would give him the opportunity to see his new friends again.

All were up early in the morning and, as soon as they had breakfasted on stale bread dipped into milky coffee, he helped Giorgio load his cart up with crates of vegetables to take over to sell in Poggibonsi.

'You've been so kind,' said Max, 'is there anything I can do for you in return?'

Giorgio and Laura protested that the company had been more than enough reward and they would be very disappointed if they didn't see him again. Then Giorgio said, 'Tell you what; next time you come you can draw a picture of Laura for me – she's as fine as any lady whose portrait is in the *Uffizi*.'

Laura of course protested and told him not to be silly, but Max was delighted by the idea and promised to have his sketch-book handy next time he got an opportunity to see them.

Chapter 3

Despite it only being the beginning of October, there was a distinct autumnal feel to the air as Max left Bargino on the unmetalled road leading across the River Pesa and up the hill towards Santa Cristina in Salivolpe. When he had climbed some way, he saw a track on the right hand side which passed through an ornamental gateway and under some trees towards the imposing house he had seen from Giorgio's window. Well tended olive trees lined the hillside to either side of the driveway which was clearly well maintained as the surface showed no sign of the rutting commonly caused by the passage of carts and cars. A curve in the drive and some strategically placed shrubs meant that it was not possible to get a clear view of the front of the house from the start of the driveway. As he reached the curve and came into full view of the house, he would have stopped to take in the view, if he hadn't been faced at a distance of less than twenty yards by a tall, well-built man holding what appeared to be a riding crop in one hand and idly flicking it against the side of his leather-booted calf.

'Buongiorno,' said Max, 'they said in the village that there might be some work here.'

'There might,' said the man, looking him up and down as if he were at a cattle market, 'Who are you and what can you do?'

'I'm English, studying the art of Italy,' said Max, 'but I've worked on farms in England, and I did some casual work in Piemonte on my way South.' What he said wasn't quite true, but having spent three days picking potatoes when he was fifteen meant that it wasn't a complete lie. He thought there couldn't be anything too difficult to do on the Estate and, if he initially struggled with anything, he could always explain it away as being due to the different crops and implements used in the two countries.

The man eyed him appraisingly, taking in the upright way he held himself and the confident look on his face. 'Go and put your pack in that building over there,' the man said. 'I'll give you a trial. If you can do the work you can stay; if you're wasting my time, you'll be gone by the end of the day - without pay.'

Twenty minutes later, Max was swinging a pick at the tangled roots of a cherry tree that had spread too far and were now blocking what was clearly a storm drain. He knew that his shoulders would be aching the following day, not because he found the pick hard to handle, but because he was aware that his shoulder muscles were out of practice for that type of movement. Most of the time, out of the corner of his eye, he could see the man who had set him on, and knew that he was being weighed up carefully. That knowledge meant that he couldn't afford to take any breaks until finally the man called over, 'Hey, *Inglese* – it's time to eat something.'

Gratefully, he put the pick down and slowly rolled his shoulders round a couple of times to flex the muscles as he stood up. He felt his right shoulder creak a little and hoped that he'd be given a different task in the afternoon. He followed the man round to the other side of the house to a shaded terrace where a rough outdoor table had been set up. The table could have seated at least twenty people, although it was clear that less were expected. Some places seemed to have been set with more care than others and Max realised that in good weather, and when there were no important guests, the family must be in the habit of eating together with the workers. At first this surprised him as being unexpectedly democratic, but then, as two more workers arrived and, with a muttered, *'Buon appetito'*, sat down quietly at the table, he realised that the arrangement allowed the family, under an appearance of benevolence, to keep a close eye on the workers at all times and limit any opportunity of talking freely together. The man who had brought Max round announced, to no-one in particular, 'This is English; he'll be working here for a bit, if he gets through the afternoon.' There were nods from the two who were clearly to be his workmates, and appraising looks from the others.

After a minute of what seemed to Max to be an awkward silence, three women emerged from a door at the side of the house, carrying dishes and pots. The first of them was well, although simply, dressed and moved with a decisive business-like manner as she put the dish she was carrying down on the table, at the head of which she then took her place. The woman following her was clearly a servant and, instead of sitting down, moved towards those who Max guessed must be members of the family and began to ladle a pasta dish onto the plates in front of them. He caught his breath as he saw the third woman; she was probably ten years younger than the other two and had wavy, raven hair that she wore loose. He didn't immediately get a good look at her face as the hair swayed forward to curtain it as she leaned over to put a large platter of cheeses, salamis and what appeared to be pickles onto the table.

'Chiara,' said the first woman, 'go and find your sister; she's late again. Tell her, if she's not here in two minutes she'll eat alone in the kitchen.' The girl turned and, as she made her way quickly back the way she had come, Max's eyes followed her and drank in the sinuous nature of her movements. Diana, the hunter, that's who he'd like to paint her as, he thought, and then quickly turned his eyes away before anyone noticed the way they were drinking in her every movement, every sway of the hips and flick of her hair.

In a few seconds the girl was back, with another, slightly younger, girl alongside her. As everyone was watching the two girls approach, he now felt safe to continue his observation, and even smile at the girls, without fear of being noticed by the rest of the family. The girls were very similar, although the younger still showed a few traces of puppy fat and wore her hair slightly longer. Both were smiling as they approached the table, although the elder girl managed to get her face under control as soon as she caught the stern eye of the woman who seemed to be in charge. As they reached the table, the woman at the head of the table stood up, followed by the others around the table. Max was only a fraction of a second behind, realising what must be about to come. 'Umberto, you will say grace for us today,' she said.

The man who had taken Max on, began to speak, and gave thanks for what they were about to receive, although it was hard to tell whether the thanks were aimed more at God or at Mussolini, who appeared to have had a lot to do with putting bread on their table. Max was not a believer but felt it was politic to play lip service and lowered his head along with the others. Although his head was lowered, he kept his eyes open and could see that the younger girl had not lowered her head and made no effort to appear engaged, while the slightly older one had her head bowed but her eyes were open and he guessed that she was no more engaged by the ritual than he was. He also noticed that she was digging the nails of one hand into her napkin as though trying to calm her nerves.

They all sat down as Umberto finished and, the family having been served by the maid, she moved the dishes down to the other end of the table where she sat down with the others who were left to serve themselves. *Penne al pomodoro* were quickly succeeded by spit roasted chicken and rabbit liberally infused with aromatic rosemary and other herbs that Max was unable to identify; a pitcher of young fruity red wine and several of water washed down the meal. There was limited conversation amongst the family as they ate, except for the youngest girl who, he was aware had cast several glances in his direction and made whispered comments to her sister, who he saw trying to repress the urge to laugh. He was unable to observe as closely as he would have liked, as the two other labourers, who seemed to have the particularly Italian skill of being able to carry on conversations while eating at the same time, engaged his attention by asking where he had come from, to which he replied by giving a somewhat edited account of his journey down through France and northern Italy. They showed no curiosity about the aspects of the journey and his experiences that he found most interesting, but seemed mainly interested in the foods he'd eaten and the variations in climate. He soon realised that all that was expected of him was that he confirm the unshakeable belief they had in the superiority of everything to do with their own area and, as this was not a task that he found difficult, he was soon able to ingratiate himself with them.

Although, he had seen many wonderful paintings, buildings, sculptures and landscapes almost everywhere he had been in Italy so far, and could well understand why most people took so much pride in their local area, it always slightly grated with him that they were all absolutely certain of the superiority of their own particular location and seemed unwilling to open their minds to the possibility that other areas could also have merit. One reason, he thought, was because most Italians did not, in his experience, move far away from the place where they were born and brought up; they either stayed put or moved massive distances to make a new life, like Rudi, or the thousands who he knew had gone to America to start anew, never to return. At least listening to their panegyric about the superiority of the sangiovese and trebbiano grapes, Val di Cecina olive oil and local chickens meant that he was able to continue to eat his food for the most part without having to say more than regular '*si*'s and appreciative grunts accompanied by sage nods of the head.

As the last crumb of bread disappeared from the workers' end of the table, Umberto stood and said to one of the men sitting near Max, 'Take English with you. I want everything ready to start getting the grapes in first thing in the morning, baskets by the end of each row and any brambles that might slow us down cleared out of the way... You,' he said, directing himself to Max, 'if Piero tells me before he goes home that you've worked hard, you can stay... at least for now'. Then, without another word to the men he turned and went towards the house. As Max rose from the table, he noticed that the elder of the two girls was looking in his direction. He smiled at her and she looked away quickly, raising a napkin to her face to hide the fact that she was colouring slightly, as if she'd been caught out doing something she shouldn't have been doing.

The work in the afternoon was far easier than it had been in the morning. Max was a quick learner and was soon able to keep up with Piero who could best be described as steady. Even though Piero was clearly not a great thinker, he was willing to talk as he worked and this made time seem to pass much quicker than it had earlier. Piero seemed to have unquestioning loyalty towards the family, for whom it sounded as if his own family had worked for several generations; the fact that he and his wife continued to live in the same very basic house that his parents, and before them his grandparents, had lived in, and had never travelled more than a hundred miles from where he'd been born, didn't seem to concern him at all. Piero told him, with obvious pride, how Aristide occasionally took him with him into Florence if there were any disturbances to be dealt with. 'See these,' he said, holding up his hands, 'they've sorted out plenty of reds who were trying to stop the boss from doing his job properly... cabbage heads'. Max had to hide his revulsion, taking it as read that the 'cabbage heads' were the 'reds' who Piero had been trained to dislike. When Max asked him what exactly Aristide did, Piero was very vague, not, Max thought, because he was trying to be evasive, but because he didn't really understand, just accepting that if the man he was used to taking orders from, and who paid him his wages at the end of every week, did something, then it must be the right thing to do. No wonder, thought Max, that the working class struggles in the cities didn't usually get anywhere; if the workers in the countryside and in the smaller businesses continued to see their oppressors as their benefactors, then there was little hope of change. For as long as the fascists could turn worker against worker, by providing some of them with a piece of bread and glass of wine, then most of their work would be done for them.

Despite Piero's simplicity, however, he picked up quite a few useful bits of information during the afternoon, most of which he filed away in his memory for possible future use, and one important piece that he decided he would ask Giorgio about at the first opportunity.

According to Piero, the grape harvest had been brought forward a couple of days because Aristide insisted that everything must be done and tidied away by the twenty-fifth.

'What's so special about the 25th?' asked Max, genuinely puzzled.

'Because its just before the 27th and important guests are coming; friends of the *Cavaliere*.' Max guessed that by the '*Cavaliere*', he meant Domenico Campolargo, Aristide's father, but other than understanding that, he was still none the wiser.'

'OK. But why the 27th? What's so special about the 27th?'

Piero seemed almost to swell with pride, 'The 27th of October was the start of the new era: the march on Rome, that swept the weak rulers we had before out of the way and made room for *Il Duce* to put everything right in the country; and this year there will be people coming to Florence from all over the world to celebrate.'

'Why Florence?'

Piero looked at Max as if he were stupid. Then said, 'Because of the martyrs, of course!' and he turned back to his work, shaking his head and muttering. Max decided it was wiser not to press him further.

Piero, Attilio, and two other workers, who had spent all day working on a distant part of the Campolargos' estates, went home when the sun started to go down and Max, who had been pronounced as '*un buon lavoratore*', a good worker, by Piero, found himself sharing a simple meal with the maid in the kitchen; a simple meal that improved as various unfinished items were returned from the family's table. Later, Max was shown to a small room with a straw mattress lain on the floor, which looked as if it had previously seen use as a store-room. The maid gave him a pair of flannelette sheets and a blanket before leaving him with, 'My room's at the end of the corridor if you need anything.' He felt that there may have been a half invitation in the words but decided that, even if there had been, it would be far better to ignore it; he could do without complications and wanted to be in Rome by Christmas. Before he went to sleep he doodled in his sketchbook and was surprised to see that what emerged from the almost abstracted pencil strokes was the figure of a dark haired girl leaning over a table. As he realised what he had drawn, he tore the page out and shredded the image, then he rolled over to sleep hoping that if his unconscious could conjure up an image of the girl when he was half awake, it could go much further in his dreams.

For the next two and a half days, the work was hard but satisfying; the sun shone, without being too hot, and everyone seemed to be in a good mood, some of the workers were even singing old peasant songs as they worked. The men worked their ways down rows of glistening purple grapes, each pregnant with the rich goodness of the Tuscan sun. At the end of each row, the wicker baskets were collected by Chiara and her sister-in-law, Virginia, and loaded onto the back of an ox wagon which was then driven by Maddalena to a large barn and emptied. He smiled at the two sisters whenever he got chance and, at one point during the day, by adjusting his pace slightly as he neared the end of a row, without being quite sure why he did it, Max managed to engineer it so that he was putting his basket down just as Chiara was picking up the previous one and their hands touched briefly. 'Let me,' he said cheerfully, taking the basket out of her hands and swinging it onto the back of wagon, and then adding the one he had just put down next to it for good measure.

'*Grazie,*' she said in a soft, slightly husky voice, the effect of which, he was surprised to find, made it feel as if his stomach was dropping down towards his boots. He smiled and, picking up two empty baskets, began to move between the rows to get to the head of the next row, ready to start picking again. It took a lot of willpower to make his way up between the vines without looking back, but he managed it.

'Idiot,' he said to himself. 'You do not want to get involved here; if she's only the slightest bit interested then it can only end in tears.' He spent the rest of the day doing the opposite of what he had been doing up until then and made sure that there were no more opportunities of meeting up. The only times he arrived at the occupied end of a row for the rest of day, they were occupied either by Virginia, Umberto's wife, who though pretty did nothing for him, or Maddalena, who he had the slightly uncomfortable feeling was laughing at him. Even at lunchtime, he managed not to look at Chiara. 'She's probably not the slightest bit interested anyway, and hasn't even thought of looking this way. As far as she's concerned, I'm just another casual labourer passing through, not worthy of a second glance.'

After Aristide told everyone that they had the Sunday afternoon to themselves, progress having been good until that point, Max decided to go down and see Giorgio and Laura. He was careful to take a somewhat circuitous route, as he felt sure that the Campolargos' view of his friends would be no more positive than was Giorgio and Laura's of them. He walked first up the hill towards Santa Cristina in Salivolpe and turned south towards Tavarnelle before cutting back and rejoining the Via Cassia, ten minutes from Bargino.

He had not forgotten his sketchpad, and made a number of quick sketches of his friends as they talked. Laura protested at first, but soon forgot about the sketches and relaxed as they chatted, as Max had known she would. Giorgio was keen to have information about the Campolargo family and Max provided slightly humorous descriptions of all of them except Chiara, exaggerating their characteristics and mannerisms, to make his friends laugh. He was not quite sure why he excluded Chiara from these descriptions and Giorgio did not notice the omission, although he felt sure from the shrewd look that Laura gave him, that she probably understood more than he did. Giorgio shook his head when Max described Piero's attitude towards the Campolargos. 'The Campolargos, and the Antinori on the other side of the valley have controlled every aspect of the lives of families like Piero Caprino's for generations. First they held them under the *mezzadria* system, convincing them that their interests were the same as the landowners; in a bad year, each peasant still had to hand over half his crops and earnings, and were evicted by the bailiff if they didn't, while the rich landowner, still had fifty percent of the earnings of thirty or forty farms coming in and, even if these fluctuated from year to year, still offered a good lifestyle for minimal effort. Now, Campolargo, as an enlightened,' Giorgio laughed without humour, 'landlord has forced out most of the tenants, repurchased the whole of the farms and employs a much lower number of people directly. The people who've gone don't matter – most of them have left the country, so they won't cause any trouble – those who are left are employed directly so they think they have guaranteed income, and the owners, like the Campolargos, have complete power. If anyone steps out of line, they are fired and lose their homes.'

Max waited for Giorgio to calm down, and Laura rocked the baby who seemed to have sensed the anger of her father. 'So, what did Piero mean about the 27th?'

Giorgio sighed and shook his head. 'In fifty years' time, if we've managed to get rid of the fascists, historians will either look back on 27th October 1934 as one of the most shameful days in Florentine history, or it will have been hidden away in a corner and people will be too ashamed to admit it ever happened.' He paused and Max waited for him to go on. 'Hundreds, probably thousands of people have been killed or injured by fascist thugs, who've almost always gone unpunished. Just occasionally, some of the thugs have got caught up in the violence they've started, and ended up being killed themselves; even more rarely, people have managed to isolate thugs and deal with them when the law won't.' He paused again. 'People have short memories and now the thugs who died while they were causing havoc before the fascists got control, are going to be represented to us as fascist martyrs... If you've ever seen one of the big church ceremonies, intended to impress the credulous, think ten times as big and a hundred times as expensive, and you'll be pretty close to what's going to happen in Florence on the 27th. The thirty-seven Florentine Fascist Martyrs. They're going to be disinterred, paraded around Florence, and then reburied in a chapel that's being built specially for them under Santa Croce. The fascists will think it's wonderful; the impressionable will be impressed, and anyone with any sense will keep well out of the way, or at least keep quiet on the day.'

'Why didn't I hear about this while I was in Florence?' asked Max.

'The intention is that the scale of it will be even more effective if most people are taken by surprise. The events commemorating the fascist takeover seem to get bigger and bigger every year, as the cult of Mussolini grows and grows, so most people haven't really paid much attention to what the fascists are planning. Those of us who actively oppose the fascists...' At this point Laura looked up in alarm and put a hand on her husband's arm.

'Giorgio.'

'Don't fret, love. I can trust Max. Those of us who are opposing the fascists have known about it for some time. We had considered a small explosion in the chapel in the run-up to the 27th, to make them cancel but, partly because the Catholics in the group were against this, and partly because a few of us argued that the fascists would just find a way of using the publicity, that they would control, as another weapon against us, we decided to let it go. What will happen, is that while almost all the fascists are there, there will be slogans put up in as many other places as possible.'

'Phew,' said Max. 'That's a lot to take in. I suppose the Campolargos and all their employees will be expected to be there.'

'Not all,' said Giorgio, there will be some muscle, as well as someone with half a brain, left here to look after the house. They're not stupid and know that we're likely to do something while they're otherwise engaged.'

'What are you planning?' asked Max.

'Nothing against the Campolargos, much as we'd like to. They control the lives of too many people round here and any reprisals that were planned by Aristide and led by Umberto would be vicious.' He paused, 'They won't take you with them: you haven't got a black shirt and, at this stage are not likely to be fully trusted.'

'Is there anything I can do to help?' Said Max.

Giorgio shook his head, 'Just let me know of anything you hear that could be useful, and make sure that no-one up at the Campolargos' knows that you are in contact with us. There's a little shop in Santa Cristina, if you need to let us know anything, leave a message there and say it's for Cecco,' he said, glancing down at his son who was happily building another castle.

Chapter 4

That evening, being Sunday, all the members of the family who were at the house, including Filippo and his wife, Carmela, but excluding the smaller children, sat down to eat together. Max was surprised, on his return, to be told by the maid, that he was to eat with them. He ate quietly, feeling grateful that his parents had always insisted on good table manners, only said 'please' and 'thank you' where appropriate and did not attempt to engage anyone in conversation; other than when he was asked whether he wanted different dishes, he was not addressed by anyone else until the food was finished. Neither Chiara nor Maddalena seemed to look in his direction at all during the meal, and Maddalena seemed unusually quiet in the presence of her eldest brother.

Finally, Aristide looked at him directly and, in heavily accented English said, 'How you are educated?'

Max paused, not being entirely sure whether to respond in English, which Aristide might not understand, or to respond in Italian, which might make it seem as if he were not impressed by Aristide's English. Eventually, he decided that the lesser of the two evils was to reply with a fairly simple English phrase and see where things went from there. 'To quite a high level,' he said.

To Max's relief, Aristide continued in Italian, 'We are to have the honour to receive three of the leaders of your Imperial Fascist League as our guests in just over two weeks' time. It is some time since I used my English and it is a little, how do you say, 'rasty'. You will converse with my wife and I every evening, so that we improve and are ready for the visit.' Having little choice in the matter, Max bowed his head to indicate assent.

He was not looking forward to the experience, as the things that he himself would have liked to say to members of the Imperial Fascist League were certainly not the type of things that Aristide would be prepared for him to say although, he reflected, as they almost certainly shared many of the same ideals as him, he would also benefit from hearing a few home truths. The dislike he already felt for Aristide grew as his association with the IFL made it easier to overcome the impression of a dedicated family man, which had, up until then, blurred slightly what he knew should be his feelings given what he had learnt from Giorgio. While Filippo and Umberto were clearly nasty pieces of work, without the brains to put on a front, Aristide mainly came across as a stern but urbane figure, with a presence that made overt aggression unnecessary. Max was nervous but realised that if he were careful he might just get some information that would be useful to Giorgio and his associates.

Before they left the table, Aristide told him that they would begin the following evening and Max, with a sudden flash of inspiration, asked if Aristide could have a newspaper with him. Aristide raised an eyebrow, then lowered it as Max explained that, as his guests would probably want to know more about the current situation in Italy, practising talking about what was reported in the papers would be a good starting point. It would also, he thought, allow him to get a better understanding of the warped way in which the fascists not only viewed events but also how they wished to present them to others.

Max took his sketchbook and made his way up the hill towards Santa Cristina where he made a couple of sketches of the imposing buildings of Montefiridolfi across the valley, partly for pleasure and partly so that he could explain his excursion if challenged on his return.

Once he began drawing, time slipped past without him noticing and it was only when he realised that he could no longer pick out details as the light began to fade rapidly that his mind returned to the real reason he was there. He closed his pad, put the pencils in his pocket and made his way towards the centre of the hamlet where he hoped the little shop would still be open. Lights were gradually beginning to glow dimly from the various windows in the houses, as he looked round remembering that in small places like this a little shop would just be a room in someone's house. As he wondered whether he should knock on a door and ask, he saw a tall, white-haired priest coming down the unmetalled road towards him and stepped out to greet him. 'Buonasera Padre. Could you tell me if there is anywhere in the village that I could buy some tobacco?' Not that he smoked but he could think of nothing else that he could reasonably wish to purchase at that time of day.

'The fourth house on the right is a *bottega*,' said the priest, 'the door will be closed now and they'll be in the back, but stick your head in and give them a shout.' Max thanked him, noticing that the priest had used the second person *'voi'*, favoured by the fascists, when addressing him. Perhaps not surprising he thought, as most appointments in the valley would be made with the tacit approval of either, or both, of the Campolargos and the Antinori, and he knew that Niccolo Antinori had recently been appointed by the fascists as their *'Federale'* in Scandicci. He made his way to the door that had been indicated to him as the priest continued down the street in the other direction.

As the priest had said, the door to the *bottega* was closed but unlocked. He pushed one side of the chestnut door open, stuck his head in and called out, 'Hello. Anyone there.' He heard the sound of pans clanking and then a wheezy, elderly sounding female voice called out, *'Momento,'* and he heard shuffling footsteps approaching him.

A wizened old woman with thinning white hair and a pronounced stoop entered the room, muttering under her breath as she did, and, seeing that it was not one of the locals, asked him rather ungraciously what he wanted and then, before he had time to reply, whether he knew what time it was. A little disconcerted, he replied that he had to leave a note for Cecco. The woman seemed to straighten slightly and the expression on her face became noticeably softer, 'Aah,' she said, 'You must be Giorgio's young English friend; Laura said that I was likely to see you soon.' She held her hand out to take the note and asked if anyone had seen him come to the *bottega*.

'I had to ask a priest where I could get some tobacco, as I wasn't sure where the bottega was,' he said.

'Then you'd better take some tobacco with you. Don Marco will mention having seen you and what you were doing; if you don't have any, it will look suspicious. He's a fascist first and a priest second, and in both of them he likes poking his nose into other people's business.' She got down a box off a shelf and wrapped up a small amount of tobacco in some paper. 'Off you go now, you'd better be getting back before they start to get suspicious.'

He left the shop with the tobacco, and began to walk quickly down the road towards the Campolargo estate wondering what he was going to do with the tobacco.

The next morning, he slipped the tobacco in his pocket and mid-way through the morning, when there was a short break for the workers to restore their strength with bread, cheese and wine, he pulled it out as he sat on the short spiky grass with Piero and Simone, the other hired hand. 'Don't get yours out. I bought you this to say thanks for all the help you've given me settling in. It can't be easy having to work with a novice,' He knew this wasn't true. Being younger and fitter than they were, after the first couple of hours on the first day of the grape harvest when he had been learning to use the cutters effectively, he knew he had been at least as productive as they had. However, he knew that that they would take what he said at face value and thought that there was no harm in gaining their positive opinion.

Midway through the afternoon, Elisabetta, Aristide's wife, came out and told Max to put down his equipment, wash himself and come to the house as soon as possible, as her husband had to go out later and wished to see him earlier than had been arranged.

Aristide was sitting behind a large, polished-oak desk, in a room that Max had not previously been aware of, next to the dining room. Full length windows opened onto a balustraded balcony behind the desk, and Max realised that the room enjoyed what was probably the best view on the first floor. Two of the walls were lined with bookshelves, full of bound volumes and bundles of paper; to either side of the full length windows were formal portraits of two men, each dressed in uniform, although clearly of different periods. One, who was dressed in what Max guessed to be an Italian officer's uniform from the Great War, appeared to be in his late fifties in the portrait but bore a clear family resemblance to Aristide; the other wore an older and more ornate uniform that Max did not recognise although the background indicated quite clearly that it must be a cavalry officer's uniform. The background to the more modern picture appeared to be mountainous, although Max was not impressed by the artist's skill as a landscapist. Above the windows, an old dark-wooden crucifix bearing a twisted Christ figure with some of its gilt peeled off, gazed down over the room. Facing the windows was the door through which Max had been bidden to enter; here, the doorway was framed with a stone arch in *pietra serena* sandstone, the apex of which pointed upwards to a picture of Mussolini, clearly facing a crowd, with his arm raised in the fascist salute. To either side of the door were two modern paintings which Max instantly recognised as products of the futurist movement; he was surprised by the two modern paintings as he would not have guessed that Aristide had a great deal of artistic sensibility; probably, he thought, the futurist works must have been the choice of his father, whom he had yet to meet.

Aristide pushed a newspaper towards Max. Max left the paper where it was and said that if the guests came into that room, they would probably want to be polite and show an interest about what was around them, before moving onto public affairs. He said that it was a beautiful room and asked Aristide to tell him about it, beginning with the picture of Mussolini.

Aristide's English was better than basic but he was clearly not used to speaking it at any length. Whenever his meaning was not clear, Max asked him to explain in fairly simple Italian, and then reworded what he had said in English, telling Aristide about the objects he had tried to describe, breaking the information down into small chunks and asking frequent questions so that Aristide himself had to use the terms and phrases he had just heard. In asking about the room, Max deliberately left until last the two objects which interested him the most, and it appeared almost as an afterthought when he asked about the two futurist paintings.

He was surprised to see Aristide swell with pride. 'These paintings were given to me personally by Pavolini as a reward for the work I've done for the party in Florence. He's a great fascist and may, one day in the future, be our leader.' It was clear that there would be other occasions to find out more about Pavolini, and Max tried to move the conversation back to the paintings. He was disappointed, but not surprised, to find that other than knowing that they were by the Tuscan artist Gino Severini, Aristide appeared to know little about them, nor did he seem particularly interested. To him the value of the paintings lay in their having been presents from his mentor, Pavolini. They had been there for almost an hour and a half before Max picked up the paper, glanced at the first article, which was about Mussolini reviewing a military base, and began to ask questions. After a few minutes, however, Aristide looked at his watch and brought the session to an end by folding up the newspaper and standing. Max understood that he had been dismissed.

As it was too late to make it worth changing and going back out to work, he decided to take the opportunity to take his sketchbook again and try to develop some of the ideas in there. He went outside and, finding a spot that was sheltered from the house by a small outbuilding, opened the book and flicked through until he came to the sketches he had made during his last visit to see Giorgio and Laura. He found a new sheet and, with the other sketches spread out before him, he began to turn the rough sketches into a portrait. He already had an idea of the composition and quickly put the outlines down. He intended to put Giorgio in the background, behind his wife, but concentrated on Laura first, very faintly pencilling in the outline of the head and roughly dividing it into eight so that he could ensure that all the main features were perfectly placed. This preliminary phase was second nature and took little more than a minute before he turned his attention to capturing Laura's eyes.

He knew he was good at eyes and it was not long before he was reasonably happy with them and moved onto the other features, knowing that he only had time to sketch them in lightly before going back into the house to eat.

He was pleased with what he had achieved so far and he looked forward to giving the drawing to his friends when it was completed, and his mind was a kilometre down the hill as he gathered his preliminary sketches together so that he could take them inside and place them under his mattress where, not only would they be out but sight but where they would also be kept flat. A voice from behind startled him out of his self-congratulatory reverie.

'I wish I could draw like that; you're very good... She lives down in the village doesn't she?'

'I think she must do. I just happened to see her with some children the other day and the idea of a picture came into my mind,' he lied, and was alarmed to feel his face flush and worried that he must be blushing. It was not just that what he had said, to his own ears, didn't sound entirely plausible, or that he was worried that his link to Giorgio and Laura might come out, it was more that it felt very wrong for his first meaningful exchange with Chiara to be based on a lie. This was not what he wanted; he felt an urge to tell her the truth but managed to dominate it. 'I like to sketch and, if I see something that I think would make a good picture, I try to get something down on paper as soon as possible,' he said, moving to a general truth and hoping that the conversation did not revert to the picture of Laura.

Chiara smiled, 'It must be wonderful to have a talent for something that you enjoy. I'd like to see your drawings but we need to go in to eat now. Could I look at them later – I'd like that very much?'

'Of course,' he said, with a smile which he was amazed he was able to produce as he thought he felt his heart miss a beat, 'although I'm sure you've seen a lot better'. She gave him a smile and turned towards the house. Tongue-tied, he watched her go and then made his way back to his room to leave his things. As he walked, he was surprised to find that he couldn't feel the ground and he felt as if something were swelling in his chest.

He was back to eating in the kitchen with Adele, the maid, this evening. A circumstance which he was very pleased about as he was sure that if he had been asked to eat with the family again just then, he would have said something inappropriate or not been able to take his eyes off Chiara. She would have thought he was an imbecile and the rest of the family would have made sure that he never had another chance to be alone with her, and he would almost certainly have been made to leave. It was difficult to understand what was happening, he was sure that he had never felt like this before. Was it sexual desire? Well obviously that had to be a part of it, but it seemed to be much more than that; he wanted her to like him, to trust him, to talk to him and surprisingly he felt a desire to protect her from anything that could possibly hurt her. It was impossible, not only did they hardly know each other but he was effectively a penniless young artist who would probably never be good enough to make a living from it, while she was the daughter of an important family for whom he felt a strong dislike and who probably already had her future mapped out for her.

'What's wrong with you this evening?' said Adele, 'Kitchen food not good enough for you now you're used to eating upstairs?'

He smiled at her, and glanced down at his plate, realising that, as he thought about Chiara, he had done little more than push his food around his plate.

'Sorry, Adele,' I was miles away, thinking about my family back in England.' Lying to Adele was far easier than lying to

Chiara, and he hoped that by introducing a new subject he would be able to stop thinking about Chiara – at least for now.

'Any brothers with eyes as nice as yours?' she asked, with clear flirtatious intent.

'No, but I'm sure you'd like my sister, Ethel,' he said, choosing to appear not to have understood the meaning underlying Adele's words. He was aware that the veiled invitation that had been issued on his first day at the house was almost certainly still open and, for a moment, wondered whether accepting it might be the best way to take his mind off Chiara. Then, feeling disappointed with himself, he rejected the idea; while he was in the same house, country? universe? as Chiara, he couldn't imagine being able be with any other woman; and besides, he had come to like Adele in the few days he'd been there, and didn't like the thought of using her – she deserved better.

'How about you?' he said, 'Got much family?'

'Five brothers and four sisters,' she said, '...there was another brother, but Ido died at Caporetto,' he was surprised to note that she put her finger on the corner of her eye as if to suppress a tear that threatened to reveal more than she wished to show.

'Were you close to Ido?' he asked, knowing that he probably shouldn't pry if talking about him upset her, but wanting to fix his mind on something other than Chiara.

'Not really,' she smiled, 'but Ido wasn't the only person at Caporetto. If it wasn't for the Austrians, I would now be Signora Rossi with lots of happy children of my own. My fiancé was – is – wonderful, but he came away from Caporetto with no legs, and when he recovered he said he wouldn't marry me because it wasn't fair on me.' She talked for a long time about Luigi, her former fiancé, clearly glad of someone new to talk to, who showed sympathy and who didn't look bored because they'd heard the story too many times before. She told him how Luigi, had a small pension for the war wounded and how he was looked after by his now fairly aged mother at the family home in Barberino. Adele had never wanted to marry anyone else and went to see Luigi and his mother every time she had a half-day off; she also gave Luigi's mother a part of her wages to help boost the meagre pension. Working as a live-in-maid meant that she could do that, as although her wage was not high, she had nothing she needed to spend it on, once she had clothed herself.

Once he had helped her clear up in the kitchen and prepare things for the following morning, they parted as friends as each went to their room, but the sexual tension that had been in the air had dissipated, and he no longer felt that she would feel rejected if he didn't find his way to her room.

Lying on his straw filled mattress, he let his thoughts drift back to Chiara, without trying to erect any further defences. He tried to put some order to all he knew of her, remembering what Laura had said when she was first mentioned, thinking about his first sight of her bringing the platter of cheese, salami and *giardiniera*, as he had now learnt that the pickles were called, to the table; thinking about their only conversation when she had found him drawing and, more than anything else, thinking of the touch of her flesh as their hands had touched in the vineyard. He had made sure that he reached the bottom of the row just as she was there loading the cart, but had he been responsible for their hands touching, or could that possibly have been her? Surely it couldn't have been; looking as she did, and with the connections she had, she must have the pick of Florentine society and, if by some miracle she was interested in him, what hope did he have? Her family would never allow anything between them. After tossing and turning for a long time, he finally drifted off into a dream filled sleep where Mussolini's clenched fist formed an insurmountable obstacle between him and a vision of two Chiaras populating a version of Titian's *Sacred and Profane Love*.

When he was woken by Adele in the morning, he felt hot and sweaty and, until he had doused himself in cold water, did not feel at all restored by the sleeping process.

The maid smiled at him as he sat down in the kitchen to spoon blackberry jam onto a large piece of rustic bread. 'Thank you for listening last night, it made me feel a lot better having someone listen to me and ...' she paused and then rushed on, 'thank you for not trying to comfort me in any other way.'

He returned her smile, 'It's nothing personal, it's just that I think I'm in love with someone else and ...' he shrugged, 'You know how it is... *Vergine, s'a mercede miseria extrema de l'umane cose già mai ti volse, al mio prego t'inchina, soccori a la mia guerra'*.

'What are you on about?' she said with a puzzled look on her face.

'Don't worry', he laughed, 'it's medieval Italian. I think I'm starting to understand Petrarch!' and he left the kitchen while she shook her head, perplexed.

Shortly after work with the vines recommenced, he saw Aristide's car sweep down the drive way with one of the girls sitting next to him. He was too far away to tell which of the girls it was, especially with the reflection of the clouds on the car's windows, but hoped that it was Maddalena who was being taken somewhere by her brother. When the rest of the women came out to remove and transport the heaving baskets of grapes, he felt a surge of disappointment as he saw that Maddalena was there and that it was her sister who was missing. Maddalena took her sister's place helping Virginia to empty the full baskets into the cart which was now driven by Elisabetta.

When, just by chance, he found himself next to Maddalena, she turned to him with laughing eyes and surprised him by saying, in English, 'Good morning, *Inglese*. There is no sun in your sky today,' then she looked innocently up at the cloud filled sky and turned away from him back to the cart. He puzzled over her words as he continued to move up and down the seemingly endless rows of grapes – had her comment been completely innocent, just slightly clumsily phrased, born out of a desire to show off her ability to speak the foreign language or, as he feared, had she meant the phrase to carry more meaning than that? Was 'his sun' meant to be Chiara, and if so, what did Maddalena know, or what had she guessed? Was it just a lucky stab in the dark, or had Chiara said something to her that indicated she had some feelings for him? He felt almost dizzy thinking about the possibilities that this latter option seemed to offer.

He felt he had to know, and tried to engineer another 'chance' meeting, but fate seemed to conspire to make sure that the opportunity did not present itself for the rest of the morning.

Midway through the afternoon, he saw the car reappear, and shortly after his heart leapt as the cart returned from one of its trips to the barn driven by Chiara and no longer by her sister-in-law. She did not, however, swap places with Maddalena, so he had no opportunity to exchange even the quickest of words with her.

As soon as he had eaten in the evening, he was called through to the study where Aristide and Elisabetta awaited him. This afternoon he greeted them politely in English, which allowed him to gain at least an initial impression of Elisabetta's fairly limited command of the language, and then passed on to the newspaper that lay on the desk in front of them. The front page was mainly given over to accounts of the assassinations of the Greek king and the French foreign minister in Marseilles, which it appeared had happened three days earlier and was still front page news. Max cast his eye quickly over the paper so that he knew what was happening, and then asked Aristide what had happened in Marseilles. Over the next half an hour, they went over the details of the article, at first with Max asking short questions and then with Aristide being able to give a short but reasonably effective summary himself.

'And what will this mean for Italy?' asked Max.

'For Italy?' said Aristide, clearly not having understood the implications of the question.

'Yes. Does the Italian government worry that your own King or politicians could be in danger?'

'In Italy, that could never happen.'

'The people love the king and our great leader, Mussolini,' added Elisabetta haughtily.

'But it has happened before, hasn't it?' said Max. 'What about Umberto the First?'

'Umberto was too good. He tried to help the people and he was then shot by an American socialist. Our country has learnt a lesson.'

'What lesson is that?' asked Max, aware that he was on treacherous ground and maybe needed to think about strategic withdrawal from the subject.

'*Credere, obbedire, combattere,*' said Aristide in Italian, puffing out his chest, and then in English, 'Believe, obey, fight – all Italians now have, what do you English call it - a bone in the back? There are not much socialists in Italy. Those who we find will be removed.'

'Backbone,' said Max, 'we call it backbone.' He was amazed that he was able to keep his voice calm after he had seen the mask momentarily slip from Aristide's fanaticism.

'What will happen in Greece?'

'In Greece they will have a new king, or the military will take over. It does not matter. Greece is weak and will always need Italian help.'

'Let's look inside the paper and see what articles there are about Italy.' He leafed through the pages and then turned back to a report of Mussolini attending an army parade. 'I can see very little about what is happening in Italy; are there no crimes in the country?'

'The people of Italy are hard-working and peaceful,' said Elisabetta, clearly parroting a party line that she had learnt.

'There are a few crimes committed by socialists, but they are dealt with. The people do not need to read about things that may upset them, so the newspapers choose to write about more uplifting events.'

'Choose?' said Max, who couldn't help himself. 'Are they free to write about whatever they like?'

'Our newspapers have complete freedom to write about anything. When they are printed, a copy is reviewed because the authorities' duty is to protect the public against moral corruption. If there is a mistake then the newspaper will not be sold. The next day they are free to write about whatever they want again.'

Max could imagine how that freedom must work. How many

publications could afford to have a complete print-run pulped? They would bend over backwards to avoid including anything that might upset the regime.

'What else should we talk about?' asked Max, keen to move back onto safer ground. Perhaps the Signora would like to suggest a topic.' Elisabetta chose an article extolling the virtues of focussed exercise for children and showing how being junior *balillas*, which Max imagined to be pretty much Italy's version of the scouting movement, would turn them into fine young adults of whom the motherland could be proud. Although, full of fairly obvious exaggerations, or at least so Max considered, this was much safer ground and the rest of the session passed off without any friction.

Over the next few days the sessions continued along similar lines, although Max managed to avoid getting into discussions where he risked revealing to Aristide that, not only was he fairly well versed in politics, but on most things their views were diametrically opposed. Aristide was fairly competent once he became used to speaking again and Max learnt that he had spent six months in London some years earlier, attached to the Italian Embassy. Elisabetta offered more of a challenge as her English had been learnt as a child, from an old English governess whose language must have been rooted in the English of the mid-nineteenth century rather than the present day.

One evening, when the session was cancelled as Aristide had not returned from Florence, Max took up his sketch-book and made his way to the spot where Chiara had previously come across him. This time she was there before him, sitting on a macintosh square on the grass leaning back on her arms and with her face turned towards the evening sun, eyes closed to protect them from the bright light.

He stopped as though rooted to the spot and marvelled at the vitality that seemed to radiate from her. Although it was mid-October, it had been a warm day and she was fairly lightly clad. A thin shawl, that had clearly been around her shoulders, had slipped and lay behind her; a linen blouse followed the contours of her upper body and Max, trying to imagine what it would be like to draw her in that position, for once couldn't imagine the comforting feel of the pencil in his hand but instead imagined tracing the lines of her body with his fingers and...

She turned round and gave him a smile that made him want to throw himself down on his knees and worship her. He didn't. He managed to pull himself together and return her smile as he moved forward from the side of the bushes.

'I didn't expect to find anyone here, you caught me by surprise. I can go somewhere else if you'd prefer.' He was aware that he was holding his breath as he waited for her to continue. If she suggested that, yes, it would be a good idea for him to go somewhere else, then remaining on the farm would become impossible. He knew, in that moment that the only thing that enabled him to put up with his sessions with the odious Aristide and his wife, was the thought that at some point during every day he would get to see Chiara, even if he didn't get to speak to her and she probably didn't even notice him.

After looking at him for a moment, she smiled, and it was as if the course of the sun had been arrested and the world warmed up again. 'But I did hope to find someone here. I think you said that you would show me your drawings. I had some time, and I know that you are not with my brother tonight, so I thought that this might be the best place to find you – you don't mind, do you?' she looked him in the eyes, and he managed to hold her gaze.

Mind! How could he possibly mind? It was as much as he could do to avoid dancing with joy. He didn't really remember having offered to show her his drawings, but what the hell. 'Of course you can see my drawings, but don't expect anything special; most of them are just sketches to form the basis of more developed pictures later on.' He put the book carefully on the floor next to her, catching a breath of lavender based perfume as he did so.

She took her time looking through the sketches, keeping her head down over the book which gave him more freedom to study her from closer range than he had ever been able to before. She sat sideways on the grass, her left hip and leg on the ground with her right leg folded on top. She slowly turned the pages with the index finger of her right hand while her left rested on the ground in front of her and took some of her weight as she leaned forwards. His gaze caressed the left hand side of her neck which was taut as she inclined her head to the right to compensate for the angle at which the book lay. Her right wrist protruded a few inches from her loose sleeve as she fingered the edge of the pages and, each time she turned a page he could see the delicate operation of the tendons beneath the alabaster skin of her wrist.

He thought that she stifled a little laugh as she came to a page where several members of her family were portrayed during various work activities. Then, as she came to the end, he saw her look quickly back through the pages and then give him a puzzled look. 'But, what happened to the picture you were doing of the woman in the village, the one you were doing when I saw you drawing last time, I was hoping to see it finished?'

Various possibilities flashed through his mind; the easiest way out would be to tell her that he'd destroyed the picture, made a mistake that ruined it and then torn it up – but he couldn't. Nor could he tell her the whole truth, but he felt that he had to stick as close to the truth as possible. 'I was down in the village the other day and I saw the woman again so I gave it to her. It seemed like the right thing to do.' He had given it to Laura, but he had not met her by chance and it had not been down in Bargino as he was aware of the difficulties it would cause if he were seen by anyone connected to the Campolargos going into Giorgio and Laura's house. They had met by prior arrangement in the back room of the bottega in Santa Cristina and he had told her as much as he had been able to learn from Aristide to pass on to Giorgio.

'I got the impression from something your brother said that he's not keen on the woman's husband, so it's probably better not to mention that picture.'

She looked at him, 'I shouldn't think I'll be mentioning any of your pictures to my family. Somehow, I don't think that they would understand – they certainly wouldn't approve of me being here alone with you. It's the sort of inappropriate behaviour that they would expect of Maddalena; she's supposed to be the one who doesn't know how to behave. We both spent a lot of time in the Val d'Aosta when we were growing up, and everything was a lot less formal there; my sister hasn't quite adapted to the change yet.'

'When I see people for the first time, I often place them in paintings. When I saw you, I wanted to paint you as Diana surprised by Actaeon,' She coloured, and he wondered which of the many representations of the mythological subject she was bringing to mind; probably not Poelenburgh's which was the only one he could think of where Diana had dark hair like Chiara's. As he thought of the representations by the likes of Titian and Rubens and the acres of naked flesh involved, the thought crossed his mind that it may not have been the best thing to say at that stage.

She looked at him and he again held his breath. Had he offended her and was he about to be dismissed? 'Could you draw me?' She said in a quiet voice with a little catch in it.

'As Diana?' he said, with a raised eyebrow, feeling a little more confident.

'I don't think so,' she replied, 'remember what happened to Actaeon.' She smiled and rose; he quickly put out a hand to assist her, which she accepted as she came to her feet. He was not sure which one of them was responsible for their hands being together for longer than was necessary; he thought it was probably him but hoped it was her.

'There's a dip just past the far end of the vines. I often go there when I want to be on my own and think. I'll go there on Sunday afternoon – if it doesn't rain.' She smiled again and, before he could react, had disappeared round the bushes towards the house.

He felt elated. The anticipation of being allowed to feast his eyes on her without having to pretend he wasn't looking was exciting; he mentally went over every detail of her face and neck, imagining the texture of her skin as he did so. He saw again a traitorous wisp of hair that he had previously noticed had a habit of escaping from the general mass that was carefully tied back, allowing him to admire her neck. He tried to rationalise the situation; was he completely and absolutely head over heels in love? Yes, of course he was; was she interested in him? It seemed like it, unless he'd completely misread all the signals – and he couldn't believe that; was there any future in this? Not a chance - her brothers and probably the rest of the family as well would put a stop to things before anything could happen; should he get out while he could before everything got really out of control? Of course he should – but he couldn't. This couldn't turn out well, but he was going to go on and see what happened anyway.

The following day he worked ceaselessly without feeling the slightest bit tired, fuelled by the sense of elation that still suffused through him. Piero, Simone and the other two workers could hardly believe how hard he worked and the cheeriness with which he did so. The bulk of the grapes had now been harvested and the process of treading and filtering had now begun. Chiara and Virginia were no longer with them and only Maddalena remained of the females, hitching up her dress as she trod the grapes and laughing as the unctuous juice squirted up her legs. Towards mid-day, as it would take too long for the workers to clean up enough to take their place at the table and, in any case, it looked as if rain was a possibility, plates loaded with cheese, ham and salami were brought out for them with a large flask of wine which was passed from person to person. Only Maddalena judiciously stuck to water and left the wine alone.

Max noticed, as he ate, how like her sister she was and, looking at the shapely wine-stained calves, imagined that they were Chiara's and that he were licking the wine off. He shut his eyes and shook his head to try and free himself of the image. He must not forget that Chiara was not one of the rough and ready country girls he had known at home; she was, he supposed, 'a lady' and although he wasn't quite sure exactly what the implications of that were, this being a totally new experience, he suspected that, at some point, it was going to make a massive difference.

That evening, Aristide told him that that was the last of the conversation sessions as his father and the three English guests would be arriving the following day. Max hoped that he would not be expected to meet them; while he had learnt to control himself and not reveal his own political thoughts while with Aristide and his wife, he was sure that he would not be able to mask the contempt and anger he felt for them, if forced to meet his fellow countrymen face to face.

He had no need to worry. In mid-afternoon he heard the sound of engines and, when he looked through the doors of the barn where the grapes were being attended to, he saw Aristide's *Balilla* making its way up the driveway followed by a chauffeur driven *Lancia Dilambda*, the powerful V8 engine of which purred like a tiger. The sun glinted brightly off the cars until they disappeared round the corner of the house so he did not catch even a glimpse of the occupants.

Neither did he see them that evening nor, for that matter, any other members of the family. Another maid had arrived at the house during the day to assist Adele and, when Adele introduced her to him as Gianna, he realised that this must be the friend of Laura who had been mentioned on his first evening in Bargino. When they were alone in the kitchen, while Adele took one of the many courses to the dining room, he asked if she had any news of his friends, but Gianna, with a quick, nervous glance towards the door, shook her head to indicate that she was worried about even mentioning them in the Campolargo house. Max understood her reticence, and let the subject drop; he realised that if she was available to be engaged at short notice, then she couldn't have a steady job and could not be expected to put opportunities of temporary employment at risk.

While he was glad he did not have to meet the English blackshirts, he was curious and would have liked to have been a fly on the wall, to find out more about them. 'Know thine enemy', he thought and then, without success, searched his mind trying to remember who had originally been credited with the saying. More than anything, however, he would have liked to have seen Chiara, who he realised was unlikely to have any chance of slipping away while the guests and her father were there. Hopefully, he would have the opportunity to see her the following evening after Campolargo and his guests had moved to the family's *palazzo* in Florence to be on the spot for the receptions and activities on the day of the ceremony itself, the twenty-seventh.

Adele was clearly exhausted when she finally managed to to slump down on a chair in the kitchen just after two in the morning. Gianna had left just before midnight promising to be back before seven. Adele had suggested that she stay, but Gianna had declined the offer as her mother was unwell and someone had to prepare her father's food for the following day. When Max had mildly hinted that maybe, in the circumstances, her father could look after himself for once, she had looked at him as if he came from another planet rather than just another country. Neither fascism nor anti-fascism, seemed to have achieved much for the status of ordinary women, he thought, but let the subject drop as he realised that it was neither the appropriate time nor place for a discussion on the nature of Italian society. He had stayed up, determined to do as much as he could to help Adele and, once the tenseness left her, he insisted that she went to bed while he cleared up the last few things. She was too tired to protest and gave him a grateful peck on the cheek as she left the kitchen.

Adele was already bustling around the kitchen when he got up just after six and soon after half past she was joined by Gianna, who shivered from lack of sleep as she entered. 'They'll all be getting up at different times, I should think. Elisabetta, Virginia and the girls went to bed just after midnight, although Signorina Maddalena didn't want to; the Conte went up at about one, but Signor Aristide, Signor Umberto and the three Englishmen carried on drinking grappa and smoking cigars until after two.'

Max gave a little snort, 'I don't think you'll see the three Englishmen at all this morning; they won't be used to grappa and will have drunk far too much, trying to show off to Aristide, and they probably didn't drink much water during the evening either. With a bit of luck they'll have very bad hangovers and feel rotten for the rest of the day.'

Adele and Gianna both looked at him. 'That's not a very nice thing to say,' said Adele, looking surprised.

'They're not very nice people,' he replied. 'They control gangs of armed bullies in England who take action against any groups of workers who try and protest about poor living and working conditions and the way they are exploited by the rich.'

Adele shrugged, 'they're the Count's guests, and for as long as they're here, I've got to look after them.' She turned away to spoon a selection of jams and jellies into ornate serving bowls. Gianna gave Max a slightly frightened look and he broke the eye contact and concentrated on breaking the left over bread from the previous day and then dropped the chunks into his caffe-latte.

He was looking forward to the evening when Campolargo would take his guests to Florence and he would have the chance to see Chiara again without the risk of being discovered by Aristide or Umberto, who he could not imagine would miss the ceremony. Two more cars arrived at the house soon before the family were due to have an early supper. One of the cars contained the Campolargo's second son, Filippo, and his wife, Carmela, and Adele told Max that the occupants of the other car were Margarita Campolargo and her husband.

Aristide had been in Florence all day and was not expected for supper, his presence in the city at that time clearly being seen as indispensable by Pavolini, the brains behind the following day's ceremony. The other three cars left the house in a line, led by Campolargo's Lancia, as the sky began to darken just after eight.

'Well, that's it until tomorrow evening,' said Adele, 'they've all gone now, except Carmela – and she won't need any looking after so long as she's happy that the house is spotless. She doesn't want Elisabetta being able to find fault when she gets back.'

Suddenly, Max felt a void in the pit of his stomach. 'What do you mean, "all"? You mean Campolargo, his guests, his sons and their wives and Margarita and her husband.' He knew as he said it that was not what she meant, it was what he wanted her to have meant; what she had meant had been exactly what she had said.

'No. The whole family has gone; they've just left Donna Carmela here in charge, as she's expecting another baby and Signor Filippo thought that the excitement might be too much for her.' She gave him a long, not unsympathetic look, and he wondered how much she suspected of his feelings.

He would have to be careful.

The following morning, as he was breakfasting, he was surprised to see a very full breasted and very clearly pregnant but otherwise physically nondescript woman walk into the kitchen. He felt her glance run over him before she addressed Adele, 'Tell, Piero and the other workers that they are all to gather in the entrance hall at nine o'clock to listen to the ceremony on the radio. Make sure that the radio is moved from my father-in-law's study and correctly set up before then.' She turned and left without waiting for a reply. Adele looked worried.

'How do I set up a radio? I've no idea how they work.'

'I should be able to do it,' said Max. 'I managed to make my own crystal set when I was at school, and a proper radio should be easier to operate.'

By ten thirty, Carmela and all the staff who had not travelled to Florence, including Max, were crowded around a crackly radio in the entrance hall, listening to an announcer, announcing in formal tones that the day would be one that Florence would never forget and one of which the whole of Fascist Italy could be proud. He talked about the great sacrifices that the Italian people had been prepared to make to give the country the structure that had allowed it to take its rightful place amongst the world's leading nations, with a leader admired and envied by all. Max would have laughed but could see how seriously Piero, Simone and the others were taking the words in, and he realised that it would not be wise to show what he thought. At ten forty five, it was announced that listeners would then hear a salute from the canons at the Forte da Belvedere as the prelude to a discourse by Canon Giulio Bonardi in the presence of Elia della Costa, the Bishop of Florence, from the Duomo of Florence.

Max was surprised to hear that the discourse of the Canon spoke only of glorious death and the great rewards that awaited those who were prepared to give everything for their country. Each of the coffins was covered with a black drape with the 'martyr's' name in white on one side and the fascist symbol on the other, however, despite the presence of the thirty seven coffins which were lined in front of the altar, death hardly got a mention.

At the end of Bonardi's sermon and after blessings from Della Costa and from an auxiliary bishop, the announcer described how, from the various sections of fascists ranged around the inside of the Duomo, groups of six fascists dressed in immaculate black shirts came out and shouldered each of the coffins and made their way slowly through the main doorway to line up in the piazza outside. Once all the coffins were lined up in a perfectly straight line, the cortège began its slow way through the city taking a roundabout route to Santa Croce, which Max imagined had been designed so that the largest possible number of people would be able to witness the occasion.

With a hushed tone, bordering on ecstasy, the announcer described the column as it set off up Via Cavour. Sixty apparently wounded ex-fascist 'soldiers' led the way in tattered uniforms dating from the period before the March on Rome. These were followed by columns of *balilla*, the Florentine fascist youth; after the *balilla* came columns of fascist university students and one hundred members of the fascist militia. The announcer explained how the column signified the power and strength of fascist Italy growing out of the sacrifices that had been made before October 1922 and the start of the fascist era. Following the coffins were the fascist action groups from each of the areas of Florence and the nearby communes, each of which carried a gilt-edged black banner fixed to a pike with a short cross baton, showing the name of one of the 'martyrs'. At the end of the individual Florentine sections, party members held up a large pennant showing both the fascist symbol and the Florentine coat of arms. Beyond the Florentines came ministers, parliamentary deputies and representatives of ninety-two fascist associations from around Italy. According to the announcer, all those in the procession except the wounded veterans at the front wore immaculate summer fascist uniforms, while the public lining the route wore the winter uniform. The announcer described in an awestruck voice how the cortège was a kilometre long, with the rear only just starting to move as the front reached Piazza San Marco where the first change of coffin bearers took place.

Knowing the city, Max could visualise the cortège as it slowly progressed from the Duomo to San Marco, from San Marco to Piazza D'Azeglio, from Piazza d'Azeglio to Piazza Beccaria, and then finally to Piazza Santa Croce; what he found more difficult, possibly because part of his mind didn't want to accept it was the description of the regular black banners stretched across the streets, each bearing the fascist slogan, *'PRESENTE'*, or the black banners than hung from windows on both sides of the street showing the words of fascist songs and anthems. The sound of cannon fire as the big guns saluted the dead, could be heard in the background and, at what seemed to be regular intervals, the assembled crowds, which were otherwise silent, broke into fascist songs, particularly *Giovinezza*.

As the rear end of the cortège reached Piazza Santa Croce, a note of awe was clearly discernible in the commentator's voice as Benito Mussolini met them. He left off describing the cortège as Mussolini inspected and then gave the Roman salute to one of the *Balilla* sections. Max was sure that the commentator was using a significant amount of poetic licence as he described the looks of devotion on the faces of the *ballila*; he may well be right, but Max couldn't imagine how he could possibly be close enough to know for certain.

The commentator described Mussolini mounting a platform that had been prepared in front of the basilica, and was then silent as Mussolini's somewhat manic, barking voice took over; *'The names and the memories of these, our comrades from the eve of fascism, are and will always remain in our hearts. In difficult times they had already adopted the proud motto, "Believe. Obey. Fight." - They believed. They obeyed. And they fought as they consecrated their absolute dedication to the cause.'* After highlighting the glory that they had achieved through their sacrifice and commanding all those present to be willing to follow the example of the martyrs to ensure the future glory of Italy and fascism, he finished his oration by telling the crowds that if they followed the examples of the martyrs in the future, then they, the Italian people, would always be triumphant no matter how hard the battles may be. He ended by raising his fist in the fascist salute and shouting, *'To whom does this century belong?'* to which the answering cry from thousands of people was, *'To us!'*

The announcer's description of Mussolini leaving the podium was almost drowned out by cries of *'Duce, Duce, Duce,'* and Max noticed that Piero's fist was thrust upwards in the fascist version of the original Roman salute.

After Mussolini's intervention, the coffins were carried one by one past Achille Starace, the national secretary of the fascist party. As each coffin approached, he called out the name of its occupant, as if taking a register, and to each name the assembled crowd roared out, *'Presente!'*

From the moment that the last of the coffins was carried into the specially restored crypt, the announcer was clearly reading from a script that had been prepared for him, as Max realised that he would not have been allowed to speak if he had been present inside with the leading lights of fascism. Presumably, Mussolini had either left, or the script had been prepared before it had been known that he would be there. The crypt was described in great detail: its walls had been relined with sheets of black and red marble, around the middle of which the word *'Presente'* was repeated at regular intervals. From the start of the nave, stretching down as far as the altar chapel were thirty seven plain sandstone arches, each one inscribed with the name, date of birth, and date and place of the 'glorious' death of one of the martyrs, and under each of which a sandstone sarcophagus awaited a martyr's coffin. Set in the wall to either side of the altar were two identical sheets of marble, each bearing the fascist pledge with the words, **God**, **Italy**, and **Duce** highlighted. A third sheet of marble, which was set into the floor of the nave, bore the text of a short speech that Mussolini had made about the Florentine martyrs three years previously. According to the commentator's script, the leading roles in the ceremony inside the crypt were played by Starace, Pavolini, who had undoubtedly been the architect of the ceremony, and Bishop della Costa.

As the radio transmission ended, Max felt a strange mixture of elation and sickness. He was disgusted by the way history was being rewritten and served up to the masses, but he had to recognise that it had been done with great skill and he could quite understand how people who wanted to hope for some kind of better future could be swept along by the emotion that had been manufactured. He recognised that even he, while knowing that it had all been false and crass had, at times, felt the attraction of it.

'You will be proud to know that my father-in-law and brother-in-law were present in the closing ceremony in the chapel,' said Carmela, bringing his mind back to the present. His fellow workers murmured their approval and then they were all dismissed by Carmela to return to their work. He wondered where Chiara had been during the ceremonies and what sort of effect it would have had on her. He didn't know how mentally strong she was or even, he realised, what, if anything, her view was of fascism.

He did not get the chance to find out that day, as the family party, now without the three English fascists, did not return to the estate until late the following afternoon.

He took the opportunity during the day to pay another visit to see Giorgio and Laura, again reaching their home by a circuitous route to avoid being spotted, even though the chances were far lower with the Campolargos safely out of the way. As usual they were delighted to see him, although Giorgio initially seemed slightly more subdued than usual. This was, as Max suspected it would be, because of the events of the previous day; although Giorgio had been out and about and had not witnessed the spectacle himself, Laura, like Max, had listened on the radio and had later given him an account, and he was depressed by the apparent fascination of the vast crowds that had been present in the city. 'How can so many people be blinded by a puffed up piece of street theatre? Why is that as soon as someone creates an idol for them and tells them something that they'd like to be true, that they stop using their brains and start bleating like sheep?' he asked bitterly.

'Surely, it's not all like that,' said Max, there must still be lots of people who aren't taken in by the fascists in Florence, people who, even if they are too scared to do anything now, will stand up for themselves at some time in future.'

'Yes, of course you're right,' Giorgio replied after a pause. 'There are a lot of good people in Florence, and at some time they will see through it all and stand up to the bullying, it's just that at the moment they're dazzled by the events that Pavolini has put on for them to stop them thinking. And he's clever, because in themselves there's nothing wrong with most of the events he's put on – not yesterday, obviously – he's brought back the annual medieval football matches played in traditional costume in the centre of the city; he's introduced a Cultural Spring with musical concerts each year in May; a lot of the ordinary people have fallen for it and don't realise that the fascists are also responsible for the loss of any individual rights, and stopping people saying what they think.'

Max let Giorgio let off steam and was glad to see that, once he had done so, he became more like the old Giorgio again. By the time he left, wanting to be back on the estate before the Campolargos returned, things were pretty much back to normal and his thoughts turned again to his own situation.

As Campolargo himself was now at the house, he thought it was less likely that Chiara would be able to get away after the evening meal which, as he had continued to give Adele a hand in the kitchen, he was aware had dragged on somewhat. However, after the last dish had been removed and Adele shooed him out of her way, he decided that he would go back to the spot where they had met before, just on the off chance that he might see her.

He was in luck. She was standing looking into the darkness over the valley where just the occasional faint light could be seen in the gloom. Although he was silent, she turned quickly as he rounded the bushes, as though some inner sense alerted her to his presence. The moon chose that moment to emerge from behind a cloud and he saw her face light up in a smile. She came towards him and impulsively he held out both hands towards her. She hesitated almost imperceptibly but then took his hands in hers although she kept them held out in front of her; he didn't mind; for the moment, just holding her cool hands and looking into the dark eyes, that seemed to suck him in like bottomless pits, was enough for him. He made no attempt to pull her any closer to him but smiled and said, 'I missed my muse.'

'I missed you too,' she said. And then, squeezing his hands before releasing them, 'Thursday is a holiday,' and she fled towards the house.

The next three days passed painfully slowly. Even though there was plenty of work to do as he and the others had now been set to cutting the grass and removing weeds and brambles that had grown since the spring around the hundreds of olive trees on the estate: even the sun seemed to move lazily across the sky more slowly than usual. He was usually able to lose himself in manual work and the hours of cutting and pulling with the sickle should have kept his mind off other things... but it didn't, and he spent half his time imagining being with Chiara in an idyllic world painted by his imagination, and the other half trying, without success, to work out how the relationship could possibly be allowed to develop in the real world.

He knew that even compared to England, which was bad enough, girls in Italy had little say in their own destiny; fathers, brothers and then husbands had complete control and usually chose to exercise it. For centuries in Italy these roles had been promoted by the Church, with the figure of the Virgin Mary there to be worshipped and to serve as a guiding light to show other women the virtues of chastity and self-sacrifice: virtues that had to be protected and venerated by the males, each of whom, in some way, seemed to identify his own mother and sisters with 'the Madonna' and was determined to protect them, whether they themselves wished it or not. This subservient role for women fitted in perfectly with the new fascist mirage of Italian men as virile national heroes who deserved a supportive home behind them. Even in what he himself considered to be a healthier relationship, like that of Giorgio and Laura, he knew that it was as it was because Giorgio was willing to see Laura as an equal and had encouraged her to see herself that way, rather than because it was natural. If the future freedom of women depended on the willingness of men to give up power, he thought, then the future looked bleak for a long time to come.

Without money and without influential connections, he knew that there was absolutely no chance of the Campolargos permitting anything to develop between him and Chiara, even if they remained in ignorance of his view of fascism. He had no doubt that with the connections of Campolargo, and particularly Aristide, he could be locked up on a trumped up charge, or even expelled from the country in no time. He could not think of any way out but, being a natural optimist and, he now realised, being so completely smitten by Chiara, that he had no choice but to go on, he tried to convince himself that something would turn up.

On the Thursday morning, Adele told him that Campolargo, Umberto, Virginia and the two girls would be going to Montecatini to spend the day with the Contessa. Max's shoulders sagged; he'd been looking forward to the day so much with its promise of some stolen time with Chiara, and now it had been snatched away from him without warning. He ate little breakfast and was taciturn for the rest of his time in the kitchen and then returned to his room where he threw himself on the straw mattress that lay on the floor. Max felt thoroughly miserable: his eyes stung slightly and he knew he was closer to tears than at any time since he'd been a child.

He knew he had to snap out of it and pulled out his sketchbook from under the mattress, then went outside. Heading up the hill at a punishing pace that made his legs ache made him feel a little better and he finally sat down on a wall to sketch the view over the valley using thicker than usual lines and then shading in angry clouds in the sky. After about an hour, the *Dilambda* made its way slowly down the driveway, eased its way around the bends on the road down to Bargino and then accelerated smoothly northwards along the Via Cassia towards San Casciano.

Feeling a little more relaxed now but still feeling desperately unhappy, he began to walk towards Tavarnelle. Before he had gone too far he realised that in his hurry to get away from the house he had not picked up his identity papers or any money. If he were stopped and checked when he got to Tavarnelle, it would cause unnecessary complications and, while the angry part of his brain would have liked a confrontation with somebody, the sensible part won out and he turned down the Via di Pergolato towards Bargino.

He was going to call in on his friends but, as he neared the small lake a few hundred metres before the village, he decided that he didn't really want to be cheered up; he wanted to wallow in his unhappiness and feel sorry for himself. Turning along a path to the left, he made his way in the general direction of the Campolargo estate.

As he entered the estate, he decided to lengthen his route by passing round the edge of the vineyards and the small hollow where he had been looking forward to spending time with Chiara. He was in no hurry, as he knew that seeing the empty place would only stoke the fires of his misery, but eventually he reached the spot.

To his amazement, the hollow was not empty, a female figure with a shawl round her shoulders sat clasping her knees, facing away from the direction he had approached from back towards the house, which he realised must be out of her sight line from within the dip.

His heart pounded and he began to run. The girl turned as she caught the sound of his feet and had almost stood up straight when he reached her, threw his arms round her and, raising her further up, spun her round before stopping to look in her eyes. 'Chiara, I...' he began, but his words were cut off as she clamped her lips on his and kissed him urgently. Finally, when he was beginning to think that he might pass out, either from excessive happiness or lack of oxygen, she withdrew her lips and rested her forehead on his shoulder.

'I thought you'd decided not to come.'

'Adele said that you were going to Montecatini with your father, to visit your mother – I was sure you weren't here – I saw the car leave.'

'I was supposed to go, but I pretended I was unwell. They waited a while, but then my father said that they couldn't wait any longer and they left me behind.'

'I'm sorry, I thought you'd gone and that I wouldn't see you at all today.' He loosened his grip on her, suddenly conscious that they were in far closer physical proximity than they had ever been before and wanting to give her time and not exploit unfairly the reaction that his sudden appearance had occasioned. She did not pull away as his arms loosened but looked up and then fastened onto his lips again with an urgency that surprised and delighted him; his arms slid down her back under the shawl and came to rest just above her hips as they kissed.

When their lips came unstuck, he knelt, pulled her down to a sitting position beside him and then sat back on his haunches still holding her hands. 'It sounds like madness because I hardly know you, but I can't imagine having to live without you. I felt as if it were the end of the world when I heard you were going to Montecatini.'

'I couldn't go, not when I hadn't seen you for three whole days; I've been counting off the minutes since I last saw you.'

'Do you really mean it? Could I really be important to you? Or am I just filling a temporary need before you get called back to your real life?' he asked, suddenly serious.

She freed on of her hands from his and placed it on his cheek. 'Yes. I mean it. I'm not sure what you mean by my "real life", but if you mean this,' and she removed her hand from his cheek and gave a broad sweep with her arm, which Max understood as being intended to encompass all their surroundings, 'then this isn't real. Everyone here is pretending to be something they're not or, even worse, believing that they're something they're not.' She paused, 'I don't think I've explained it very well but... but you're different... even though you're not in charge, you seem to have dignity – self-belief...' She tailed off and leaned her forehead on his shoulder.

He looked at her, unable to speak for a moment as his throat seemed to constrict then, the dilemma that had tormented him for the last few days returned to him. Maybe she had thought about it and come up with an answer. 'How are we going to manage it? Your family would never allow us to be together and will do everything they can to split us up as soon as they find out.'

'We'll find a way... we have to!' He was touched by the strength of her belief and wanted to believe her, to trust in her blind faith in the power of her conviction. He was determined to find a way and not to let her down.

'For the moment we'll just have to be very, very careful and not give anyone any reason to suspect,' and then, determined to lighten the atmosphere, 'perhaps I should throw them off the scent by taking up Simone's invitation to go with him on his next visit to the *case chiuse* in Florence.'

She punched him on the arm.

'All right, all right, no *case chiuse*, I give up,' he said, putting his hands in front of his face as if to protect himself, and looking at her through his fingers.

'Have you ever... I mean... you know ... the *case chiuse*?' She reddened as she asked the question, and he thought again how beautiful she was as she lowered her face and looked at the floor half dreading the answer.

'He stretched out his left arm and gently lifted her chin until her dark eyes flowed into his, 'No, I've never been to the *case chiuse*, and I can't imagine that I ever will. There's only one woman for me,' he smiled, 'and now I'm going to do a picture of her before she disappears again.'

She laughed, 'I feel like Cinderella at the ball, knowing I've only got limited time.'

'Then the picture will have to be your glass slipper.'

'How do you want me?'

A series of visions flashed through his mind, each more attractive than the last, but he managed to push them to one side to peruse later, and swallowing to free his tongue, which suddenly felt very dry, replied, 'Just as you are... Maybe let the shawl slip down a bit so that I can see your right shoulder.' She complied, and he was soon lost in his drawing which, unlike the earlier angry sketch he had done when he thought that Chiara had gone away, was carefully crafted and delicate, as he tried to put the love he felt into every line, highlight and patch of shade.

'You don't like my family, do you?' she asked suddenly.

He hesitated, but decided that they were now past the point where lies, even little white lies were an option; if she were going to have to adapt to a completely different lifestyle to the one she was used to, then she had the right to know why and, he was desperate that she should love him for the person he really was, not as the rustic farm labourer she probably considered him. 'I don't like what they stand for. I can't accept the idea of wealth passing down the generations and accidents of birth determining whether people have power and luxury or whether their whole lives are a continual struggle to survive. And, I don't like fascists; I've seen how they treat other people who have different opinions and it sickens me.'

She said nothing for a minute, then, 'Do you think we're all like that?'

'If I did, I wouldn't want to spend the rest of my life with you.'

'But, how do you know I'm not just the same as the others. I might have a crush on Mussolini – I hear that he's not averse to keeping a lover or two?'

'Young ladies who secretly help the families of those who have been put out of work by the regime, because they wouldn't carry the party card, make unlikely fascists.'

She was obviously surprised and a little embarrassed: 'But how did you... who told... Gianna shouldn't have...' she was clearly flustered.

'Gianna didn't tell me anything, she was almost too scared to talk about anything but work when she was here last week. Someone else told me before I met Gianna; a friend who, I think, suspects that I may have a particular interest in the subject.... Anyway,' he said, preferring to redirect the conversation, 'how could you tell that I'm not keen on your family?'

'Don't worry, I don't think anyone else has noticed, except maybe Maddalena, and she doesn't like the others anyway, so that's all right. You can't spend as much time as I have over the last few weeks studying someone without learning things about them... You really dislike my brothers, don't you?'

'Yes, but for different reasons. Umberto is a typical bully, the type you find everywhere, no matter what the political system; his social position gives him status and he uses it to dominate others. He's a fascist because they are the dominant force in Italy at the moment and their modus operandi fits perfectly with the way he likes to treat others, and they need people who will just do as they are told unquestioningly, like him. Aristide is far more dangerous because he's a lot cleverer; he knows that fascism will sustain the class differences and he knows how to make himself indispensable to Pavolini and the regime. He believes in fascism because he knows it's the ideal system for clever, rich unscrupulous people like him. I haven't seen much of Filippo but I suspect that he's very similar to Umberto.'

She bowed her head and he waited to see if his honesty had offended her. Then she raised her head and looked him steadily in the eye, 'The room that I share with Maddi is next to Umberto and Virginia's room. Sometimes at night we can hear her cry and Umberto laugh. He hurts her, but she's always refused to talk about it whenever I've tried. He's a brute who shouldn't be allowed to live with humans. Aristide isn't really like a brother at all. Maddi and I hardly saw him while we were growing up; our mother has been ill ever since Maddi was born, probably even before that, and she was sent away for specialist cures soon after the birth, when I was only four. As soon as Maddi no longer needed the wet-nurse, she and I were sent away to live with a cousin of my mother's in Val d'Aosta. Our father sent us birthday and Christmas presents and came to see us once a year; sometimes our other sister, Margarita would come with him, and once or twice, when he was younger, he brought Umberto as well.'

'And your mother?'

'We didn't see her again until two years ago, after our father decided that it was time to bring us back here. We were taken to see her on Assumption day on the fifteenth of August and expected to display affection. She sat in a chair in the gardens of the thermal baths with a maid whose job it seemed to be to wipe the corner of her mouth clean when she dribbled. My father sat by her for a while and then went off to play blackjack in the casino, leaving us "to get to know her".' Chiara smiled ruefully. 'She just about knows who my father is and she smiled at Umberto, but she was completely blank when Maddi and I spoke to her; she just looked through us, as though we weren't there.'

'You poor thing,' he said, and then playfully, 'so your 'illness' wasn't just for my benefit this morning then.' She laughed, and the sound made him feel good.

'Poor Maddi. She probably won't speak to me tonight after abandoning her to her fate today.'

'You must be very close to her after all those years away together.'

'We tell each other everything – well, almost everything,' she said glancing at the ground, 'even though she's four years younger than me, she's really clever. For as long as I can remember she's always had her own opinions and is prepared to argue about them with anyone. Up in the Val d'Aosta there was a young priest who was a bit rebellious and had been sent there from Torino, because he'd got too close to some of the communist workers. He was supposed to teach us the catechism but Maddi would start to question everything and want detailed explanations for everything, and she wouldn't accept anything that he couldn't prove. Sometimes, when he had to resort to, "you just have to have faith, my child," she would just laugh and shake her head, and all three of us knew that she'd won the argument. The only person she doesn't argue with here is Aristide, because she's scared of him; she ties Umberto up in knots and leaves him furious, and he can't do anything about it without looking stupid.'

He flicked his finger over the cross-hatched shading he'd done on one side of the image he was drawing to make the join between cheekbone and hair look natural, then turned the paper around to show her.

She gasped, and then laughed, 'You've made me look beautiful!'

'I can't make you look as beautiful as you really are.'

She slid towards him and rested her cheek on his thigh; he ran his fingers through her hair feeling every contour of her skull.

Neither spoke for a while, each lost in their thoughts, then Chiara stirred, 'I've no idea what time it is; I only seem to have been with you a few seconds, but the sun seems to have moved a long way. I told Elisabetta that I needed to go out for a few minutes to get some fresh air; I wouldn't want her to send anyone out to look for me.'

They embraced tightly before he reluctantly gave her a push in the direction of the house. 'Go on; I'll wait a few minutes so no-one sees us together.'

He watched her go and then looked at the portrait again for several minutes before tucking it behind some landscapes and beginning to make his own way back to the house, making sure that he arrived from a slightly different direction.

Adele commented on his cheerfulness as he entered the kitchen for a bowl of minestrone, taking her by the waist and waltzing her across the floor as he did so. 'Get off you daft ha'porth,' she said, waving a ladle at him, ' a day off work and it addles your brain. What's got into you?'

'Nothing; it's just been a lovely day. I've had a nice walk through some beautiful countryside.'

Adele shook her head and ladled the thick soup into his bowl, muttering about all foreigners, and especially Englishmen, being mad.

He retained his good humour as he worked through the next two days, singing half remembered songs from his childhood as he hacked away at the weeds that, if not removed, would make the olive harvest much more difficult. Even though he only caught the occasional glimpse of Chiara, he didn't mind because he knew that she loved him and that they would find a way to be together again on the Sunday.

Usually, if he were free, he would try and give Adele a hand clearing up in the kitchen but on Sunday, he excused himself as soon as he'd finished eating lunch and, telling Adele to leave something for him to do later, he hurried off with the excuse that he wanted to catch the light before it changed, for a picture he had in mind. He collected his sketchbook from under his mattress and made his way to the hollow and sat down to wait.

While he waited, he amused himself by doing rough re-creations of some of his favourite mythological scenes: Botticelli's *Birth of Venus* and *Venus and Mars*, a dark haired *Venus* by Dante Gabriel Rossetti that he had seen in a gallery in Bournemouth and exquisitely executed nudes by the French artist, Suzanne Amaury-Duval, an exhibition of whose he had managed to get into as he passed through Paris on his way south. In each of these pastiches he substituted the background with the Val di Pesa and, although he only included a few light lines to indicate facial features, the outline of the hair on each of the figures was remarkably reminiscent of that of the woman whose image filled his mind.

'I'm here, at last,' said Chiara, breathlessly, as she came quickly down into the dip, checking herself just in time to throw her arms around his neck. Max pushed the pencil and sketchbook to one side and responded eagerly to her embrace.

They held each other close for several minutes, saying nothing, just enjoying the feeling of being alone together. Finally she released him and turned round, sliding down so that she lay with her head on his lap looking up into his eyes. He felt that the muscles in his face had taken on a life of their own and that he'd never be able to stop smiling again. With his right hand he pushed aside a wisp of hair that lay across her face just below her nose and joked, 'I think I prefer you without a moustache.' She smiled and closed her eyes as he lifted her hair and let it slide through his fingers before carefully ensuring that it framed her face perfectly. His fingers traced over her cheekbone, along the line of her jaw and then, very softly, down the muscle in her neck to finally rest on her collar bone. He felt her give a little shudder and he began to move his hand away aware that it was still very early for the intimateness of the contact. As soon as she felt him begin to withdraw, however, her own hand came up and unerringly locating his, even with her eyes still closed, pulled his hand back down and replaced it where it had been.

'They always told me that nice young ladies were very reserved, and that even a kiss was a lot to hope for before marriage,' he said, trying to sound shocked but not succeeding.

Chiara's eyes opened and locked on his, 'Then either, "they" didn't know what they were talking about, or I'm not a nice young lady!' She rolled off him and moved into a sitting position with her head leaning on his shoulder. 'What are we going to do?'

'In a few weeks' time, when the olives are in, they won't need me anymore here, and I'll be expected to move on. Because my Italian is reasonable now, I'm sure I'll be able to find enough work to do in Florence or Siena to let me survive through the winter; there must be some things where they need someone who can speak English.' He put a finger on her lips as she started to object, 'I'll get hold of a push-bike and I can be here every Sunday. Then, next year, when you're twenty-one, we'll go away together.'

Chiara shook her head, 'Just because I'm twenty-one won't mean that I'm free of my family. My father and Aristide know people who can arrange anything, no matter what the law says. Even though Luigi, my mother's cousin in Val d'Aosta, carried the party card and said all the right things in public, I used to hear him complaining to Laurette, when they thought that Maddi and I were asleep. The daughter of the town's prefect used to come into the school and give extra lessons to some of us students, then all of a sudden we didn't see her any more. I heard Luigi telling Laurette, that she had refused to marry the "suitable" person chosen by her family – they locked her away in a safe hospital for a few months until she got "better", then she came out and married the man her father wanted. It wouldn't be any different for me.'

A tear rolled slowly down her cheek and he leaned forward to kiss it away. 'I know what Italy's like, and I know what your father and brothers could do. I know that your being twenty-one will make no difference here, but if we can get out of Italy, your being twenty-one will mean that no-one can touch us.'

Max leaned back and looked at her, anxiously waiting for her reaction, to the idea that after days of thinking was the best he could come up with. He knew that he was asking her to exchange a life which, while repressed, was still full of comfort and luxuries, for one where nothing was certain, where there would be no maid, little sunshine, poorer food and where she would be an outsider.

He saw that tears were now rolling freely down both cheeks and reached out his arms to pull her towards him. She did not immediately allow herself to be drawn forwards but looked him in the eyes and said quietly, 'You'll really love me for ever?'

'For ever,' he said, and then she came towards him and grasped him tightly.

'I love you, so much.'

'And I you.'

They sat, clasped together in perfect unity for a long time, before she said, 'Now, I want to see what you were drawing before I arrived,' and she reached out and picked up the sketchbook from where he had pushed it to one side when they had first embraced. She smiled as she saw the adaptations of Botticelli and the other painters. Her dark eyes sparkled as she looked back at him, 'They're not very good...' she paused for effect, 'you've missed off my birthmark.'

For a moment his mind was a whirl as he wondered how he could possibly answer, 'I thought I wasn't meant to know about that until our wedding-night,' he said, trying to sound innocent.

'Now you're being cruel; first you tell me that I have to wait until next year before you rescue me from captivity, and then you tell me that I have to wait until then for a bit of affection as well. Call yourself a knight in shining armour!'

'I'll go and fight the dragon now if you like, but I'm not sure I'd win. They say you need patience and persistence to reach the Holy Grail.'

'My Galahad!' she said, throwing her arms around him again.

The next hour, which was all the time they dared spend together, passed quickly, as they held hands, embraced, kissed and generally talked lovers' nonsense. Finally, they separated and, as before, allowing an interval of a few minutes to pass, Max followed her back in the direction of the house.

As he reached the house he saw Virginia collecting herbs from the terracotta pots in the kitchen garden. She looked at him as he approached and, feeling well disposed towards the world in general, even the less important members of the Campolargo family, he greeted her cheerily before entering. She did not return the greeting and he shrugged his shoulders and returned to thinking about Chiara, completely unconcerned by Virginia's lack of manners; no-one could put a damper on his happiness.

He was in such good spirits, that once again, the following day, he hardly noticed the hours passing by and, when it was finally time to return to the house, he was surprised that the day was over.

As he entered his room, he noticed that he had left the corner of his sketchbook sticking out from under the mattress. His head still full of Chiara, he bent down to push it carefully further underneath – then his head exploded. There was a swishing sound, a sudden sharp pain on the side of his head and then concentric zig-zag multi-coloured circles spread out into the blackness that filled his field of vision before fading into uniform black nothingness.

Chapter 5

He hurt all over. He tried to lift his arm but couldn't. A dim light showed between his eyelids but he couldn't force them open; it was as if there were no room for them to move within the confines of his eye-sockets. He tried to speak but only a low inarticulate sound came out, and his ribs felt as though they were on fire. 'Shhhhh,' came a soft soothing voice, and he drifted back into unconsciousness.

The next time he awoke, or at least the next time he was aware of being awake, his eyes would open a little further, although everything still seemed very fuzzy. Cautiously, he tried to formulate a word, 'Wh... what...'

The indistinct female shape that was sitting next to his bed turned and bent over him and, in a voice that seemed familiar but which took him a few seconds to place said, 'Don't try to talk now. You need to rest to get some strength back,' and a cool damp cloth wiped his forehead. 'After a few seconds he said, 'Laura,' and then closed his eyes again.

'You owe your life to Adele Lucchesi,' said Giorgio. 'She sneaked out in the night and told us what had happened and where to find you.'

'What did happen? I don't remember anything.'

'Umberto happened. I think you must have done something to upset him. He told Adele to stay in the kitchen and not to come out for any reason until he told her she could, then he must have ambushed you somewhere. Luckily, because he's stupid, he was just below the kitchen window when he told two of his men to put you down by the side of the bridge, so that the animals could finish you off during the night. He told them that he'd have some communists arrested after the body was found, and blame them. Adele heard what he said and, as soon as everyone else was in bed, she sneaked out, knocked us up and told us where to find you. The rest is history, as they say'.

'I have to go. You'll all be in trouble if they find me in your house.' Max tried to rise but a stabbing pain shot through his ribs.

'I don't think so. But don't worry; you're not in the house. You're hidden away at the back of a friend's barn. And, just in case you're still thinking of being a hero and leaving, you have several broken ribs, possibly a fractured skull, a broken wrist and someone seems to have stamped on your fingers. A friendly doctor has had a look and he says that you're not even to get out of bed unaided for at least three weeks and it will be at least another month before you are reasonably fit again. So it sounds as if you'll have to spend Christmas with us.'

Max lay and thought while Giorgio watched him. 'Is there anyway I can get a message to someone?' he asked.

'Someone inside the Campolargo house by any chance?' said Giorgio with a smile, placing his hand with surprising delicacy on Max's shoulder. 'Laura said that that would be the cause of this... it's already been taken care of.'

'How? When?'

'A little note in her room saying just, "Alive but injured. Say and do nothing. Be courageous", written in a hand that no-one there will recognise. I wanted to put "be patient" instead of "be courageous" but Laura said that if it fell into the wrong hands that it would tell other people that you are still around.'

'But, she'll think I've gone.'

Giorgio shook his head, 'Laura also said that if she's worth loving, that she won't lose faith in you. Women eh! Will we ever understand them? But if Laura says that it's like that, then I trust her, and you should too.' And that was the best Giorgio could offer him.

Chapter 6

Two weeks later, Chiara found a three word note under her pillow. 'Improving slowly. Wait', and she let out a little cry that drew the attention of Maddalena.

'What is it?' said the younger girl. 'You look as if you've seen a ghost.'

'It's nothing,' said Chiara, pushing the small note inside the back of her skirt waistband before her sister caught sight of it, 'just something I remembered.'

'Chiara,' said her sister, making sure that the door was closed and lowering her voice, 'we've never had secrets up until now, you've been big sister, substitute mother and best friend all rolled up into one, but that means I know you better than anyone else. I saw the way you looked at him, and he looked at you when each of you thought the other wasn't looking and, once the pair of you had worked up the courage to talk to each other, I could see how happy you were.' She took Chiara's hands, 'I don't know what you argued about that Monday that made him leave, but I want you to be happy... and I want you to trust me; I'll be sixteen in a few days, I'm not a baby anymore.'

She felt a flood of relief that finally she could share what she was feeling with someone else; she hadn't realised just how much of burden it had been to keep up a pretence of normality at all times. 'Oh, Maddi!' she said, putting her arms round her sister, 'I do trust you, but it's dangerous. We didn't argue. Max didn't leave by choice. He was badly hurt and thrown in a ditch because someone found out about us, and now... I've just been told he's starting to get better.'

'Go to him. Run away. Don't come back here!' she said passionately.

Chiara smiled and hugged her sister even more tightly, 'Dear Maddi, it's not as simple as that; I don't know where he is, or even for sure how he is getting messages to me. I don't think he's far away but he must have been really bad as he's not fully recovered yet,' and then, as a thought struck her for the first time, 'and what about you, Maddi? How can I leave you behind?'

Maddi pushed Chiara to arms length, while still holding her arms, 'No, that's no reason, Chiara. If you've got the chance to go, then go; don't worry about me, I can look after myself. My chance will come and I'll find you again sometime. Don't make me feel that I'm stopping you taking what might be your only chance of happiness.'

The two sisters embraced tightly, and Chiara was glad that at last she felt she had an ally.

Despite the reassurance of the note, she began to feel more and more on edge as the days passed by without any further news. Finally, she received another note, again hidden under her pillow saying, 'Sunday hollow'. Her mood lightened immediately and she had to work hard to conceal her happiness. 'Well,' said the perceptive Maddalena, as soon as they were safely ensconced in their room that evening, 'tell me.' Chiara told her about the note and what it meant.

'On Sunday afternoon, I'm going to have an argument with Umberto and Virginia, that should keep them busy, and give me something fun to do.'

'Be careful. Aristide will probably be here and you don't want to upset him,' said Chiara, concerned that her sister would find herself in trouble.

'Don't worry, I'll get Umberto to say something really stupid, so if Aristide wants to join in, he'll have to join in on my side. It'll be the best fun I've had for ages!'

On the Sunday, Chiara put her coat on to protect her from the cold and, taking a very indirect route, made her way to their hollow. To her chagrin she saw that their plans had been foiled. On the edge of the hollow were a woman and a toddler playing with a ball; he wouldn't risk coming if there were other people around. She was about to turn round and retrace her steps when the woman kicked the ball towards her son a little too hard and it eluded his flailing arms and rolled on towards Chiara. She hesitated, wondering whether to retrieve the ball and throw it back, or whether it was best not to draw any attention to herself. As she wondered, she recognised the woman as the woman from the first picture she had seen Max draw, and she felt a surge of excitement.

She stepped forward and bent to pick up the ball which she then held out to the woman. The hand that the woman held out contained a scrap of paper. *'You can place absolute trust in the bearer of this note,'* the note was unsigned but she recognised the handwriting, which was very different to that taught to Italian children. 'Make it look as if we're talking about my son. We haven't got much time,' said the woman.

Chiara leant towards the toddler but said to its mother, 'Go on.'

'Firstly, I need to know if you still feel as strongly about Max as you did before.'

'Of course.'

'I thought so, but I needed to check... His hands still hurt him which is why he hasn't written more. He wanted to come today, but we needed to know if it is safe; someone else is watching to see if you've been followed. If you haven't, then you'll get another message telling you where to go next Sunday... And, start to go out for walks more regularly so that nobody takes any notice of the important walks... maybe at least one where you are in view of the house at all times.'

Chiara started to thank the woman but she shook her head and said, 'Now go... and be patient just a little bit longer. He loves you,' and she turned and, taking the toddler by the hand, set off up the hill towards Santa Cristina.

During the week, she took the woman's advice and went out for a long walk every day except Thursday, trying not to establish a pattern. In front of the family, Maddalena made fun of her for her new found sportiness, 'Aristide and his friends will put you on display as an example of vigorous Italian womanhood, a shining example for others to follow.' Aristide narrowed his eyes slightly, aware that his sister was mocking the system, but not sure that he could do anything about it.

'You ought to come with me,' said Chiara and, smiling sweetly, 'how about you Virginia?'

Virginia shuddered as she thought of the cold outside, 'Maybe when the spring comes,' - but Maddalena said that she would come for a walk, as had been previously agreed on by the sisters.

As a consequence, Maddalena accompanied her sister on both Wednesday and Friday, for the second of which they plotted a route that meant they were never out of sight of anyone who might be watching from the house for more than a few seconds. On the Friday, another brief note appeared under her pillow, *'Riverbank. Uprooted tree. 200m north of bridge'*.

On Sunday, large flakes of snow were drifting lazily down out of the sky. Elisabetta told the girls that they should not go out, and then, when they insisted, reminding her that they had grown up in the Val d'Aosta, changed to insisting that they should wrap up well, be careful, and not stay out too long. It took great will-power not to walk directly down towards the river, or to walk too fast. She had made sure that the previous day, when she had walked alone, that her walk took in the river and she had been relieved when she had seen that there was only one uprooted tree, she had tormented herself all day with the thought of missing him as she waited in the wrong place.

As they reached the trees that screened the western bank of the small river from any casual onlookers, Maddalena sat on a wall and took off one of her shoes. 'Go on. And if anyone comes I'll call out, "Chiara – I'm getting cold -I want to go back," she waved her sister away as she saw she was about to give her a hug of gratitude. 'Go on – now – don't waste any time.' Chiara looked at her, smiled, and then turned and disappeared into the trees.

He was there before her, leaning on the trunk of the uprooted tree. She smiled and moved towards him feeling suddenly shy. As he pushed himself up from the tree she was shocked to see how much he had changed over the last few weeks: his cheeks seemed sunken; there was a red weal running down one side of his face; one hand was bandaged and the other had two fingers strapped together; he seemed to move very stiffly. She could not help putting her hand to her mouth in shock, then all shyness passed and she rushed towards him as a surge of tenderness ran through her.

They embraced, but she pulled away immediately as he failed to stifle a gasp of pain. He kissed the tip of one of his free fingers and put it gently to her lips as she was about to speak. 'I had a few broken ribs, and they're not quite healed yet, but it's nothing to worry about. I'll wake up one morning soon and they'll just feel normal again,' he paused and then, removing his finger from her lips, 'you'll just have to behave like a good girl for a while!'

'What happened? Tell me everything.'

He shook his head, 'Not now. I will tell you everything, but later when we have all the time in the world. There's nothing to worry about: no permanent damage apart from a couple of teeth that won't be growing back.'

She looked him in the eyes, noting that a glint of steely determination had replaced the trustful innocence that had been there before and had been one of the things that had initially attracted her to him. Now, he seemed to have grown up and she felt that she desperately needed to show that she was able to grow with him. 'Tell me what we need to do... Tell me what I need to do.' He smiled, 'and don't smile at me like that, or I won't remember anything.' He kissed her, then gently pulled her over to the tree trunk where he sat down, leaving room for her to sit next to him.

He hesitated for a moment and looked at her earnestly, 'Are you prepared to give up everything you have: your nice home, money, a life of luxury where you can have almost anything you want?'

Chiara did not hesitate before replying; she thought that she'd never felt more certain of anything in her life, ' "Almost" means everything except what I want more than anything else, so Yes, I am.'

'And are you prepared to do it soon – not waiting until you are twenty-one?' He studied her face carefully, his heart in his mouth as he saw conflicting emotions fighting for possession of her.

'Yes – but Maddi is waiting for me just outside the wood, so that she can warn me if anyone comes – I can't just leave her there.'

'Oh, you are wonderful,' he said, attempting to hug her and then wincing as his ribs reminded him of their presence. 'Not quite that soon. I need to be fit before we go because the journey won't be easy. Between Christmas and New Year, I should be ready – can you be?'

She tried to think rationally and ignore the heightened sensation of her heart and all her pulses pumping blood around her body. 'My father always spends Christmas here and expects all the family to be there – the big happy Italian family. But, if it's the same as the last two years, he'll be going to Montecatini on the twenty-seventh and then directly from there to Rome for the New Year. Once he's gone, Aristide will be busy with

Pavolini, organising New Year festivities in Florence, so no-one really knows what's going on in the house.'

'How much time do you think you'll have before anyone realises you've gone?'

She thought, 'Probably about half a day before anyone misses me, apart from Maddi. Maddi's going to be a problem... not because she'd give me away, but because she'll be in big trouble if she doesn't say anything. I don't want them to take it out on her.'

He sat back and looked at her; this was one more problem that he hadn't thought of - of course she had to protect her sister – it just made him love her even more, if that were possible. He sighed; there was some serious thinking to be done.

They sat looking at each other considering the practicalities, for what seemed like a long time, but which in reality was less than five minutes, then she jumped to her feet, 'I think I know how we can do it. I need to talk to Maddi, but I think we can do it,' she said excitedly. 'I'll go now.'

'No. Wait. There's too much risk in going and then coming back. Tell me now, then go and talk to Maddi, and let me know.'

'All right. Maddi loves choral music and every year, around Christmas and New Year, there are concerts by the two choral societies in Siena. One of them, the 'Mascagni' is supported by Baldo Brandi, who's a lawyer and sometimes works with Margarita's husband. Alfonso tries to go to all the concerts because he likes to be seen in the right places. Margarita, hates going and tries to get out of it whenever she can. If Maddi insists on going to stay with Margarita so that she can go to the concerts, everyone will be happy; Margarita gets to stay at home; Alfonso doesn't have to sit in his box on his own or with a moaning Margarita, and no-one can accuse Maddi of having anything to do with my escape.'

'Brilliant, if Maddi agrees, and if she's allowed to go.'

'Oh, she'll be allowed to go; she can make herself very irritating when she wants – they'll be glad to get rid of her in the house.'

She smiled at him and he embraced her gently without putting too much pressure on his recovering ribs. She smothered his faces with kisses until, reluctantly, he pushed her away. 'Go now. Next week, I'll meet you two hundred yards downstream, so you can approach from a different direction. If Maddi agrees, wear something blue when you go for a walk tomorrow. Someone will be watching.'

She turned and ran out of the trees towards where she had left her sister, knowing that if she looked back, she would not be able to leave him.

Maddi was shivering when she reached her, and Chiara felt guilty for having left her for so long. She put her arms round her sister and held her tightly, hoping to put some warmth back into her. 'Well someone looks a lot happier now. If I'd been here much longer you'd have had a dead body to explain away.'

'I'm sorry. I don't deserve a friend like you, let alone a sister. Thank you, thank you, thank you!' and she hugged her even more tightly.

'Let me put my shoe back on. We'll have to go a bit more slowly on the way back; I rubbed the side of my foot to make it sore so that I had an excuse for sitting here waiting for you, if I'd needed one.'

'I love you Maddi, but now I need to ask you to make an even bigger sacrifice.'

'Go on. I'm listening – but you know the answer's going to be "yes", don't you? Even before you ask.'

Before she asked her sister if she would help them with her plan, she told her about Max and his injuries and the initial shock she had felt.

Maddalena looked shocked and there were tears in her eyes; 'All that and they haven't managed to scare him away. It sounds as if he might be good enough for you; I didn't think it was possible that anyone could be,' she said, linking her arm through her sister's, 'Now, what do you need me to do?'

'When papa leaves, after Christmas, Margarita and Alfonso will go back to Siena with the kids. I want you to go with them because you want to go to the concerts.'

Maddalena responded with mock horror, 'I see what you mean about the ultimate sacrifice, spending time with moaning Marg and arrogant Alfonso... and I'll have to be nice to them and their spoilt brats while they here, otherwise they won't take them with me.'

'That's not the sacrifice, Maddi, and you know it. The sacrifice is that I'll be gone when you come back and, unless we're caught, I won't see you for a long time.'

Chiara waited for Maddi's response for a while then her sister looked at her with tears in her eyes, 'I said before that the answer's yes. I'll do anything to make you happy.'

'Thank you,' said Chiara, 'I'll see you again. I promise.' Maddi shook her head sadly.

The two sisters spent as much time as possible together over the next few days talking about everything and anything, except for the one subject that was closest to their hearts: that was taboo.

The following Sunday was one of the days that Maddalena did not accompany her sister on her walk. They had been careful not to establish any kind of pattern and Maddalena said that she could hardly sit on the edge of the wood again pretending that her boot hurt her foot. Instead, she decided that she would start to work on Margarita and Alfonso, who were visiting with the children.

Chiara was relieved to see that Max was looking much stronger with the passage of another week. He looked a little less gaunt, and only the hand that had previously been swathed in bandages, now bore light strapping to provide a visible sign of the violence he had endured for her. She was also pleased to feel that he could now embrace her tightly without suffering discomfort and she ran her hands over him beneath the greatcoat he wore. There were still some areas where he was sore, but he assured her that in a few more days he would be as good as new.

Although, as she had worn the blue coat on two occasions during the week, he already knew that Maddi had agreed to help them, he listened keenly as she recounted her conversation with her sister and updated him on Maddalena's charm offensive towards Margarita and Alfonso. He laughed as she told him of Elisabetta's irritation when Maddi continually played records by Mafalda Favero, Giovanni Martinelli and José Luccioni, and her claims that she might become an opera singer herself. 'They really will be glad to get rid of her after Christmas, although I'm not sure how keen Margarita will be to have her.'

Max went over the plan in detail, just in-case anything prevented them from meeting the following Sunday, which was just two days before Christmas. He stressed that if there were things that she was expected to do and that she would normally have done, then it was far better if she did them to avoid raising suspicions. He hoped that, a month having passed, they would be less on their guard, but they couldn't be too careful. One of the benefits of his being, in their view, "a nobody", was that they would find it hard to believe that Chiara could have any real interest in him, and hopefully assume that there had been nothing serious on her part. If the opportunity arose, Chiara should try and give credence to this assumption by showing an interest in other people, 'without going too far!' he said, looking at her sternly to elicit a smile.

Having already gone over the plans proved to be fortuitous, as a few days later, Aristide announced that they would all be attending a special pre-Christmas mass in Florence on the following Sunday. Maddalena protested that she had far better things to do but was informed stiffly by Aristide that it was up to families like theirs to set a good example, and also that it was good for them to be seen there. To Maddalena's surprise, Chiara did not protest and seemed to accept missing her weekly meeting with Max without putting up a fight. She shook her head and muttered, showing that although Aristide had made it clear that they would all be going, she still wasn't happy about it.

'Why didn't you back me up?' she asked later in an argumentative tone, 'You've got more reason than anyone not to want to go on Sunday.' She glared at her sister.

Chiara took hold of Maddalena's hand and kept hold of it when she tried to pull away. 'The last thing I want is for Aristide, or any of the others, to think that I have a reason for not wanting to go to Florence on Sunday. If they think I'm not bothered about being here then they won't watch me as closely next week... and there was no way that Aristide was going to change his mind.'

'Oh, Chiara, so I nearly messed everything up for you, I'm...'

'No, Maddi, you were wonderful, because you were natural and behaved just how they all expected you to behave.' Max knows that things were likely to come up this weekend, so he won't mind too much. Think of these next few days as being our time, because when you've gone to Siena, it will be a long time before we see each other again.'

'Alright', said Maddalena, 'I don't mind going to the boring mass then, because I'll be with you... but I'll have some fun moaning about it before we go. I can't seem enthusiastic about it, or they'll think I've had a damascene conversion and am well on the way to finding my true vocation as a nun.'

Although they spent most of the Sunday together, they did not get to sit together during the mass. Aristide had arranged it so that Chiara was sitting next to an immaculately dressed cousin of Pavolini. He had slicked-back brown hair and a close clipped moustache which he was obviously very proud of. Undeniably handsome, he was clearly fully aware of it and behaved as if it was his right to be worshipped by everyone. As they knelt for the prayers she noticed his hand push the kneeling cushion slightly closer to hers so that as they knelt, she was aware of the proximity of his leg to hers. She did not move her own leg, remembering the advice that she should appear interested in other suitors.

When the time came for the congregation to take communion, he did not move so, although she no longer believed and, over the last few years, had only taken communion at Easter, as a way of placating her family, she excused herself and joined the queue waiting for the *'ostia'*; the slight sense of guilt she felt at taking communion under false pretences was heavily outweighed by the relief she felt at having escaped from his presence for a few minutes.

At the end of the service, Elisabetta made her way over to them. 'Gian Giacomo, what a pleasure to see you again,' and she kissed him on both cheeks, 'how are your family, especially your dear mother?' then, without waiting for his reply, 'but how rude of me; I haven't introduced you to my sister-in-law. This is our dear Chiara. Chiara, this is Gian Giacomo Melluso, a cousin of Alessandro.'

'Ah, I had the pleasure of sitting next to your charming sister-in-law during the ceremony; my thoughts were so distracted that I was unable to go and take communion at the end.'

'It's a pleasure to meet you... any friend of my brother and Elisabetta is a friend of mine.'

He looked pained and with a slight bow said, 'I hope that on further acquaintance you will find that I have merits over and above the approbation of others to recommend myself.'

She smiled, secure in the knowledge that in a few days she'd be gone and safe from any 'further acquaintance' with this insincere playboy. 'I hope that after the festive season is over, you will be able to come out and visit us in San Casciano. And now,' she smiled, 'I must go and find my younger sister. If you'll excuse me.' She turned, glad to escape from Melluso's presence, and made her way through the crowd to where Maddalena was being talked to by some friends of their father, seeing that she definitely needed rescuing. 'Good evening. Good evening, *Marchese.*' They greeted her in their turn but, before they could recommence their words of advice to Maddalena, she said, 'I'm afraid I'll have to tear my sister away from you, we need to find our brother who will be driving us home. Have a very pleasant Christmas,' and she pulled her sister away, acknowledging the return greetings as she did so.

'So, which of our wonderful brothers is waiting to whisk us out of this theatre of the absurd? You weren't making it up were you?'

'Of course I was. Should I have left you at the mercy of the great and the good? Anyway, I don't care which of our brothers leaves first, but I want to make sure that we are in the car with them. It will probably be Filippo, as small talk isn't his thing.'

'Then let's go and find him and pretend he's our favourite brother.'

Chiara laughed, 'If you think about it, he probably is – but that's almost certainly because we see less of him than the other two.' Maddalena giggled.

The following evening, the whole family was again in church for the midnight mass, but this time in the small church of *San Colombano* on the hillside above Bargino. First, however, the family sat down to the traditional Christmas Eve meal, for the preparation of which both Chiara and Maddalena had been seconded to help Adele during the day, Gianna being unable to help as she was ill. When they joined the others at the table, being sure that Adele could cope with what was left to do in the kitchen and serve, Chiara was asked to say grace by her father, which, as they all stood up, bowed their heads and, with the exception of Maddalena closed their eyes, gave her the opportunity to study them well for what she hoped would be one of the last times. No, she definitely would not miss any of the others. 'For what we are about to receive...' Once the grace was said, the glasses were filled, not with the estate's own wine but with a *Barolo* from Piemonte.

When she and Maddalena had been in the Val d'Aosta, she had looked forward to the meals at Christmas which had been abundant and made with high quality ingredients, but which felt genuine and wholesome and did not give her the feeling that appearance was more important than reality.

The marathon meal began with a vast assortment of antipasti: slices of lightly toasted rustic bread rubbed with garlic, smothered in chopped anchovies, and dripping with their own olive oil; tartlets of olive paste, baked aubergine mashed with oil and garlic, and chopped pickled artichokes. She thought of the millions of less privileged people in the country, for whom this antipasti on its own would constitute unimaginable luxury, and felt a sense of guilt. The *antipasti* were followed by two *primi*. The first was a large bowl of spaghetti with *vongole*, which had been brought specially from Livorno that afternoon, along with the mixture of seafood that gave the flavour to the other *primo* which was a creamy *risotto alla pescatora*. There were a few minutes respite before the main course arrived, made up of sea-bass and gilthead bream which had been carefully wrapped up in paper parcels with thyme and a sliver of oil and then roasted; these were served with rosemary sprinkled roast potatoes and deep fried pieces of cauliflower and marrow, not forgetting the large bowls of salad that had been placed within reach of either end of the table. Despite the roast fish being the part of the meal that she liked best, she found that she had been drawn into eating too much of the *antipasti* and *primi* and so did little more than pick at a piece of sea-bass, making sure that she kept her plate well filled with salad, to mask the lack of the more filling elements.

They drove down to the village using all three cars and ascended the hill on the other side of the valley, parking a hundred metres short of the church. Led by Domenico, with Elisabetta on his arm, they then completed the short distance separating them from the church on foot, allowing the other people heading towards the mass to admire and pay their respects to Domenico and the other leading members of the family. At the door of the church, the priest, clearly warned of their imminent arrival waited at the door to greet them.

Once the priest had paid his obsequious respects, including several references to the family's contribution to the rebuilding of the bell-tower, the family were led to the front pews which had been left for their use. As Chiara made her way up the aisle alongside Virginia and with Umberto and Maddalena behind them, a woman who was on her feet at the start of one of the rows, bent over a toddler to re-button his coat, straightened up and took half a step backwards into the aisle knocking against Chiara and causing her to pause. The woman half turned and put out her hand as if to steady herself. As she did so, Chiara realised that it was again the woman from the picture, and tried not to let surprise show on her face. The woman apologised profusely for having bumped into *la signorina*, and as she did so, Chiara realised that a small piece of paper had been slipped into the cuff of her glove. She smiled and insisted that it was of no consequence and that she understood how distracting it must be having to look after a small child so late at night.

'Chiara, you're holding everyone up,' said Umberto behind her, and she gave Laura a smile and moved on.

Afterwards, Chiara couldn't remember a word of the service. She managed to get through the next forty minutes, mechanically responding in the right places, even though she would normally have just moved her lips so that she would appear to be participating, while secretly despising the whole piece of theatre. All she could think of was the piece of paper in her glove; she had pushed it further in, and although she knew that there was no way it could come out without assistance, she was terrified by the thought that when she removed her glove it would be gone, and everything would go wrong because she didn't have some important piece of information.

Even when the ceremony finished, she still had to be patient: everyone seemed to want to pay their respects to Domenico, Aristide, Elisabetta and, to a lesser extent, Umberto and Virginia. Except for smiles and nods of the heads and brief formulaic greetings, most people seemed to ignore her and Maddalena, for which she felt very grateful. She looked around for the woman from the picture, whose name, she realised, she still did not know, but could not see her anywhere. Presumably she had used the toddler as an excuse to slip away as soon as possible, maybe even before the end of the service.

She was impatient to get back to the house, back to her room, and able to look at the slip of paper in her glove. Eventually, all the family's social obligations seemed to have been fulfilled; Aristide's youngest child had fallen asleep in Elisabetta's arms and everyone was ready to go.

Saying how tired she was, she excused herself and went straight up to her room when they got back. Having closed the door behind her, she leaned against it so that she could not be surprised and ripped her glove off. On the slip of paper was drawn a little cherub which seemed to be pointing its arrow straight at her heart, and the words *'Hands recovered for you. 2 am Friday morning -the hollow.'*

She closed her eyes and leaned back on the door for a few seconds suddenly feeling warm all over as she thought of his artistic fingers and what it would feel like to be really touched by him. She pulled herself together and began to carefully, though regretfully, shred the note into the smallest pieces possible so that not a single letter remained legible. Kicking her house-shoes off, which she had slipped on after taking her boots off in the entrance hallway, she let herself fall backwards onto her bed still fully clothed, and pulled the bolster cushion onto her, trying to force her imagination to believe that it was Max. A click as the bedroom door closed made her jump up guiltily, but she relaxed as she saw Maddalena standing looking at her with a smile on her face. 'Oh, it's you.'

Maddalena's smile widened, 'Who did you expect? Now... I want to know everything.'

'What do you mean?' 'Chiara, you have four insensitive, heartless brothers and sisters, not five. That woman in the church - the one with the baby - she gave you something, didn't she?'

She felt Maddalena's quick dark eyes bore into her and she felt that her sister was able to peel away the different layers of her soul as if she'd been an onion. Then she felt a stab of alarm, 'Did, Umberto...'

'Umberto wouldn't have spotted anything even if he hadn't drunk at least a bottle of wine. You were very quick and very sneaky about it. If I didn't know you almost as well as I know myself, you would have fooled me as well, but your eyes gave you away.' Chiara didn't know what to say and her sister continued, 'Do you remember when we went to Rome with *papa*, and were shown around the main sites?' Chiara nodded, 'Well your eyes would have fitted perfectly into that statue by Bernini, the one they call *'The ecstasy of Saint Teresa.'*

Chiara laughed; they had both been very impressed by the statue and she had wondered how anyone could be so possessed by religious fervour. Now, as she remembered the statue, she wondered whether it had been something other than religion that had been so dramatically recreated by Bernini.

Alright,' she said, 'I wouldn't have kept it secret from you, it's just that after more than a week, I just wanted to savour the moment a bit before sharing it.' Maddalena came and sat next to her and hugged her. 'You're right, there was a little note. He still loves me and he's going to take me away.'

'Well, he'd better make sure he loves you as much as you love him, or it won't just be the rest of our family who will want to kill him.'

Feeling relieved at not having to keep the secret, Chiara forgot about the long day she had just had and, enthused by the twin powers of love and hope, talked to Maddalena at great length about her hopes for her and Max's future, until she realised that her sister had fallen asleep, at which point she guided her, half asleep to her own bed.

The following day, Christmas Day, was another day of Lucullan excess, with free flowing wine, this time from the family estates, and seemingly endless meat dishes throughout the day. They were joined before lunch by Margarita, Alfonso and their children, and whenever they were not helping Adele, Chiara was amused to see Maddalena's renewed charm offensive on their elder sister and her family. By the end of the day, after her efforts had been assisted by the combined influence of bottles of *spumante, vin santo* and *grappa*, Alfonso thought it was an excellent idea, and Campolargo himself appeared to look on the prospect with benevolence. Only Margarita seemed less than convinced by the idea. On Boxing Day, Margarita's eldest boy came off worse in a scuffle with his cousin, Benito, and Maddalena solicitously comforted him before returning him to her sister. By the end of Boxing Day it had been agreed that Maddalena would go with them on the evening of the twenty-seventh.

Throughout the twenty-seventh, Maddalena was a blur of perpetual motion, laughing, joking, playing with the children, rushing to help Adele in the kitchen, the epitome of life, youth and happiness. Only Chiara was not taken in; she knew that Maddalena was trying to fill up every minute of her day so that she didn't have to think about the forthcoming separation. She herself felt a strange mixture of emotions that she had not expected: she was desperate to feel Max's arms around her and to be taken right away from the family whom she viewed as her jailers and yet, at the same time, she felt sad to be leaving her dear Maddi, not knowing how long it would be before they could meet again.

Campolargo left with his chauffeur at five o'clock, after embracing the other members of the family one after the other although, Chiara noted, with varying degrees of warmth. As soon as his car disappeared down the driveway, Margarita told Maddalena that she needed to be ready to leave at six, and that if she wasn't, they would go without her.

'Yes, Margarita,' said Maddalena and turned to go to her room followed by Chiara. Most of Maddalena's things had already been carefully placed into a leather valise so all she really needed to do was to change for the journey, which would only take a few minutes. The two sisters held each other tightly for a long time before speaking. Chiara could feel the salty tears mingling on their cheeks. 'I just want you to promise me that you'll both be happy, Chiara.'

'I'll write. I don't know how but I'll write.'

'And how do I write to you?' said Maddalena, 'I won't even know where you are.' 'We'll find a way. If the people Max knows can help us get out of the country, then I'm sure that letters will be a lot easier. Now, go and rinse your face, you look a mess.'

When she had done her best to erase the signs of crying, she looked at her sister and said, 'What about you? You can't come down and see me off looking like that, they'll think I've beaten you up before leaving!'

Chiara shook her head, 'I'm not coming down. I don't think I could bear it. Tell them I've got a headache and will come down for a glass of milk later.' She looked at her sister and committed every detail to memory then, feeling that she was going to cry again and fearing that that would start Maddi off, she kissed her and pushed her towards the door, 'Go on. Don't keep them waiting – you're enthusiastic, remember.'

Maddi did her best to put on a brave face, 'I love you, Chiara. Be happy and don't forget me.'

'I will, and I'll never forget you – I love you too,' and she closed the door behind her sister.

Although she did not go down to see her two sisters off, she stood at her window watching the car's tail-lights slowly disappear, and then fixed the last spot she'd seen them for a good five minutes more, with her sister's image etched on the inside of her eyelids.

She looked pale when she went down for a glass of milk and nobody questioned her claim that she needed a good night's sleep and would see them the following morning. After the excesses of the past few days, and with another evening of overeating and drinking ahead of them, she was confident that none of them would be up early in the morning, and would assume that she too was sleeping in late.

Ideally, she would have slept for three or four hours, to help prepare her for what lay ahead during the night, but she was too tense and didn't sleep at all. She sat in the most uncomfortable chair in the room near the window, which she kept open so that the warmth of the heating system didn't lull her into sleep. Any time she felt her head begin to droop, she sprang up and walked around the room several times. She heard other people move past her room on their way to bed and then finally, by half past twelve, she was confident that they had all gone. Still she sat, listening intently, until the clock in Aristide's study struck one and she knew that she hadn't heard anyone move in the house for more than forty minutes. She very quietly placed the few things she was going to take into a canvas travelling bag and then, as the clock struck half past one, gently eased the door open and slipped through into the corridor.

Moving very slowly, she made her way along the corridor to the back stairs, hardly daring to breathe as she passed Umberto's door. If he were still awake and heard her, what then? But he didn't. As she rounded the corner and gained the top of the stairs, she leaned against the wall and exhaled, then breathed deeply several times before beginning to carefully descend, feeling her way along the wall in the near complete blackness. Reaching the bottom of the stairs without making any noise she began to feel more confident. Having the layout of the house and its distances fixed firmly in her mind, she began to move more quickly towards the outside door.

Suddenly, her foot met something soft and there was a noise between a miaow and a loud hiss. She froze. The cat. Was she going to be defeated by the cat? She heard movement in the room to her left and then saw a glimmer of light appear as the door opened. She looked horrified, straight into the eyes of Adele.

Adele smiled, inclined her head towards the door and mouthed something which Chiara thought was, 'God go with you', and then withdrew back into her room.

Chiara felt a wave of gratitude, and moved forward determined not to waste this reprieve. As she was about to draw back the several heavy bolts that secured the door she stopped, if Adele didn't report finding the door open first thing in the morning then she would be in trouble, and Chiara didn't want that. She retraced her steps and tapped softly on Adele's door and a few seconds later she was whispering her new plan to the maid.

Chapter 7

Max shivered and held his watch up to the moonlight. Five past two. She had to be here soon or all the carefully thought out plan would begin to unravel. Then she was there, in his arms, appearing out of the vines like a phantom.

As they separated, he took her bag in one hand and led her with the other. He headed uphill for a few minutes along the verge of the road and then stepped onto the harder surface and turned and headed down towards the Via Cassia and Bargino. 'It probably won't make any difference, but if they look for footprints it's better that they're going the other way.' She nodded, trusting him completely.

On the outskirts of the village, Max guided her into a small barn where she saw that another man was waiting in the darkness. The man, whose face she couldn't see well, held out a coat. 'I need you to swap your coat for this. At ten past six, a young dark-haired woman wearing your coat, and a young man with fair hair will catch the early morning coach to Florence. It's cold and dark, so they'll be well wrapped up with scarves and hats and easy to remember but difficult to recognise. Once they're in the city they'll separate, dispose of your coat somewhere safe, and go home separately by other means.'

Max could see that Chiara was impressed and also very tired, having been operating on nervous energy since early the previous morning. 'We're going to rest here for a few hours then we're going to leave in a different direction. If we avoid doing the things they expect, and lay a few false trails, we can do this.' He eased her coat off her shoulders, and then wrapped the coarser cloak that Giorgio held out around her. He nodded thanks to Giorgio who left the barn without saying another word.

Who is he?'

'Not now. If we get caught, the less you know the better – I'll tell you everything when we're safe. Just rest now *amore*. He smiled as he said the last word, savouring the long central vowel sound.

He woke her with a kiss on her forehead, four hours later. 'We need to go,' he said, we have a three hour walk to do, and we need to get started while there's no one about. In half an hour we'll be off the road and on the old mule tracks, but until then we have to be very careful.' He led her towards the main road then told her to start walking south and that he would follow in two minutes, which would eliminate the risk of anyone in Bargino remembering seeing a young couple.

Soon after he caught her up, they turned off the main road and shortly after onto a track which ran roughly parallel to the Via Cassia until reaching a fork above Sambuca. We go left here,' he said 'and when we get near to San Donato, we'll need to split up again, for safety. Are you all right with all the walking?' 'I grew up in the Val d'Aosta, remember. I can walk all day, over difficult terrain, if I have to.'

'That's good, as you might have to end up carrying me, if I can't keep up.'

A look of concern showed in her face, 'Your injuries. Are they still hurting you?'

He laughed, picked her up and spun her around, 'Good as new... you'll have to get used to my English sense of humour,' and then tenderly, ' I'm sorry. I didn't mean to worry you.'

She smiled, 'Come on then, let's see who needs carrying first,' and she strode off up the left-hand fork.'

At San Donato, they decided it was best if one skirted the castellated village to the east and one to the west. They were to meet up again at their destination which was an impressive seventeenth century church surrounded on three sides by a terracotta veranda, supported by five arches at the front of the church and three to each side.

The church lay in the hamlet of Pietracupa just to the South-East of the village and the sounds of children playing could clearly be heard coming from a large building attached to the rear. As Chiara, being Italian, would appear less noteworthy than him, he asked her to go to the large building and ask for Sister Antonia, with the excuse that there was a message for her from her father. Max waited under the veranda on the southern side of the church, which was out of the sight-line of the nearby houses.

Within five minutes, Chiara was back with a very severe looking nun, who Max thought could have been almost any age between twenty-five and fifty. 'Good morning, Sister Antonia. I think you were expecting us.' The nun gave a half smile and indicated that they should follow her.

A rough, but clearly fairly well frequented track ran down by the side of the church. Sister Antonia led them along the track for about three hundred yards to a point where, a countryman sat on the grass by the side, smoking a pipe. The nun broke into a genuine smile, that made her look far less severe, embraced the man and then, turning to Max and Chiara said, 'This is my brother, Aldo. He will take you on the next stage of your journey. May God go with you. I will pray for you.'

'Thank you, Sister, for what you have done for us, said Max', and Chiara leaned forward and kissed the nun on the cheek.'

'Come on then, your carriage awaits,' said Aldo.

They followed him to where two oxen were grazing and a flat bottomed cart was tucked into the trees at the side of the road. 'Up you get,' he said, 'You sit at the front next to me, signorina, and you go in the back. Keep low down and, if I say "down", pull the sacks over you and don't say a word. If anyone asks,' he said, addressing himself to Chiara,' you're my shy girlfriend, so you'll need to stay very close and, if we have to put on a show, I'll put my arm around you and pull you towards me. That will help to hide your face...' 'Perks of the job, I'm afraid,' he added, addressing this last remark to Max, and making an apologetic hand gesture.

'Come on, let's go,' I'll trust you unless you start suggesting taking us further than the plan!' responded Max with a friendly grin.

There was only one moment that gave rise to any alarm on the ninety minute journey along the rutted track. As Aldo rounded a bend he saw that, on their left, two young men were harvesting the fruit from an olive grove. 'Down… Chiara, put your head on my shoulder, and try and keep your face facing down. They haven't seen us yet, but I know them and it will look suspicious if I try to go past without saying anything.'

'Hey, do you two never stop working. The rest of the country's having fun between Christmas and New Year. Are you after a medal from Mussolini for your productivity?'

'Sod off, Aldo. The olives don't know it's Christmas and they won't wait. We can't all just swan around waiting to be given a load to carry... Where are you off to anyway?'

'Never you mind. You're not the only ones who can find fruit that's ripe for the picking.' All three men laughed and the two olive pickers sent him on his way with a few well chosen ribald comments.'

'Sorry about that, just trying to appear natural.'

'Don't worry. I enjoyed the show,' responded Chiara.

'I'll have to go back a different way, or the word will get round that I'm losing my touch,' he added with a laugh.

He pulled up next to a small farmhouse with a lean-to barn alongside. A vicious looking hunting dog strained on its chain and growled in their direction, and Chiara moved closer to Max. 'His bark's worse than his bite, Miss,' came a voice from behind them. An old farmer stood at the corner of the house with a gun, which Max thought was probably the oldest he'd ever seen, slung over his shoulder. Aldo took his cap off and held out his hand.

'It's good to see you, Signor Bruni. You're looking well.'

'I'd be better if we could get rid of these fascist scum. You mark my words, they'll drag us into war sooner rather than later. But don't just stand there, come inside and have something to eat, you must be more than ready.'

Both Max and Chiara realised that they were, in fact, very hungry. The old man led the three young people inside, pulled the cork out of a flask of wine, placed a large form of bread in the middle of the table and ladled generous helpings of *ribollita* into four earthenware bowls. As they ate, the old man asked

Aldo how his sister was doing and about other common acquaintances. Max noticed that he did not show any curiosity about Chiara and himself. As they neared the end of the meal, Chiara commented that it had probably been the tastiest *ribollita* she had ever had. The old man was obviously pleased by the compliment, although he tried hard not to show it.

'I only eat my own produce. I'm not paying any more taxes than I have to to the blackshirts. Everything you buy in the shops, or even in the markets, they take a cut of. And anything I can do to fight back, I will.'

'What do you grow?'

'Signor Bruni grows everything that you could possibly imagine. He waves his hand over the land and all sorts of fruit and vegetables spring up. No one else round here manages to grow half the things he does.'

'Huh, what would you know, young-man. You'd run a mile before getting your hands in the soil.'

When they had finished eating, Chiara insisted on cleaning the plates for Bruni, giving Max a quick little smile as she adopted the role that she knew would be expected of her by most men. Bruni and Aldo filled Max in with the details of the next stage of their journey. Early the following morning, a lorry laden with olives was travelling to Arezzo. They would be hidden in the back until a couple of kilometres before the city, where they would be handed over to someone else. Bruni did not know what was happening after that. He hadn't asked, because the less anyone knew, the safer it was for everyone. Although Max didn't know the details of the route, he knew that the idea was that they would cross the Adriatic to Greece and travel back to England by sea. Agreeing with Bruni's sentiments about it being safer for people not to know too much, he judged it better not to share this information. He would rather people jumped to the obvious conclusion that they planned to make their way north, although giving Florence a wide berth.

'For some reason, the local Mayor, a loyal follower of his excellence the *Duce*, has taken a dislike to me and got into the habit of sending police round to call at all hours of the night, so I'm afraid it's better if you don't sleep in the house tonight. There's a hayloft in the barn that should be safe. The animals down below will provide a little bit of warmth. It's not long since most of us lived that way in the countryside, with our own living space on top of that of the animals.' They assured him that they didn't mind at all and that they didn't want to do anything that would bring the wrath of the authorities down on his head. He was already taking a big risk for them. He assured them that the police would never bother to check the barn as it would mean going close to the dog, and they couldn't be sure how long its chain was.

Aldo left when the light began to fade and he judged that his olive picking friends would have given up for the day and it was safe for him to return the same way. Shortly after he had gone, the old man showed them out to the barn and handed them a pile of old blankets. He then showed them up a sturdy handmade ladder and held his lantern aloft while they burrowed down into the straw and made a cocoon with the blankets.

After Aldo had withdrawn, placing the ladder out of sight, there was just enough moonlight filtering through the terracotta air-bricks at the end of the barn for them to see the vapour every time they breathed. Chiara, gave a nervous laugh as she snuggled closer to him, 'Did you know that every girl dreams of what the first night she spends with the man she loves is going to be like? I never, ever imagined that it might be like this. There is absolutely no way that I'm going to take any clothes off tonight - if I do, I can't guarantee to be alive in the morning!' He hummed the music to the opening of the third act of *Rigoletto* and, as she realised that he was making fun of her, she gave him a hard pinch on his chest where her hand was resting under his coat, ' Just you wait! I'll give you *"la donna è mobile!"* and they both laughed, snuggling even closer together.

He was relieved when she awoke early in the morning as the animals began to stir down below; for the last hour he had been aware his right arm had become completely numb, trapped as it was beneath Chiara. He knew that his hand was resting on her flesh somewhere underneath the various layers of clothing and blankets, but for the moment he could feel absolutely nothing except for a dull pain. 'Could you just roll over so I can get my arm out, it's gone numb – you must have eaten too much at Christmas!'

She stuck her tongue out at him and taking care to put as little extra pressure as possible on his arm, she gently lifted herself off him. 'It must be my guardian angel protecting my virtue,' she said and leaned to kiss him.

He grimaced as he lifted his right wrist with his left hand and rolled his right shoulder until circulation returned, sending daggers of pain down his arm to be followed by pins and needles. 'Can you tell your guardian angel that I promise to be good, at least until we find somewhere a bit warmer, please.'

'I'm not sure. I think my guardian angel and I may have different views on the subject, so I can't promise to be good.'

Half an hour later, they heard the dog growl and then fall silent at a command from Bruni. He invited Chiara into the house, telling her that she would find a jug of hot water in the back room, but that they needed to be ready to move in fifteen minutes. Shortly after, a van-backed Fiat commercial vehicle creaked to a halt by the house, driven by a taciturn young man wearing a flat cap and a military style great coat. A scarf was pulled up over his face leaving only a pair of green eyes visible. He nodded to Bruni. 'The man in the back and the signorina in the front for as long as she can stand the cold, then they can swap over for a bit, but I want her in the front every time we go through a town.' He addressed neither Max nor Chiara directly but directed all his comments to Bruni. Although, the back of the vehicle, which Max suspected was a relic of the Great War, was enclosed, the cab was exposed to the elements and Max thought it would not be long before they were swapping paces. He could understand why the Italian was so well wrapped up.

Three and a half hours later, Max, who had eventually been jolted to sleep during his third spell in the back, was woken by van stopping and the engine being turned off. Then the back door was opened and Chiara called him out. The taciturn young man spoke for almost the first time that morning, indicating a bridleway on the right. They were to walk for about five kilometres, always keeping the city of Arezzo visible on the horizon. Then, when the track met a road that was ascending steeply away from the city, they were to follow that for another kilometre until they reached a small travellers' inn. In the Inn they were to ask if anyone could give them a lift towards Sansepolcro. Between two thirty and three, there would be someone there who was expecting them and would offer the lift they asked for. Having delivered what for him seemed to be a very long speech, he climbed back up onto his cab and continued along the road towards Arezzo, giving only a slight nod of the head when they tried to thank him.

Although the air was still cold, it was a bright sunny winter's day and they set of on the first part of their walk, hand in hand, feeling more relaxed than they had for days. After three and a half hours of the rickety, uncomfortable van, they felt re-invigorated by the walk and were in a good mood when they found the inn. Chiara had brought as much money from home as she had been able, including two hundred and fifty lire that she had taken from a roll of banknotes in Aristide's desk, with the justification that Max had not been paid by the family for the work he had done on the estate. As they had made good time and reached the inn by ten past two, they ordered some wine, some *bruschetta* and some bread and cheese to fill in the time and also to assuage the first pangs of hunger that had been induced by their walk. A large piece of seasoned *pecorino*, flavoured with black truffle was carved off just over half a large wheel of cheese which was wrapped in cheesecloth behind the counter, and the host poured out two generous glasses of wine from a two litre flask.

Soon after their arrival, two lorries pulled up outside with a gap of a couple of minutes between them, and both drivers came in and ordered a bite to eat and a glass of wine. Max assumed that one of them would be their next contact and hoped that they weren't both going to Sansepolcro. Luckily, when he went over to the landlord just after half past two to pay the bill and casually asked if he had any advice on how they could get to Sansepolcro, only one of the drivers called over to say that he was going that way and would be happy to give them a lift if they didn't mind waiting until he had finished. Max thanked him and told the landlord that when the lorry driver was ready, he would pay his bill.

Fortunately, this lorry was more modern than the previous one and had an enclosed cab with ample room for three people, so the next stage of their journey was accomplished in relative luxury. Unlike their previous helper, this driver was also a talker; he chatted away for the whole journey, making jokes about the regime and its leader that would have got him arrested if he'd made them in public. 'I never realised that so many people are against the regime,' said Chiara, 'all we're ever told is how popular the Duce is, and how successful all his policies are'.

The driver, whose name was Alfiero, but who had told them he preferred to be called Alfi, laughed, then apologised for any offence his laughter may have caused. A lot of people will go along with anything they're told, so just accept the regime; some people know that if they are part of the mechanism of the regime that they will have power over all those people who just accept it... and the rest of us want to do something, anything, to make life fairer for everyone. A few people are brave enough to stick their heads above the parapet and either end up in prison like Gramsci, or in exile like Togliatti; most of us just do what we can, when we can, and hope that it makes some sort of difference.

Alfi told them that, as far as he knew, there was no active search for them in Umbria, but that the further away they got the better it would be. He gave them a note to give to an uncle of his, who lived on a farm outside Gubbio. His uncle had no interest in politics, was illiterate, and saw few people except on market day when the main arguments of conversation would be sheep, cheese and grain while Alfi's aunt left the farm even less frequently than her husband. He dropped them near the station in Sansepolcro from where they were to take the train to Umbertide and then, if there were no obvious sources of lifts, they would be able to get a bus to Gubbio. From Gubbio, they would have to walk the two miles south to the farm near Santa Cristina.

As it happened, there was a bus just about to leave for Gubbio from in front of the station in Umbertide so they had no hesitation in taking that. From Gubbio, a straight narrow track ran across the plain to the south of the town. In the gathering gloom they could just make out distant hills and prepared themselves for a long walk to end the day. Distances, however, are deceptive in the dark and, less than forty minutes later, having crossed a larger road, they were climbing up the first of the gentle hills towards the isolated farmhouse that was their destination.

Alfi's uncle and aunt were clearly not in the habit of receiving visitors, and his uncle looked on them with suspicion, one hand on the collar of a large dog, as they tried to explain that Alfi had told them to go there. Max held out Alfi's note and the uncle called back over his shoulder, 'Teresa,' and his wife appeared. He passed her the note and Max could see her lips moving silently as she worked her way slowly through it, then she smiled.

'Move out of the way and let them in, or we'll all freeze to death,' and then to Max and Chiara, 'I'm sorry, but we have to be careful these days. But never mind that; you come in and sit by the fire. No don't take your boots off, you'll catch a chill from the floor... How is Alfi? We've not seen him for a while, but I'm sure he'll be along to see us soon. Come on. Get yourselves warm while I go and warm some broth up.' Her husband shook his head with a slight smile on his face as she fussed and flustered over the unexpected guests, in a way that made it difficult for anyone else to get a word in edgeways. Her broth turned out to have the consistency of a farmhouse vegetable soup rather than the consommé that they had been expecting, and they ate it gratefully, mopping the dishes with chunks of the traditional unsalted country bread.

They had decided, together with Alfi, who knew his aunt's disposition well, that they had to have a convincing reason to give their hosts for their travelling at that time, one which would sate her curiosity, while at the same time providing an explanation for Max not being Italian. Max was quite happy to leave most of the talking to Chiara while he sat looking into the flames of the fire. Because of her upbringing, it was hard to place Chiara's accent, although she was well able to pass for either a Florentine or a Val d'Aostan when she wished, and it was the latter which they had determined she should use until they were completely safe. Max heard her tell how she had left the mountains and been employed as a nursemaid in a well off family in Pisa with close connections to the clergy. Max, or Marsyas, as he was now to be known, was Greek and had been employed by the same family after the Greek vessel on which he had been working, had left suddenly during the night after the port authorities in Livorno had threatened to impound both the ship and its cargo if various import duties remained unpaid. They had got to know one another, had received the blessing of her family, and were now making their way to Ancona to get a boat over to Greece so that she could meet his family. They were hoping to get across in the next two days, in order to celebrate the New Year with his family.

Alfi's aunt was spellbound, and even Max found himself almost convinced by her narrative, even though he knew it was a complete invention. He would have to tease her as soon as he got the chance.

Soon, Alfi's uncle began to shuffle his feet restlessly and his aunt, understanding immediately, announced that they should all be going to bed. The only decorations around the room were religious icons and both understood that Chiara's guardian angel still had decidedly the upper hand and was not to be outwitted for at least another day. To Max's surprise, Chiara asked, in her most winning voice, 'could we just have a couple of minutes to look at the tree, it's something I've heard a lot about and have always wanted to see.'

Max was feeling comfortably warm, and had no real wish either to get cold again, or to put out Alfi's aunt and uncle, so he said, 'Let's leave it till morning, I'm sure we'll be able to see everything better in daylight.'

To his surprise, the other three all laughed, even Alfi's uncle, who had said little all evening. 'Go on, lass. Take him out and show him.'

Outside, he put his arm around Chiara and made to kiss her, but she moved away and, pulling him by the hand, moved along the front of the house and round the corner to the side facing over the plain towards Gubbio.

'Look,' and he looked, mouth open and eyes transfixed in amazement. Across the plain, the lights of Gubbio picked out key features of the main buildings: the Palazzo dei Consoli, the Palazzo Ducale and the Cathedral. The effect of the city itself with its twinkling lights was impressive, but it was not that which grabbed the attention; the outline of the mountain immediately behind the town was roughly triangular in shape and all the way up each side were a series of lights, presumably fires, that gave the mountain the appearance of a giant Christmas tree with the old town at its heart. 'How does that please your artistic eye? Worth coming for?'

He looked at the view without speaking for more than two minutes before responding. 'I'm surrounded by beauty,' he said, turning away from the tree and embracing her. 'Come on. Time to go in and be pure!'

A bed had been made up for Chiara behind a curtain in Alfi's aunt and uncle's room; it had been where their own daughter had slept until she married, they explained, and Max was given some blankets so that he could sleep on some matting on the kitchen floor near the fire.

After breakfasting on Alfi's aunt's apricot, fig and blackberry jams they said a warm goodbye to the couple and set off down the road to the main road they had crossed the previous evening. They had been hopeful of getting a lift onwards in Ponte delle Assi which wasn't much more than a mile away, however, when they got there, they saw two large saloons, one with a pennant on top of the radiator, parked in the centre of the village and, although Alfi had said that they weren't being actively searched for in that area, decided that there was no point in taking any risks, and continued on foot for another two miles until they came to the main road. Here, they were soon able to flag down a lorry driver who, although he was unable to take them on to Fabriano, which was where they had determined to catch the train, said he could take them as far as Fossato di Vico: they took his word that this was on their way and cheerfully climbed in for the twelve mile journey which took around forty minutes.

When they reached Fossato and headed for a road signposted, Fabriano, they were pleased to see a smaller sign indicating that Fossato had its own station, which was situated in the opposite direction, about five hundred metres to the south of the historic centre. A bored looking functionary informed them that there was a train for Ancona which would be passing through in about twenty minutes, but that it was an express and wouldn't be stopping before Fabriano. The first regional train would be stopping in Fossato in an hour and twenty minutes. It would then get them to Ancona in just under three hours, stopping at every little station on the way. If he had been on his own, Max's restlessness would have convinced him to get back on the road and make for Fabriano, hopeful he could pick up another lift on the way. However, he was aware of how much walking they had done since leaving Bargino, and decided that, as they may still have more walking to do, it would be better to wait for the train in Fossato.

They filled in the time by walking into the centre of Fossato where Max managed to acquire a pencil and a small piece of paper, both sides of which he filled up with sketches of the town. The centre was made up of a number of narrow streets filled with rough stone buildings that had clearly been added to through the centuries. The stones used for all the buildings, including the church and the civic buildings were made up of fairly small flat stones, carefully fitted together using what he presumed had originally been drystone walling techniques. Rough stone arches joined buildings together across streets and enabled him to provide his sketches with natural frames, enhancing the compositions. Everything about the village architecture contrasted with the classical elegance he had found in many of the traditionally wealthier northern cities, and he wondered whether the people here were as susceptible to the illusions created by fascism.

They decided that it was wisest to sit separately on the train as they still did not know how thoroughly they were being searched for. This proved to be a wise precaution; the ticket collector on the train was accompanied by a well-dressed man, wearing a fascist badge on his lapel and an air of authority on his face. He looked intently at every passenger as their ticket was punched, and asked several of them to see their papers. Max was one of those whose papers were requested. Fortunately, when he had been left by the bridge after his beating, his pockets had not been emptied, so his papers, although a little battered, were in order. The official asked him where he had been, and Max told him he had been in Rome for the past few weeks before leaving that morning. When asked where he was going, he replied that he intended to make his way up the Adriatic coast to Venice. The man handed Max back his papers, advising him to take better care of them in the future, then moved on to catch up with the guard who was now checking the tickets further along the carriage.

As they had decided to travel third class, the carriage was open plan with hard wooden seats. Chiara was at the other end of the carriage and he knew that there was a greater risk of discovery if her papers were checked than his. He knew that they had no photograph of him, probably didn't remember his surname, and had no proof that he was involved in Chiara's disappearance, or indeed had survived their attack. With Chiara it was different; they knew her name and had probably circulated her photograph. He watched the official give her the same penetrative stare he gave everyone else in the carriage, and then turn slightly and ask the woman sitting next to her for her papers. He noted with relief that Chiara had not looked the official in the eye; if her photograph was circulated later, he didn't want her to be remembered.

They joined up again a hundred metres from the station and headed up the hill behind, where Max relied on Chiara having memorised the directions that Alfi had given them. After twenty minutes they passed the *Cittadella* Public Park and after that the climb became less steep then, after having to ask directions once, they crossed *Via Montegrappa*, which Max remembered having been mentioned in the instructions. Shortly afterwards they descended slightly to a cluster of small houses by the *Parco del Cardeto*, with its magnificent view over the Adriatic. They found the door they were looking for, but there was no answer to their knock.

'Too early,' surmised Max, we'll try again later, we don't want to draw attention to ourselves, and certainly don't want to draw attention to the people who are helping us.'

'Let's go and sit in the park. You can either get your paper and pencil out and draw the sea or you can give me a cuddle to keep me warm.'

Leaving the houses behind them, they retraced their steps a little until they came to an entrance to the park. A little way into the park, a stone bench faced the sea and also offered an oblique view of the entrance to the park. They didn't expect any problems, but they had learnt that it was always best to be prepared for any eventuality.

The advantage of it being cold was that there was no-one else in the park to disturb them. As they sat down, she snuggled up to him and looking up into his face said, 'Well, what's it to be, Rembrandt?'

'He gave the impression of thinking then smiled, said 'My fingers are too cold to hold a pencil properly,' and slipped his hand between the buttons of her coat and up beneath her top. She shrieked at the touch of his icy fingers on her warm soft flesh, but brought her arm across pinning his hand to her.

'Brute... I might change my mind and go home if you do that again!' He laughed and kissed her. 'Now keep your hand still until it's warmed up enough for you to move it around without giving me a heart attack.'

The next two hours passed quickly and it was with some reluctance that they headed for the park entrance as the last of the light faded. A glimmer of light could now be seen behind the shutters of the house they were aiming for. This time they were obviously expected, as the middle-aged man in a thick green fishing jumper, who let them in, knew exactly who they were and why they were there.

Without standing on ceremony they were ushered through to a table in the back room and given a fish based stew with layers of stockfish and potatoes, flavoured with diced onions, carrots, celery and rosemary. While his wife plied them with food, Aldo, their host, explained that they would be leaving very early the next morning; as it was the thirty-first of December, there would be no Italian boats crossing the Adriatic only Yugoslavian and Greek ones anxious to get home in time to celebrate. The controls at the port would be laxer than usual, and it would not present too much difficulty for them to be got aboard in the midst of a group of apparently drunken Greek seamen. Chiara would be in the middle of the group with a greatcoat collar turned up, and wearing a fisherman's woollen hat.

After what seemed like a very brief sleep, they were woken by Aldo at half past two and then, slipping from shadow to shadow, led down to a bar half hidden along a shady side street not far from the port. Ten minutes later they were part of a group of singing, cheering Greek sailors, swaying their way back to a freighter at one end of the docks. A young Italian soldier tentatively asked for papers as they entered the docks and was met with laughter and a volley of what Max guessed to be Greek insults, as the sailors ignored him and pushed past. Max saw the soldier finger his gun but then think better of it, shrug his shoulders and turn back into warmth of the guard room.

As they got to the end of the gangway leading up onto the deck of the ship, a burly seaman detached them from the rest of the group and led them towards the stern of the ship. He lifted a hatch and again beckoned them to follow him down the ladder below. Soon they were in the cargo hold and the sailor indicated a space between some packing cases and showed them with his torch where there was a loaf of bread and a bottle of water. 'Thirty six hours,' he said, and left them in the almost complete darkness.

Three times during the voyage, the sailor reappeared and, indicating that they should make no noise, led them, one at a time to use a toilet – even so, the voyage seemed interminable and it was hard to believe that it lasted for less than two days. Eventually, however, they had the impression that the ship was no longer moving and lay in calm water.

It was still, however, at least an hour before the sailor appeared, accompanied by another man who did not look anything like a sailor.

Chapter 8

To Max's surprise, the man addressed them in English. 'Welcome to Greece, and a happy new year... although, of course, these heathens don't celebrate for another few days as they still use the Julian calendar.' The man then said something to the sailor in Greek and then they were finally led off the ship down the rear gangway. The man, who was dressed in a suit and tie, looked them up and down and said, 'I think the two of you could do with a good clean up before you meet my wife.' Max, still almost speechless at the unexpected turn of events, managed to express his thanks and followed the man through the town and up a hill to a white house swathed in bougainvillea.

'Could I ask where we are?' he managed to ask finally.

The man laughed, 'Igoumenitsa. I'm the Honorary British Vice-Consul,' he held his hand out, 'Bertie Frizzell-Smyth.' His answer left Max even more confused; he had never heard of Igoumenitsa, and had no idea why the British Government was involved. He decided to just let events take their course for the moment and work out what was happening afterwards.

An hour later he was sitting with a cup of tea, in a reasonably comfortable chair which had been pulled in in front of a fairly ostentatious polished oak desk in the man's office. Another similar chair awaited Chiara, who was still cleaning herself up.

'Now,' said the man, with a smile, 'You're going to have to bring me up to speed with the situation. All I know is that I was told that two of His Majesty's citizens had arrived, stowed away in the hold of a boat after having had a bit of a contretemps with some big-wigs in Italy. If you haven't broken any British laws, then we'll ship you off to Blighty as soon as possible and we'll all get on splendidly.' At that point, Chiara was shown into the room by a Greek maid. The Honorary Vice Consul, got to his feet, came round the desk and, with a flourish, ushered Chiara into the other chair. 'Tea?'

'Yes, please.'

Max was glad that there was no trace of an Italian accent in the two words. This wasn't going to be straight forward, and he much preferred to be able to have some influence on the direction of the conversation, rather than allow the Vice Consul to make his own discoveries.

When the cup of tea had been poured and passed over, Max said, 'We're really grateful for what you've done already. I certainly wasn't expecting to be welcomed to Greece by a representative of the British government.'

'I'm not sure you quite understand the role of the vice consuls. I can only very loosely be described as a representative of the British Government. I run a small shipping business here and, as I'm viewed as a respectable citizen, I'm paid a small honorarium each year, and given the grand title of Vice Consul, to assist any British Citizens who may require help. In fact, you're the first people I've needed to do anything for, for nearly five months.'

'Perhaps that's just as well, as I'm not sure to what extent you'll be able to help us.' The Vice-Consul raised an eyebrow. 'I don't think either of us has broken any British laws,' he continued, with the emphasis on "think", what I think will prove to be the problem is that Chiara, my future wife,' and he took her hand, 'is not a British citizen. She's Italian.'

The Vice-Counsel relaxed, 'Easily dealt with. I don't know when you'd planned on marrying, but the civil part of the ceremony can be done here. Once you're married, your wife,' and he bowed his head respectfully towards Chiara, will become a British Citizen. I can do the paperwork and request that a passport be issued by the embassy in Athens.'

'You are very kind, but...' said Chiara.

'Chiara is not twenty one until May, and there is no way that her father will give his permission for her to marry.'

The Vice-Consul leaned back in his chair, folded his arms and, rolling the end of his moustache around the index finger of his right hand, sat and contemplated them for a while. Chiara looked worried and Max sat impassively waiting to see what the Vice-Consul proposed to do.

'If I do my duty as Honorary Vice Consul, for which I am paid the princely sum of one hundred guineas each year, I should pick up that telephone, dial my Italian equivalent and tell him that I have one of his citizens here, who should be returned to her parents,' Max felt Chiara tense and stroked her hand reassuringly; he was sure that the Vice-Consul was not going to follow that course of action. 'Or I could take the easy way out, and let you walk out through that door and pretend I'd never seen you.' He waited for a reaction, which was not forthcoming. Max looked at him calmly, Chiara nervously.

'Our government, has good relations at the moment with Mussolini, they admire the way that he keeps his country in order and is building up their prestige, however, being somewhat closer to Italy than are our politicians in London, I see things differently – in fact I see a lot of things I don't like about Italy, so I won't be picking up the phone and speaking to my Italian counterpart whom, by the way, I detest.' Max smiled and Chiara relaxed. The Vice-Consul held up a hand, 'However, the Italians are very influential here. The Greek government is impressed by the reports, which I believe to be exaggerated, about Italy's military might, and will bend over backwards to ingratiate themselves with the Italian government.' He leaned forward, put his elbows on the desk and rested his face on his hands for a few seconds, almost as though he were praying, then he leaned back looking decisive. 'I think I can work something out. Now please go back to the room where you changed and be ready to join my wife and I for dinner at eight. You will be our guests tonight. Oh, and while you are here, could you please not disabuse the maid's view that you are both English. We don't want Signor Cassano, the Italian representative, knocking on the door and demanding the return of his citizen.' He brushed away their thanks as they withdrew.

While they had been with Frizzell-Smyth, someone, presumably the maid, had removed the clothes that they had been travelling in and neat piles of additional clean clothes now lay on the bed. They checked through what was there; the sizes appeared to have been estimated with a fair degree of accuracy, and they did the best they could to appear respectable for their dinner with the Vice-Consul and his wife. When they left the room, half an hour later, the maid materialised as if from nowhere and led them to a tastefully furnished drawing room decorated with lively colourful scenes, clearly influenced by the expressionist movement. Chiara sat down while Max studied the paintings which, he noticed, had been hung tastefully by someone with a good sense of colour and balance.

'Ah,' came their host's voice from the doorway, 'You like our little collection... splendid.' I'll tell you about them later. Now,' he continued as Max turned to face him, and Chiara rose, 'let me introduce you to my wife,' A slim, dark haired woman stepped forward from behind him and kissed Chiara on each cheek before shaking hands with Max, 'This is Cora…. Cora these are our guests, Max Caddick and his future wife, Chiara.'

'You are very welcome in our home, and I hope that your stay is a pleasant one. Please, sit down.' Max noticed the casual elegance of her dress and decided that she must be responsible for the decoration of the room, an assumption confirmed by

Frizzell-Smyth shortly afterwards, when the conversation turned to the pictures.

'I know what I like. And if I like something and also think it's going to be a good investment, I'm quite happy to buy it, but they never look quite right until Cora decides where to put them, and what needs to go next to what. Take that one, for example,' and he indicated an almost abstract, cubist influenced painting hung between two impressionist seascapes. 'I wanted to put it with the other picture by Yiannis Morales over there,' and he waved a hand vaguely towards the wall facing the window, ' but Cora said it had to go between those two pictures by Spyros Vassiliou, and she was absolutely right'.

A bottle of ouzo appeared and both Frizzell-Smyth and Max enjoyed a glass of the aniseed flavoured liqueur over ice, as an aperitif, while Chiara and Cora both chose freshly squeezed orange juice. When the maid called them through to the dining room, they found a round table, with a loaf of bread, a block of feta cheese, a jug of water and two carafes of wine, one white and one red. To these the maid quickly added five small dishes, the contents of which looked unfamiliar to Max. Mrs Frizzell-Smyth said, 'we almost always eat in the Greek style when we are home, both Bertie and I prefer it, and the results can be unpredictable if we ask our maid to produce anything else.'

'Wherever you go, local customs and local foods are always the best,' said Chiara, ' but I would be interested to know what we are eating.'

'Together these dishes are known as *Mezes*, I think in Italy you would call them *antipasti*; this one is baked aubergine mashed with olive oil and garlic; this is *bamies*, a small vegetable, which I'm afraid I don't know the Italian name for and the English don't have a name for, stewed in tomato; this one is stewed octopus; these are *pites*, which are pastries stuffed with cheese and spinach, and this last one we call *tzatziki* which is chopped garlic and cucumber in a yoghurt sauce; our meals always begin with a variety of *mezes* and everyone just dips in and helps themselves. As they began to spoon the mezes onto their plates, Bertie picked the loaf up, tore off four large chunks of bread and distributed them around the table.

'You need to know,' he said, that in Greece, it is considered rude not to talk while you are eating, so please forget your English manners and just enjoy yourselves. Max did his best to do justice to the food and join in the conversation at the same time but was happy to leave most of the talking to Chiara who seemed in her element. He noticed that Frizzell-Smyth also talked far less than Cora, and wasn't sure whether this was because of his English upbringing or because he wanted to listen to everything that Max and Chiara said, so that he could make his mind up what it was best to do with them.

After a while, the *meze* dishes were removed and replaced by a large dish of rabbit, cooked with shallots in a red wine sauce heavily spiced with cinnamon, and a large dish of salad made of slices of tomato and cucumber mixed with kalamata olives and liberally doused with olive oil. Before serving the salad, Cora cut a slice of cheese off the block of feta in the middle of the table, crumbled it into the bowl and gently stirred a few times so that both the cheese and the oil were well distributed. Both the wines were very different to varieties that Max had tried previously, and he complimented their hosts on the quality of the wine. Frizzell-Smyth seemed pleased with the compliment,' I'll let my brother-in-law know that his wines are appreciated; he grows *malagousia* grapes to make his white wine and *xinomavro* for the red. His reds are very popular but his white is more difficult to sell because not many people know the *malagousia* grapes.'

'How many vines does he have?' Chiara asked Cora.

'We have seventeen hectares altogether, although they are not all productive.'

As Chiara continued to talk with Cora about the vines, in a conversation that showed that both women were knowledgeable on the subject, Frizzell-Smyth said to Max, 'It's a shame she won't be able to make use of that knowledge in England... or are you planning to go back to Italy at some point?'

Max shook his head, 'Chiara's family is very influential... not just in Tuscany... her father and brother both have very important friends in the regime and I don't think that anywhere in Italy would be safe for us in the foreseeable future.'

'What will you do in England? Do you have connections who can help you out?'

Max considered before replying, 'My brother-in-law has a secure job in a bank, and we will be able to stay with them while we get sorted out. I have administrative experience and now have good language skills, which I am sure will be needed somewhere.'

Coffee appeared at that point, and Frizzell-Smyth warned them that it was very different to Italian coffee, was already sweetened, should definitely not be stirred, and should be drunk with extreme caution as the bottom half of the cup was filled with coffee grains. After the coffee, Frizzell-Smyth offered them *tsipouro* or *raki* to help them digest, but Cora objected that both were far too strong to give to unwary guests, and suggested that instead she should go and make *rakomello* for everyone. She excused herself and reappeared a few minutes later carrying a small tray with four glasses of steaming liquid. 'This is *rakomello*,' she said as she handed the glasses round, '*raki* mixed with honey cinnamon and cloves and then warmed up on the stove. It's very popular in winter and nothing like as strong as neat *raki*.'

'This is wonderful,' said Chiara, *'sas efcharistò.'* Cora gave a big smile, clearly not being used to being thanked in her own language by guests of her husband.

'Now... I've been giving some thought to your little problem, and I think I've come up with a solution. I can't get you to England because Chiara doesn't have a British passport and, as a minor, should really be given into the care of Signor Cassano, who I am sure would have her on the first boat back to Italy.' He looked at them, 'However, as I mentioned before, being a Vice-Consul is just a little sideline, my main activity is making sure that boats, some of which I own a share in, get from one place to another around the Mediterranean with suitable cargoes. Now, although I deal with various places, the place I deal with most is Malta, where I have an office and a warehouse. If you are happy to spend a few months in Malta until Chiara comes of age, then I can find work for Max to do in my business and, as there are many Italian immigrants in Malta, I'm sure that we could find Chiara some work, teaching English to their children. How does that sound?'

'I don't know what to say. It sounds ideal. I don't know how to thank you.'

'You can thank me by keeping this delightful young lady out of the hands of Mussolini and his friends. Officially, I can't know anything about you of course. When you reveal yourself to the Consul in Malta in a few months' time immediately after your marriage, and he contacts me to complain that I have been employing people without carrying out proper identity checks, I will have to tell him that my manager in Valletta will be severely reprimanded for his carelessness. You will, of course, be sacked, and the Consul in Malta will have no choice but to remove you both to England.'

Their room was light and airy with a view over the bay. Lights showed dimly through shutters in many of the buildings between the house and the shore, where he could see an array of boats of all different types and sizes. The black outlines of the hills encircling the bay were visible against an indigo, star-filled sky. A crescent moon gave off just enough light to allow him to pick out a few of the features of the boats. The faint sound of singing could be heard in the distance from a *kafenion* near the port, and nearer by, the silence was broken momentarily by the sound of laughter from a nearby house.

As he leaned on the balcony, drinking in the calm atmosphere, he did not hear the bathroom door close or the sound of bare feet moving silently across the floor towards him; the first he knew was when a pair of delicate hands infiltrated themselves under the back of the loose shirt he was wearing and slid round the front and up through the hairs to gently caress his nipples, then he felt a head rest against his back. He stiffened and, removing his hands from the balcony, began to undo the buttons of his shirt. As the last of them opened, Chiara withdrew her hands and stepped back so he could turn.

He stopped in awe; she was completely naked and, her perfect skin seemed to glow in the pale moonlight. He dropped to his knees and held his arms out. She moved forward and he embraced her, resting his cheek against the dark triangle between her legs. After a few seconds he turned his head and kissed her. He felt her give a little shudder and then she placed her hands on either side of his face and pulled gently upwards. He was completely hers and rose gently until he was facing her. He put his arms round her and kissed her, feeling her lips open to let his tongue slide between her teeth. As they kissed, her hands moved downwards as if by instinct and began to undo the buttons of his fly. She pushed downwards and he felt the trousers fall; she put a finger on his lips to indicate that he should say nothing and then, slowly moved backwards towards the bed while resting her left hand on his hip, 'I think my fairy godmother is still on the boat, but she'll come back if you don't keep me warm...'

At breakfast, Frizzell-Smyth told them that they were to leave later that day. 'This is a fairly small town and news, gossip and speculation get around very quickly. Sometimes, it can be useful when you want people to know something, but if you've got something you want kept quiet it causes complications. I'm sure that everyone who is anyone, here in Igoumenitsa already knows that I have guests and will be making enquiries as to who you are. Everyone is going to see me drive you down the coast-road, as if I were taking you to Arta, where I have business interests. What they won't see is that part way there you'll be transferring to a van coming in this direction with some items that I'm shipping to Malta tonight. You'll help to unload the van and, when you carry boxes on board, you'll stay there. The crew is Maltese, and last time they were here one of them got into a fight with one of the Greek dockers, so they won't be meeting them socially any time soon and chatting about their passengers.'

Everything went as smoothly as the Vice-Consul had predicted. The seven hundred and fifty kilometre journey took just over thirty hours; Chiara helped the cook in the galley while Max, who tried to be helpful, soon discovered that he could be most helpful to the crew by keeping out of the way, and so spent most of the daylight hours sketching different parts of the ship and the crew going about their business.

In Valletta, Max gave the manager of Frizzell-Smyth's office the introductory letter that the Vice-Consel had handed him before leaving. 'Can you do accounts?' he asked.

'I worked in an office for two years in Manchester, so I had to learn book-keeping as well as general admin.'

'In that case there's no problem – I need someone in the office, so you can start on Monday morning.' They were then directed to a small, somewhat seedy looking hotel near the port for the night, the cost of which would be taken out of Max's wages. The manager said he would speak to someone who had a couple of apartments that they let out to tourists during the summer season. He was sure that for a small consideration the owner would let them out until Easter as an apartment that was lived in was usually kept in better condition.

Luckily, Easter was quite late that year, not falling until the twenty-first of April, and the owner agreed that they could stay there until the week before, which only gave them a month for which they needed to find alternative accommodation. By the time they had to vacate the apartment in the Floriana district of Valletta, one of Max's fellow workers in the office, had suggested that they rent one of the rooms in her widowed mother's house until they found something more permanent. Max accepted gratefully, feeling only slightly guilty in the knowledge that they weren't looking for anything more permanent as they hoped to be leaving the island in a few weeks' time.

Max found the work in the office, easy but dull; life in Valletta was far less intense than it had been in Manchester, and this spilled over into the workplaces. It was not as easy for Chiara to find work as had been anticipated and most weeks she only managed to find four or five hours' worth of private lessons to give. However, she busied herself in learning how to run a house, looking for the best value foods in the local markets, reading as many English books as she could to improve her grasp of the language, and going for long walks in all weathers.

Partly because they were aware of Chiara's vulnerable legal status, but mainly because they enjoyed each other's company so much, they did not mix much socially and by the time May came around, Max knew that they had enough money put aside to allow them to obtain steerage class passage on a boat back to England. He was pleased about this as it avoided the need to go cap in hand to the British Consul, and expose Frizzel-Smyth and his manager to any sort of sanction.

Getting married, however, turned out to be more difficult than had been anticipated. When they went to the registry office in Merchants Street, they were surprised to be met with hostility by the prim woman, dressed in grey, who faced them across the desk. 'No, Civil marriages did not exist in Malta – No, it was not possible for anyone baptised as a Catholic to marry in anything other than a full Catholic ceremony – No, the young lady could not get married without her birth certificate even if she did have her Italian identity card – No – No -No.'

Chiara had been feeling unwell for several days, particularly in the mornings, and Max put an arm round her protectively as they left the building.

'Don't worry, we'll find a way, even if it takes longer.'

'It's not that... I just wanted to do it as long as possible before the baby's born.'

Max was trying to think of a solution to the problem and had taken a few more steps before what she had said sank in. He came to a stop suddenly, turned and got hold of her free hand with his and said, 'Say that again.'

She smiled and looked him in the eye, 'I want to get married as long as possible before the baby is born.'

He stood looking at her for a couple of seconds then pulled her towards him and gently embraced her, 'Why didn't you tell me? How long have you known? How...'

'I'm not sure I can answer the third question while we're standing in the street... but if you can wait till we get home, I'll show you.'

'I didn't me...' Her lips silenced the rest of the words

'I wasn't sure at first, it's not something that's ever happened to me before, and I didn't want to say anything until I was sure.'

'So when?'

'Yesterday, I had a cup of tea with Mrs Lipari, after I'd been to the market. She's always been very nice so I talked to her, and she was sure. I wanted to wait until we'd sorted things out today to tell you... a sort of early wedding present... You don't mind, do you?'

'Mind! How could I mind? I want lots of lovely little girls, all just like you. But, are you tired? Do you need to sit down? What can I do?'

She laughed, 'Just behave normally. There'll be plenty of time for fussing when I'm big and fat and look like a hippopotamus. Now, let's go home.'

Max spoke to Frizzell-Smyth's office manager the following day and explained their dilemma. The manager was relieved that Frizzell-Smyth's original plan of being married by the Consul, with all that implied, was not possible, but was left perplexed by the issues raised by the Public Registry. Unfortunately, contrary to popular belief, sea-captains were not permitted to conduct legal marriages so they could not, as Max had hoped, be married on their way to England. After some thought, he said that there was one possibility, but that he was not completely sure whether it would work or not. He believed that the formalities in Gibraltar were much more relaxed than in Malta, partly because the authorities on the Rock had experience of formalising cross-border marriages where one of the parties came from over the border in Spain, sometimes against the wishes of the Spanish families. As it seemed to be their only chance of marrying before reaching England, they decided it was worth trying.

Nine days later, more than half expecting to face new obstacles, they entered the registrar's office, through a wide but low stone archway, half way down Secretary's Lane in Gibraltar. When they emerged after forty-five minutes their faces were wreathed in smiles and Chiara tightly held the Special Marriage Licence which, provided they could produce two witnesses, would allow them to become legally man and wife at 10.45am the following day.

Chapter 9

They got off the tram close to the end of the suburban street, just outside Nottingham, where Stan had recently been appointed as manager of a fairly small new branch of the bank. Max checked the address on a bit of paper and, insisting on carrying both their bags, walked down the street with Chiara at his side, until they came to number forty-seven.

'I'm scared... I feel more worried now than I did when I escaped from home. What if she doesn't like me?' He squeezed her hand and smiled. He felt the urge to kiss her but was aware that public displays of affection outside his sister's house, were probably not the best way of announcing their arrival. He led her up the short path that dissected the small, but immaculately tended front garden, and then rang the bell.

'Well, look what the cat's dragged in,' said Ethel, as, half embarrassed and half pleased, she accepted a hug before pushing him away. She looked at Chiara, who was standing slightly behind him, and then back at Max and then back at Chiara. 'I am very glad to meet you, please come in and make yourself at home,' she said slowly, speaking louder than usual and making sure to separate each of her words. Max smiled, amused at his sister's assumption that she needed to speak like this.

'Thank you very much, Mrs Sykes. I'm really pleased to meet you, and thank you very much for letting us stay with you.'

'Mrs Sykes! It's Ethel, love. Now get in here, take the weight off your feet and have a nice cup of tea,' efforts to make allowances for her new sister-in-law being foreign, already forgotten. Max stepped slightly to one side, allowing his sister to lead his wife through into what was clearly a rarely used front-room. Ethel took Chiara's coat and sat her down on a new settee in chintz.

'Take the bags upstairs... third door - that's your room,' and then, in a whisper, as she brushed past him on her way through to the kitchen, 'she's lovely.'

'I know.'

The house was a typical modern semi-detached with small garden at the front facing the road, a tiny porch leading into the kitchen which led to a hallway and stairs. Two doors opened off the kitchen; the first one, Max guessed, would be the sitting room where Ethel and Stan would eat and spend most of the time; the second one was the more elegant room they had been shown into, which would be used to receive guests and on special occasions. He wondered how long it would be before he and Chiara were relegated to the sitting room: not long, if the change in Ethel's manner of speaking to Chiara was anything to go by. At the top of the stairs was an indoor bathroom, which he guessed must be their pride and joy, and a landing with three more doors leading off it. The first, he assumed, which was above the sitting room, would be Ethel and Stan's bedroom, the second was the guest bedroom, and the third must be a small box room that could become a bedroom if required, although, as they had now been married for twelve years, he realised that the likelihood of an extra bedroom being needed was now slim. Behind the house was a larger piece of garden which they had obviously not yet got around to landscaping.

Back downstairs, he sat in one of the armchairs rather than next to Chiara on the cottage-settee; he wanted to leave the space next to her for Ethel, to help the two get to know each other. This was a good move, as in no time Ethel was conquered by Chiara's gentle nature, and was soon asking all about the wedding and about what it was like to live in Italy. Her disappointment at not having been at her brother's wedding was assuaged when she heard about the very basic ceremony which had been celebrated in front of two witnesses who had been more or less dragged off the street.

'But it is legal, isn't it?' she asked for at least the third time.

'Would you like me to go and get the certificate signed on behalf of the Governor of Gibraltar, who is appointed directly by the King. Would that convince you?'

'Oh, don't be silly,' she said, but she didn't ask the question again.

Stan arrived home just after half past six. He wore a dark suit with a waistcoat, across which a watch-chain was visible, and when he came through the door, he carefully hung up a bowler hat and umbrella in the porch. The necessary introductions were made and Stan went to change out of his suit before dinner.

'I've made a potato pie,' said Ethel, 'I hope it's still your favourite. Max made an appreciative noise and Chiara said how much she was looking forward to English home cooking. Max suppressed a smile, knowing how low the reputation of English cooking was in Italy.

Stan was, by nature, reserved and formal and it was not until each was sitting with a cup of tea after the spotted-dick that followed the potato pie that he finally relaxed, and the real kind gentle Stan emerged from under his reserve. He was surprisingly well informed on what was happening in the world and not only was he able to bring Max up to date on what was happening in British politics, but was also able to update him on what was happening in Europe. He was very concerned about speeches that the still relatively new German Chancellor had made decrying and ridiculing the terms of the treaty of Versailles and, in his view, Mussolini was headed for war with Abyssinia. Whether it was at home or on the continent, Stan saw the political and economic landscape as bleak, and the only hope he had was that governments such as those of Britain and France would see the success of 'New Deal' introduced by Roosevelt in the United States, and adopt similar measures themselves. Max was pensive; although Stan wasn't a man of action he was good at analysing situations and risk. If Stan was worried, then the future for Europe looked pretty bleak. Ethel, while enjoying the feeling that her husband was intelligent and that her brother and his new wife obviously thought he was worth listening to, got bored with the political and economic discussion after a while and managed to redirect the conversation back onto topics that she was more comfortable with.

At one point, Max saw Chiara push her shoulders back and flex her back and realised that she had been sitting for far too long. 'If you don't mind, I think we'll call it a day. It's been quite tiring, especially for Chiara with all the new people and places to take in.'

'Of course. I'm sorry, we've been really selfish. You must be worn out after the journey, love. You go up and get ready for bed and we'll see you in the morning.' Max smiled at his sister, and nodded to Chiara that she should go ahead. Stan rose politely as Chiara left the room, and then sat down again and looked at Max.

'You've got a good one there. You make sure you look after her.'

'Oh, I will, don't you worry about that.' and then, 'There's something I need to tell you,' Although, Chiara was now nearly four months pregnant her nascent bump was only really visible when she was naked and they had decided it was best if he broke the news to Stan and Ethel when she wasn't there, to give them time to get used to the idea. They had decided not to let them know before they arrived as they felt that their marriage was already a big enough piece of news to give them. 'We're expecting a baby,' he said.

Stan's eyebrows raised while Ethel smiled and said, 'I did wonder. There's always something just slightly different about a woman who's pregnant – another woman can always tell.' Stan's eyebrows seemed to rise even further, then he grinned, 'Congratulations... time to open that bottle of sherry we were keeping for a special occasion.'

The last two months of Chiara's pregnancy were difficult and there were several days when she felt too ill to get out of bed. Stan had managed to find Max an administrative job in the export department of one of the bank's larger clients, and he was out of the house every weekday from seven thirty until six thirty, at which point he would rush to Chiara to comfort and reassure her. The doctor who was called in for a two guinea fee, had a quick look and said they didn't need to fuss, it was just that is was obviously going to be a big baby and Chiara was naturally slim.

The labour started early on in the evening of the twenty second of December and continued throughout the night and morning. Ethel rushed about looking fraught and did her best to keep Max out of the room. Stan had been sent to run for the midwife during the night, but when she came she shook her head and said that it would be a few hours before she could do anything and that she would be back in the morning. Max was tortured by the sounds of Chiara's screams and felt that his place should be by her side, but the midwife was immovable and he was forced to prowl the sitting-room below like a caged animal.

Through the morning he was convinced that Chiara's cries were becoming weaker, although more frequent, and he clenched his hands tightly, digging his fingernails into his palms, desperately trying to shut out her pain with some of his own, but to little effect. Ethel brought him cups of tea but he forgot to drink them as he became more and more terrified of what was happening in the room above his head.

Finally, there was a scream that was louder, longer and more desperate than the others and then after a few seconds of absolute silence, he heard a baby cry.

He rushed up the stairs, taking them three at a time and burst into the room. The midwife was standing wrapping the baby in a towel at the foot of the bed while Ethel, looking pale, stood as if rooted to the spot, eyes filled with wonder as she stared at the infant. Although his mind registered the presence of the baby, Max went straight to Chiara who lay softly moaning on the bed, drenched in a mixture of sweat and tears. A weak smile just about managed to make it through the pain and she said, *'il mio bambino.'*

Max, kissed her gently on the forehead and, as she feebly held out her arms for the baby, tried to dry some of the sweat off her face and shoulders. The midwife gently placed the bundle into her arms but continued to support the weight as it was lowered down to rest on Chiara's breast.

'It's a boy,' she said, as she stepped back and allowed the new family a minute together before stepping forward again when she ordered Max out of the room while she cleaned up Chiara. 'Just a few loose ends to tie up... You can come back in a few minutes.. Now, go and make us all a nice cuppa.'

He went downstairs and into the kitchen, feeling drained. He had expected to feel excited, elated at having become a father, but all he could think of at the moment was the suffering that Chiara had gone through. The regular screams over the last few hours and the pain he could see etched on her face as it lay on the pillow framed by the tangled, sweat-matted mass that had previously been her beautiful flowing hair, were things that he thought his mind would never be free of. He realised that there were tears on his own face and, managing to pull himself together, he put the kettle on and then washed and dried his face at the kitchen sink while he waited for it to boil.

Back upstairs, he managed to smile as he entered the room. He placed the tray with the tea things on the small table by the bed, and poured Chiara's out straight away as she took hers black and very weak. He replaced Ethel in the chair beside the bed and bent over Chiara who was lying, propped up by pillows, with the baby at her breast. She smiled, 'He's beautiful, isn't he?'

I think I'm supposed to say, "he looks just like you", and you're supposed to say, "Oh no, he's got your nose," or something like that. I'm sure he will be handsome when he's older, especially if he does take after you, but at the moment, he's just a baby, who's very special because he's ours,' she tried to look disapproving but squeezed his hand weakly, as he continued, 'it's his beautiful mother who I care about most at the moment... and I'm sure she always will be.'

He picked up the baby and held it rather awkwardly, not being sure where to put his hands, how to support the head that he felt was in imminent danger of falling back and breaking the neck, or how to respond when it made a gurgling sound.

'John.'

'What?' he said startled.

'John. I want to call him John, like your father.' They had talked and talked and talked about possible names for the baby. If it had been a girl it would have been easy as they would have called it Madeline to form a link with her sister. Boys' names were more difficult; he had suggested trying to find a name that was similar in both English and Italian but the choices were limited. Of the available names, their favourite was Daniel, but the Contessa's brother, the bishop, was called Daniele and Chiara said that she didn't want to think of church services every time she looked at their child. She had asked about English names and he had talked her through every one he could think of, explaining the connotations each of them might have. They had remained undecided, and now, suddenly she had decided. He was happy with the choice but curious to know why she had made it.

'I'm English now, or I will be when we've been married for long enough for me to be naturalised, so an English name is right, and your family has been so good to me; I want Ethel to know that I really belong, that I'm putting down roots in the family.'

'John it is then.' He turned and leaned over the cot that Stan had borrowed from his sister, 'Welcome to the family, John Caddick, Junior,'

Chiara pinched his hand, 'Don't you dare call him Junior. He laughed and turned back to kiss her gently.

Soon after, Chiara fell sleep and, after making sure that she was well covered, he went downstairs to have a quick bite to eat.

'Here,' said Ethel, placing a glass bottle containing white liquid, and with a rubber teat in his hand.

'What is it?'

'Milk formula. The midwife told me how to make it before she left; condensed milk, cream, honey and water. Chiara needs to sleep tonight to try and get some strength back, so when the baby wakes up, instead of waking Chiara, feed him with this. Try to sleep with the bottle right next to you to keep it as close as possible to body temperature.'

'You're wonderful, sis. I don't know what we'd do without you. Oh, and by the way, we've decided to call him John, like Dad.' He saw Ethel's eyes mist over and, as he left the room, added, 'It was Chiara's idea.'

In the middle of the night, Max was woken by the sound of laboured breathing. He moved his hand over to Chiara and felt that her skin was burning. He quietly slipped out of bed and went downstairs to heat some water and bring it back in a bowl with a towel. Chiara's breathing became more and more ragged and her head turned from side to side; Max tried to soothe her and moisten her lips with water but, without waking up she seemed to become more and more agitated. The door opened behind him and Ethel, with a lavender coloured dressing-gown wrapped tightly over her nightdress, moved alongside him and picking up one of Chiara's wrists, felt her pulse.

'I'll send Stan to get Doctor Langdon. Make sure she doesn't throw the covers off; we need to keep her warm.' and she left the room.

When Stan came back, with the news that the Doctor would be there as soon as possible, Ethel told him to move the cot with the baby into their room, and sat down with Max to try and keep him calm. Chiara continued to worsen and it became more difficult to force any water between her lips, even though her skin continued to burn and was damp with sweat. Doctor Langdon was in his sixties, had a bulbous red nose that suggested an over-familiarity with port and had fingers that felt icy to the touch when Max briefly shook his hand. He was clearly somewhat disgruntled at having been almost dragged from his bed on a wet winter's night, and Max wondered if he would have deigned to come out before morning, if it hadn't been his bank manager who summoned him. His manner with his patient, however, seemed to be professional and he carried out what seemed to Max to be a fairly thorough examination.

His face was grave when he stood up. 'She's suffering from a severe infection of the genital tract contracted during a prolonged labour; you must make sure that she is kept warm and well hydrated – try to give her barley water rather than plain water as it will help to keep her strength up.'

'Do we need to get her to the hospital, Doctor? Is there any medicine you can give her?'

Langdon shook his head, 'There are no medicines that can help her and I'm sure she'll get better care at home than in the City Hospital, without being exposed to the cold damp air on the way there. All we can do is hope, and give her as much care and attention as possible. Regular doses of aspirin will make it less painful for her, but they won't cure her.'

At intervals, Chiara seemed to half wake and at those times she became delirious, Max could pick out his own name and Maddi's name, and once or twice he thought he heard her say 'John' but the rest of her ravings were incoherent to him. Only once during the course of the following day did she appear a little calmer and when Max, whose head had slumped forward on his chest in the chair next to the bed, opened his eyes and lifted his head, he found her dark eyes fixed on him. Her lips moved but her voice was so soft and her lips so dry, he couldn't make out what she said. He leaned forward so his ear was close to her lips. *'Ti amo tanto,'* she breathed, and he turned to reassure her that he loved her too, but the effort had obviously been too much for her and she had lapsed back into unconsciousness.

In the late afternoon and early evening her breathing became more regular as she slept and Max dared to hope. Ethel took his place by the bedside, insisting that he go downstairs to eat some of the stew she had prepared, and step outside to get some fresh air. He did as he was told, although he had no appetite and ate only a small portion, without any enjoyment.

Ethel had told him to stay away for at least half an hour but he was back to retake his place and hold Chiara's hand under the covers before twenty minutes had elapsed. Later in the evening, Chiara's breathing became more uneven again and she tossed and turned in the bed. She was again delirious and rivulets of sweat ran down her neck. Max gently mopped away at her face and neck with the cloths that Ethel had given him, and tried to force some of the barley water between her lips. In the early hours of the morning, Christmas morning, she seemed to become calmer again and he did his best to rearrange her matted hair on the pillow around her face. He thought over the fifteen months since he had first seen her, and every look and every word of hers in that time seemed to be etched with crystal clarity on his mind. He saw her carrying the platter of cheese and salami to the table; he saw her come through the vines into the hollow towards him; he saw her in her nakedness, completely open and trusting as she stood before him in the bedroom in Igoumenitsa and he saw her standing next to him in the Registry building in Gibraltar and....

He wasn't sure at what point he fell asleep and the memories became dreams, nor was he aware of what woke him, but he was suddenly fully alert. He saw Chiara's head raise slightly from the pillow, neck muscles taut and eyes wide open and staring at the ceiling, then a strange guttural sound came from her throat, there was a long exhalation of breath as she fell back on the pillow as if every last breath of air was being squeezed out of a balloon, and she lay still, with her eyes still seemingly fixed on the ceiling.

Feeling empty inside, he mechanically checked for the pulse he knew he wouldn't find, and then after kissing both her eyes, gently closed them, and putting his head on her still hot shoulder, cried quietly.

Chapter 10 - July 1943

Max straightened the collar of his uniform and brushed some dust off his left sleeve before knocking at the door.

He had been surprised and somewhat irritated when he received the message ordering him to leave his front-line unit and get a lift twenty miles in the wrong direction to Siracusa. Despite a determined counter attack by an Italian tank regiment, which had led to significant damage in the suburbs, the swiftness of the initial allied advance had left the centre of the city relatively unscathed and, as Max had entered the city he felt a pang of regret for his sketchbooks that had lain gathering dust in Ethel's attic since Chiara's death. He had tried to shut himself off from the things he had done while they had been together because the memory of his loss was still too painful. On arriving in Sicily, the first time a lull in the fighting had allowed him to take in his surroundings, he had found himself in front of one of the many tabernacles with sculptures of the Virgin Mary that were to be found on street corners. It struck him that his love for Chiara was now very similar to the Catholics' devotion to their religious idols, placed on a pedestal, idealised and de-contextualised. Maybe, if he survived this war, and he realised that he didn't really care whether he did or not, he would try to draw again, and maybe, if he could bring himself to do that again, it would help him to talk to his son about the mother he had never known.

John was happy with Ethel and Stan, and Max knew they had been good for each other; John took the place of the child of their own that they hadn't been able to have, and they had taken the place of the parents he had lost: his mother because she was dead and his father because he reminded him too much of his loss. Max wanted to do the things that other fathers did with their sons, but something inside him seemed to clam up when he was with John and make him tongue-tied and sad. Perhaps if there hadn't been loving substitute parents so easily available, Max would have had to break through the barrier earlier on and give his son the love he needed but, as it was, it had been too easy – a coward's way out.

'Enter.'

A smartly dressed officer with the epaulettes of a colonel stood behind a desk with his back to the door as he looked out of an open full-length window over the town. His hair was completely white and Max guessed that he was probably in his sixties. 'At ease, Staff Sergeant, and take a seat.'

Max did as he was bid and sat upright in the chair, holding his cap in his hands and waiting to know why he had been sent for. Then the man turned round and, while managing to maintain his military posture, Max could not prevent surprise from registering in his eyes. Even with the strong sunlight from the window behind him, he recognised Bertie Frizzell-Smyth.

'Hello, Max,' said Frizzell-Smyth, with a smile.

'Yes, Sir.'

Frizzell-Smyth did not sit at the chair behind the desk, but instead moved round and sat at another chair on Max's side so that Max did not have to look into the sun. 'Forget the "Sir" while the door's closed. Neither of us needs to impress anyone here, certainly not you with your record.'

'My record?'

Frizzell-Smyth picked up a buff folder from his desk which Max saw said "Staff Sergeant Maxwell Caddick: 8th Army, Infantry Brigade, XIII Corps" on the cover. He didn't open the folder, clearly being familiar with its contents. 'Volunteered for service August 1939; promoted to Corporal December that same year; showed conspicuous gallantry during the Dunkirk débâcle putting your own life at risk to save five others who were pinned down by machine gun fire – should have been decorated if CO had not tempered report by referring to a tendency to insubordination – what did you do to upset him?' Max opened his mouth to reply but Frizzell-Smyth waved his arm dismissively. 'Rhetorical question. Showed outstanding bravery again at Heraklion while with the 14th infantry brigade in May 41, while somehow managing to also distinguish yourself by your resourcefulness at Babani Khani shortly afterwards. Promoted to Sergeant on arrival in North Africa and Staff Sergeant after further examples of bravery and resourcefulness in Tunisia, where you were involved right from the very start, in May last year. Does that sum things up, or have I missed anything important?'

Max said nothing, having no idea where this conversation was leading to.

'No. I thought I'd covered most things. Now, first can I say how sorry I was to hear about Chiara.'

Max looked up, 'But how did you...'

'It's my business to know things; that's what they pay me for. Especially to know things about people who I hope are going to work for me... I know you well enough to know that I can rely on your absolute discretion, even if you decide not to accept my proposal – which you have every right to do.' He paused, and Max nodded to indicate that he should continue. 'My job is to obtain intelligence that will hopefully enable us to shorten the duration of this awful war. I have no doubt that now the Americans are alongside us we can fight our way up Italy, over the Alps, and all the way to Berlin, metre by metre if necessary but, we could do it a lot faster and with less loss of life if we knew more about what the enemy are doing on their side of the lines, and if the rising discontent that there is amongst the Italian civilian population could be encouraged to rise a little faster. Now, do you know how many soldiers in the British Army speak fluent Italian?' Max shook his head. 'Not many, despite the Italian immigrants who have come to Britain over the past fifty years. Many of them have been interned as aliens for the duration of the war, a decision which I personally think was mistaken, and half of them have been brought up by parents who wanted to fully integrate and discouraged their children from speaking Italian – yet another decision which I view as foolish and misguided – however..' and he shrugged his shoulders resignedly. 'When your name appeared on a list of potential recruits that was provided for me, my initial thought was to discount you because the risks are very high and I didn't want the chance of Chiara losing you to increase by my doing – then I saw the word "widower".'

'I'm happy to serve in any way I can. I have a son, but he is looked after by my sister and her husband and will hardly notice if anything happens to me.'

'You do realise that if you are captured, while working for my section, you will be shot, possibly after undergoing torture to find out what you know.'

'There are still plenty of limbless and shell-shocked ex-servicemen who have been hidden out of view in nursing homes since 1918. My only fear is going home like them, to be conveniently forgotten or, even worse, pitied. I'm not afraid of death.'

'No,' said Frizzell-Smyth with a sigh, 'that's what your record would suggest.'

By the time Max left Frizzell-Smyth's temporary office, two hours later, he had been promoted to Warrant Officer Class One, 'Best I can do, I'm afraid, to boost the money that will go to your son if anything happens. In the last war, I could have promoted you to Lieutenant or even Captain, but you have to have done the officer's training course now.'

He was airlifted back to Tunis the next day and then on to London for briefings and training. He passed both the physical and psychological tests with flying colours, as Frizzell-Smyth had predicted, and spent most of his time being brought up to date with everything that was known about the current situations in Naples, Rome, Florence and Bologna, and in getting used to his false identity. It was made clear that he would primarily be used in Tuscany as that was the area he knew best, although he had to be prepared to be moved elsewhere should the need arise. He had acquired a slight limp after taking a bullet in the leg while in Crete, and he was taught to accentuate it, to give him an excuse to walk with a stick, as a healthy young man walking about the streets would draw unwanted attention to himself.

A contact name and address was provided in Pescia for use in absolute emergencies but, other than that, it was decided that it would be safest if Max worked completely independently of the existing operations. He was encouraged to use any existing contacts he had, and to try and develop new ones, although Italy was effectively in a state of civil war and it was hard to know who could be trusted. Different groups united only by the common interest of fighting against the Germans and the representatives of the Reppublica di Salò could not always be relied on not to turn on each other, and he would need to be very careful about who he chose to work with. Gradually, moving between the four cities of Livorno, Pisa, Lucca, and Pistoia with occasional visits to Florence, taking great care not to establish any set patterns of movement, he was able to get a feel for the public mood and also to help set rumours going that would help swing the undecided to the allied side. Occasionally, he was stopped in spot checks, but his false papers proved to be up to the job. It was easier if he was stopped by the Germans as they did not pick up the defects in his accent; on the two occasions he was stopped by Italian officials, he had to rely on the fact that although his ID card said that he lived in Florence, it also said that he had been born in the Val d'Aosta, and he could remember everything that Chiara had told him about growing up there.

He resisted the temptation to go out to Bargino for a long time. He thought that the possibility of him being recognised was so remote as to be inconsequential, but he was wary of doing anything that might put the people he knew into any greater danger. Finally, with the allied advance having already passed Rome, he decided that he could resist no longer and needed to know what had happened to his old friends, and to urge them to lie low until the allies reached the Val di Pesa. There were regular troop movements going south towards the front and, as an apparent invalided ex-soldier, it was easy for him to get a lift with a lorry full of very nervous young Italians who happened to have found themselves in the wrong place at the wrong time when the Reppublica di Salò had been created. They were generally defeatist and he felt sorry for them, having been conscripted into a cause that was doomed to failure, likely to be either killed during the allied advance or picked off by partisans if they tried to run, having left it too late to stop believing in Mussolini. He didn't think he had anything to worry about from the soldiers but, in order to protect the people he was hoping to see, he went beyond Bargino, telling them that he needed to get to Tavarnelle.

They left him in the central square in the town, where he sat quietly, without drawing any attention to himself, in the shadow of the church. He allowed himself to doze, knowing that he had a long night ahead of him and feeling fairly secure where he was.

When the light began to fade, he carefully checked in all directions to see who was about, and then, after a group of children had left the square, quietly slipped out down one of the narrow streets. Making sure not to be observed from any unshuttered windows, he made his way to the track that led to Santa Cristina in Salivolpe. The *bottega* that had previously been used to pass messages between him and Giorgio was boarded up, and there was no sign of life around the back. He had been hoping to get news there, but now realised that he would have to proceed with even more caution than before and make his way down into Bargino.

Giorgio's door was locked, as he had expected, but there was a faint glimmer of light showing through one of the shutters. He thought he could hear voices inside. Checking around him, he knocked gently. Nothing. He hadn't knocked hard enough. He knocked again, a little harder, and everything went silent inside. He knocked for a third time.

'*Chi é?*' came a voice from inside.

'An old friend,' he said.

There was a pause and he heard the lock being turned. The top half of the door opened slowly, but the child who opened it then stepped quickly to one side. Facing Max, at the far end of the corridor, was Laura, pointing a hunting rifle at him.

'Hello, Cecco, you've grown a lot since I last saw you... *Ciao*, Laura. I'm glad to see you can look after yourself.'

'Who...' she started, looking uncertain.

'Max, the Englishman. Have you forgotten me?'

She didn't lower the gun. 'Cecco, check if there's anyone else outside, and if there isn't, let him in then close the door behind him, but keep out of his reach.'

Max kept his eyes on her as the child opened the lower part of the door and moved past him to check outside. 'Come forward, slowly,' she said and he started to move down the corridor as he heard the boy close and bolt the door behind him. She backed into the kitchen and across to the other side so that the light was between them, then she put the gun down and rushed across the kitchen to embrace him. 'It is you, I couldn't believe it.'

After a few seconds of holding each other tight, he gently moved away, allowing his arms to slide down the back of her arms until he held her lightly by the elbows and could get a good look at her. She had aged significantly in the eight and a half years since he had last seen her: her hair was no longer a healthy chestnut but was now mainly grey with only the slightest hint of its former lustre. Her cheeks were sunken as a result of the privations of the war and also, he thought, of some sadness that seemed to begin at her eyes and extend over her whole face. She tried to smile at him, but it was the smile of someone who has forgotten how to smile, and he pulled her close again and lightly guided her head down onto his shoulder where she could let the tears flow without having to look him in the face. When she had recovered somewhat he steered her to the bench where Cecco sat watching them, his hand, Max noticed, resting on the hilt of a kitchen knife.

'You won't remember me, Cecco, you were very young the last time I was here with your Mamma and Babbo. They looked after me after I got hurt, and helped me to get away from some people who were looking for me.'

Laura collected herself and put her hand on Cecco's shoulder, 'Cecco's a big brave boy now. He's not scared of anyone.' The boy smiled, pleased with the compliment, and allowed himself to be pulled towards his mother and enfolded by possessive arms.

The embrace lasted slightly longer than was comfortable for the boy and he wriggled free, 'Mamma!'

She looked at him fondly, 'I'm sorry, I forget how grown up you are now. But, you still need to get plenty of sleep to make you grow even bigger and stronger, so say "goodnight" to Max and go to bed now.'

'Buonanotte,' he said to Max, then giving Laura a big kiss, 'Buonanotte, Mamma. Call me if you need anything. Max managed not to smile at the boy who still couldn't be more than twelve years old, confidently asserting his right to protect his mother. He watched the boy leave the room and close the door behind him.

'Giorgio?' he said, with an air of urgency.

'Laura shook her head. 'He was called up early on but managed to get the call-up put off for as long as possible. When he couldn't avoid it any longer, he got on the bus, reported in to the command post in Florence and then walked out again. He said he had to report in and then desert rather than just avoiding the call-up, because he thought that there would be less repercussions on us if he didn't go missing from here. - He was wrong. He made the mistake of assuming that they think like decent human beings – but they don't. They knew all about Giorgio and had a folder with some of the things he'd said at various times written in it. They came late at night, kicked the door in and searched all through the house with torches in one hand and guns in the other. Anywhere where a man could have been hidden they ripped apart, I was sitting on the bed trying to tell the kids that it would be alright – or probably, trying to convince myself that it would be alright. When they didn't find Giorgio hiding, the one in charge told two of his men to bring me in. I got up straight away because I didn't want the kids to see their mother mistreated, but it didn't make any difference.'

She paused here and two big tear-drops rolled down her face, Max held out his hand to take hers but she ignored it, or didn't see it, as her own eyes were fixed on a scene that had remained indelibly impressed on them. 'Sara wouldn't let go. She clung to me as I got up, and one of the *squadristi*, swatted her off like a fly so that she fell on the floor, then they dragged me out, with me screaming for Sara, Sara lying still on the floor, and Cecco just looking as if he were rooted to the spot. When they let me go three days later, Signora Bosco was looking after the children but there was something very wrong with Sara; she must have hit her head on something as she fell. She had stopped talking, couldn't walk anymore and hardly ate, just sat there looking out with vacant eyes and drooling. Every few weeks they come back to check if there's any sign of Giorgio but never find anything. Once there was a man in plain clothes with them; he said he was a doctor, took a quick look at Sara and said that they'd be coming back the next day to take her away because she needed to be in an institution. After they'd gone, I read her *Capucetto Rosso*, because it had been her favourite story, even if she didn't understand it any more – then I put her down in her cot, gave her a kiss and pressed the cushion down over her face.'

'You brave, brave woman – you did what every parent should have done but most wouldn't have had the courage to do. That was the very best thing you could have done for her. Being disabled is one thing, but being taken and put in one of their institutions is another thing entirely.'

They sat in silence for a few minutes, each lost in their own thoughts. Max had mainly managed to cordon off his memories of Chiara's death from the happy memories, locking the painful memories away in a safe room at the back of his mind, insulating himself as though it had never happened. Now, Laura's pain had breached his defences and the memories of his loss came flooding through. She should have been thirty now, a mature, happy, smiling woman, a devoted mother whose body would have filled out slightly with motherhood, but whose smouldering dark beauty would still turn heads everywhere in

England where the default mousey blonds with their poorly-cut clothes would have paled into insignificance beside her.

'Mamma,' came a small plaintive voice from beyond the door, and Laura, who was clearly used to this, shook herself free of her memories and with a, 'He still has nightmares,' got up and quickly slipped out of the room.

Cecco's voice made Max think of John, and he realised that the reason he had not been able to have the relationship he knew he should have with his son was that, in a way, John was the key to the safe room where the memory of his loss was stored. He thought of what Laura had done for her daughter with awe and felt ashamed that he had not given John the love he deserved. It would be different when he got home he promised himself. He would be a good father to John, no matter how painful it was at first.

'Does Giorgio know?' he asked, when Laura came back into the room.

She nodded, 'For more than two years we used to meet occasionally, sometimes by arrangement, others he would surprise me; he said it was safer like that.'

'Said...?'

She gave a small smile, which didn't extend to her eyes, and shook her head, 'No. He's not dead – as far as I know – but after the armistice, he joined up with the partisans in the Apennines, said that he wanted to kill as many fascists as possible to make them pay for Sara.' The small smile had disappeared now. 'But I'm scared. The German fascists are bad enough but the hard core home grown ones are worse; they caught a partisan from Greve a few weeks ago and they didn't just kill him, they went to his home, raped his sister and hung his parents... That's why I had the gun ready when you knocked at the door tonight.'

They talked for much of the night. Laura tried to console him when she heard about Chiara's death, but quickly understood that it was not something he wanted to talk about. He asked about the other people he had known. The old lady with the bottega in Santa Cristina had fallen ill and been taken to live with a sister in Florence; as far as Laura knew, she was still alive but unable to recognise even close family members. Sister Antonia was still at the convent school in San Donato, making sure that the children, particularly those whose parents had been taken by the fascists, were as well cared for and educated as possible. Aldo, like Giorgio was with the partisans and she had heard that Bruni had been arrested.

He had been hoping that, through Giorgio, he may have been able to establish a new cell, collecting information which he could ensure was transmitted to Frizzell-Smyth and his shadowy superiors in their Baker Street office. However, now he was there, he felt it wrong to expose Laura and Cecco to any more risk than they already ran. Laura gave him the name of a farmer in Montefiridolfi who she thought might be able to help, but then he wouldn't let her get any further involved.

His other reason for coming back to Bargino had been to find out what Chiara's family were up to. As leading fascists, any news about their activities could turn out to have some use for the allies. Again, what he heard was discouraging but not, on the whole, unexpected; Aristide was by Pavolini's side while Elisabetta and their children were somewhere in the north of the country with Domenico. La Contessa had died, in Montecatini, the previous year and Filippo was reported to be either missing or dead, having been with the Italian Army in Kefalonia at the time of the armistice. Umberto was an official in the army of the Republic of Salò, but she didn't know where. She did know that Virginia had left the estate a few weeks before and had last been seen driving northwards with an army motorbike escorting her. Rumour had it that apart from Virginia, the car contained the majority of the more easily transportable family valuables and it was hoped that they wouldn't be seen again. Adele had left the house the day after Virginia, taking with her enough silver cutlery to cover the value of the wages that she was sure would never now be paid.

'And Maddalena?'

Laura hesitated, then, 'When you left, Aristide had just introduced Chiara to Gian Giacomo Melluso, a cousin of

Pavolini's. Aristide and Pavolini had intended Chiara to marry Melluso. The match would strengthen Aristide politically, and be good for Pavolini socially. Melluso is a very handsome socialite, and completely insincere, making a "good" marriage was useful for him and, once Chiara had gone, he was encouraged to transfer his attentions to Maddalena. She was only just sixteen and desperate to get away from her family. When you're sixteen, the grass is always greener on the other side of the fence; she was always headstrong and I'm sure she thought that she could turn him into a reliable husband – they eventually married just a few days before Italy joined the war. He's fairly important with the police now, based up on Via Bolognese.'

'Aren't the police based in the new *Questura* in Via Zara?'

Laura gave a mirthless laugh. 'The regular police are, but the *Banda Carità*, with their "special" responsibilities for "National Security", share a building with the German Police at the corner of Via Bolognese and Via Trieste. People who are arrested and taken there, don't come out again. They say that...' But Max was no longer listening, he was thinking about Maddalena. Even though they had rarely had occasion to speak to each other, and really, he'd hardly noticed her, having eyes only for Chiara, he knew that Chiara had been close to her and cared for her. How old would she be now? He did the sum: twenty-five or twenty-six; he probably wouldn't recognise her. How would her life be, married to someone important in Fascist circles with all the right connections? He tried to imagine, but couldn't.

In Florence, the situation concerned him. The air itself seemed brittle; everyone's nerves seemed to be taut like violin strings with the audience on the edges of their seats waiting for a discordant note. Children were conspicuous by their absence as their mothers tried to keep them indoors and out of harm's way. There was a shortage of food in general and bread in particular. Bands of police, both German and Italian roamed the streets, stopping, questioning and searching people on the slightest pretext with fingers on triggers read to mete out summary justice should they deem it necessary. The Italians were worse than the Germans, feeling the need to prove themselves to their allies. On the seventeenth of July, five people including an eight year old boy were seized when members of the *Banda Carità* swooped on Piazza Tasso, determined to crush the spirits of the population of that poorer area of Florence where there had been significant unrest and where a number of rebels were believed to be hiding out. The five were executed in the piazza where they were arrested.

On the twentieth of July, Max came out of a bar in Via dei Cerchi where he had been arranging for a wounded partisan to be hidden. He rounded the corner into Piazza dei Cimatori just as a group of police entered the piazza from the other end. He pressed himself into a doorway hoping that he hadn't been noticed but luck was not with him.

'Alt la!'

Max ran. Even if his papers would stand up to a reasonable level of scrutiny, the mere fact of being out on the streets was enough to render him suspicious and, if he were subjected to any kind of search, they would find the M34 Beretta pistol he had recently begun to carry. A shot rang out behind him, but the police had not had time to take proper aim and he neither knew nor cared where the bullet went. He heard the pounding of running footsteps, a whistle blowing which was then echoed by more whistles from different directions. The tangle of narrow streets in the historic centre made it easier to keep out of sight, but they also made sound deceptive and he could not tell which streets would not lead him straight into the arms of the converging groups of soldiers. At the end of one street he almost ran out in front of a group of soldiers rushing towards where they judged the whistles to be coming from. He pressed himself back into a doorway and then turned in the other direction. Normally there would be a shop, a bar, an unlocked door he could slide into – but not today, almost everyone was hiding behind locked doors unless they had no alternative. He was determined not to be taken alive. If the worst came to the worst, he would make sure he killed some of them but the last bullet in the chamber was for him – but first, he would do anything he could to get away.

In Piazza dei Donati, he desperately tried one of the other streets leading off it – shouts approaching; then the next – whistles and shouts. The sound of running footsteps could be heard from at least two of the alleys leading to the square. He looked around for somewhere he could make his last stand, somewhere he could put his back to the wall so that he couldn't be taken from behind. Then, a voice from the other side of the small square called, 'Here!' He looked up and saw that less than ten metres away a door stood slightly ajar. As he sprang towards it, the opening widened just enough to allow him passage and then clicked smoothly closed behind him. It was all over in less than two seconds, but that two seconds changed not only his destiny, but that of many others as well.

Chapter 11 - August 1944

On the twenty second of August, just as dawn was breaking, Max slipped out of the trees above the orchards and olive groves behind the Church of San Francesco in Pescia. He moved very carefully into the fruit trees and did his best to remain under cover as he continued to move downwards towards the town. He saw a lorry full of soldiers emerge from a narrow street on the other side of the almost completely dried-up river and cross the bridge towards him. He stopped and crouched even lower, ready to make a dash back to the denser woodland behind him, if necessary. However, as the lorry disappeared from view behind the buildings, he could tell from the sound of the engine that the lorry had turned in front of the church towards the hospital.

Still crouching, he half walked, half slid down the remainder of the slope until he reached the edge of the orchard. After two minutes scanning the edge of the town ahead of him and particularly the end of the road where the lorry had disappeared, he made a dash across the road and pressed himself against the wall of the nearest house. The house, like the others between it and the church was completely silent in the early morning and he hoped that he would not have to knock too hard to attract the attention of the occupants. He took a deep breath and tapped lightly with his fingers on the shutters covering what he assumed must be the kitchen window. Nothing happened and he tried again slightly harder. He was nervous. In all his time in Italy, he had relied on his instincts to decide who could be trusted; now, for the first time, he was going to use the emergency contact he had been given and it made him feel uncomfortable and very exposed. He would have much preferred to continue to live on his wits and develop his own contacts in his own time, but the situation no longer permitted him that option; the papers he had with him had to get to the allied commanders as soon as possible – if they didn't, then a significant number of extra lives would almost certainly be lost as the Allies pushed up the coast and moved inland to attempt to breach the Gothic Line.

The fighting to the South and South-East of Florence was now intense, as it was on the coast, and his only chance of getting through to the allies in time was to go through the *Padule di Fucecchio* where the marshy terrain was impassible for modern military vehicles and even unsuitable for foot soldiers. To get through the *Padule*, however, he needed a guide and, given the relative proximity of Pescia to the *Padule*, the emergency contact was the best option he had. Finally, he heard a noise above his head and a wooden shutter with fading green paint was pushed open a few inches. He caught a glimpse of a face and then the shutter was pulled closed again. Thirty seconds later, the door of the house was half opened and gratefully he slid inside.

A grey haired man in his late fifties faced him with a pistol in his hand that was trained steadily on his heart. He looked pretty much as Max had imagined the contact would look and, turning his hands palms upwards in front of him to show he wasn't armed, he said, *'Professore di Biagio?'*

The man nodded his head, without lowering the gun. 'Who wants to know, and what are you doing here?'

'British Special Operations. I was told that I could contact you in an emergency, and the emergency has now arrived.' Di Biagio looked quickly at the door behind Max who realising that what he had said had been misconstrued shook his head, 'No. Don't worry. I haven't brought them to your door, and there's no extra danger to you, but I desperately need your help to be able to complete my job.'

I'm pretty sure that there's no-one else outside, so he doesn't appear to have been followed,' said a female voice from some steps to the teacher's right. Di Biagio lowered the gun, although without putting it down, and waved Max through the door to his right into a kitchen and then followed him in. Seconds later they were joined by the owner of the female voice who Max assumed to be the man's wife.

Three glasses appeared on the table and then a bottle of clear liquid. Max raised an eyebrow.

'Sorry I can't offer you a coffee – *grappa* will have to do. I'm afraid we'll have to sit in the dark for now; we don't want to attract attention by opening the shutters or putting a light on at this time.' Max allowed her to put a small amount in his glass then made a stop gesture near the glass with his hand and nodded his head in thanks.

'Tell us your problem,' said the man. As succinctly as possible, Max did so.

Di Biagio and his wife quickly grasped the seriousness of the situation and began to draw up a plan of action. Max, having spent the last two weeks, painstakingly making his way carefully west from Florence, travelling mainly by night, was exhausted and was soon struggling to keep up as the di Biagios threw ideas around, naming places and people that meant nothing to him. The *signora*, or as he assumed she would be used to being addressed, *professoressa*, noticed how he was struggling and insisted that he go upstairs to get a few hours' sleep.

When di Biagio woke him, shortly after two, he felt refreshed. There were now three people sitting in the kitchen; the di Biagios and a boy who Max judged to be fourteen or fifteen years old. The boy was fairly roughly dressed with a frayed shirt that may once have been white and a rough pair of trousers that looked as if they may well have been his father's.

'This is Riccardo,' said Professoressa di Biagio, 'he's one of my most intelligent students and certainly the bravest. We call him the Scarlet Pimpernel because he seems to be able to get out of any situation. He also has the advantage that he spent the first ten years of his life in Anchione, which is as close to the heart of the *Padule* as it's possible to live. If anyone can get you safely through the *Padule*, he can.'

Max looked the boy in the eye for a minute and found that Riccardo held his gaze. 'You realise that this will be very dangerous? It's one thing being able to get through on your own but having to take someone else through more than doubles the difficulty.' The boy shrugged. 'What about your family? What if you're killed?' Although the boy was clearly brave, Max was uncomfortable about the risk that he would be facing; he did not want another innocent death on his conscience.

'My name is Riccardo del'Orefice. Does that name suggest anything to you?' said the boy in a quiet but firm voice. Max shook his head.

'No? Well it would if you were Italian, especially a fascist Italian.' Max shook his head.

'I know what the name means, but that's all.'

'In the period when most surnames were assigned, the profession of *orefice*, was one which was usually carried out by Jews, just as in England you have your "Goldsmiths" and one of the highest concentration of Jews is in "Golders Green". Riccardo is a Jew.'

Max was surprised and a little disappointed, he hadn't thought that the di Biagios would be the type of person who would discriminate on racial grounds and suggest that it didn't matter if a Jewish family lost a son.

Di Biagio obviously read, and correctly interpreted, the expression on Max's face; 'Riccardo, I think that our friend is making judgements based on incorrect assumptions. Tell him about your parents.'

'My father, was a notary until the *'leggi razziali'*, the racial laws were passed in 1938. After that, when he was no longer allowed to follow his profession, he worked as a clerk for the Notary who had taken over his practice, doing most of the work in the practice and being paid very little for it. After two years, the notary made a mess of a file he was dealing with on behalf of the Prefect of Montecatini. He publicly blamed my father, even though it was one of the few cases that my father had not worked on. My father was arrested, as was my mother when she went to protest. Along with other Jews, they were put on a train for Germany last year. I don't believe they will ever come back.'

Max was left speechless by the calm composed way in which Riccardo summarised his parents' fate. At first he felt he should be shocked, then he thought about his own reaction to Chiara's death and realised that the boy didn't care whether he lived or died, he just wanted to get some sort of revenge. He knew he should try and persuade the boy that there was always something worth living for, especially now that he himself had finally realised he wanted to live and to rebuild his life, but he knew that it would be pointless – knew that there was nothing anyone could say that would change the boy's position, nothing that anyone could have said to him that would have persuaded him that life had a point after Chiara's death. He held out a hand for Riccardo to take, and when he did, he brought up his other hand so that the boy's was enclosed in both of his. 'I understand. I couldn't have a better guide,' and then to the di Biagios, 'I'm sorry I jumped to the wrong conclusions; I should have known better.'

They left the di Biagios shortly after five and took the road through the 'Florentine Gate' towards Montecatini, avoiding Piazza XX Settembre where the imposing *Casa del Fascio* made it the hub of the regime's power in the town. Riccardo seemed to have a sixth sense for danger and twice pulled Max into gateways while official vehicles went past, seeming to be aware of them and their dangerous cargo before Max had even heard the engines in the distance. He soon realised that he should trust Riccardo completely and do exactly as he said. At times they left the road and made their way through olive groves as Riccardo skirted around places where there were likely to be roadblocks or controls. Because of the many pauses and the careful route choices made by Riccardo, it took them over four and a half hours to reach Ponte Buggianese on the edge of the *Padule*, by which time night was closing in.

Flashes were visible in the distance to the South and the faint sound of heavy guns could be heard. Keeping close to the walls, Riccardo made his way to a house in Via Battisti, knocked and pushed at the door. It was locked. He looked worried but said nothing and led Max back down the street and through the town to another house on Via Fosso alle Torri. Here Riccardo's knock was answered and they were ushered inside. Straight away, Riccardo asked about the people in Via Battisti. The woman who had let them in explained that because of the danger of bombing, particularly at night time, many inhabitants of the village and other surrounding villages had left their homes and moved into the *Padule* for safety. She wasn't going anywhere; in her view there were people just waiting for the opportunity to do some looting, 'and not just fascists,' she added darkly. She offered to put them up for the night but Riccardo was keen to be moving on. If there were already people wandering about in the *Padule* they would be less noticeable.

By the time they reached the edge of the *Padule* it was very dark and Riccardo insisted that they rest until first light in the shelter of a small barn which had suffered significant damage at one end, but which still served to hide them from the track. Max slept with his back against the wall facing the breech in the wall; Riccardo went to sleep lying alongside the soundest of the barn's remaining walls.

Max woke first as the earliest rays of light crept over the top of Montevettolini, silhouetting the tower of the ruined castle. He waited a few minutes, wanting to allow Riccardo a little more rest and then shook him gently when he felt that it was better that they delayed no longer. They ate some of the bread that the di Biagios had sent with them and washed it down with water from their bottles then, looking round cautiously as they emerged from the ruined barn, walked in the opposite direction to Anchione and further into the *Padule*. As the first part of the track was long and straight, where anyone walking could be seen from a long way away, they dropped down and made their way through the tall sunflowers that filled the fields to either side.

They had not been going for much more than ten minutes when they heard the sound of a vehicle bouncing its way along the track heading further into the *Padule*. Riccardo looked puzzled, 'What do they think they're doing in the *Padule*? The partisans will hear them coming and clean up.' But as the sound of the engine grew more distant, they could hear the sound of running feet and German voices, and they thought they could hear other engines in the distance. Then they heard the first shots – machine gun fire. Soon they came to a small clearing on the edge of a wooded area. A small stone hut stood at the intersection of three small canals or drainage ditches which disappeared into the thick vegetation. The sun had now risen above Montevettolini and a brilliant light glinted off the little stagnant water that remained in the base of the ditches after the hot summer. Half a dozen flat bottomed boats, narrow with pointed ends, rested uselessly on the dried up mud of the banks. One had had its bottom kicked through, and the sides of two more were perforated by a curved line of regularly spaced holes, each roughly the size of a finger-tip. The sole of a rough peasant boot could be seen protruding around the corner of the hut.

Max put a hand on Riccardo's arm indicating that he should stay where he was while he crept forward, pistol in hand, to make sure that it wasn't a trap and, if it wasn't, to see if anything could be done for the body that he was sure he would find attached to the foot. He listened carefully, pressed against the side of the hut until he was fairly sure that there was no-one else there then, finger poised on the trigger of the *beretta*, he moved cautiously round the corner.

His arm dropped and the gun slipped from his fingers as he dropped to his knees by the side of the body. The foot they had seen belonged to a man, in rough peasant dress, who he judged to be in his late forties or early fifties; the curved line of regularly spaced holes that had perforated the sides of the boats continued across the man's side, changing direction suddenly as he had obviously fallen through the bullets. What was particularly horrifying was that the man lay on top of a boy, who he had clearly tried to shield. The eyes of the boy were wide open and, for a moment, Max hoped that he might still be alive but, as he rolled the father's body to the side, he saw that three bullets had passed straight through the father and into the son. He looked and tears came to his eyes as he thought of the senseless loss of life - and of John.

'*Bisogna andare*,' said Riccardo, gripping his shoulder as he urged him to move on, 'They might come back this way and I can hear more shooting.' Max managed to pull himself together and nodding his thanks to Riccardo, picked up his gun again and began to follow him through the trees. Ten minutes later there was a crashing noise behind them and they dropped down behind the nearest tree trunks; even though they provided inadequate cover, they might at least gain them a few seconds and mean that they weren't taken by surprise from behind. As the crashing noise grew nearer, they could hear a strange keening noise and Max imagined that they would soon see a terrified wounded animal come into view; the keening noise sounded primal and wild and Max hoped that the animal died before it reached them... Then he saw that it wasn't an animal, it was a girl, dress badly torn by the vegetation she had been running through, and blood on one side of her face.

'No!' Riccardo leapt up from behind his tree and rushed to meet the girl, who tried to run straight through him as if he weren't there. He managed to get hold of her waist and they span round and fell to the ground together as the impetus of her mad rush knocked him off his feet.

'Maria! Maria! Maria! It's me, Riccardo. Shhhhhhh. Shhhhhhh, Shhhhhhh.' Gradually the keening subsided into a whimper and then she began to cry.

'What happened, Maria? Tell us what happened.'

She shook her head, but said nothing.

'You're with us now, you'll be safe,' said Riccardo sounding much more reassuring than Max thought he had any right to be.

'They're all dead.'

'Who are all dead?' said Riccardo. The girl was wracked by sobs then, as they subsided, *'La Mamma, Babbo, i Nonni, tutti!'*

'Your whole family!'

'No, you still haven't understood. Not just my family. There were about fifty of us who slept in the Tobacco drying store last night. This morning, Signor Rossi went outside and then there were shots. The next thing, two German soldiers burst in shouting, *"Raus! Raus! Raus!"* Everyone pushed towards the door scared of what might happen. An old lady fell over and her husband stopped to try and help her up. One of the Germans shot him in the head and yanked the old lady up by her hair. She tried to pull back to get back to her husband, so they shot her as well.' The girl paused, obviously reliving the scene in her mind and Riccardo pressed her face against his chest. After a minute, she lifted her head away and continued; now she had started to tell her story she clearly needed to get it all out, 'Outside there were about ten of them all waving their guns at us and shouting in German. The one who seemed to be in charge said something to one of the others and he lit a brand and threw it in through the door onto the straw where people had been sleeping. We all started to line up, because that seemed to be what they wanted us to do, a couple of metres in front of the *Tabaccaia*. I was on the end of the row, nearest the end of the building; my dad gave me a push and said run, so I did. I saw him step forward so that he was in their line of fire until I got round the corner, then there was lots of shouting and shooting.'

She stopped and Max understood that her mind was working through what she had experienced again, and creating horrifying visions of the worst things that could possibly have happened behind her as she ran. He wanted to help her, reassure her that it was probably only her father and the old couple who were dead, but what sort of reassurance would that be? Even in the best case scenario, the girl had lost her father and, he shuddered to think about the worst case scenario. He felt useless – there was nothing he could say or do to help the girl.

'Riccardo, how much further do we have to go to get through to the allied lines? Could I make it on my own?'

The boy looked up from where his eyes had been fixed on the girl's face. He shook his head, 'We should have been able to get through to the Arno in about three hours, if the *Padule* was as deserted as it usually is, now... who knows... Listen...' Max listened, having previously been captivated by first the cries and then the voice of the girl; from all directions the sound of intermittent shooting could be heard, some of it sustained. 'It sounds as if, for some reason, they've decided to surround the *Padule*. Our only hope is that they haven't got anyone with them who really knows the *Padule* well. If they are determined enough, and have enough time they can do a fairly thorough sweep, but there are places where they would still need a lot of luck to find people hiding. We need to go on because here isn't safe, but we'll have to take Maria with us – I'm not leaving her here.' Max nodded. 'Maria,' said Riccardo gently, 'will you come with us? You'll need to be very quiet and do everything I say. Then, as soon as we can, we'll go back and find out who else escaped.'

Maria nodded and Riccardo lifted her up and began to lead her by the hand.

Although it had been a hot summer and much of the *Padule* was dry, there was still mud amongst the thicker vegetation and Riccardo stuck to that, at times carefully testing the ground before them with a stick. Several times, after prodding the ground, he turned to the side and skirted round patches that to Max were indistinguishable from the ones they were slowly moving through. At the first patch of thick, brackish mud that they met, he made them lie down and roll in the mud so that their clothes took on the hue of their surroundings. Both his own and Riccardo's already blended in well, but Max understood that Riccardo was aware of the danger posed by Maria's white dress and felt that the easiest way to get her to camouflage it was if they all took the same action. Twice, he made them all drop to the ground in the mud as the sound of heavy boots and guttural but nervously excited German voices passed within thirty yards of them. He could only catch glimpses of the field grey uniforms through the dense vegetation and was fairly confident that, unless they turned and almost stumbled over them, they were safe. As they were about to pass out of sight, one of the Germans raised his gun and let off a burst of machine gun fire into the vegetation on the other side of the path they were following, clearly so wound up that even the slightest noise was enough to make them fire. Max realised just in time that Maria was about to scream and clamped his hand over her mouth in time to prevent any more than the initial noise from passing her lips. Fortunately, the strangled beginnings of her cry were covered by the noise of two birds that rose out of the marsh nearby, disturbed by the shooting.

He kept his hand clasped firmly over Maria's mouth until the group of Germans had moved out of sight and Riccardo was holding one of her hands while putting his finger over his lips with the other. They waited another five minutes before moving on, aware that even being careful and staying out of sight of the soldiers might not be enough if they were going to loose off random rounds into the vegetation.

Although they heard the sound of shooting from all directions, the highest density seemed to come from the East and Riccardo told him that many German soldiers were based in Monsummano and that almost certainly the action had been co-ordinated from there, but that it wouldn't have been possible without the help of Italian *'repubblichini'*, many of whom had scores to settle with locals who didn't support Mussolini's republic.

Later in the morning, there was no longer any sound of shooting and, telling Max and Maria to remain well hidden, Riccardo cautiously moved out of the marshes to reconnoitre the hamlet of Massarella, to find news and see if there was a safe way out, He came back half an hour later and confirmed that the Germans seemed to have withdrawn, but only after massacring hundreds of people; no one seemed to know how many, and the estimates he had heard had varied widely. In Massarella itself, six people had been killed, including four members of the same family; there seemed to be no logical reason why they had been chosen rather than others, they weren't partisans and had just lived quiet lives on their farm, without any involvement in politics. Those he had spoken to had told Riccardo that the group who had carried out the killings in Massarella had not penetrated far into the *Padule*, clearly fearing finding themselves outnumbered by partisans while on unfamiliar territory.

'There are groups of partisans in the *Padule?*' asked Max, but Riccardo shook his head.

'There is only one very small group that operates out of Ponte Buggianese, and they are very careful not to do anything that could bring reprisals down on the rest of the people. If there were any in the *Padule*, they will have moved northwards or westwards when the refugees moved in. The partisans operate in the hills to the north of Pescia, where they can do most to stop the Germans reinforcing their Gothic line.'

Riccardo then led them out of the marshes to a house in Massarella where the first thing they did was to wash the mud off themselves and their clothes. He knew the woman slightly and explained to her how Maria had escaped from the massacre in the tobacco drying store and that all her family may well be dead. Max had expected the woman to respond with horror, but she just shook her head and took Maria's hand.

'Yesterday, I wouldn't have believed it – couldn't have believed that humans could be capable of such things. Now, I would believe anything – after what I've seen and heard today, nothing will ever surprise me again. We're all related, you know... here in the village... everyone is someone's cousin, or married to someone's cousin.... Most people never move away... if you're born here, you'll probably die here. Five of the six here, were some sort of cousins of mine.' She took Maria's other hand, 'There are people going into the *Padule* to look for the bodies. I'll ask them to find out what news they can about the *Tabaccaia*.'

They tried to persuade Maria to go to bed but she was terrified of being left alone and each time she closed her eyes, the images returned to her eyes. Eventually they persuaded her to lie on a mat on the floor where she curled up into a foetal position with her shoulders in contact with the woman's leg.

Max again attempted to persuade Riccardo to remain behind and let him go on alone, but the boy insisted that he had to go because Max would stand far more chance with someone who knew the lay of the land to help him find the way. Although Max felt guilty about the continued danger he was subjecting the boy to, he knew that he was right, and that if he were to get his information through to the allies he still needed help.

They left the house, soon after five which still gave them another four hours of daylight to reach the river and try and work out the best way of breaching the German line and crossing the river between the two armies. They started off by walking westwards up into the gentle wooded hills separating the *Padule* from the plain around Bientina, and then turned south west to shadow the road towards Pontedera. They kept the road in sight at all times to make sure that the direction was right. The only vehicles they saw were German military trucks heading northwards and Max was pleased to see that they seemed to be pulling back, or at least preparing to pull back.

The walk passed without incident, in contrast to the morning's journey, and by eight thirty, having turned eastwards, they were standing in the shadow of the walls of Santa Maria a Monte, looking at the Arno less than two miles ahead of them. The German defences were clearly visible from their vantage point in the village and he could see that there were a couple of places where it might be possible to get through them in the dark. The sentries would have their eyes focussed on the far bank of the river and for one man, moving very very carefully, it should be possible to sneak past them from behind, particularly if there were some kind of bombardment, which was entirely possible.

They rested until after eleven and the occasional exchanges of fire that had taken place earlier became more sporadic. Deciding that they were not going to get the bombardment they had hoped for, they carefully set off towards the river, moving one at a time, from one patch of cover to the next. From their previous vantage point, Max had spotted a small island in the middle of the river, at a point where there had obviously once been trees on both banks. Although these were now blasted and blackened stumps they would still offer some degree of cover if they could reach that point.

A damaged farmhouse stood at the end of a track less than a hundred metres from the bank of the river facing the small island, and Max could see the barrel of a large gun protruding from one of the windows. Motioning Riccardo to remain where he was, he inched forwards on his elbows to the edge of the property. One minute, two minutes, three minutes... then his patience was rewarded; there was the glint of light on steel as a match flared and momentarily illuminated the face of a German soldier about thirty metres away from him, by the corner of the house. He watched for a few more minutes to make sure that there were no more and then inched his way back to Riccardo.

'There's only one sentry. If we can get rid of him, silently, we can get all the way to the river bank without being seen. The gunners are probably taking it in turns to sleep and those who are awake, will be watching the other bank.'

'Why don't we take the men out who are inside with the gun, once we've got rid of the sentry?'

Max put a hand on Riccardo's arm, 'Two reasons: firstly, we couldn't do it without making a noise and we can't be too far from the next gun points in both directions, and secondly, we've got no way of dealing with any prisoners.'

'But why don't we...'

'No!' he interrupted sharply, 'If we do that, then we're no better than them, and if we're no better than them then we shouldn't be fighting them.' Riccardo looked truculent. 'Listen, Riccardo. You're one of the bravest men I've ever come across, but you need to understand that the reason you can be so brave and so determined is because you know that what you are fighting for is right. If you get to the stage when your actions could be seen by anyone else as unjust, you won't be able to do it anymore. You fight because what happened to your parents and what happened this morning was unfair. We have to kill the sentry because not only do our lives depend on it, but because it's my duty to get the information I have to the allies, and it's his duty to try and stop me. The duty of the soldiers inside is to try to stop the allies from crossing the river; they're probably scared stiff, and in any case it looks as if the Germans are getting ready to pull back. We leave them be.' He waited a few seconds, then Riccardo nodded and held out a hand, which he clasped.

After lying watching for a further fifteen minutes, Max began to ease himself forward again on his elbows, adrenaline making him oblivious to the rough surface that took his skin off and left both elbows and knees bleeding. This time he made for the opposite corner of the building to that at which the guard, on whom he kept his eyes fixed, was stationed. Five minutes later, he reached the building and, raising himself into a crouching position, made his way carefully along the side to the front. At the front, he carefully surveyed the damaged wall and the muzzle of the gun that protruded over a sill where a window had once been. Very very carefully, he eased himself along the wall, crouching low as he passed under the window. No matter what he had said to Riccardo, he strongly suspected that if he had had a grenade, he would have found it very hard to resist throwing it in, and smiled grimly, glad that he didn't have that temptation to resist.

Having reached the corner beyond the gun, he carefully eased his head around to check where the sentry was. He was still where he had been before, leaning against the wall at the far end of the building, cigarette in one hand and the other holding the strap of a rifle that was slung loosely over his shoulder. Max switched the *beretta* to his left hand and grasped a rough stone, about the size of a large apple in his right, then he began to inch his way along the wall, hoping that the German had no reason to turn around. The next two minutes seemed like hours, and Max hardly dared breathe as he inched along, closer and closer to the sentry. If the sentry turned round, Max's gun was trained on his head, but it would alert the soldiers inside and probably others who wouldn't be too far away. At one point, a stone shifted slightly under his foot and he froze, finger tightening around the trigger. Then, all of a sudden, it was all over; launching himself off his left foot, he brought his right arm round in a fast swing parallel to the floor so that it hit the sentry on the top of the backbone just beneath his helmet. Without letting go of the *beretta*, Max followed with his left arm, managing to clamp his forearm over the sentry's mouth as he fell, minimising any noise he might make as he died.

Max stood up and, after waiting a minute to be sure that he had not attracted any attention from the soldiers inside the building, he beckoned Riccardo forwards. Almost invisible in the gloom, Riccardo glided across the distance that separated them. Fingers on lips, Max indicated a point just over halfway to the river bank that Riccardo should make for while he covered him. As Riccardo slipped across, Max concentrated on the low voices of the soldiers inside the building, but as there didn't seem to be any change in their voices it was safe to assume that they were still unaware that anything was wrong. Once Riccardo had reached the point he had indicated and lain down just over the brow of the slight rise before the land sloped gently down to the river, Max ran across bent double and slipped down beside the boy, his *beretta* in one hand and the dead German's gun in the other. He handed over the Beretta and pointed to the spot on the river bank where he wanted Riccardo to move to next, while he trained the German sentry's gun on the window housing the heavy duty gun. Once Riccardo had made it, he himself slithered backwards towards the river, keeping the gun trained on the window as well as he could while he did so, until he was able to slide down the bank so that his boots were in the water.

Before swimming the first half of the river across to the small island, Max showed Riccardo the oilskin pouch that was taped to him. 'This must get to the allies... whatever happens... it could save hundreds, maybe even thousands of lives... or it could be completely useless,' He shrugged and Riccardo nodded to show that he had understood. Again, Max insisted that the boy went first, while he lay ready to try and provide some cover should it be necessary. Being dressed only in a light pair of shorts and a thin shirt, Riccardo accomplished the crossing easily, swimming on his back, using only his legs so that there was no noise, and holding the pistol just above the water. For Max it was more of a struggle as his clothes absorbed more of the water and the rifle also hampered him. Rather than lying on his back as he would have wished, he was in an almost vertical position and had to kick strongly to lift his head each time he needed to take a breath. Eventually, however, he reached the island and Riccardo stretched out to grab the muzzle of the gun and pull.

They lay for more than ten minutes on the little island until Max felt he was able to continue. This time he went first, taking the *beretta* but leaving the rifle on the island; this made swimming much easier and he was soon at the opposite bank and safety. He stayed low and beckoned Riccardo across.

When Riccardo had almost made it, their luck ran out. There were shouts from the damaged house where the gun emplacement was. The guard had obviously been found. Seconds later, as he was pulling Riccardo out of the water, the machine gun opened up, strafing the area in front of the house as far as the river. The gunners clearly could not see a target but were firing at random, hoping to avenge the dead sentry; then, two more guns opened open, one to either side of the original. From the southern side of the river, allied guns began to respond and Max ducked down as the air above his head filled with metal. Then, as he pulled Riccardo alongside him there was a thud and the boy's eyes opened wide with surprise as a hole appeared in his chest a couple of inches below his collar bone where the bullet that had caught him in the back exited his body.

Riccardo groaned as the initial shock passed and the pain kicked in. Max rolled him over the top of the bank and then, pulling himself up, began to shout "English, English, don't shoot," and picking up Riccardo began to run towards the allied lines. He didn't know when the first bullet hit him, or the second, but the third one brought him to his knees and he was back in his room at the Campolargo's feeling Umberto's boots crashing into his ribs.

A very blurred nurse bent over him as he opened his eyes and tried to smile. Nothing hurt any more, and it was very light around him. He struggled to focus on the nurse's face; it was Chiara – no it was Laura – or was it Ethel – he hadn't realised they all looked the same. 'The package?' he managed to whisper.

A man appeared behind the nurse. 'Please don't try to talk.... The boy showed us the packet before he died. It's been passed on to the right people.'

Riccardo dead as well. Max shut his eyes. Before he drifted into unconsciousness, he heard the nurse say, 'Will he live, Doctor?' Max didn't hear an answer, but he didn't need to.

End of Part 1

Part 2 1985

Chapter 1

The young border guard dropped his magazine, carefully rested the bottle of *orangina* down on the ground next to him, replacing it in his hand with his standard issue sub-machine gun, and levered himself up from one of the two deckchairs that had been placed outside the hut alongside the barrier officially controlling the high route into Italy from Switzerland. He lazily waved the red disk on the end of a stick to indicate that the young man at the wheel of the slowly approaching vehicle should pull over to the side. Once the driver, a lightly-bearded, fair haired, athletic young man with intense dark eyes, had turned the ignition off and coasted gently to a halt, the guard walked all around the old MG Midget until he was again facing the slightly tarnished chrome of the front bumper. 'Please. You open,' said the guard in halting English. The driver pulled the lever under the dash that sprung the catch, and watched as the guard lifted the bonnet and looked at the hot little engine. It was clear that the guard had only stopped him because he wanted a look at the car and not for any purpose that was likely to cause any problems. He had nothing to hide, apart from the four packets of leaf tea which, for some unfathomable reason, could only be taken into Italy in minuscule amounts without attracting ridiculous import duties. It would be a shame if the guard found the tea and confiscated it, but he thought it was unlikely; probably, even on top of the Great Saint Bernard Pass, young Italians doing their military service as border guards, had better things to do than cause a fuss over two pounds of tea.

The guard finished his inspection of the car without even asking for the boot to be opened, half turned to go back to his seat in the sun then, remembering what he was supposed to be there for, turned back, *'Passaporto'*.

Picking up the slightly dog-eared document from where it lay on the passenger seat, the driver watched as the border guard made a show of looking through it. Not much to see really: Surname – Caddick, First-names – Paul John, Date of Birth – 21st May 1962, Place of Birth – Glossop, Height – 5 feet 11 ½ inches, Eye colour – dark brown, Profession – Student, Passport number – L9006317, Issued – Liverpool 8th August 1984, Expiry – 8th August 1994; lots of blank pages and the 'emergency contact details' with his mother and father's names and address.

The guard handed it back shaking his head, 'Liverpool – English hooligans,' and Paul realised that it was less than two months since thirty nine Juventus fans had died in the Heyssel Disaster at the European Cup Final. He wondered for a second whether to reply in Italian but decided that he would be on his way sooner if he allowed the limited schoolboy English of the guard to be their medium of communication. He opened his passport at the details page and pointed, 'Passport Liverpool – me Glossop,' the Italian would have to have a very detailed knowledge of football, to have any dirt on North End; then, for good measure, he smiled, gave a thumbs up sign and said, using the rhythm he knew was used by Italian football fans, *'Rossi, Tardelli ed Altobelli'*. The smile was returned by the guard as he heard the names of Italy's three goalscorers from the most recent World Cup Final, and he gave a little salute and waved Paul on his way.

Paul started the engine and giving the guard a friendly wave moved away from the barrier, past the little souvenir stalls and the chalet style restaurant at the southern end of the little lake that nestled beneath the head of the pass, and disappeared round the left-hand bend where the road began to wind its way down to the valley.

A couple of miles below the summit he pulled off the road outside a robustly built bar with a dozen round plastic tables outside. He blinked as he went from the bright sunlight into the gloom inside the bar where the small windows, which could be securely sealed to protect the building against the heavy winter snowfalls, let in only a small amount of light.

'Buongiorno. Un caffè, per favore.'

He watched, saliva moistening his mouth as the man behind the counter replenished the coffee holder, pushed it against a machine which both refilled it and tamped the grains down, and then pushed it up into the bottom of the large coffee maker giving a half twist to secure it, before flicking a switch. During the twenty seconds it took for the machine to fill the tiny cup with the dark brown nectar, the barman had slid a saucer and spoon along with a sugar dispenser, in front of Paul. Then, 'Eccolo,' as he placed the cup on the saucer.

Paul resisted the temptation to drink down the espresso in one go, deciding to savour it for a few seconds longer by taking three small drinks before he emptied the cup and replaced it on its saucer, letting out a sigh of satisfaction.

'The best thing about coming to Italy is that first coffee,' he said as he placed a five hundred lira note onto the counter.

The barman smiled but said nothing as he pushed Paul's change across, but then said 'Buona giornata e buona permanenza,' as Paul made for the door.

'Buongiorno. Arrivederci.'

When he reached Étroubes, he pulled off the road into the petrol station on the right and, using one of the coupons he had pre-purchased and a few thousand lire in cash, had the Midget filled up to the top, which he thought would get him beyond Genoa before he needed to top up again. Then he crossed the road to a general stores, bought himself a litre carton of milk and three bananas and continued on his way.

Down in the valley he skirted the edge of Aosta, avoided the green signs that urged him to take the motorway, and picked up the relatively traffic free main road that snaked down the valley along the northern bank of the River Dora Baltea. Small vineyards clung by their fingertips to the edges of rocky precipices, and whenever there was a flat ledge a stone barn roofed with scales of rough-hewn, unevenly shaped slate, seemed to have been crammed in. Outside the villages, most of the traffic on the road seemed to be either old fiat five hundreds, or the quaint little three wheeled pick-ups built around Vespas, which chugged along puffing out oily black smoke from their two-stroke engines. The valley was an area he loved travelling through, with the many strategically placed castles dominating the pinch points and reminding him of the Napoleonic campaigns he had studied during 'A' Level history.

He stopped for a while in Bard to admire the imposing castle that had required a surprise night attack by Napoleon's troops to break its resistance. He had hoped to visit the castle but a note on the outer gate informed prospective visitors that it was *'Chiuso per restauri'*, and he had to make do with a walk around the outside.

After Bard, he made fairly good time, zipping along the country roads in the little MG, and stopping occasionally in the small towns along the way to fill up his water-bottle or boost his caffeine levels. Beyond Masone, the road twisted and turned through wooded mountainside, passing under the significantly straighter elevated motorway on numerous occasions, as it dropped the thirteen hundred feet down to sea-level. Before entering Genoa itself, he took the motorway, as everyone he had spoken to had advised him against following the Via Aurelia around the eastern half of the Ligurian coastline.

At the first service area after leaving Genoa, he pulled in, topped the car up again and then pulled over to park in front of the *"Autogrill"*. Paying for a crispy *focaccia* filled with *prosciutto crudo* and *mozzarella*, he asked if he could have some *gettoni* as part of his change. The cashier gave him four of the double grooved alloy disks that were needed to operate the public telephones, and which were also regularly used as substitutes for fifty lire coins.

When the payphone was free, he pushed the four *gettoni* into the slot at the top of the phone, dialled 055, the Florence area code, and then, looking at the scrap of paper he'd pulled out of his pocket, the number that his old schoolfriend, Gary, had given him. For almost thirty seconds the phone gave him a metallic, brrrn, brrrn, brrrn, until finally,

'*Pronto.*' He heard the four *gettoni* cascade down through the phone's innards.

'*Ah, buona sera. Parlo con Simon?*'

'*Si. Chi parla?*'

'Hi Simon, my name's Paul Caddick. We've never met but I'm a friend of Gary's... Gary Bright's. He said that you were a good person to contact when I first got to Florence.'

'OK, boyo,' the very correct Italian had now been replaced by a strong Welsh accent, 'where are you now?'

'Not quite there yet. I'm still on the motorway, near Rapallo – I should think I'll be in Florence at about eight. Can I ring you again at about nine, after I've found a *pensione* and somewhere to put the car, or will you be out?'

There was a little laugh, 'Of course I'll be out. Listen, before you book into a *pensione*, come along to the Gran Café San Marco in Piazza San Marco, I'll be there having a beer with a few friends. You can't miss me, I'll be the only male redhead in there. There are plenty of cheap *pensioni* in the area, and if you leave it till later, you're likely to get a better deal.'

'OK. I'll see you then. I've got a Che Guevara t-shirt on, by the way.

'Yeah, and so has half of Florence. Find me, it's easier,' and he rang off. There was a clink as the phone deposited the one remaining *gettone* into a curved metal slot at the bottom and he smiled to himself as he scooped it out.

Result. From what Gary had told him, he was fairly sure that unless Simon already had someone staying with him, he was likely to be offered a bed for the night.

As he entered, he saw that the bar was crowded, mainly with young tourists, most of whom seemed to be English speaking. He stood for a moment inside the door scanning the tables for redheads; there were four altogether but, as Simon had said on the phone, only one of them was male, and he made his way over to a table where four males and two females sat laughing.

Each had a *birra media* in front of them and a pile of small plates indicated that most of them had had one of the sandwiches or mini-pizzas that were in evidence in the display counter under the bar.

'Simon?' he asked, as he approached the group and caught the red-head's eye.

'The one and only. You must be Paul; grab a seat.'

'I'll just get a beer first. Anyone ready for a top-up?'

'Sit down,' and then half turning towards the counter, where two young men and one young woman were serving, 'Hey Suzy – *un altra birra per mio amico.*' The girl, who was in the middle of serving two, obviously American, teenage girls with cocktails, nodded to Simon, to show that she had understood, and a couple of minutes later brought over a half litre of blond beer to the table.

Simon slipped an arm around her waist and said, 'Are you finally going to give way to my charms tonight, or are you going to continue breaking my heart?'

She turned, slipping out from his arm and, laughing as she turned back to the bar, said over her shoulder, 'In your dreams,' and they both laughed.

'Cheers,' said Paul, raising his glass, 'I take it you're a regular here.'

Simon nodded, 'Once or twice a week. It'll be better in a couple of months when most of the summer tourists have gone, and only those who are serious about Italy are left. Suzy's a good laugh – we have an ongoing joke, but actually she's married with a kid – I play football with her husband.'

'Gary said that you were a part of the community now.'

'How's my old mate Gary doing? I told him he should stay and have fun, but he never quite got the idea that you get the most out of life if you live for the moment – *carpe diem*- as they say. Until he had a few glasses of wine inside him, he was always very serious about building a career.'

Paul laughed, he could just imagine Gary talking earnestly about his future plans. He'd been amazed when he'd announced that he was taking a gap year after university, even more amazed that he'd really enjoyed it, and not at all surprised that exactly at the end of the time he'd originally said he was going for, he'd left Italy and gone back to England. 'He's a lost cause I'm afraid. He's got a job as a management trainee with the Derbyshire Building Society.'

Simon shook his head. 'How about you? What are your plans? Are you just doing a year then going back to be a sensible adult, or are you staying longer?'

'At the moment, I have no plans for the future. I've done an intensive TEFL course and, from the beginning of October, I'll be doing twelve hours a week in a private language school near Piazza Vieusseux, although I'm not quite sure where that is yet. That will just about keep me alive but I need to find a bit more work somewhere else.'

'That shouldn't be a problem. There are loads of language schools in Florence. To get into some of them, you need a bit of luck and also to know the right people, but there are always some of the smaller ones that are desperate for staff. Go through the yellow pages tomorrow, then go and knock on a lot of doors; sooner or later you'll strike gold.'

Simon introduced the others as, Baz, an English language assistant from the *Liceo Scientifico Gramsci* in the Coverciano area of Florence, Chuck, an American 'getting life experience', Lucio, a Calabrian student of Engineering, with whom Simon was currently sharing a flat, Gabriela, Lucio's girlfriend, and Clara, a fairly plain friend of Gabriela's who was clearly trying far too hard to impress Chuck. Chuck was friendly but very much matched up to Paul's stereotype of an American tourist; he had an opinion on everything, a very limited knowledge of any history before the twentieth century and a clear belief that money could buy everything in life. Baz was very self-assured and very keen to let everyone know how he expected to be fast-tracked into the diplomatic service after he had done his year abroad and completed his degree. Paul picked up the contemptuous look in Simon's eyes when Baz spoke about his wonderful future, and guessed that he was unlikely to see Baz in Simon's company again. Lucio was quiet and only rarely joined in the general conversation which was taking place in English, talking mainly with Gabriela.

By half past ten, Simon was obviously satisfied with Paul and, after confirming that it was OK with Lucio, suggested that until he found somewhere of his own, Paul should stay at their place.

Paul was delighted to agree and assured them that he would start looking around the next day. Lucio then advised him to leave it until the following Tuesday when the weekly edition of 'La Pulce', a magazine packed full of small ads, came out.

Chapter 2

Simon was still asleep when Paul got up in the morning, but Lucio was already up and sitting with a large Archaeology text book on the table in front of him, trying to memorise the differences between the archaic and classical period styles of Etruscan *bucchero* pottery. He gave a slight nod to Paul but continued reciting the details out loud for another five minutes before stopping and controlling the text book to see if he'd missed anything. Then he said, '*Scusami*, I've got an exam on Etruscan pottery in the September session and, any picture they show me, I have to be able to talk about fluently and explain how it fits into the overall tradition.... *Caffé?'*

'Mmm, that'd be good.'

'OK, I'll put the *macchinetta* on. I need one to keep me awake. There's bread and jam on the side in the kitchen if you want.'

Lucio chatted away as Paul ate, as if he were keen to take his mind off Etruscan pottery for a few minutes. Paul let most of it drift over him, only really paying attention when Lucio told him that his girlfriend, Gabriela, had said that she thought Paul would be popular with the girls in Italy. He raised an eyebrow and paused with a teaspoonful of jam poised over a biscuit. 'What does she base that on?' Lucio laughed and told him that a lot of girls seemed to prefer people with fair hair just because it was unusual amongst Italian men, and also that Paul would stand out because the combination of fair hair and very dark eyes was unusual and then, of course, he wasn't full of himself like Baz was.

Paul smiled, 'Hopefully, I've got more going for me than just my hair and eyes... but I suppose that if they give me a head start, then I shouldn't complain.'

Before Lucio began to study again, he asked, 'Why Florence?'

'There are a few reasons; first of all, there are hardly any jobs for Arts graduates in England anymore, so there was no point staying there, and then the obvious reasons like... it's a beautiful city; I'm interested in art and Florence is full of it. A friend of mine was here last year and was able to pass on a few contacts, but I think really, I wanted to find out about a part of my background that's a bit of a mystery.'

Lucio raised an eyebrow in interrogation, so Paul continued, 'I'm actually a quarter Italian. My grandmother was Italian but died when my father was born, and then my grandfather went off and got killed in the war so my father never really knew either of them. He was brought up by my grandfather's sister and her husband and he always called them Mum and Dad. It wasn't until her funeral four years ago that I found out she wasn't my gran. The vicar, who was taking the service said what a wonderful woman she was and how she'd brought up my dad as if he were her own. I asked my dad and he confirmed that my gran was really his aunt and not his mum, but as far as he was concerned it made no difference because she'd always been a mum to him. He had only a very vague memory of his real father and had never wanted to find anything out about his real parents because he didn't want to seem ungrateful. He's never even been to Italy, and couldn't understand why I switched from Spanish to Italian as one of my two main subjects at University.'

'OK, but still the same question: why Florence, there are other beautiful cities?'

'Oh, sorry. I didn't mean to miss that out. After my gran died, my dad was clearing her loft out and came across a shoebox with a few things in relating to my real grandparents. There was a Military Cross and a letter addressed to the woman I'd always thought was my gran, telling her that her brother had been killed in Italy, and the medal had been awarded posthumously for conspicuous gallantry; there were a few tatty photographs and my grandmother's death certificate. The death certificate only showed her married name, but the following summer I went down to London and spend a day in the Public Records Office until I finally got hold of a copy of their marriage certificate. That certificate, which for some reason was issued in Gibraltar, gave me her maiden name and told me that she was born in Florence in 1914.'

'So there might be family here in Florence.'

'It's possible, but the one thing my dad did know was that my gran had told him that after my real grandparents came to England, there was never any letter from Italy, nor was any family ever mentioned.'

'You could start by having a look through the phonebook, it might be as simple as that,' suggested Lucio, turning reluctantly back to his textbook.

'I'll leave it until this afternoon; there are a few things I need to do this morning. Is there anything you want me to get while I'm out?'

Lucio thought, started to shake his head, then stopped and said, 'We're running a bit low on *passata*; you could get a couple of bottles if you get chance, but if you don't see any, don't worry.'

The first thing Paul needed to do was to retrieve his car from where he'd left it in Piazza dell'Indipendenza. Once in the car, he pulled out his map of Florence and checked how to get from where he was to Piazza Vieusseux where he would be working from the start of October. He was pleased to find that it wasn't too far, but forty minutes later, after having finally managed to negotiate roadworks and a temporary one-way system, he wished he had left the car where it had been parked and walked. He was going to have to get hold of an old pushbike to use in the city – the car was not really a practical option.

He eventually found the school in Via Barbera, after having left the Midget parked in Piazza Leopoldo, which was the nearest space he could find without embarking on a second battle with the one-way system. An ornate brass plate resembling a shield was set in to the wall by the side of an imposing double door surmounted with a half-moon window made burglar proof by the artistic wrought iron grill that covered it. The door and window were enclosed by a thick carved stone frame that came to a point above the window, and where arriving visitors were protected from the elements by a pillared stone balcony that protruded around the first floor window. The façade of the four-storey building had obviously recently been re-rendered and, as other buildings in the street appeared to have undergone similar treatments, he assumed that he was in a relatively well-to-do area of the city, close enough to the centre to make it easily accessible, but just far enough away to guarantee a more peaceful environment.

There were eight bell-pushes on the ornate plate, in four rows of two which he assumed corresponded to the floors. The bottom and the top two rows of bells showed family names next to them, engraved on mini brass plaques that had then been riveted to the back plate; on the second row, however, two plastic name tags, each showing, *"Academia Globale di Lingue"* appeared to have been glued over the original name plates, and one of the two bells was covered with a piece of tape. He pressed the uncovered bell-push and then leaned closer ready to speak into the grill when his ring was answered.

No voice answered his ring but there was a buzzing sound from the grill, a click, and one side of the door sprung open a crack. He pushed and entered a marble tiled, beech panelled entrance hall where he pressed the light switch before closing the door behind him. A door on either side led to the two ground floor apartments and beyond them he had the choice of taking the stairs or the lift, which stood doors open in front of him, indicating that the last people to use it had been going out. He took the stairs.

On the first floor landing a printed notice was fixed to the first of the two doors that opened onto it: *"Academia Globale di Lingue* – Please use other door."* The other door again bore a notice announcing itself as the *"Academia Globale di Lingue"*, and this door stood slightly ajar.

'Permesso', he said, as he pushed the door open.

A young black woman, her hair pulled up inside a colourful headscarf was mopping the floor inside the entrance hallway.

'Buongiorno. I'm looking for Signor Malesano. I'm a new teacher here.'

'Boss, through there,' the woman said, in English, jerking her head towards the door at the far end of the hallway.

'Thank-you,' and he walked over to the door again and knocked.

'Venga,' came a voice from the other side, inviting him in.

The owner of the voice was a swarthy middle aged man balding on top but with long sideburns as if he were a throwback to the seventies. Paul couldn't help the image of a 1970s TV cop coming to mind. When the man spoke again, Paul thought he recognised that the accent was southern, although his ear wasn't well enough attuned to the many Italian accents to tell precisely from which area of the south. He was fairly sure that it wasn't Sicilian but couldn't exclude anything else. 'What can I do for you, young man?' he asked, carefully placing the manila folder he'd been looking at onto the desk in front of him.

'My name's Paul Caddick. I think we spoke on the phone a few weeks ago when you offered me a teaching job from the beginning of October.'

'Ah, yes, Mr Paul. Pleased to meet you, although you're a little early aren't you.'

'I thought it would be a good idea to have some time in Florence before I started, so I can find some accommodation and get to know my way around the city. I was wondering if there were any teaching materials I could take away to have a look at, before I start.'

'A very sensible idea Mr Paul. Unfortunately, the materials for the English courses haven't been run off yet. Do you by any chance speak Spanish, or French?'

'Yes, I do, a little bit of both, although my French is better.'

'Wonderful, wonderful. All our courses, in all the languages we teach here, follow the same simple structure – one which I designed myself about fifteen years ago. All students are issued with one of these folders when they arrive for their first lesson: blue for Spanish, green for French yellow for German or red for English,' he picked up an A5 folder, made of shiny blue cardboard and with three flaps attached to the edges of what was presumably the back of the folder. When the students register at reception before each lesson, they are given the worksheet for that lesson, containing key vocabulary, a new item of grammar, and some exercises based on the vocabulary and grammar on the sheet. The teacher's job is to go through the sheet with them to make sure that they understand the lesson and can pronounce all the words appropriately. Although the English materials are not yet ready, I can provide you with a full set of worksheets for our "Beginners French" course. Obviously, you will be teaching "Beginners English", but the principle is exactly the same.

It did not sound, to Paul, like a very stimulating, or very effective way to learn a language, but his first visit to the school did not seem like a very good time to express that view, so he politely complimented Malesano on the efficiency of his system and said that he'd be delighted to work his way through the French course to familiarise himself with the method. He asked how big the classes were and was told that it varied between ten and twenty, but received the impression that the true answer was, as many as could be persuaded to sign up for the course. There was no entrance test, and students decided for themselves whether they were beginners, intermediates, or higher level. Paul was to teach one intermediate and three beginner classes; the intermediate group had lessons on Tuesday and Thursday evenings from six to seven thirty, while the lessons for the three groups of beginners would be on Mondays and Wednesdays, at six o'clock, seven thirty and nine o'clock respectively. The courses would commence on the first Monday of October and continue for fourteen weeks, with a two week break for Christmas. Further courses began part way through February and again ran for fourteen weeks which, taking Easter into account, meant that they finished in late May. Paul asked how many teachers were employed and was told that there was an Australian, who had been with them since the school opened, an American lady who had been there for two years, and that there was currently one vacancy, although he was interviewing another American girl the following day, and hoped that she would prove satisfactory. Paul noted that one of the Americans had been described as a "lady" and the other as a "girl" and wondered what Malesano's criteria were for distinguishing between them. Again, he decided that that was not something to delve into on his first visit. He thanked Malesano, and telling him how much he looked forward to working for him, left with an A5 green folder containing "Beginners French".

Checking his watch, and bearing in mind how long it had taken to find a parking space, he decided to put off the other things he had planned to do until later in the day and instead, after finding the nearest shop that sold *passata*, find his way back to Simon and Lucio's apartment on Via Antognoli. He managed to find a small store not far from where he had parked the car and bought the *passata*, a *ciabatta* loaf, some *gorgonzola* and a flask of *Chianti* to take back with him.

Lucio had gone into the university library when he got back, but Simon was now out of bed and lying on the sofa reading a copy of Orhan Pamuk's *'The White Castle'*, which had just been translated into English and which he had been sent a copy of for his birthday. Finding it heavy going, he was happy to put it down and share some bread and cheese with Paul.

'Gary never told me that you were Florentine!'

'I wouldn't quite say that. A grandmother who nobody seems to know anything about, and who died nearly fifty years ago when my father was born, hardly puts me in the same league as Dante. I have some Italian blood in me – that's about as far as it goes.'

'It's better than most of us,' said Simon, even though I've been here for six years now, I still hardly know any Florentines well enough to be invited into their houses. They don't really mix with the foreigners except on a very superficial level, and you English have a very bad reputation for your loose morals, and that spoils it for us nice Welshmen, because they don't know the difference.'

'I thought you just said I was Florentine - make your mind up.' They both laughed.

'So what's the plan for this afternoon?'

'I need to find somewhere to get a few copies of my CV made, so I can start dropping them off at Language schools tomorrow.'

'Good luck with that; there are at least fifty spread out around the city. You can forget about the better known ones: The British, and The Wall Street Institute, just concentrate on the smaller ones, and make sure you speak to someone; if you just leave your CV, it'll end up in the bin.'

Simon told him how he'd started off working for four different small schools, as well as earning a bit of extra money by distributing leaflets. He'd picked up quite a few private lessons where anxious parents were desperate to avoid their offspring having to repeat the school year or, even worse, cut short their summer holidays so that, if they had only failed one subject, they had the chance to resit that exam in September. At the start of his third year in Florence he'd had the amazing luck to get taken on in a temporary capacity by the *Giovanni Pascoli* secondary school, after one of their English teachers had an accident. Before the teacher could be properly replaced, the cash-strapped Region had blocked new appointments in schools and so he had found himself there for much longer than anticipated and had now become permanent, ways of circumnavigating the regulations having been found.

He was directed to a *copisteria* where he got his photocopies done, and then caught a bus into the centre where he got off next to the station. From there he made his way through the crowds of tourists up Via dei Panzani until the slight turn to the left where the road becomes Via dei Cerretani and the magnificent sight of the Duomo with Brunelleschi's cupola sitting proudly on top bursts into view. He paused for a few seconds to take in the view, despite the buffeting from a group of Japanese tourists who swarmed past him following a small plastic Japanese flag on the end of a stick, and clicking away with their Nikons and Pentaxes as they did so. He would have liked to take a picture himself, but not just a tourist snap, he considered himself a reasonably good photographer and wanted time and space to set his shots up properly.

As the road widened out in front of the Duomo, he saw that there was no point even trying to get near the bronze doors sculpted by Ghiberti and Andrea Pisano, surrounded as they were by at least four guided tour groups. He wondered how many of the tour leaders rushing people from Venice to Milan, Milan to Florence, Florence to Rome and so on, could even tell the difference between the doors by Ghiberti and those by Pisano.

There were less street vendors and tour groups to his left as he looked at the Duomo, as the almost obligatory route for the groups was along the pedestrianised Via dei Calzaiuoli leading to the Piazza della Signoria and the Uffizi. He was glad of this as he was intending to go in the opposite direction anyway. He dodged across the road between two of the orange buses that somehow negotiated the mainly narrow streets of central Florence, and made his way round to Via dei Servi and then, after crossing Via dei Pucci, turned right under the Medici coat of arms into Via del Castelluccio, which he knew led to the main part of the university.

After a hundred metres the narrow road broadened out to become Piazza Brunelleschi, dominated by the Renaissance architect's stunning round church at the northern end, and the high outer wall of what had once been a convent but was now the seat of the university on the right hand side. Large iron gates that were set into the wall stood open and, despite it being summer, plenty of students were still moving in and out of the former cloister beyond the wall. Paul joined them and moved inside to study the hundreds of notices that were attached to the left hand wall of the cloister.

There were adverts for almost everything imaginable: some were clearly official posters that had been put up by local businesses desperate to tap into the student market, some were handwritten – *"non-smoking girl wanted to share room with female History student, price negotiable"* - *"woman's bike for sale, 20" wheels"* - *"wanted home for kitten"* - *"Fourth year student can help you with your English or French"* - *"50cc Vespa for sale – smoky engine"* *"Sensual massage by experienced attractive woman"*, *"Drama group – all welcome"* - *"Concerto – string quartet – Poggio Imperiale, 11am Sunday, 3,000 Lire"*, all followed by telephone numbers.

After browsing the adverts for ten minutes and failing to find any suitable accommodation advertised, he had an espresso at the university bar in the cloister, and then went inside the building to look for the library. He was directed by one of the students along the corridor behind the stairs and then down another, shorter one to the left. Two women were sitting behind a counter to the left of the entrance, and further into the library a few students sat silently at tables, some reading, some taking notes from books and some just writing, with no books at all in front of them.

'I'm looking for information about life in Florence during the nineteen thirties,' said Paul, to one of the women, who looked up when he went in. She waved him over towards a rank of filing cabinets containing index cards, directing him over to three drawers in particular where she said he might find something useful. Nothing seemed to fit the bill exactly but he did find cards detailing a few books about the city in general during that period. He chose one and took the reference card over to one of the librarians, who disappeared with the card through a door behind her.

Some minutes later she returned with the volume that Paul had ordered and he thanked her and went over to one of the free desks to read.

He found the book engrossing and, after two hours, when he finally put the book down, he felt that he had a much better feel for the atmosphere in the city during the period, however, he had not come across any reference to anyone called Campolargo. Before leaving, he asked the younger of the two women if she had any idea where he might be able to find out any information about a family who he knew had lived in Florence during the 1930's. Having ascertained that he had no idea which *quartiere* of the city the family had lived in, she suggested that his best bet may be to try the new Communal Archives in Via del Oriuolo. He was lucky, she said, that it was nineteen eighty five as the archives had been closed to the public since the great flood in 1966 and the new seat of the archives had only recently opened. 'However', she said, 'many original documents were destroyed by the floods, so you still might not find what you're looking for.' He thanked her for her help and made his way back through the building to re-emerge under the bright sunshine of Piazza Brunelleschi.

When he went to the archive the following morning, the archivist manning the public desk was less than helpful. Yes, they had all the surviving original records of births, marriages and deaths; no, they hadn't been catalogued yet; yes, he could look through them himself but only if he turned up with a formal request from a recognised academic institution stating that he was engaged in an approved research project. Paul tried to explain that this was a matter of personal interest, that he was trying to trace his family rather than conduct an academic research project, but the only response from the archivist was that in that case, he would have to wait until the records had been catalogued and made publicly available. 'And when is that likely to be?'
'We anticipate that it is likely to be either nineteen ninety one or ninety two.'
Somewhat dispirited, Paul decided to put his research on one side and concentrate on finding somewhere to live and some more work. The next two days were spent walking from

language school to language school, using a list he had created from the business pages of the telephone directory. Some were polite but didn't need anyone at the moment – they would keep his details on file; some didn't need anyone and made no effort to be polite in informing him of the fact; some of the ones on the list just didn't exist, or certainly didn't exist at the addresses shown in the phone book; one, which he had walked a considerable way out of the centre to find, turned out to be a canine beauty salon specialising in Old English Sheepdogs and incorrectly listed in the directory; three said that if he was prepared to work at short notice, they would call him whenever they needed a cover teacher and two were definitely interested but, of these, one put on lessons at times that clashed with his lessons at the *"Academia"*.

The final one agreed to take him on. It was run by a charitable organisation dedicated to providing extra-mural cultural experiences for the city's many students. He was to take two two-hour lessons each week, from one until three on Monday and Wednesday lunchtimes. Like the *Academia*, this school insisted on its own method being followed, but at least this time Paul had more faith in the method. The teaching was to be done entirely orally with audio-visual aids. Students were to be immersed in situations that approximated to real life and discouraged from writing anything down. Paul was only ever to speak English with the students, and it was best if they didn't even know that he could speak Italian. Theoretically wonderful, but fraught with practical difficulties thought Paul; he would toe the line in the first lesson when the school's director would be in the room but, after that, he would be prepared to deviate slightly from the puritanical approach if he were convinced that it was for the benefit of the students.

The day after he finished his tour of the language schools was Tuesday and he followed Lucio's advice, got up at six and went out to get the latest copy of *'La Pulce'*. By eight o' clock, when he felt it was reasonable to start calling people, he was standing by the phone in a nearby bar, with a list of eight possible rooms and a stack of eight *gettoni* by his side. Three of the rooms had already been rented out before the first copy of *'La Pulce'* hit the news-stands, two were only prepared to accept female tenants, one involved sharing a room with four other people in a house with sixteen people in total and just a single bathroom, which left him with two rooms to go and see.

'Three hundred and seventy five thousand lire a month, with two months' rent in advance, no pets, no guests in the room after eight in the evening and no noise to be made after eleven o'clock... is that acceptable?'

'I'm very interested, but there's one other room I promised I would see, and it would be rude of me not to even give them the courtesy of looking, although I'm sure I'll be back in touch with you later today. Thank-you so much for your time, *Signora.'* The room was a very pleasant, well maintained room in a nice area, but it was a long way out of the centre, out near Coverciano, and the terms were restrictive; while he was currently unattached, remaining so was certainly not part of his long term plan. He fervently hoped that the other room would prove to be more suitable.

At five in the afternoon, he stepped into a bar in Borgo La Croce and asked for Signora Vaccherini. The barman indicated an elegantly dressed woman in her mid to late forties sitting at a table in the corner, long bronzed legs crossed as she gazed out of the window at the passers-by, a slim, probably designer cigarette poised casually between the middle and index fingers of her right hand. Sizing her up as he moved towards the table, Paul prepared himself to be disappointed; the obvious care that she put into her own appearance suggested that the conditions attached to this rented room might be even more onerous than the previous one.

Appearances can be deceptive, however, and he told himself after, that he needed to be more careful about judging on appearances.

'Mi scusi. Signora Vaccherini?'

She looked round and smiled, 'Ah *Signor* Caddeek. Sit down, please... let me get you a coffee,' and then without waiting for his acceptance, called over to the barman, 'Mimmo... a coffee for the gentleman and a decaf for me...*Grazie*, Mimmo'. She offered him a cigarette and, when he declined, telling her that he didn't smoke, she stubbed out her own and apologised if the smoke had disturbed him at all, she hardly smoked, she said, it just felt more comfortable to have something in her hands when she was sitting alone in public.

The coffees arrived almost straight away and, as soon as the barman had returned to his post, she turned the conversation to the room while finding out as much as she could about Paul himself, to satisfy herself that he would be a suitable tenant. She asked him how long he thought he would be in the city and whether his parents would be supporting him. He told her that there was no time limit on the length of his stay, that no, his parents wouldn't be maintaining him, but that he had already obtained two jobs teaching English and was confident that he could supplement that income, either by finding more jobs or more likely by giving private lessons in his free time.

'Maybe I'll need to brush my own language skills up at some point,' she said, uncrossing and then recrossing her legs, an action which called for a lot of will-power on Paul's part for him to keep his eyes on her face – most of the time.

'And will you be on your own in the room, or will your girlfriend be coming over to stay with you?' He was going to have to be careful here, he realised that the wrong answer could lose him any chance of getting the room, on the other hand he wanted to make it clear that he wasn't prepared to state categorically that there would never be anyone else there.

'Lots of friends, back in England, said that they wanted to come over and see me at some time, but I think it's highly unlikely that any of them will.'

She smiled, 'It's difficult to resist the charms of Florence'.

'Yes,' he said, unable to help thinking about her legs, 'I'm discovering that. Would it be possible to have a look at the room before I decide?'

'Of course. - Mimmo! ... I want to pay, please.' A minute later the barman brought over a receipt which the woman dropped into her bag without even glancing at it and, giving the barman a two thousand lire note said, 'Keep the change.'

'*Grazie, Signora*'.

'Prego'. Then she picked up a *Fendi* bag, which Paul guessed was an original, rather than one of the cheap imitations available on the temporary street stalls near the station and at either end of the *Ponte Vecchio*, and glided between the tables towards the door, giving an airy wave behind her as she did so.

Paul followed her, giving the customary '*Buongiorno*', as he exited.

The woman stopped almost immediately and pulling a bunch of keys from her bag, looked quickly through them until she found the right one, which opened an outer doorway onto a flight of stairs, the first narrow ramp of which rose up before him and then turned to the left as if going above the bar. The ramp of stairs leading to the left was a short one, just six steps and then a gloomy corridor with no natural lighting. There was a door on each side of the corridor and an opening on the right at the far end where another ramp of steps led up to the second floor. The *signora* pushed a light switch which immediately began clicking as at began its countdown towards the moment it would turn itself off. The dim twenty-five watt bulb gave just enough light for them to make their way along to the next flight of stairs and up to the second floor, where the layout was identical, except that the next flight of stairs now disappeared to the left at the end of the corridor.

This time, she didn't lead him to the end of the corridor, but stopped outside the door on the right and, with a pair of keys that somehow seemed to have materialised in her hand as they had made their way through the gloom, unlocked the door. The first lock, which had a chunky looking black key, was clearly a security lock and, as she turned it several times, Paul could hear the steel bars inside the door being wound out of their sockets in the door frame. The second lock was a simple Yale type lock, although even with this one, Paul noticed that the key was rotated through four hundred and fifty degrees before the door swung open and revealed a spacious room, almost as big as the bar on the ground floor.

One end had been partitioned off to create two smaller rooms. The one nearest to the corridor had been turned into a small bathroom, hardly much bigger than his parents' downstairs toilet back in England, although with a shower head protruding from the wall above the space between the toilet and the sink. He noticed that the floor here sloped slightly towards the centre and that there was a grate in place of one of the terracotta tiles. An electric water heater and storage tank had been mounted on the wall over the sink, which backed onto one end of the other small room that had been created. This room was a narrow, elongated kitchen. The layout was a little odd, he noted, with the sink at the end furthest from the window. A work surface with a three ring hob, over a small oven with chipped enamel, that looked as if it had originally been designed for a caravan, a small fridge, and a storage cupboard beneath it covered most of one wall. The kitchen's best feature was at the end nearest the street where one of the two large windows of the original room provided lots of light over a table that had been built in across the end of the room. There was a bar type stool at the table but Paul judged that you could quite easily squeeze two people in, if you wanted to.

The main room was fairly sparse. A table and two chairs were set against the wall on the street side; a bed that Paul noted was wider than a single, but not as wide as a double, was placed along the wall furthest from the kitchen and bathroom, and the furniture was completed by a small wardrobe set between the doors to the kitchen and bathroom. The floor was tiled with simple old terracotta covered with red wax, while the ceiling had exposed beams supporting smaller beams which had been laid at ninety degrees to the main structural beams, and which themselves supported a layer of terracotta which Paul was glad to see had not been covered in red wax.

The rent was four hundred thousand lire a month with one month in advance, although the *signora* said that she would only charge him two hundred thousand for the current month as it wasn't a full month. She showed him where the electricity meter was and told him that although the bills would arrive at her address and she would pay them, she would then recharge it to him within a week, if that was alright with him. The three gas rings ran off a gas bottle which he would be responsible for replacing when it ran out. This was not complicated, she explained, as all he had to do was take it down to the bar where Mimmo always had two or three spares in the cellar.

Paul had no doubts that this room was a far better option than the one out in Coverciano and agreed to take it on the spot. He gave *Signora* Vaccherini fifty thousand lire as a down-payment and agreed that he would meet her again in the bar at ten the following morning to pay her the remainder of the first month's rent and a further four hundred thousand as his month in advance. In return the *Signora* would hand over the keys for the room and a copy of that for the street door and, he assumed, buy him another coffee.

In the morning, he left early, hoping to find a parking space not too far away for the Midget, and managed to find one in Piazza d'Azeglio which was only about ten minutes' walk away. This meant that he was in the almost deserted bar just after quarter to ten where he leaned on the bar chatting to Mimmo, a Sicilian who had moved to Florence ten years previously. Mimmo told him that the *Signora's* husband's family owned and rented out several buildings in Borgo la Croce, including the bar itself and the six bedsits above, but that it was usually the *signora* who dealt with tenants.

Finally, at about a quarter past ten, *Signora* Vaccherini arrived, more heavily made up than she had been on the previous day and wearing a shorter skirt and longer heels. When he saw her he wondered if she were going to offer to help him settle in, a suspicion that grew deeper as she kissed him on both cheeks as if they were old friends. However, yet again she confounded his expectations by apologising for not being able to help him settle in as she had an appointment with a friend on the other side of Florence at eleven. She said that at the beginning of the following month she would let Mimmo know when she would be around to collect the rent and, if there were no convenient times then he could leave the money in an envelope with Mimmo for her.

After she had gone he wasn't quite sure whether he was pleased or disappointed that she hadn't decided to seduce him. Certainly, she was a long way from the type of attractive, shy, dark haired young beauty he had imagined meeting in Italy but... on the other hand... it was very difficult to take your eyes off the various areas of flesh that were exposed by her summer clothes, and he could imagine receiving plenty of envious looks from passers-by if he were to be seen with her on his arm – particularly if his old university friends from England could see them.

'No! Don't even think about it. You wouldn't even give her a second glance if you were still with Linda, or had found someone else to take Linda's place – well, OK, maybe a second glance, but no more than that.

He'd met Linda during Freshers' Week at university and they'd had an on-off relationship for most of the time they'd been there, although both of them knew that it was never going to last. She'd been too wrapped up in her work to have time to find a replacement and he, with his athletics in the summer and cross-country in the winter, had been in a similar position. When she'd announced that she had been awarded a scholarship to do a PhD at Yale, he had been genuinely pleased for her and wished her all the best for the rest of her life. They had drunk a bottle of cheap Spanish bubbly to celebrate her gaining her place, spent a last energetic night together, and then said good-bye over toast and marmite in the morning. Each had gone their separate ways with no recriminations and no regrets. That had been five months ago, just after Easter. Since then he'd seen her once, at the degree ceremony; they had embraced briefly and then shaken hands with each other and each other's parents, and got on with their lives.

Chapter 3

Once he'd unpacked his few possessions, he went out and found a shop down a backstreet near the Sant'Ambrogio market that sold household goods at reasonable prices and bought himself two pairs of sheets, two rough blankets, a pillow, two pillow cases and a tea towel. Later on he could buy a cheap bookcase and a few posters to make the room feel more like home.

After installing his new possessions and making the bed, he left the bedsit again and went down to the bar where he ordered a glass of red wine and a toasted sandwich and leaned on the bar rather than sitting at one of the tables, to allow him to talk to Mimmo. He explained that, he needed to put an advert up to enable him to pick up a few private lessons but that he really needed somewhere where people could contact him.

'If I put down the number of the bar and give you a thousand lire for each one who calls, would that be OK?'

'Are there likely to be many calls?'

'I'll be amazed if there are ten altogether, and when I've got a few hours, I'll take the notice down and rely on word of mouth.'

'Then, of course you can give this number... and don't even think about giving me anything for answering, it'll be a pleasure... although obviously, there will be times when I'm busy and can't answer.'

'That's great, I don't know how to thank you.' Mimmo shrugged, indicating that in his view it was a matter of no consequence, and ending the conversation.

From there, Paul walked back to Piazza Brunelleschi and the seat of the university, where he attached three copies of a notice advertising his services amongst the many other notices. He would have to find a way of advertising to school students as well, but university students would do to start with. As it was still early, he decided to have a wander further into the centre and have a look round some of the less frequented sights. His first port of call was the *Palazzo Medici-Riccardi* where he wanted to see again the magnificent frescoed *Procession of the Magi* by Benozzo Gozzoli. There were hardly any other visitors and he was able to linger in front of the painting and admire the rich detail of fifteenth century Tuscan life. It was a shame, he thought, that artists during the fascist period had not left a permanent artistic record of the people of the times, it might have helped him locate his family.

Outside the Palazzo he turned to the right and was about to head towards San Lorenzo when the second hand book stall on the opposite corner caught his eye. He crossed the road and began browsing; most of the books were fairly shabby art books with a few old novels piled up to one side of the stall. He rummaged casually through the novels, looking for some fairly light Italian reading to fill in any spare time he had and to improve his vocabulary at the same time. He couldn't see any novels that appealed to him but towards the bottom of the pile was a very tatty book with half its front cover torn off. *Il Mio Viaggio Attraverso il Fascismo* by Ferru... and the rest of the author's name was missing, It was only five hundred lire and just might have some interesting information about the period he was interested in, so he handed over the three coins he needed, and pushed the paperback volume into his pocket.

Later, when he got back to the bedsit he threw the book down on the table and made himself a large mug of tea, having decided that until he could find a way of replenishing his stock, he was going to limit himself to one proper cup of leaf tea a day. He spent the five minutes for which he let the tea brew, leaning on the window-sill watching the people and the traffic moving about on Borgo La Croce below. Then, when he decided that the tea would have developed sufficient body, he added a drop of milk, sat down at the table and picked up the book. The first chapter was very heavy going, not because the content was difficult, but because it was written in a very flowery style, full of pompous rhetorical flourishes. When he had ploughed through the first chapter, he felt that he couldn't face any more for that day, and just flicked half-heartedly through the remainder of the volume, promising himself that he would read the rest another day. Just as he was about to put the book down, something caught his eye that brought his full attention back to the book.

He wasn't sure what he had seen but he knew it had been important. He carefully turned back through the pages scanning them as he did so, hoping that he would again find whatever it was that had half registered before. He had gone back fifteen pages from the point where he had stopped flicking through when he found it: *"On the aforementioned eighth day of May in the tenth year of the new era, I was summoned to a meeting in Palazzo Vecchio with Alessandro Pavolini; also present was his assistant, Aristide Campolargo of San Casciano."* There it was, when he hadn't really been looking for it – the first clue. He turned back to the start of the second chapter and, notebook and paper open in front of him, he began to skim read, not stopping to understand or really take anything in unless any of the key words: Aristide, Campolargo, Alessandro, Pavolini and San Casciano caught his eye, in which case he read the whole page or as much as was required to understand the reference. There were a lot of different Alessandros mentioned and he soon refined his search criteria by eliminating the first names. He got through three chapters before deciding to call it a day; there had been no more references to Aristide Campolargo, or any other Campolargo, but plenty of references to Pavolini, and if, as the first reference to catch his eye had said, Campolargo was Pavolini's assistant then it was reasonable to assume that, in broad terms, wherever Pavolini went then Campolargo would also be present. He decided that the following day, he would find out more about Pavolini and take the Midget for a drive out to San Casciano.

He had arranged to meet up with Simon and Lucio in the 'Pizzeria – Spaghetteria' at the junction of Via Sant'Egidio and Via dell'Oriuolo, having insisted on buying them a meal to thank them for their hospitality; Simon had suggested that they meet there as it was central, easy to find, reasonably priced and made good pizzas.

When they had finished their pizzas and were sitting with their second *'birra grande'*, Lucio said, 'I was chatting with the Assistant Professor who's supervising my thesis earlier on, and I was asking if they knew of any way to find information about families who used to live here before the war. She said that the City registry is not likely to be much use but that, Church baptism records and cemetery registers are much easier to access. Obviously, the problem with the churches is that there are so many of them, but cemeteries should be a lot easier as there are only thirteen in Florence, and some of them are very unlikely to be the ones.'

'Why so?'

'Because the list includes the monumental cemetery in Piazzale Donatello, known as 'the English Cemetery,' and the Porte Sante Cemetery next to San Miniato where, unless you've had a family tomb for centuries, you don't get buried.'

'That's really helpful, thanks for asking for me... it could turn out to be really useful, but I found something just by chance, this afternoon'. And he told them about the book he had bought and the reference to Aristide Campolargo.

Simon immediately offered to come out to San Casciano with him, fancying a ride in the Midget and Paul happily accepted the offer of company. Lucio said that Paul's task was very similar to archaeology except that he had significantly more chance of finding a few bones with flesh on them. He told them what little he could remember about Pavolini and said that it would be easy for him to find out more the following day.

Shortly after that, a group of twenty or so female students came in and sat down where a row of tables had been pushed together and a *"riservato"* sign placed on the top. Lucio waved at one of the girls then excused himself and went over to have a chat for a few minutes. When he came back, he explained that they were all archaeology students, some from his year, but most from the first and second years. The girl he knew best, who he had been chatting to, was currently studying for the same exam on the Etruscans.

The following morning, Paul went down to the bar for a *latte macchiato* and a doughnut and to browse the day's papers. When he'd done he remembered that he still hadn't checked the phone directory and asked Mimmo if he could borrow it for a minute... Nothing, no Campolargos and not even any Pavolinis. He handed the thick volume back to Mimmo. 'How do you go about tracking someone down who's not in the phone book?'

He hadn't expected to receive anything more than a shrug of the shoulders in reply, his question having been pretty much a rhetorical one, so he was startled when Mimmo said, 'Electoral Registers.'

Electoral Registers! Why hadn't he thought of that? He knew that he would have done if he'd been in England.

'How stupid of me. I hadn't thought of that. You're a genius. Are they easy to get hold of?'

'Simple. Write three copies of your request on franked official paper, available at any good tobacconist and then send them by registered mail to the *"Servizio Anagrafico"* and wait between six months to a year,' Paul's face fell, 'or, I can ask a friend of mine whose wife works in the *Servizio Anagrafico,* if a way could be found for a copy of the registers to find their way out in the next few days'.

'That sounds much more appealing,' said Paul with a smile, feeling very relieved.

'I might need to slip my friend fifty thousand lire to make things run smoothly.'

'That's not a problem.. I'll let you have them later on today.'

He spent much of the day continuing to go through his book. There were a lot of references to Pavolini who, he got the impression, must have been a very complex character. His studies at university had equipped him to identify bias and process source documents effectively; he knew that most people in history tended to be portrayed as either black or white, whereas in reality, once you had looked at different sources and peeled back the layers of bias on each one, most people were actually different shades of grey. Although he only had the one source available, Pavolini surprised him, instead of being a very dark grey, as he would have expected Florence's leading exponent of Fascism, and a valued friend of Mussolini to be, he seemed to be made up of black and white stripes. Certainly, he was ruthless and committed to the fascist cause, but he was an intellectual, and seemingly a great promoter of the arts. Clearly, much of this had been done because he believed that developing the arts was of major benefit to the regime, but some of it seemed to have been done because he believed in the value of art in general.

Unfortunately, the three new references he found to Aristide Campolargo were only brief mentions of his presence at various events, and did not give him any further information. Nevertheless, he made a note of each mention and what meeting it was that Aristide had been present at. He did find one other Campolargo reference which was a mention of a Domenico Campolargo who appeared to have been with a group of important visitors from Rome. There was no other reference to Domenico Campolargo so he wasn't sure if the shared surname was just a coincidence, or if the family was to be found in Rome rather than Florence.

When he called into the bar late in the afternoon, Mimmo waved two slips of paper at him – 'Numbers to ring of people wanting to learn English.' Then he turned back to the coffee machine where he was preparing four cappuccinos for some American tourists who had wandered in. The Americans, who had recognised the word for English at the end of Mimmo's greeting, looked him quickly over and then, clearly deciding that he wasn't elegant enough to be brought into their conversation as a fellow anglophone, shifted their bodies slightly on their chairs making it clear that they wished to exclude him. Paul smiled to Mimmo, he could imagine nothing worse than getting dragged into their conversation about how cute the city was, despite its narrow streets.

He ordered a coffee and got two *gettoni* from Mimmo, but waited until the Americans had left before making the calls.

The first woman he spoke to, after telling him that her neighbours' daughter had told her about Paul's advert, spent ten minutes complaining about the quality of English Teaching in Italian Schools, and then telling him that the private schools running courses were a waste of money run by thieves and cheats; her son had been studying English for three years at school and done a course at the British Institute and didn't seem to have learnt anything – would he be able to help? Probably not, he thought – it sounded as if the boy was either not very bright or, just as likely, had no wish to learn English - but he had no intention of saying that to the mother.

'Of course, *Signora*. There are lots of young people who find it difficult to learn in large groups but who can thrive on a one to one basis.' ... 'When am I free? Let me think. Would Tuesday at eight o'clock be OK, beginning next week?'... 'No, I'm afraid I can't earlier; I'm working until seven-thirty'... 'Oh. Eat with you and then do the lesson as soon as we've finished eating. Well, we can give it a try, *Signora*, and see how it goes.'... 'Yes. I should be there by about a quarter to eight, and the address is.' ... 'Thank you, yes, the same to you. *Buona serata.*'

He pushed the cradle of the phone down and then released it and dialled the second number. This time he didn't manage to get a meal out of it but the lesson itself sounded far less like hard work. The caller was a university student who had been offered a one month placement with a firm in England in January. She wanted to make sure that her spoken English was up to scratch before she went and could pay ten thousand lire an hour for two one hour lessons each week until Christmas. She was free in the afternoons so they agreed that he would go round at four o'clock on both Monday and Thursday, but she was quite happy to be flexible if ever he needed to change.

He was quite satisfied with his day as, with the two jobs that had already been arranged, the private lessons he had now arranged would mean that he wouldn't have to scrimp and save, and he was sure he would be able to pick up more. Back in the bedsit he made himself a large bowl of *spaghetti con olio, aglio e peperoncino* with plenty of grated parmesan, and then settled down to read with a glass of *Chianti*. Having finish his scan of all the book's chapters for the key words, he had now gone back to read it properly to increase his knowledge of the period. Once he had got used to the dense prose used by the writer, he found it much easier to read and, by the time he put the book down and turned the light out, he could almost imagine himself back in 1930s fascist Italy. If you had no conscience and were prepared to throw your weight around, people at the time must have enjoyed very comfortable lifestyles, but if you wanted to think about issues deeply, or do anything that was seen as being in any way different, life must have been very difficult.

There were no new messages on the Friday but Mimmo reminded him that that following night was the night of the month when the streets were cleaned in the area where he had parked his car. He advised him to find alternative parking in good time, as if it were still there at midnight it would be towed away and he would have to go out to Via Salvatore Allende to get it back by handing over several banknotes to the city authorities. Paul thanked him and made a mental note to find somewhere different to park the car later, when they came back from San Casciano.

Chapter 4

Simon's school finished at one thirty on a Thursday so he made his way round to the house just before two, being lucky enough to find a parking space almost opposite the door. Simon lightly toasted some bread to make bruschetta and, when Paul declined wine or beer as he was driving, and knew that they would probably need to visit several bars in San Casciano during the afternoon, made him a cup of tea with a fairly flavourless Italian teabag.

Progress was slow around Florence's inner ring-road until they had passed over the Ponte della Vittoria and, after a few hundred yards along the road towards Scandicci, taken a sharp left and followed the outside of the old city walls until Porta Romana. There, they took the right turn towards Siena and climbed to the top of the hill before descending along a road lined with several large petrol stations until they reached the bottleneck of Galluzzo. Once clear of Galluzzo, the road climbed up again past the imposing fourteenth century fortified monastery that had once protected the southern approaches to the city, before dropping down amongst roadside stalls selling fresh vegetables, fresh fruit, and roast suckling pig sandwiches.

At the large roundabout where the road reached the Greve valley, he took the second exit onto the Florence-Siena *'superstrada'*. Once he was round the first tight corner and the road became a dual carriageway, he was able to put his foot down and give the Midget a proper run for five miles before taking the second exit to wind up the hill through a mixture of small-vineyards, olive groves and chestnut woods interspersed with restored farmhouses, some of which had become luxury restaurants.

Once within the built up area of San Casciano he parked the car in a car-park on the left, beyond which olive groves dropped away towards the bottom of the valley. In the bar opposite the car-park a bored looking young man leaned on the counter behind the till, watching two others who appeared to be in their late teens playing pinball. The young man looked as if he were about to stand up straight and make an effort to serve them, but Simon stopped him with a gesture. 'Sorry, just need some information. Could you tell us which of these roads leads into the historic centre, please? There doesn't seem to be a sign.'

'Take the road to the right of the Cassia, but there's no point driving in, unless you just want a quick look and then out again, You won't find anywhere to park.'

'Is it far?' asked Paul.

'Only about two hundred metres,' the barman said, with a shrug.

'OK. Thanks a lot for your help,' said Simon and then, when they were outside again, 'sorry for taking over but I think we'd have been wasting our time if we'd had a coffee and asked them about your family.' Paul nodded his agreement, and they started to walk down the street that the barman had indicated.

After a while the street opened out into a small piazza where several roads met. They tried one of the two nearby bars and ordered a coffee. The woman behind the bar was in her early thirties and shook her head when they asked about the Campolargos; her customers had also never heard of the family, but one of them suggested that the best place to ask might be the butcher's just along the street.

The butcher's was a traditional one with the partial carcasses of several animals hanging on big hooks at the back, behind the marble counter. Framed posters showing the different cuts of beef, lamb, pig (or boar) and horse, were on the sidewalls. An old fashioned till stood at one end of the counter, and at the other, on a large chopping board, the butcher himself, a man who appeared to be in his late fifties with a florid face and hands that were slightly swollen from too frequent washing, was jointing a pile of chickens, making the job look effortless.

'Buonasera,' they both said as they entered.

'Buonasera. What can I get you?' said the butcher, as he ran his hands under the tap and then dried them on a towel.

'I'd like four hundred grams of veal liver,' said Simon.

'And when you've dealt with him, I'd like a couple of the fennel flavoured sausages,' said Paul.

After the butcher had served them, putting Simon's liver in a light plastic bag and then wrapping both purchases in brown paper parcels, Simon paid and then, as Paul was paying, he asked, 'Have you been here long?'

The butcher pointed at the window where Paul could read the back of letters that said, *"Macelleria Giunti dal 1897"* 'Quite some time. And I've been here for more than half that time. I stopped going to school when my father was called up in forty one and came in here to help my mother. I've been here ever since, and will be for a good few years yet.'

'You must be looking forward to retirement.'

He snorted, 'Retirement. What would I do if I retired, sit at home all day with my wife and watch Brazilian soap operas, or go and sit at a table in one of the bars and drink myself to death? No thank you, I'd rather be here; I get to talk to everyone, and so long as I don't poison anyone and give the regulars a little bit extra sometimes, everyone likes me.'

Paul laughed, 'Sorry, I didn't think it through before I spoke but... listen... you might be able to help me. Did you ever hear of a family in San Casciano called Campolargo? I think they may have lived in San Casciano about fifty years ago.'

'Campolargo. Now that's a name you don't hear very often anymore, and there are still some people around here who'd prefer never to hear it mentioned. You need to be very careful when you ask about the Campolargos. Why do you want to know?' The butcher's jovial smile had now disappeared and he appeared wary.

Paul suddenly had to take a decision that he hadn't expected to have to make; was he going to be completely open, or would it be better to be more circumspect? Instinct told him that while the butcher might not be one of those who'd prefer never to hear it mentioned, he was certainly reluctant to talk about it. He decided it was better to hold back for the moment.

'I'm doing a PhD in History and, as part of my research I was reading a book about Alessandro Pavolini yesterday and it mentioned an assistant of his, an Aristide Campolargo of San Casciano, I just thought that as I was passing through, I'd see if I could pick up any more information – I'd never heard of Aristide Campolargo before.'

The butcher shrugged, 'Your book was wrong, the Campolargos weren't from San Casciano, they were from Bargino'. Just then the door opened and two women came into the shop; the butcher gave a hearty *'Buonasera'* to the two women and then a somewhat less enthusiastic one to Paul and Simon, making it clear that they were dismissed.

'Well, well!' said Simon once the door had closed behind them, 'there's something in your family history that worries people. - I'm starting to get interested.'

"Well, well." Just about sums it up. I got the impression that if I'd pushed him any further it could have been counter-productive, but if I can't find any other information, he may become my regular butcher until he's told me everything he knows. Let's see if we can find anyone else who might have known the Campolargo family and see what reaction I get from them. We'll try someone else in San Casciano and then try to find out where this Bargino place is.'

'Don't worry about that; it's just a few kilometres further towards Siena. It will only take a few minutes to get there.'

They walked through the town until they saw another butcher's, and then a little bit further to the next bar. 'Hopefully, the people here will use their local butcher, so the other one won't get to hear that I'm still asking.'

Four old men sat at one of the tables, playing cards, each with a pile of coins in front of him and an empty glass by his side. Paul and Simon got a litre carafe of wine and sat down at the table next to them and chatted while keeping an eye on the old men.

After about fifteen minutes, they finally finished their game and it was clear that it was up to the winner to go to the bar and get their glasses replenished. As he was getting up, Paul leaned over towards them. 'Sorry for interrupting, but I made a mistake and ordered more wine than we needed. Let me fill your glasses up.' They accepted gratefully and asked if they were tourists. Simon said that he had been in Florence for a few years, while Paul said that he'd only been there for a few days, and allowed them to get the impression that he was a tourist without stating so specifically. 'An old man back in England told me that he'd been in this area during the war, but his memory wasn't very good and I didn't really understand much of what he was telling me. He mentioned a name a couple of times though...

Campolargo it was... is that a place? Maybe where one of the battles took place when the allies came down from Siena?'

One of the four gave a hollow sounding laugh, 'A place! It would have been better if it had been. No, the Campolargos owned a lot of land, mainly around Bargino but not just there, and controlled a lot of people's lives as well. They were in the area for centuries, lording it over everyone, until the last lot got what they deserved – fascist bastards every one of them - stayed with Mussolini right until the end.'

'Some of them did... One of them, Umberto I think, was killed somewhere in Greece in forty three.'

'It was Kefalonia, wasn't it, but surely it was the older brother, who had his own place near Barberino, not Umberto – it was Umberto who sold everything off when they let him out of prison in forty six and then left the country'.

'Yes I think you're right. Do you remember when...'

Paul and Simon sat back at their table and let the old men reminisce, transported back to the days of their youth. The men very soon seemed to have completely forgotten about the presence of the two young men at the next table and continued for more than twenty minutes bringing out memories, agreeing or disputing details and flitting quickly between events. One of them reminded the others of a parade of *Balillas* that seemed to have taken place in San Casciano and inspected by 'old' Campolargo himself, who had turned up in a large chauffeur driven car accompanied by two uniformed officials. He remembered how a certain Beppe had cried because he'd torn his black shirt while climbing over a fence and wasn't allowed to go to the parade. 'He asked if he could borrow mine, because we lived next door. I told him I hadn't got one and wouldn't lend it to him even if I had. He slapped my little sister at school the next day and the teachers didn't do anything because they knew that while Beppe was a little fascist, my father was a communist. My mother was so angry that she walked down to Bargino to complain. They didn't even let her in; one of the men who worked there, told her she'd be horse-whipped if she was ever seen there again, and then slammed the door in her face.'

At length, the conversation began to drift away from the Campolargos to other more general reminiscences and Paul decided it was worth risking intervening to see if there was any more useful information to be gleaned. 'So were all the Campolargo either killed during the war or left the country afterwards?'

The men looked round, all seeming surprised that they were still there. There was a pause during which Paul tried not to show how important the question was to him, and the men looked at each other, clearly trying to remember if they had said anything they shouldn't have. Finally, one of them replied, 'Most of them. One of the wives, a widow, stayed on a farm they owned near Barberino; Margarita, the eldest daughter lived in Siena until she died, and I think there was a younger daughter, but I've no idea what happened to her.' The others shook their heads.

Paul decided to leave it there; he got the impression that it would not be wise, in present company, to say that he was effectively a Campolargo himself, or at least assumed he was, and in any case, he knew where to find them if he needed to speak to them again. He commented on what a pleasant place San Casciano was and how it must be much calmer living there than in the city, moving the conversation back onto safe ground. Shortly after, he and Simon wished the men a good day, pushing the remainder of the flask over to them, said '*Buongiorno*' to the bar in general and left. Simon looked at him, 'Barberino?'

Paul looked at his watch, 'How far is it?'

'Between fifteen and twenty kilometres, I think'

Paul shook his head, 'No. I don't think so. It would be nearly six before we get to Barberino, then we'd have to do more detective work to find out where she lives, and even if we strike lucky it's going to be too late before we get to her.'

'OK. I'll ask Gabbi if she knows anyone on her course from Barberino'.

Back in Florence, Paul dropped Simon off and then made his way back towards home, remembering not to park the Midget in its usual place and instead finding a place in Via Nardo di Cione, on the other side of the inner ring-road that had been built over the site of the most recent circle of city walls, when they had been removed to allow the city to expand. It only took just over five minutes to reach the bar on Borgo La Croce where he called in to see if there were any more messages from prospective students.

Mimmo shook his head – 'No messages today, but Signora Vaccherini was looking for you earlier on', he said with a grin.

'Any idea what she wanted?' Paul asked, reminding himself that he'd already jumped to hasty conclusions about her twice, and trying to resist doing it again. Mimmo shook his head again. Then they talked about football and the new season for a few minutes before Paul decided it was time to go upstairs and cook his sausages.

He carefully peeled two cloves of garlic and placed them in the bottom of a frying pan with a little olive oil while he boiled a little water in a saucepan – the first time anyone in England asked if he wanted them to bring him anything, then he would have to ask for a small kettle, as well as further supplies of tea and marmite – once the water had boiled, he removed the frying pan from the flame for a minute and added the three sausages, giving the pan a shake so that they rolled and were covered with oil on all sides, then he poured in the boiling water until it came half way up the sausages, added a little red wine, placed the pan back on the heat, which he had reduced to the minimum setting, and covered it with a heavy lid. Having done that, he put two further cloves of garlic in the pan where the water had been, browned them in oil, poured in some *passata*, brought it to the boil and then added a sprig of rosemary and a drained can of cannellini beans. He waited until the pan began to bubble then turned the heat right down, poured himself a glass of wine and sat down with *'La Strage Dimenticata'* a short historical novel by a Sicilian writer called Andrea Camilleri, who he had never heard of but who, one of his university lecturers had assured the students, would be the next big thing in Italian literature.

Ten minutes later, the doorbell rang. It took him by surprise at first, partly because he was engrossed in the book but mainly because he hadn't realised that he had a doorbell and, even if he had, he certainly wouldn't have expected anyone to ring it. By the time the bell rang again he had located it and pressed the button next to it. 'The *Signora*' he thought quickly straightening the bed covers where he had been reading, and slipping his t-shirt back on. 'Ah well,' he thought, *'che sarà, sarà.'*

Then he heard a male voice, 'Which is your room?'

'Second floor – the door's open.' And seconds later, Lucio appeared.

'Well, this is a surprise. Come in. Have a glass of wine.'

Lucio came in but shook his head to the offer of wine. 'I was just passing and I thought I'd call in because I've found something that might be useful.' He sat down on one of the chairs at the table by the window. 'Not far from here, in Via Carducci, near Piazza d'Azeglio, there's a private foundation that was originally set up to help the families of partisans and victims of fascism after the end of the war. Over the years, it's become more of a research centre gathering together as much information as possible, not just about the victims and opponents of fascism but about anyone who was involved in any way. If this Aristide Campolargo was local, and worked with Pavolini, then they'll have information on him.'

'That's fantastic, Lucio. If you can give me the address, I'll go round in the morning.'

'The address is Via Carducci 5, it's between here and Piazza d'Azeglio, but there's no point going in the morning, you'll need to go on a weekday morning. Apparently, it's run by volunteers so it's not open all the time.'

Later, after finishing the novel by Camilleri, which was set in Sicily in 1848, the year of revolutions throughout Europe, Paul decided that he needed to put down on paper all the facts and half-facts he had managed to accumulate so far. He tore four A4 pages out of a note pad and tried to set out all he knew in a logical order. There had been at least three brothers and two sisters: the Aristide who he had first come across and who had been closely linked with Alessandro Pavolini, Florence's leading fascist intellectual; another brother who had been killed in Kefalonia in 1943, but who had left a widow who was almost certainly still alive and living near Barberino; another brother, called Umberto who had gone to live abroad after the war; a sister, Margarita, who had lived in Siena; and a younger sister, who he presumed must be his grandmother. Mimmo was going to get him copies of the electoral registers for Florence, although they would probably turn out to be not much use if the family was based in San Casciano. He had the address of a research institute that he could visit on Monday where he might be able to find out about the family in general and, if he could get to see the widow near Barberino he would have tracked down a great-aunt and finally be able to find out more detailed information about his grandmother.

He decided that, over the weekend, he would dedicate one day trying to track down the woman near Barberino, and then give himself a day off and head across to the coast and have a swim at either Torre del Lago or Tirrenia.

Chapter 5

Friday had been a good day and he felt he had made lots of progress; Saturday was not a good day and, by the end of it, he felt that he had been knocked backwards again. The morning had been fine. He'd collected the Midget, put the hood down, and followed the *Viale* round and up the hill past the panoramic Piazzale Michelangelo. He pulled over at the end of the piazza to enjoy an eight hundred lire tub of banana, *gianduia*, and fig ice-cream while he took in the view over the city, marvelling at the clear reflection of each of the bridges in the Arno, under the perfect azure sky. He wondered if he should pay a visit to the Porte Sante Cemetery while he was less than a quarter of a mile away, but then decided that he'd be far better going straight to

Barberino, as it was possible that the woman there would be able to tell him everything he needed to know.

Instead of taking the *superstrada* he took the old Via Cassia from the big roundabout beyond the fortified monastery, thinking that that would have been the road that his ancestors would have had to take before the *superstrada* was opened. The first bit of the road was slow as it passed through Tavarnuzze before straightening out for a while. Part way along this stretch was an impressive entrance flanked by two marble blocks; the front of the first marble block bore a sculpted eagle while the other showed the words "Florence American Cemetery and Monument". The entrance between the blocks led through an avenue of trees to a series of enclosed fields which together formed the shape of a fan on the lower slope of the hillside beyond the river. On the nearside of the river were some parking areas, again symmetrical and surrounded by some of the best tended grass he'd ever seen in Italy; it wouldn't have looked out of place on a top golfcourse. Somewhere he needed to visit another day, he thought.

Beyond Fornaci, he had to slow down as the road began to climb and, after a while he passed the point where he had exited the *superstrada* the previous day. From there he climbed the road again, left behind him the car-park where he had left the Midget previously and, after passing between the older and newer sections of the town, began to descend again as the Via Cassia twisted its way down through woodland into the Pesa Valley. Once the road flattened out, he passed through a small group of houses, and then the village the road went through was Bargino. He slowed right down but decided not to stop as it would be better to get as much information as he could from the old lady before looking at the places where his grandmother had grown up.

In Barberino, his day began to go downhill. It was more than two hours before he could find anyone who could confirm that he was on the right track. The Campolargo name had obviously been so unpopular after the fall of fascism that no one he spoke to could remember the widow ever having used it, and it wasn't until he was almost ready to give up that he found an old man who admitted to remembering the husband. He spat on the ground when Paul mentioned the name and muttered something that Paul didn't quite catch but was along the lines of her being better off as a widow. Don Filippo Campolargo had lived on a large farm about a kilometre and a half along a minor road that went across country before rejoining the main road towards Certaldo, '...but, you won't get much sense out of her.' He shook his head, muttering again, and Paul started to make his way to the car.

Initially, he took the wrong road out of Barberino and had to turn back and try again, before eventually pulling up outside a large former farm house. He studied it for a while before getting out of the Midget. There was a relatively small area of land around the house, that looked as if it only underwent the bare minimum of maintenance to keep the worst of the weeds in check. There were half a dozen olive trees, but even to his untrained eye it was clear that they hadn't been pruned for several years. Most of the windows had tightly closed shutters with faded green paint, although two pairs of shutters had been opened, one on the ground floor and one, which stood partially opened and hadn't been fastened back, on the first floor above it. A dusty black twenty year old *Lancia Fulvia Berlina* with a flat tyre was parked under a lean-to shelter by the side of the house, while a much cleaner bright red 50cc *Vespa* was parked next to it, looking completely out of place in the dilapidated surroundings.

He approached the door and pressed the old brass button set into the doorframe enclosing the door, which he now noticed also had peeling varnish. After a minute the door was partially opened and a young woman, who clearly was not Italian came to the door and looked at him enquiringly.

'*Si?*' she said, in a tone that implied 'No'.

'Is it possible to see *Signora* Campolargo,' he asked with a smile.

'Campolargo?' she answered and shook her head, 'No *Signora* Campolargo'.

'The *signora's* husband was Filippo Campolargo, so when he was alive she was *Signora* Campolargo, I know that she uses her maiden name.'

'*La signora non puole,*' she said, in imperfect Italian which took him a few seconds to work out.

He smiled again, he hadn't dared to think that he would just be waved in and re-establish contact with his relative just like that.

'I've come a very long way to see her,' and he waved his hand towards the Midget where the English plates were clearly visible. I think that she is a distant relative and I'd like to ask her about my Italian grandmother.'

'*Signora, non puole,*' said the woman again shaking her head and starting to close the door.

'Wait! Do you speak English?'

'Yes, I speak some,' and she began to open the door again.

He spoke slowly and clearly in English, 'My grandmother was the sister of the *Signora's* husband, but she died a long time ago. I am trying to find my relatives in Italy and the *Signora* here is the first one I have managed to find. I would be very grateful if she would see me, and I promise I won't take up any more of her time than she wants. Could you please ask her if I can see her?'

The woman shook her head but indicated that he should follow her into the house. She led the way through a door on the right of the entrance hall into a nineteen sixties style kitchen that looked a little dated but was clearly functional and spotlessly clean, in contrast to the exterior of the house.

'Sit down please... Would you like coca-cola?'

'Yes, please,' he generally avoided fizzy drinks but accepted on the grounds that it's harder to rush someone into leaving if they're holding a drink you have just given them.'

The woman sat down opposite him, 'You can see *Signora* Carmela, but she will not be able to tell you anything,' he looked puzzled and was about to say something when she continued, '*Signora* Carmela has Alzheimer's; she cannot talk to anyone. I'm sorry.'

He reflected, 'Don't people with Alzheimer's sometimes remember things from a long time ago, even if they no longer have short term memories?' He realised he was clutching at straws.

She shook her head slowly, 'In beginning it is like that. Later they remember nothing – can say nothing. Come,' and she stood up and led him through a door leading out of the side of the kitchen. A woman who could have been any age from seventy to ninety lay propped up on cushions on a hospital style bed which had had the back wound up to raise her almost into a sitting position. Her grey hair was cut very short revealing a fine boned face which, despite the wrinkles and the blank listless eyes, he thought had probably once been very attractive. The shoulders were hunched forwards and the Filipino carer, as he now realised she was, moved behind her and, after wiping away the saliva that drooled out of the corner of her mouth, kneaded her shoulders until the muscles relaxed. '*Signora* Carmela, Carmela, there is a visitor for you.'

'Hello, said Paul. *Buonasera.*'

The old lady gave no sign at all that anything had registered, and her unfocussed eyes continued to stare blankly into the distance.

'Do you remember Chiara, or Umberto, or Aristide?' he asked, hoping that the names might trigger something, 'What about Filippo?' Absolutely nothing. He sighed and retreated to the kitchen.

'I'm sorry,' said the Filipino, who told him that her name was Cheskka.

'No. I'm sorry for disturbing you. Is there anything at all that you can tell me about the family?'

'I know that she has three daughters. One lives in New York, one is in Milan, and one is in Geneva. The one in Geneva comes for an hour once every two months; the one in New York comes once a year and the one in Milan never comes. If I need anything, I have to contact a lawyer in Siena.'

'OK. You've been very helpful. Could you give me the name and address of the lawyer in Siena?'

'Of course'.

He had tried ringing the lawyer from a call box in Barberino but, being Saturday afternoon. There was no reply. On his way back he called into the bar in Bargino but, the owner wasn't there and the woman behind the counter said that she hadn't been in the area for long and didn't yet know many people. The customers at that time were all fairly young so he didn't think it worth asking.

He knew that Simon was visiting friends on the Sunday and assumed that Lucio would either be studying for his exam or relaxing with Gabriela, so he didn't bother contacting them on the Sunday morning, just grabbed his swimming things and made his way around the *Viali*, which were fairly quiet at that time, and followed the signs for the A1 and A11 motorways. At the first barrier he paid his five hundred lire for she short stretch leading to the junction of the Firenze-Mare, and the main A1 North-South artery. As he didn't enjoy the constant arrogant flashing in his rear mirror as the larger cars honed in to within touching distance of his rear bumper, as if expecting him to suddenly develop extra horse-power, or to conveniently slot in behind the old Fiat Five-hundreds and Autobianchi Bianchinas in the inside lane, he turned off the motorway almost immediately at the Prato Est exit and followed the dual carriageway which marked the previous course of the motorway. At least until Pistoia, he would not only save money on the tolls but could be sure of a mainly fast straight road. After Pistoia he knew that progress would be a bit slower, particularly through Montecatini and around the city walls of Lucca. However, he didn't mind and thought that he might even park just outside one of the gates of Lucca and have a walk along the old walls to enjoy both the sunshine and the view.

Spending ten minutes behind a tractor and trailer as he descended the steep twisty road after Serravalle, made him change his mind about stopping in Lucca. While it was generally fine in the Midget with the hood down, when he had to go very slowly under a hot sun it could be uncomfortable, and he wanted to get out on the open road beyond Lucca and cool down again. The road over the coastal spur of the Apennines separating Lucca from the coast was an enjoyable road to drive on, twisty enough for him to get the Midget's tyres to squeal on some of the corners but with enough straights to allow him to pass slower traffic or, on one occasion to allow him to be passed by a bright yellow Alfa Spider whose driver gave him a little wave as he eased off and made sure that he was well over to the right, so that he could be passed safely before the next bend.

After dropping down through the trees from Montemagno he continued straight on, across one main road, under the motorway, across the Via Aurelia and through an increasingly busy Viareggio until he reached the promenade with its many bathing establishments. He had no intention of paying for the privilege of placing his things on a deckchair while he swam, or of sitting under a parasol while he dried off after each swim, so he turned left and drove along until he was forced back into the town where the tourist harbour stretched inland. He was soon able to cross the river that led to the port and make his way back down to the seafront, passing the little football stadium, where there were still signs up for an international youth tournament that had taken place three months earlier. Once near the sea again, the road continued as a dual carriageway for another kilometre and then came to an end at a large turning space which also served as a parking area. It was clear that most people then went back the way they had come, for the only other road leading away from the parking area was a much smaller road leading inland.

Once he had squeezed the Midget into a small space between a Volkswagen Beetle and a Fiat 127, Paul put the hood up to give the inside a little shade, but left the windows open to let a bit of air circulate. He then took his bag into one of the several bars around the turning space and, after ordering a coffee, slipped his trunks on under his shorts in the toilets. Outside, he went round the edge of the last bathing establishment and began to walk south along the beach.

At first the beach was still crowded with families, many of whom had brought their own umbrellas and chairs and claimed their own little bit of the free beach. After about a hundred and fifty metres, however, the people began to thin out quickly and, after five hundred metres, it was very sparsely populated. He walked a bit further, being happy with his own company and wanting to spend as much time as possible swimming or reading. Soon he realised that he wasn't going to get solitude as, if he continued, the numbers would begin to increase again as he got nearer to Torre del Lago, so he found a patch of sand without cigarette butts or other detritus, placed his towel carefully and took off his shorts.

He put factor eight sun-cream onto as much of his body as he could reach and lay down, propped on his elbows, determined to resist the allure of the water until he had read another chapter. Once he had finished that next chapter, he slipped his watch under the corner of his towel and walked down to the edge of the sea. His father had always referred to him as "nesh" as he'd sat, wrapped in a towel, watching his father rush whooping into the breakers at Blackpool or Morecambe, transformed for two weeks every year from the timid clerk known and generally taken for granted by all at Glossop Council, into a hearty beach-bum out to enjoy himself and insisting that everyone else did too. Paul had only found it easy to get in to the sea in England when there had been waves; he had really disliked the gently sloping beaches where the icy water gradually rose higher, inch by painful inch, and it was ages before it was deep enough to throw yourself in and begin to enjoy yourself.

Here, although the water always felt cold at first because you were usually coming out of hot sun, it only took seconds before your body adapted. Once the water reached his thighs, he used his hands to rub water over his stomach and shoulders and then dived forwards, rolling over onto his back after a few strokes. It took about thirty seconds for the last of the tiny air bubbles that remained on his skin to disappear, but then he felt comfortable and began to swim slowly out to sea. When he was sufficiently far out to be well away from the shore, but not so far as to risk having a lifeguard sent out to him on a *pedalo*, he lay on his back and floated, watching the wispy clouds pass in front of the seemingly snow covered mountains which rose steeply behind Carrara.

He thought about Michelangelo leading a team of porters up into the marble quarries, carefully selecting the blocks he wanted and shouting orders as they lashed them on top of first sledges and then carts to take them down to the town. He wondered if they would then have been transported over Montemagno, taking the road he had taken earlier, or would they have first been taken down the coast to Pisa and then pulled on barges up the Arno to Florence. How many famous people had passed over those same spots at different times, he wondered... and what would it be like to have HG Wells' time machine to see them all together. That led him on to thinking about his own family; how close had he been to the places where they had been? Had he stood on the same spots? Seen the same sights? Maybe even thought the same thoughts?

Once his brain had begun to follow this rather unproductive train of thought he found it difficult to relax again. Rather than enjoying the day and taking it as a complete break from the task he had set himself, he found himself going over and over the conversations he had had over the past few days, the places he had been as he tried to find out about his grandmother.

When he emerged from the water, stepping carefully to avoid impaling the sole of his foot on any of the little twigs that had been blown out of the pine forest and into the sand over the preceding months, he saw that despite all the space, a couple in their early fifties had chosen to lay their towels down less than twenty metres from his. The man, almost completely bald except for some greying tufts on each side, was sitting reading a copy of the *Gazzetta dello Sport*, keeping the paper down with one hand and smoking a cigarette with the other. His wife, or at least Paul assumed it was his wife, lay on her back with one leg slightly raised and inclined outwards where it was bent at the knee, and with her hands clasped behind her head, allowing the inside of her arms to catch the sun. The man wore a pair of fairly nondescript trunks, the colour of which matched the bikini bottom of his wife, but not the bikini top, as the position she was in made it very obvious that she wasn't wearing one. From the look of her body she must have lapped up almost every single ray of sunshine there had been since the spring, and he doubted if she had ever worn the top of the bikini.

Ten years previously as a repressed teenager in England, he would have been excited by such a sight. One of his friends, whose father had been a 'business' man had been on an exotic foreign holiday to Benidorm, unheard of for the rest of them and, when he'd come back, he'd regaled them for weeks with tales of all the unimaginably beautiful girls he'd seen, all of them topless and most of them wanting to share a glass of sangria with him in the evening. They hadn't really believed him, were sure he was exaggerating wildly, but you could never quite be sure and they'd all wanted to listen. Now, although he couldn't resist an appraising glance, he was indifferent; if anything, what came to mind when he saw her was a piece of meat that had been left in the oven too long, or a tray of blackened buns. He laughed at the image as he sat down on his towel and the man looked up from his paper.

'*Prego?*'

'Oh, sorry. Nothing. I was miles away, talking to myself. *Buongiorno.*'

'*Buongiorno,*' responded the man and looked back at his paper as Paul sat down, glad that Italians were used to hearing students repeating things under their breath to learn them off by heart – hopefully the man would just assume he was a student preparing for an exam.

Twenty minutes later, Paul had almost dropped off to sleep in the sun, his head full of images of demented old women giving the fascist salute to Mussolini when...

'*Mi scusi*'. He turned his head to the right and opened his eyes just as the woman who had rolled over onto all fours started to push herself up, filling his eyes, which automatically squinted against the sun, with burnt cupcakes. He pulled himself together.

'Would you mind keeping an eye on our things while we go for a swim? We won't be long,'

'No. Of course not. Take as long as you like.'

The man thanked him as they walked down to the sea. His eyes followed them, particularly her, and he noted that despite a slight sag, she looked pretty good for her age from the back. He thought of *Signora* Vaccherini, remembered that Mimmo had said she had been looking for him and almost hoped that she would try again that evening.

He smiled and lay back, 'Hah, the thoughts that come to you when you see a woman and a man together'. He closed his eyes, "a woman and a man together... a woman and a man together".

He sat up suddenly – a woman and a man – he'd spent all his time concentrating on the ghost of a woman, and he hadn't thought about the man. His grandfather, Max, had died in Italy during the war... surely he must have left some trace. He'd gone past the big American Military Cemetery the day before, even thought about going back to visit some time – if that was for the Americans, where were the British buried? Of course, there would be more than one for each nation in the whole of Italy, but he was fairly sure it wouldn't be like France where the number of First World War cemeteries was almost countless – and if there were one for each region, he felt that his grandfather would be in the one nearest to his wife's home. There was no logical reason for thinking this; his grandfather could have been killed and buried any-time during the Italian campaign, but he was sure he was right... it was as if he felt it in his bones.

He was impatient for the couple to come back; he was going to grab a sandwich and make his way back to Florence and see what he could find out. When they finally sauntered out of the water and back towards their towels, he smiled at them and said he hoped that they'd enjoyed their swim. Then, after a couple of minutes, so that he didn't give the impression that he was only leaving because of them, he asked if they could recommend any of the bars for a snack, and then slipped his shorts and t-shirt back on, packed up his towel, book, bottle of water and sun-cream, bid them good-day and left.

After a cold but fairly tasteless Italian beer and a *panino* with a Milanese cutlet inside it, he was back in the Midget and heading towards Florence. One advantage of setting off back early, rather than soaking up every last drop of sun was that he was ahead of most of the traffic and was back in Florence by six.

Mimmo shook his head, 'I'm sure I've heard one mentioned but I've no idea where... but I would think that most older-people would know. Hang about a few minutes and I'm sure that there will be someone in who can help. Paul sat on a stool by the bar and ordered a lemon tea while he waited.

Less than five minutes later, two older men, who Paul had noticed there before, came in and sat down at their habitual table in the corner. As soon as they had appeared on the threshold, Mimmo had pulled out a bottle of prosecco from the cool cabinet under the counter, removed the vacuum cork and poured out two glasses.

'*Buonasera*. Here you are – your usual for a Sunday evening.' And then, as they grunted their thanks, 'This young man was asking me if I knew where the British Military Cemetery is, from the war. I couldn't tell him, but I thought one of you would probably know'.

'Isn't it that one in the *Viali*, in the middle of Piazzale Donatello?'

'No. That's not a military cemetery. That's full of poets. It's been there for hundreds of years. The military one is out on the Via Aretina, towards Compiobbi'.

'Is that far?'

'Five kilometres maybe. The number fourteen goes out that way'.

'Bus,' added Mimmo, helpfully.

Back upstairs, Paul added the name, "Jack", to his chart. Time to give his parents a ring; it would make them happy and he'd been meaning to do so since he got there. Instead of asking Mimmo for a big pile of *gettoni* and calling from the bar, he decided to walk over to Piazza della Repubblica and make his call more privately from one of the booths in the SIP.

He looked at his watch. Just after seven. That was OK, they would have finished their Sunday tea and his mum wouldn't keep him on the phone too long because *'Open All Hours'* would be starting soon. He waited until the assistant told him that booth four was free and then went in and dialled the number. It rang for nearly half a minute and he was just about to put the phone down when his brother-in-law's voice answered.

'Oh, hi Al, didn't expect you to answer – are mum and dad OK?'

'Yeah, they're fine. Your dad's doing the washing up and I was drying. Your mum's upstairs changing Luke's nappy, yelling at us to get the phone. How's it going with the pizzas the vino and the *señoritas*? Having a good time?'

'Pretty good thanks, except I'd be worried if I found many *señoritas* here – they're Spanish. How are things at home? I thought I'd better call and let them know I'm still alive and settling in'.

'Everything fine. No-one's ill. Nobody's lost their job. Liverpool beat Everton in the Merseyside derby yesterday, City drew at home with West Ham and United put five past West Brom, at West Brom... Hang on, your mum's here now. She wants to swap Luke for the phone, so all the best...'

'Hello, Paul. How are you? Is everything alright? Have you found somewhere to live? Are you eating alright – getting plenty of greens?'

'Yes, mum, everything's fine. I just thought I'd give you a quick ring to make sure you were all OK'.

'Us? Well of course we're OK. We're at home. Tell me about your journey... was the weather nice?'

'Yes, mum. I'll write you a nice long letter and tell you everything. If I stay on this phone too long I'll be bankrupt and have to go begging in the streets.'

'Begging in the streets!'

'Only joking mum – I can sell my body if I have to.... Listen.' he cut her off as he heard her make a tutting sound as a prelude to speech, 'There's something I need to ask Dad before I go. If he can't come to the phone, can you ask him if he can remember when his father was killed during the war, and if possible where.'

'John!' he heard her shout as she only partially covered the mouthpiece of the phone, 'Our Paul wants to know if you know when and where your dad was killed in Italy,' There was a pause and then his mother removed the hand that was partially covering the phone, 'He says it must have been in forty four, but he doesn't know where... he says Italy's Italy.'

'OK that's fine, Mum. Tell him "thanks." I'll write and then I'll ring again in a couple of weeks. Good to hear your voices. Byeee!'

'Bye. Love you lots.' And he hung up and went over to the counter to pay.

"Sometime in 1944," so that would work; if Florence was liberated at the end of August, there must have been fighting first to the south and then to the north of the city for some time around then. His grandfather could easily have been killed there, and his grave might be just a few kilometres down the road. That was another thing to go on his 'to do' list.

Chapter 6

Monday was the day of the week when the bar was closed so, when he left his room he went straight to the Midget and drove to the Arno and then followed the road eastwards as it followed the course of the river. Most of the traffic was going towards the city so he made good time out to the cemetery which was just outside a small village, a kilometre before Compiobbi itself. He noticed immediately that although the style was similar to the American Cemetery he had noticed on the way to Barberino, this one was significantly smaller. He approached a gardener to ask if there was a way to find particular graves and was directed to the custodian, who sat in a little office with a sign saying

"Commonwealth War Graves Commission" and giving the opening times.

Paul was a little surprised to see that, even outside the custodian's working hours, the cemetery was open to the public although there was no vehicular access at those times. There was also a sign giving visitors a phone number to ring if they required assistance when the custodian was not present. When he was invited to sit in front of the custodian's desk, he expressed surprise at this, as he had generally found that closing times tended to be strictly adhered to in Italy. The custodian smiled at him, 'I may be Italian by birth, but my father was English and I work for the Commonwealth War Graves Commission. As many of the soldiers fighting in this sector were from all around the Commonwealth, we often get visitors who have come from the other side of the world, and may be on a tight deadline to catch flights back. Their relatives made the ultimate sacrifice for their country and, by coming here, many of them have also made sacrifices, although of a different nature. It would seem a little unfair to say, "sorry we close at six-thirty, come back another time" wouldn't it?'

Paul acknowledged the point that the custodian had made and explained that he was there because firstly he wanted to establish whether or not his grandfather was buried there, and secondly, if he was, whether it was possible to visit his grave. The custodian handed him a form to complete: name, date, address, reason for visit etc. - 'We do like to keep a record of who's been, and who they've been to see. But while you're filling that in, I'll see what I can find.'

He opened up a large drum shaped card index and began to rotate it, 'There are one thousand six hundred and thirty two cards here, one for each soldier, all divided into nationality and then alphabetical order. So long as no one has taken one out and put it back in the wrong place. ... I should... Yes! Here it is – just where it should be.' He carefully unclipped the card, replaced it with a blank marker card and brought the original over to the desk. 'Maxwell Robert Caddick,' he read, 'Warrant Officer Class One. Date of birth, second of April 1912. Date of death, twenty-seventh of August 1944. Place of death, Santa Croce sull'Arno. Next of kin, Ethel Sykes (sister)'. He stopped and Paul detected a slight frown on his face.'

'Is there something wrong?'

'No. There are just a couple of things that are unusual – you see I have a lot of time to read up about the campaign while I'm here – it means I can be more helpful to visitors. As far as I knew, none of the liaison officers who were with the Americans were killed, and Santa Croce sull'Arno was very definitely in the American sector.'

'You said, "a couple of unusual things", what was the other?'

'There's no regiment. We do have a few here who were not with regiments, but they don't have ranks either, whereas your grandfather was a Warrant Officer Class One.'

'You'll have to excuse my ignorance, but what's a Warrant Officer Class One.'

The custodian gave a little laugh, 'If you'd been born a bit earlier and had to do National Service, you'd have known what a Warrant Officer was. The officers you'll have heard of, the lieutenants and captains and so on, all had commissions to make them officers – most of them had been to university, or would have gone to university if they hadn't joined up. The men who come up through the ranks and become officers because they have shown that they are good at what they do, can't generally get commissions, so they have to find another way of promoting them. It's a bit easier now, because they can be sent on courses to become officers and gentlemen, which you don't have time to do in wartime. You'll be pleased to know that if your grandfather was a WO1, it means that he was a very good soldier.' Paul nodded his thanks for the custodian's words. 'But I'm intrigued by the lack of a regiment -very odd – very odd indeed. ... Are you in the area for long?' And, when Paul confirmed that he intended to be there for the foreseeable future, 'I'll make some enquiries and, if you can come back in a week, hopefully I'll be able to tell you more.'

'That's very kind of you, but please don't put yourself out. Just knowing where he is will be good.'

'Oh don't worry, young man – I'm not just doing it for you; I want to know all there is to know about the young men whose care has been placed into my hands. Now, let me show you where the grave is.'

When they reached the area where the lines and lines of headstones stretched out ahead of them, he counted his way up to the correct row and told Paul that it was the seventeenth one along. 'I won't come to the grave with you as many people like to have a silent moment there but, if there's anything you want to ask, please don't hesitate to call in and see me before you leave.'

The grave was one of the many immaculately clean white stone headstones, each row straight as a die and joined by a narrow groove cut from grave to grave in the well-watered green turf. Each headstone bore a sculpted image of a regimental badge, then a service number, the soldier's rank and name, date of death and age. In the middle of each headstone was a cross and, at the bottom, just above the grass was a phrase or quotation, which seemed to be different for each soldier, but he knew that under each stone was an individual and that each of those individuals had their own story and meant something different to the people they had known. He wondered what his grandfather's story was; he hadn't really thought about it before, but now his search seemed to have become even more complicated; all the headstone told him about his grandfather was that Warrant Officer Class One Maxwell Caddick had died at the age of thirty-two on the twenty-seventh of August 1944 and that he had striven to extend an olive branch.

Before he left, the custodian, who clearly appreciated having an appreciative audience filled him in with more details about the battle on the Arno and the campaign in general, so when Paul left, he had a much clearer idea about the history of the period. He also thought he was starting to understand why it was so difficult to obtain information. He had expressed surprise that relative to other campaigns in the Second World War, very little seemed to a have been been written about the Italian campaign. 'Speaking with my Italian hat on,' the custodian had said, 'we didn't really cover ourselves in glory during the war, so we'd much prefer to forget about it and, the Allied powers were too worried that we would vote communist to encourage us to do anything other than forget.

Back in Florence he decided to locate the private foundation in Via Carducci as it lay between Piazza d'Azeglio, where he parked the car, and Borgo La Croce. He walked past it the first time, and it was only on his second, slightly more attentive walk down the street that he found the small nameplate next to a narrow opening leading into an elongated courtyard between two commercial buildings. A second nameplate by a door at the far end of the courtyard told him that he had found what he was looking for. He rang the bell and, as he expected, there was no answer, but he did notice that a list of opening hours did suggest that it was possible to contact the institute by telephone up until five thirty. Having seen that, he changed his mind about going home for a bite to eat, and instead turned right by the Church of Sant'Ambrogio and made his way towards the centre. He stopped on his way at the *'tripperia'* under the arch of San Pierino, and had the Florentine speciality of hot lamprey sandwich dipped into its cooking liquid and smothered with a spicy sauce, then found a drinking fountain to rinse his hands.

Inside the SIP, there were quite a few students on gap years waiting for booths to phone home so he took a ticket, looked at the number and then decided he had time to nip out for a quick coffee. The nearby bar was quiet and he was tempted to use a *gettone* to ring the Institute from there, but decided it wasn't worth the risk of missing his turn. As well as ringing the Institute, which he thought would be a fairly brief call, he also had to ring the solicitor's office in Siena which could turn into quite a lengthy call and, if he got put on hold, require a large supply of *gettoni*. There were only two people in front of him when he got back, and one of those was allocated a booth almost immediately so he knew there wouldn't be long to wait.

'*Buonasera*. Guerrini and Becalossi. How can I help you?'

'Oh, good evening. I'd like to speak with someone who deals with the affairs of Signora Carmela di Lollo in Campolargo.'

'May I ask the purpose of your call, Sir?'

'Of course. The *signora* is a distant relative by marriage. I called to see her yesterday but found that she's no longer,' he paused, as he tried to work out the best way of phrasing it, 'she's no longer in complete control of her faculties. I was told that your firm dealt with her affairs.'

'OK. Hold the line please; I'll see if anyone is able to speak with you,' and he was put on hold for what seemed an interminable time. The music he was played as he was waited seemed to come from a compilation of songs about the law and lawyers in a variety of languages, although the only ones he recognised were *'Jailhouse Rock'*, *'Will your lawyer talk to God for* you' and Jackson Browne's *'Lawyers in love'*; the compilation of eight songs had just started for the third time when,

'To whom am I speaking?'

Startled out of the torpor the music had lulled him into, Paul initially found it difficult to find the right words, 'I'm... I just... Sorry, let me start again. My name is Paul Caddick. My grandmother, who died in England at the end of 1935 was related to Carmela di Lollo in Campolargo who, I am led to believe, has her affairs administered by your firm.'

'I'm sorry, I'm not able to discuss the affairs of clients. I'm unable to help you.'

'No, wait. Just a minute. I don't want to discuss the *signora's* affairs. I was just wondering if you were able to put me in contact with any of her other relatives.'

'I repeat, I'm sorry, Mr Caddick. I am unable to discuss any aspect of the lady's affairs or even to confirm whether or not she is a client of this firm. If you have any specific queries, please ask your own legal representatives to address them to us in writing, using the appropriate channels. *Buonasera*, Signor Caddick,' and the phone was put down.

Pensively, he reattached his own phone. He thought about ringing the Institute but decided that, after that phone call, he really needed to sort his thoughts out before making the next phone call. The best way to do that was just to walk, so he set off walking through the centre and then headed out away from the crowds. A couple of hours later when he decided to head for home, he realised that he was beyond Rifredi and could easily cut across under the railway line to call on Simon and Lucio.

Simon answered the bell and buzzed him in. Then, when the door to the flat itself opened and Simon saw him he said, 'Ah fantastic. Come in. Come in. Lucio's a great cook but he has no idea of portion sizes; he's just put a *melanzane alla parmigiana* in the oven that's big enough to feed an army.'

'Good planning. Consider me a regiment, or a battalion, whichever is bigger. It's ages since I last had a good *melanzane alla parmigiana*. Let me just pop down and get a bottle of wine. … No. No. I insist. I hadn't come here to scrounge a meal, but since it's working out that way, I need to get something.'

'Before they ate, Simon opened some cans of Guinness that the supermarket had in as part of "World Awareness Week," 'I usually brew my own from kits I buy back in Wales, but it's not as good as the genuine article.' Lucio opened a bottle of Peroni, 'I haven't got him properly trained yet... but I will.' They all laughed.

Paul gave them as full an account as he could about developments over the last couple of days, with the others questioning him closely about every little detail.

'So what's next?' asked John. 'You start work next week.'

'I've still got Lucio's Institute to see; that may lead somewhere else, then I need to go back to the War Cemetery in a few days. I doubt that knowing more about my Granddad will really help, but you never know.'

'How did your grandparents meet?' Paul shook his head. 'And what did he do before he was in the army? Knowing that might help you work out how they met.'

'As far as I know, he worked in an office doing accounts and general admin. Hardly the type of job that's going to find you a mysterious Italian bride... unless he worked for a firm that specialised in importing wine and olive oil.'

'Sounds like the type of job that would be ideal for me,' said Simon.

'It's a thought,' said Lucio. 'You import plenty of olive oil and wine -so why not?'

'We do now, but the amounts involved in the mid-thirties must have been minuscule. My grandma keeps a little bottle of olive oil for softening earwax, before she goes to have her ears syringed. She must have had the same bottle for more than twenty years.'

Lucio shook his head, obviously thinking that Simon was pulling his leg. Even the British couldn't be that barbaric!

The *parmigiana alle melanzane* was very good and Simon had been right about the portions; even with three of them, it was all they could do to finish it off. After they had eaten they played Risk until almost midnight when Paul, refusing the offer of a bed, set off on the forty minute walk home.

By the time he had cut across along Via Vittorio Emanuele and crossed the River Mugnone to emerge on the *Viali* at Piazza della Libertà it was almost half past twelve and there was very little traffic about. He crossed over and had done about a hundred metres along the *Viale* when an Innocenti Mini drove past, braked and then reversed up to him. The side window reflected the light from a neon sign advertising an insurance company so he could not see in until the door was pushed open by the driver leaning across from the far side. 'Paul! What a surprise! Get in; I'll give you a lift home.'

From there, it took less than five minutes to reach Borgo La Croce and, as the Innocenti was small, it could just be squeezed into a space less than fifty metres from the entrance to Paul's stairway. 'A gentleman would invite me up for a drink to thank me.'

'A lady would refuse.' he said, and leaned across to meet her lips.

She pulled back after a moment, 'Not here. Let's go to your room – quickly.' and she slipped out of the driver's door and, before he had even shut the car door behind him, had opened it with her key and disappeared up the stairs.

By the time he had reached his room she was stepping out of her skirt which was on the floor around her ankles. He went to close the shutters but she shook her head, 'I need to see you,' He stepped up to her and kissed her again, then gently pushed her back so that she was sitting on the edge of the bed, then he dropped to his knees between her legs and carefully undid the buttons of her blouse while she pushed up his t-shirt. When the last button was undone, he raised his arms and she lifted the shirt right off, giving one of his nipples a playful nip as she did so, then he fumbled with her bra-strap while she started on his belt and fly. She won the race: he was still struggling with the last hook when she came to his aid with her practised hands...

Two hours later, he woke to find her dressing. She smiled and continued to dress as he watched, then she came over to the bed and lightly kissed him on the lips. 'Don't worry. This never happened,' and she turned, blew him a kiss from the door, which she closed quietly and was gone. Two minutes later, he heard the engine of the Innocenti and then, all that was left was the lingering scent of Signora Vaccherini's jasmine flavoured perfume on the pillow.

In the morning, when he awoke, somewhat later than usual, he half wondered if it had all been a dream and had to press his face into the pillow to recapture the smell of jasmine before he was finally convinced. He wondered what difference, if any, it would make, to his time in Florence; would it complicate his life or could he take her at her word when she had said that it 'never happened'? He knew that in his present circumstances it was an experience he would have no objection to repeating, but he didn't want it to become a routine or anything that couldn't be stopped at any time with no hard feelings if he happened to meet someone he really liked. He decided to take her at her word and not worry about it.

When he went down to the bar it was at least an hour later than his usual time.

'I thought you weren't coming,' said Mimmo, bending down behind the counter. Then, re-emerging, 'Look what I've got for you. This'll keep you busy!' and he put down a pile of computer paper more than three inches high. Paul looked quizzically. Mimmo checked who else was within earshot, and then said in a lowered voice, 'Electoral register for the Comune of Florence, correct as of lunchtime yesterday. My friend's wife came up trumps.'

Paul's face must have shown the alarm he felt as he looked at the large pile – if the name he was looking for was on the very last page, it would take him weeks – and if there were no Campolargos at all it would all be for nothing. 'Under eighteens won't be on there, so if you're lucky, you might only have four hundred thousand names to look through,' said Mimmo with a smile.

'Thanks, Mimmo. You never know, they might be on the very first page – but just in case they're not, can you make me up a couple of rolls with *prosciutto* and *mozzarella*. I'm going to sit in the Boboli Gardens for the day. If you see me before this evening it will mean I've succeeded.'

As Paul left the bar, Mimmo called, 'Good luck. Hope to see you for lunch.' He waved over his shoulder, without turning and made his way along the Borgo and the succeeding streets until Via Verdi, where he turned and made his way past Santa Croce and down to cross the Arno over the Ponte alle Grazie. Once over the river, he made his way along the Lungarno towards the Ponte Vecchio. Instead of joining the flood of tourists heading from the Ponte Vecchio towards the Pitti Palace and the main entrance to the gardens, he turned left up the steep Costa San Giorgio towards the *Forte da Belvedere* and the little used top entrance to the gardens. A few intrepid tourists had found their way to the top of the gardens, aiming for the Ceramics Museum but most had not made it any higher than the ornamental pool where he could see about thirty people around the edges, lining up, posing for family photographs in front of the statue of *Neptune*. Later, he would wander down to the lower levels of the gardens to see Michelangelo's *'Prisoners'* in one of the grottoes, but for now he had work to do.

He found a bench at the top of the gardens in the shadow of the Forte and began to run his finger down the columns of names. It didn't take long for him to realise that the task he had set himself was likely to be one of the most boring he'd ever done. The only thing he could think of that ran it close had been revising for his 'A' Level Maths exam, but then he'd had *Emerson, Lake and Palmer, Genesis, The Who*, and *Uriah Heap*, to make life bearable. Now, all he had was a fantastic view, but if he looked at that, he lost his place on the page. Once, he fell asleep and only the soft sound of the computer paper hitting the floor woke him up. Luckily, each sheet was attached to the next so he was sure he hadn't lost any, but it still took him a while to find his place again. After that, he began to put a tick on the corner of each completed page – just in case.

By half past four, he decided he'd had enough for the day. While he could sit for hours with a good novel or studying paintings, looking at a list of names and addresses was definitely a very different matter. After he'd gathered up his things, he wandered down to the grotto to look again at the copies of the incomplete sculptures in the Grotto del Buontalento. In the imperfect light of the grotto it was almost impossible to tell the difference between these copies and the originals that had been removed to the Galleria dell'Academia before the First World War. From there, he made his way home, avoiding the bar as he preferred to put off having to talk about his fruitless day for as long as possible. Once inside, he made a cup of tea and changed into his running kit as it brewed. As soon as he had drunk his tea, he left his room, turned left along the Borgo and began to run. He had to stop to wait for the right moment to thread his way through the slow moving traffic on the *Viale* but then was able to move freely, keeping in the shade as much as possible as he headed out past the Italian Football Federation's base at Coverciano and up the hill to Settignano. It was still fairly hot, and he hadn't run for a few days so he kept the pace steady and stopped for a drink at the drinking fountain in the centre of the village. From Settignano he climbed a bit further and then followed the road along the side of the hill towards Fiesole. EM Forster must have known this road, he thought, as it had to have been somewhere along here that he had set the famous kiss amongst the violets in *"Room with a View"*. He had heard rumours that a film would be made of the book in the near future and wondered whether it might be possible to get a role as an extra, as part of it would have to be filmed in Florence. He'd have to work through his address book and see if anyone might have the right contacts.

By the time he got to Fiesole and was able to stop at another drinking fountain, he was starting to feel the effects of his recent lack of training, and decided to take it very easy down the steeply sloping Via Fiesolana Vecchia. It was nearly half past eight by the time he got back and slipped under the shower. He knew that his calves would be sore and his hips stiff in the morning, but he felt much more relaxed, and the thought of continuing with the electoral registers the following day no longer filled him with dread.

Wednesday did, in fact, turn out to be very similar to Tuesday. He didn't go back to the "Prisoners" and he ran out to the south of the city taking in Pian dei Giullari and Arcetri before dropping down to Porta Romana by way of Poggio Imperiale. The only real variety in his day was provided by Mimmo who gave him the phone number of a student who had called the previous afternoon wanting English lessons. He was only available to be called in the evenings and so it was not until after his run and shower that Paul was able to call him.

Giulio turned out to be an Architecture student who was obliged to include a modern language exam amongst the portfolio of exams that he had to complete before he was able to begin work on his thesis. Giulio explained that the exams in non-core subjects were completed orally. What he had to do was select two from a long list of approved texts, read out sections chosen by his examiners and then answer questions about the two texts. The trick, he had been told, was to choose fairly obscure texts as the examiners who were almost always the 'lettori' or language assistants in the Faculty of Letters could hardly be expected to know all the texts off by heart. When Paul asked how many texts were on the approved list, he was amazed to hear that there were sixty novels as well as the complete works of Shakespeare; the only restriction students faced was that they could not turn up and ask to be examined on two different Shakespeare plays as their two texts. Giulio was intending to take the exam in the December session so they agreed that up until then, Paul would do two two-hour sessions with him each week, from three-fifteen to five-fifteen on a Wednesday and from three until five on a Thursday, to begin on the following day. At least, Paul thought, it would mean that he didn't have to spend all day poring over the electoral register. The private lessons he now had set up also meant that, until Christmas, he had enough work to keep him going and still had every morning as well as Friday, Saturday and Sunday free.

The following morning as he made his way to the Boboli Gardens, he called into the university building and took down the notices he had put up about private lessons. He had told Mimmo that if anyone else called in the meantime that they should be told that he was fully booked until after Christmas. Hopefully, if his existing students were satisfied, they would pass on his name to other people anyway.

At eleven thirty four he found what he was looking for. His brain was virtually on automatic pilot and it was only as he was ticking the corner of the page that he realised what he had just seen and looked at the page again. There it was: Campolargo Maddalena, Palazzina dei Gerani, Viuzzo delle Corti, and at the same address: Conte Guido, Conte Rosanna and Melluso Lia. He read the entries twice more, just to make sure; he had got so used to finding nothing over the past couple of days that it was hard to believe that he finally had what he was looking for. He wanted to rush straight round there, although he had no idea where Viuzzo delle Corti was. It was probably just as well, he thought; he wanted to be well prepared this time and not just blunder in as he had with his great-aunt Carmela. Finding out where Viuzzo delle Corti was, turned out to be more difficult than he had anticipated. He asked several people, including a traffic warden, as he made his way back towards his room, but none of them had heard of it. It was not until he got to Mimmo's bar, and Mimmo got his street map out, that he managed to locate it.

'Very nice,' said Mimmo, 'I wouldn't mind living up there. It must be just behind San Miniato and either have views over open countryside or over the eastern side of Florence towards Settignano.'

'I think I'm going to go up and have a look, before I make contact. See if I can get an idea of what sort of family they are.'

Before he could do anything, however, he had his first lesson with Giulio which was over in Poggetto, exactly the opposite direction to that in which he wanted to go. He thought about taking the car but decided that parking near Giulio's house could be a problem and he was better off on foot. It took him a little longer than he'd estimated and he had to apologise when he arrived, but Giulio's mother, who opened the door, assured him that it was fine. He was shown through into a study which he assumed must be Giulio's father's. His mother offered him a coffee and shouted for Giulio, who appeared immediately.

Paul explained to Giulio, in Italian, that he would be speaking almost entirely in English and that when there was anything that Giulio did not understand, he would try and explain it using simpler English, rather than translating. He would only use Italian if, when they were looking at the two literary texts, there were concepts and ideas that required an understanding of some aspect of English culture if they were to be interpreted correctly. Even then, if he thought that it was possible to explain in English he would do so. He asked Giulio to tell him how much English he had already studied and whether he had any experience of the language outside the classroom. When they had talked about Giulio a little, he asked him to show him the list of approved texts, then told him a little bit about what some of the texts were about so that he could make an informed choice. He advised against choosing obscure texts, arguing that even if the *lettore* didn't know a text well, they would be able to tell whether the student was talking nonsense or not unless the student was extremely fluent and, 'if you're extremely fluent, you have got nothing to worry about, so you may as well read books that you enjoy'. Giulio saw the logic behind this argument and they decided that he would read *"Lucky Jim"* and *"Passage to India"*; he would purchase the texts and start reading one of them before the next Wednesday when they were next to meet. At the end of the two hours, Giulio called his mother who gave Paul twenty thousand lire, the first money he had earned since arriving in Italy.

An hour after leaving Giulio's house, Paul emerged on to the *Viali* near Piazzale Michelangelo from the steps up from the Arno. He crossed the *Viale* and continued up to San Salvatore al Monte and then round the side into an area of Florence he hadn't even known existed previously. Less than a quarter of a mile from the hustle and bustle of Piazzale Michelangelo, and even closer to the steps where coachloads of tourists were disgorged at the foot of the steps leading to the main entrance to San Miniato, was an oasis of peace. Immediately behind the two churches were two lanes which could have been in any small Tuscan village. A few houses, mainly individual but not all, were scattered along the narrow streets, all painted in shades of ochre and most with window boxes trailing geraniums. One house had a mass of bougainvillea trailing over the wall providing contrasting colours. One of the two roads came to an end in a small courtyard, the far end of which was borded by a low wall separating it from an olive grove that fell away down the hillside.

There were not many houses so he soon identified the one belonging to the Campolargo/Conte/Melluso family; it was not one of the larger ones but a high wall that continued from the end of the house along the side of the street showed that it must have some garden – a rare luxury in a city where most people lived in apartments and relied on balconies for their outside space. As with all the other houses, the windows facing the lane were protected by metal bars, at least on the ground floor. A footpath ran into a wood behind the high walls of the grounds of San Miniato and he sat on a bench near the start, where he could just see what he assumed to be the main entrance to the house. After about an hour a Fiat Mirafiori pulled up outside a gate in the wall. A few seconds later, an orange light began to flash on top of the wall and the gate slowly opened to let the car in. Because of the angle he was at, Paul could not see through the gate and the view he got of the car's occupant was only sufficient for him to feel fairly confident that it was a man. Feeling that he had not learnt much in the last hour, he got up and made his way back to Borgo La Croce.

Rather than just turning up and knocking at the door, Paul decided that it would probably be better to telephone first. He considered ringing straight away but realised that the family would probably be eating by now and decided that ringing during the day might be more sensible. For the moment he satisfied himself with finding the number in the directory: Conte.G, Viuzzo delle Corti; he would ring in mid-afternoon the following day.

Chapter 7

In the morning he decided he would try the Institute, and accordingly, at a quarter to ten rang the doorbell in Via Carducci. The lock clicked open – he suspected that there must be a camera somewhere so that visitors could be subjected to a minimum of scrutiny before they were admitted – and he entered to find himself in a small reception area. An earnest looking receptionist or secretary sat behind a desk which was almost entirely covered by a typewriter, a pile of buff files, several sheets of paper and a telephone.

'*Buongiorno.* Can I help you Sir?'

'*Buongiorno, Signorina.* I'm trying to find some information about a family in the nineteen-thirties who I believe were heavily involved in the fascist movement in Florence'.

'Is your research for study purposes or is it a private matter?'

'It's a private matter. I'm led to believe that I am related to this family and wanted to find out more about them.'

'Most of the information we have here is information on the partisans. We do have some information on the fascists but it is less easily accessible. If you wish, you can consult the indexes of documents we hold on microfiche. Alternatively, or preferably in addition, if you would like to complete one of these forms, one of our researchers will try to find the information you require as soon as they are able.'

'OK. Thankyou. I'll fill the form in and then see if I can identify anything helpful on the microfiche.'

The form didn't differ too much from the one he had filled in at the military cemetery although this time he was entering all the details he could of the Campolargos rather than of his grandfather. He spent an hour looking through microfiches detailing lists of publications and documents but it wasn't very fruitful as he didn't really have much of an idea what type of documents might be relevant. During the time he was there, only two other people were researching in the study room, both of them elderly but otherwise differing greatly from each other. One was fairly distinguished looking, wearing a light summer suit and armed with a slim crocodile leather briefcase, leather bound notebook and Montblanc pen; he had a pile of old pamphlets in front of him which he appeared to be systematically scanning and taking occasional notes from. The other man was much less well presented with a pair of brown trousers that looked as if they had been badly ironed and an off-white shirt to which a narrow brown tie was held with a tie-clip; the shirt, Paul couldn't help noticing, was fraying at the cuffs and had a stain on the underside of the right forearm. What surprised Paul most about this second man, however, was that, in all the time Paul was there, he only had one hand-written document in front of him, which he read through again and again, every so often stopping to wipe a tear from his eye. The contrast between the two men made Paul appreciate even more just what a sensitive area he had almost inadvertently stumbled into; while for some, such as the distinguished man with the Montblanc pen, it was a fertile area for academic research which presumably led to the publication of academic tomes and the presentation of well remunerated talks on a lecture circuit, for others, this was a subject that was still very alive and full of memories seared with strong emotions of all kinds.

By the time he left the Institute he felt he had achieved absolutely nothing; there didn't seem to be any point in his returning there unless he knew exactly what he was looking for. Hopefully, if making contact with Maddalena Campolargo of Viuzzo delle Corti went as well as he hoped it would, he would be able to find out everything he wanted to know without needing to go back there.

After having some lunch, he again made his way over to Piazza della Repubblica and the SIP. It wasn't the time of day when the tourists tended to think of ringing back to their home countries and, he had found that, for some reason, Italians making phone calls from the SIP tended to do so in the morning, so he was directed straight away to a free booth. He knew that he would get a contemptuous tourists-don't-know-what-they're-doing look from the cashier when he went to pay at the end, as it would have been much simpler to make the call within the city from any phone in the street or in one of the many bars that had a phone available for public use, however, he wanted the privacy of the private booth for this call.

'*Pronto.*' A cheerful sparkling female voice. Too much to hope for that it was Maddalena Campolargo herself.

'Good afternoon. Mrs Conte?'

'No, I'm her daughter. If you'll just hold the line a moment I'll get her – Oh, who's calling please?'

'My name is Paul Caddick, although I'm afraid that won't mean anything to her at the moment.'

'Oh. OK. I'll see if she's available'. Paul noted the change in the wording and, as he waited, wondered if he hadn't inadvertently caused a problem for himself. He couldn't really blame her if she didn't accept a call from someone who might turn out to be selling vacuum cleaners, or insurance or...'

'*Pronto.* To whom am I speaking?'

'My name is Paul Caddick. I'm from England but I think that I am related to your family.'

There was a pause, and then, 'And how might that be, Mr Caddick?'

'My grandmother, who died a long time before I was born, was called Chiara Campolargo. I know very little about her except that originally she was from Florence. The name Campolargo seems to be rarer than I thought it would be and the only member of the family I have been able to identify lives with you. I would really like to know more about my grandmother and wondered whether it would be possible for me to call and see Signora Campolargo.'

'Mr Caddick. I'm sorry to disappoint you but, although I can confirm that my mother does live with us, I'm afraid it will not be possible for you to see her.'

'Oh, I'm sorry. Is she unwell?' he said, thinking of how he had found his 'aunt' Carmela.

Signora Conte ignored his question. 'Although, my mother was born with the name Campolargo and has to use it on official documents, she has always made it clear that it is a name she does not wish to use and she has made it very clear that she has no wish for any contact with members of her family – nor, would she wish me to be talking to any of the family, so I'm afraid I'll have to say *buongiorno* and leave you. Goodbye, Mr Caddick'.

'But....' He looked at the now silent phone in his hand and felt a surge of anger which he knew must have reddened his face. He banged the phone down onto its cradle and then waited a minute and took several deep breaths before leaving the booth and going to the cashier to pay. He was so angry and frustrated that he even forgot to pick up his change.

Sod them. Sod them all. He didn't need to find out about the family; he'd survived perfectly well without them for all these years and they quite clearly didn't feel any need to get to know him. He'd go back to the military cemetery in a few days to find out about his grandfather, but other than that, he would use his spare time to enjoy himself instead of chasing ghosts – or possibly poltergeists!

That evening he made his way into the centre towards the *Birreria Centrale* in Piazza dei Cimatori where he knew that, as it was Friday, there was a good chance that he would find Simon. Simon had explained to him which were the most convivial bars, pizzerias and trattorias in the centre and had told him what was fairly close to being his weekend routine. In fact, as he passed the windows on his way to the door, he could clearly see Simon at a table with a few other young people. One of the others seemed vaguely familiar although Paul couldn't remember where he had come across her or if, indeed, he was mixing her up with someone else.

He ordered himself a large *birra scura* and then made his way over to the table where the two young women and one young man, who were on the side facing Simon, shuffled up to make room for him.

'Hi Paul,' glad you could join us. Do you know Claire? She's another of this year's crop of language assistants, but she's from your old uni.'

So that was it. The Italian department at Leeds wasn't too big so he would almost certainly have passed her in the corridor between lectures. However, if she was doing a year as an assistant now, they would have only been there for one year together as he would have been doing his year abroad when she was in her first year. 'Hi Claire, I thought you looked familiar, but I couldn't place you – sorry about that – how's it going so far?'

'Not too bad. The staff at the *liceo* are all very supportive so I'm feeling fairly confident for when I start to see groups of students on my own. I remember seeing you around the department occasionally, but I think I probably saw you more often on the sports pages of *Leeds Student*.'

'Ah. You didn't have to do much to get on the sports pages of *"Leeds Stupid"* – If the club you belonged to had a publicity secretary who could write, they'd print anything. Anyway, if you were a regular reader of the sports pages you must be either sporty yourself or have had an interest in someone else who is.'

'I do a bit of fencing, so I usually look at the sports-pages and read all the reports except the rugby. I'm afraid that however much I try, rugby just bores me.'

'Leeds has a pretty good reputation for fencing doesn't it? There was a lad called Gordon who used to come out for a training run occasionally to keep his general fitness up.'

'Yes, I know Gordie, he's a friend of mine.'

They chatted away for the next couple of hours, comparing experiences of different lecturers and aspects of student social life in Leeds, although it soon became clear that while Paul had tended to go to the pub when he had gone out, Claire had spent most of her time either in the Student Union bar or in one of the various night clubs around the city. Soon after ten, Claire excused herself and went to the station to meet her Italian boyfriend who was arriving that night from Bari.

Once she had left, Simon looked at Paul, 'Bit of an improvement on Baz. Shame about the boyfriend.'

Paul laughed, 'Yeah. Nice girl – but not my type so, if the boyfriend disappears at any time, I won't be getting in your way.' They clinked glasses and then, Paul, noticing that the glasses were nearly empty, drained his and went to obtain replacements.

'So how's the genealogical research going? Found that you're heir to a fortune yet?'

'Huh. Well, I managed to track down the remaining Campolargo – who must have been the youngest daughter that the old guys in the bar mentioned – unfortunately, when I rang the house, the name Campolargo turned out to be as popular there as it was with the butcher in San Casciano. Apparently she only uses the surname when she has to, and the family won't have anything to do with anyone who is any way connected with the Campolargos – and that includes me. So I've decided to give up.'

'Why?'

'What do you mean "why"? I've tracked down the two people remaining who would have known my grandmother. One of them's completely demented, and the other one refuses to have anything to do with me – she's hardly likely to suddenly change her mind and say, "Oh, let's sit down and have a cosy chat about your grandmother," is she?'

'I don't know,' said Simon thoughtfully, 'that depends really what she's got against the rest of her family. We worked out from the bits that people were prepared to say in San Casciano, that the family were fairly influential fascists, but if the one you've found in Florence will have nothing to do with the rest of the family then, to me, that suggests that she's not a fascist and, as you don't appear to be one either, then you may well have a lot in common.'

Paul thought about it. 'Maybe,' he said, 'Maybe you're right, but I'm so pissed off with all of them at the moment that I'm going to give it a rest for a bit.'

''S'up to you, boyo, but if I were you, I wouldn't be able to let it rest.'

'We'll see. You never know,' said Paul, who had no intention of recommencing as that only ever seemed to result in frustration. 'But I will see what else there is to find out about my grandfather.'

As the following two days were the last completely free days he had before starting to teach, he decided to have a run down to Santa Croce sull'Arno the following day, to have a look at the area where his grandfather had been killed. A guide book to Tuscany he had said very little about Santa Croce, except that it had been established in the thirteenth century and was well known for furniture manufacturing.

When he got there, he parked down a side street, and asked an old woman who was walking down the street for the way to the centre. After he had followed her instructions, he found himself in a nondescript piazza surrounded by nondescript buildings. He picked a bar with a middle-aged bartender on the basis that the older the person he spoke to, the more likely they were to know something about the war.

Although he would have preferred a coffee, he ordered a latte macchiato as that would give him more of an excuse to linger over his drink. 'I expected Santa Croce to be more historic... I read in a book that it has been here since the thirteenth century.'

The bartender shook his head, 'The town might have been here since the thirteenth century, but the buildings haven't. Artillery fire and then a herd of Sherman tanks saw to that, back in forty-four.'

'I hadn't realised that there was so much damage. I thought that the Germans just blew all the bridges up, except the Ponte Vecchio.'

'That was just in Florence. Just because Hitler fancied himself as an artist and declared Florence an 'open city', they got off fairly lightly. Apart from the bridges and the buildings they blew up to block access to the Ponte Vecchio, it was mainly installations used by the military that were targeted. Outside Florence, however, in places that had buildings that were just as old but not as famous, they just flattened everything that was in the way – and Santa Croce was in the way.'

'So was that the English?'

'No. The English were on the other side of Florence. It was General Clarke's Americans who came through here. The Germans set up machine gun posts and mortars in as many buildings as possible, so the only safe way through for the Americans was just to flatten everything.'

'What happened to the people?'

'I was only small at the time, so I don't really remember, but people knew the battle was coming and so most people got out well before. Most went to stay with relatives in the countryside.'

Although the conversation with the barman had been more useful than he'd dared to hope, given recent experiences, there wasn't really anything else for him to see or do in Santa Croce so, as the weather was still nice, he decided that he'd have a drive round and see a few of the lesser known sights.

A road sign informed him that it was only ten kilometres to San Miniato and, as he vaguely remembered that the town had been in some way connected to Napoleon, he decided to pay it a visit. Although there was a newer section of the town in the wide valley bottom, unlike Santa Croce, enough of the old centre remained on the hillside to the south to make it an interesting place to have a wander round for a couple of hours. A castle with what appeared to be a well preserved tower, dominated the town from the hill behind, but when Paul read the plaque giving information, he discovered that although the castle dated from the thirteenth century, and had been mentioned by Dante, the tower and the other higher sections had been rebuilt in 1958 after having been blown up by the retreating Germans in 1944. The link between the dantesque location and the Second World War made him wonder if he would ever find out exactly how his grandfather came to be killed in the American zone, and if he did, whether his death would have been as dramatic as that of Pier delle Vigne, whose decision to kill himself by repeatedly banging his head on the floor of the castle when wrongly accused of treason, had given him pride of place amongst the suicides in Dante's Inferno.

The link to Napoleon turned out to be a little looser than he'd remembered, although there was a statue of the emperor at the centre of the attractive Piazza Buonaparte. Reading about the link in a small pamphlet he purchased about the town revealed that, it had been Napoleon's ancestors who had lived there, before his branch of the family had emigrated to Corsica. On the whole he decided that he liked the town and, when he left, he decided that he would come back and visit again, almost certainly in the second half of November when a number of posters informed him that the town would be host to the annual white-truffle fair and gastronomic experience.

According to the pamphlet he had purchased, it was less than twenty kilometres to Vinci and as he still had at least three hours before the light started to fade, he decided that he might as well make the most of the opportunity and visit Leonardo's home town before returning to Florence.

At some point north of the Arno, he missed a turning and, by the time he realised that he was on the wrong road, it seemed more sensible to go on and visit somewhere else, rather than turning round and looking for the Vinci road. Montecatini seemed to be a sensible alternative destination so he continued to head northwards. As he travelled, driving slowly so that he could look around as he drove and pulling into the side regularly to let other vehicles pass, he began to notice what appeared to be gravestones by the road, each flanked by a pair of cypresses. At first he thought that they must mark spots where people had died in road accidents, however, when he saw the third he realised that that explanation didn't really make sense as the road was quiet and did not seem the sort of place where fatal accidents would be a regular occurrence.

Intrigued, he stopped for a coffee in Cintolese and asked for information. 'The stones and the trees mark the places where victims of the *eccidio* were found.'

He shook his head, still puzzled, 'What is an *eccidio*? It's a word I've never come across before.'

'It's not a word you really want to come across, but it's one that everyone round here, and in some other places such as Stazzema and Marzabotto, have grown up with and will never forget. An *eccidio* is a massacre of innocent people by soldiers.'

'I'm sorry for not knowing but, what happened, and when?'

The woman sitting on the bench whom he had asked sighed, 'Sit down young man. A lot of people still won't talk about it but, I think that even though it's painful to talk about, those of us who survived have a duty to tell people, to make sure that what happened is never forgotten, even though some people find it inconvenient to remember.' Paul sat down.

Back in August forty-four, the Americans had been making their way northwards and had dug in temporarily on the south bank of the Arno. There were regular bombardments of the German defensive positions, most of which they deliberately set up close to towns, probably hoping to use the civilian population as shields - not that that seemed to make any difference to the Yankees. We all knew that the bombardments would only get worse until the Germans had retreated, so a lot of people decided to leave their homes and move into the Padule...'

'The *Padule*?'

'The *Padule* di Fucecchio,' and she waved an arm vaguely indicating the countryside that stretched out ahead of her to the west, '"*Padule*" is the Tuscan variant of the standard Italian "*Palude*" or marsh. The *Padule* of Fucecchio is the largest area of marshland in Italy. There are no roads that go all the way through, and unless you know what you are doing, it's very easy to get lost in there. We thought that we'd be safe. The Americans wouldn't bomb there and the Germans wouldn't risk getting lost in there. But that's not how it turned out. Early in the morning of the twenty-third of August, German soldiers, mainly based in Monsummano and Chiesina Uzzanese surrounded the *Padule* and then went in intending to kill everyone they found, and they found a lot of people. Some people managed to escape, or were injured and left for dead but recovered. One hundred and seventy three people were murdered in less than three hours: eight of them were below two years old at the time.'

Paul saw that tears were streaming down the woman's face although she seemed unaware of them. 'And you were one of the ones who escaped?'

'It didn't feel like escape at the time; I lost both my parents, my grandfather and my little brother. For a long time I wished I'd died with them, but I knew I had to live to be a witness, and because my father had deliberately sacrificed himself to let me escape.'

Paul didn't know what to say, and they both sat there for nearly five minutes before he managed to say, 'I didn't know... I never thought...'

'No,' said the woman, rising. 'That's the problem; nobody knows. But now that you do know, make sure that you tell others about it. Don't let the dead be forgotten,' and she walked off down the street without looking back.

Paul knew that he would not forget. One day, he thought, I'm going to bring my children here to make sure they know what humans are capable of doing to each other.

He gave up on the idea of stopping in Montecatini - that would have to wait for another day- and turned towards Florence once he had passed Monsummano.

Back in Florence he parked the Midget illegally in double file outside the bar, while he nipped upstairs and put his running clothes on, then, five minutes later he was back in the car driving out towards Careggi Hospital. Leaving the car on the road outside the rear of the hospital, he began to run up the road that took him towards the top of Monte Morello, passing through the little village of Cercina on the way. It took him an hour to get to the top and then another fifty minutes to get back. From the top, the sunset was spectacular, but it soon became dark and he had to go very carefully on his way back down the hill. However, ten minutes after reaching the Midget, he was parking again in Piazza D'Azeglio and jogged the remaining four hundred metres back home. He put a pan of water on to boil, put a cassette in his cassette player and had a quick shower to the strains of '*A horse with no name.*' Once out of the shower, he rapidly diced an onion and put it to soften in a centimetre of olive oil with a crumbled dried chilli, poured some *penne* and salt into the now boiling water, beat two large eggs and grated about a fairly large chunk of parmesan into it. Once he judged that the penne were done, he drained them and tipped them back into the empty pan which he placed on the smallest flame. The egg and cheese mix was then stirred in, followed immediately by the hot oil and onion. As soon as he was satisfied that the heat from the oil and the small flame had started to turn the egg in the mix, he tipped everything into a large bowl and poured himself a large glass of wine to accompany it.

Chapter 8

As the following day was the day before he had to begin teaching, he spent most of it going over the teaching materials he had been provided with and double checking any points of grammar that he wasn't sure of. He was really glad that he had had his year as a language assistant as that had been the first time that he had really had to apply any more than basic grammatical terms to his own language. Although it was perfectly possible to speak English well as a native speaker, he had soon learnt that speakers of languages with more complicated structures often felt the need to learn rules. He had been baffled by a private student who had asked him if he could explain how to use the second pluperfect in English, and was sure that the student had not stayed with him long as a result of his obvious confusion. It had only made him feel slightly less foolish when he had looked it up and found that the second pluperfect only existed in German: he knew that, at the time, he would have been equally helpless if the student had just asked about the pluperfect – now he didn't intend to get caught out again.

With settling into his new routine, it wasn't until the following Friday and the start of his three-day weekend when he returned to his enquiries. Unfortunately, it was raining heavily, so he was unable to put the Midget's hood down as he headed out of the city, back towards the British Military Cemetery. He had to drive slowly as the rain overwhelmed the flimsy windscreen-wipers of the Midget and there was the constant risk of finding a puddle too deep for the low-slung car to make it through. However, he was fairly confident that there would be very few other visitors at the cemetery and he wouldn't have to wait before seeing the custodian.

Having experienced Italian rain during his year as an Assistant he had acquired an umbrella to keep in the car but it was raining so hard that the raindrops seemed to be bouncing up off the floor and reaching the underside of the umbrella in the seventy metres from the roadside spot where he left the car to the custodian's office and water was dripping off him as he pushed the door closed behind him.

'Can I help? … Ah, it's you, Mr…Caddick. Brave of you to turn out on a day like this.'

'Brave, or more likely foolish – I don't think I've ever seen rain like this. I think I'd better stay standing or you'll never get your seat dry again.'

'Oh, don't worry about the seats, they'll soon dry off. Sit down. Can I get you a cup of tea?'

'Real English tea?'

'The very best. I have it sent out by a friend in London. I usually keep it for myself, but I think that after venturing out on a day like this, you deserve a cup. Just excuse me a moment,' and he disappeared through a small door that blended into the rear wall of the office.

When he came back he had a mug of tea in each hand, one of which he pushed over towards Paul as he sat down and gestured vaguely towards some sachets of sugar which had obviously been accumulated from various bars he had visited. 'Now. You want to know if I've managed to find out any more about your grandfather.' Paul nodded. 'It wasn't easy to work out, but I think I managed to get a fairly good handle on it eventually.' Paul could see that the custodian was looking forward to telling the story and nodded encouragingly. 'So, how much do you already know already about your grandfather's service record?'

'I only really know the bare bones. I know he joined up in thirty nine, so probably as soon as war was declared. I know that he spent some time in North Africa, that he died in Italy in August 1944, and that he was posthumously awarded the Military Cross – that's about it really. Anything else you can tell me will be a bonus.'

The custodian smiled. 'You're right about him joining up: he volunteered in August 1939 and by December had been promoted to Corporal. By that time he was over in France with the B.E.F. – Oh sorry, that's the British Expeditionary Force –

During the retreat to Dunkirk, he appears to have distinguished himself by taking out a German machine gun post single handed, saving the lives of at least five men. He also, by the way, appears to have been put on a charge for insubordination at around the same time. The charge seems to have been withdrawn after his heroics during the retreat. The next significant entries on his record are from the following year, by which time he had been posted to Crete. Again, he was mentioned in despatches for outstanding bravery both in the defence of Heraklion and an action at Babani Khani and, when the remnants of the British forces regrouped after being evacuated to North Africa, he was promoted to Sergeant. By the time Tunis was taken he had been promoted again to Staff sergeant, just in time for the invasion of Sicily. It's after the invasion of Sicily that his record starts to get interesting, or rather – it doesn't.' Paul looked at him quizzically.

'I'm afraid I don't quite follow.'

'No. That's because we're not meant to. Ten days after arriving in Sicily, Staff Sergeant Caddick was promoted to Warrant Officer First Class – somewhat odd, as he he appears to have missed out Warrant Officer Second Class. After that his records have been redacted – there are just several pages of blacked out writing, until his body is transferred by the Americans, with limited details stating only that he died from wounds received in the course of his duty.'

'Was that a usual occurrence? Were many soldiers' records kept confidential during campaigns – surely military historians know almost every move that was made in the campaigns?'

The custodian gave a self-satisfied smile and Paul realised that he still had more to add but was wanting to make the information he had to give even more dramatic. He waited for the further revelations that he was sure were coming.

'You said that you knew your grandfather was posthumously awarded the MC, do you know why?' Paul shook his head.

'No. Even if you had seen the citation, you'd be none the wiser. In almost every case, MCs are awarded for specific acts of bravery – a specific act of bravery that is detailed in the citation. Very unusually, your grandfather's just says "for conspicuous bravery over and above the call of duty" – not much use you may think, however...' and he paused for effect with his right hand raised, index finger pointing upwards, 'the citation does say who it was who recommended him for the honour. Do you know who was in charge of the British and Commonwealth Forces in Italy?' Again Paul shook his head.

'At the time, it was General Alexander, shortly after to be Field Marshal Earl Alexander of Tunis and Supreme Allied Commander Mediterranean. Your grandfather's citation was signed by Alexander personally, something that was almost unheard of. What does that tell you?'

'Could he have been some sort of Aide de Camp?' hazarded Paul.

'Very unlikely. Can I ask whether your grandfather spoke Italian?'

'I assume so. I believe that he spent some time in Italy and almost certainly met my grandmother here.'

The custodian nodded his head with a satisfied smile.' I thought he probably did. There was a special section of the security services based in Baker Street in London. One of those sections that everyone knows exists but no-one will admit to officially. After the allied invasion of Sicily, they identified soldiers who were both intelligent and spoke fluent Italian, and used them for special duties. This was generally liaison work but could involve sabotage and other belligerent acts. I've no idea what your grandfather did but I'd put money on it that he was one of the 'Baker Street Boys' and that it was what he did undercover that earned him the gratitude of Alexander,'

'Wow. That's incredible. Have you found any proof of this?'

'I'm afraid not. I've just gone on the balance of probabilities and I can't think of any other explanation that links together the facts that we already know.'

'Are there no government records in the Public Record Office that would confirm this?

'I'm sure there are, but I'm afraid you'll have to wait until 2044 before you're able to access them; the MoD gets very possessive over its secrets. If you're extremely lucky, you just might come across someone who remembers your grandfather during the last year of his life, but I would think that it's extremely unlikely, particularly as he would have been undercover, and we don't know what name he used.'

'You've done a fantastic job. I didn't expect anything like this. I don't know how to thank you.'

The custodian smiled, 'I think I said, last week, that I like to know everything about all my charges and, even though everyone has their own individual story, they are usually fairly straightforward. I have to admit that I enjoy it when I come across a challenge like your grandfather. He's certainly added some variety to my last week – so it should really be me who's thanking you.'

Paul stood up, smiled and held out his hand, 'I think we can agree to differ about who has got the most out of this. I hope you find some more interesting cases to look into and, if I do happen to find out any more about the last year of my grandfather's life, I'll let you know, so that you have the full story. You deserve it.'

Paul was very pleased by what he had found out about his grandfather. He didn't see any point in trying to find anyone who had known his grandfather during the last year of his life, assuming that as a task it would prove to be impossible, and he'd had enough of that in searching for his Campolargo relatives.

Chapter 9

For the next two weeks he was quite happy settling into his two teaching jobs and preparing lessons for his private students, with all of whom, he found he got on. It was at the end of his fifth week in Florence that there was an unexpected development, or rather two unexpected developments.

During the Friday he had taken the Midget down the motorway and spent most of the day looking round Cortona and taking photographs of picturesque corners of the town, experimenting with two new filters he had bought for his camera. When he got home he considered developing the film in his sink and having a look at the negatives, but then decided that it could wait for a rainy day, and went out into the centre.

Being Friday, the obvious place to head for was the *Birreria Centrale*, where there were bound to be some of the people he had met through Simon, and probably Simon himself. As it happened Simon wasn't there but Lucio was, with Gabriela and the inevitable Clara; Paul was slightly surprised to see Lucio as he'd noticed that the Calabrian only usually mixed with the British and Americans when Simon was there – maybe Clara was setting the agenda he thought.

He greeted a few people he'd come across before and then sat down with his beer next to Lucio. 'What's this – a conversion to beer as your drink of choice?'

'Not quite. I don't mind the odd one now and again so I'm quite comfortable here but, the main reason why I came here tonight was that I was hoping to see you.'

'To see me! I'm honoured.'

'And so you should be. Especially when you hear what I've got to tell you,' Paul raised his eyebrows, ' I think that, just by chance, I – or rather Gabbi – may have found you a way into your family.'

'I'm all ears; tell me more.'

'Not now – it's too complicated with this noise – Can you come round in the morning – but not too early,' he looked across to where Clara was telling an American student where were the best places to buy handbags, then in a lowered voice, 'Gabbi will be there too. Her parents are away for the weekend, so once we've got rid of the bodyguard, she'll be coming over.'

Lucio and the two girls left about half an hour after Paul's arrival and in less than an hour after that, when he had finished his second beer, Paul also excused himself and made his way home. He put a Genesis tape on when he got home and settled down with *Lo Specchio Cieco*, a novel by Michele Prisco, determined that he wasn't going to get his hopes up too high, only to have them dashed again.

'I had an exam on Monday,' said Gabriela, ' and, you probably don't know, because it's different in England, but before the exam, people's nerves get to them in different ways: some just want to sit quietly and not speak to anyone, while others are really chatty and just want to talk about anything to take their minds off the exam. Well, on Tuesday, while we were waiting I was talking to one of the chatty ones – yes, OK, Lucio, I know – pot calling the kettle black and all that – well anyway, we were chatting and the other girl, Rosa, was saying that she'd answered the phone a few weeks ago and passed the caller to her mum. It seems that someone claimed to be a distant relative from abroad – which she didn't think could be right – but that her mum had been really unfriendly with the caller and had refused to discuss it later. Apparently she'd even told Rosa that if the person rang again, she should hang up straight away.'

'And you think that this phone call she was talking about was my phone call to the house of the people who I think are my relatives? It could be – what's her surname? There was a Rosanna on the electoral register – could Rosa be short for Rosanna?'

'I'm afraid I don't know her surname, she only started at the University a few weeks ago. It's only because I wanted to redo one of the first year exams, to improve my overall mark, that I know her at all. But Rosa could easily be short for Rosanna.'

'Did you mention to her that you know me?'

'No. It didn't mean anything to me at the time. It was only later when I was talking to Lucio that we made the connection.'

'I could do with talking to her,' said Paul thoughtfully, 'but I'm not quite sure how to go about it, especially if she's been told to have nothing to do with me.'

'Leave it to us. We know some of the group who she hangs out with at the University, so we'll be able to talk her into meeting you. Just give us a few days to sort things out. I'll call round and let you know as soon as I've arranged something.'

'That's great. If I'm not in, you can leave a note with Mimmo in the bar downstairs.'

It was Mimmo who provided the second unexpected development when he called in the bar on his way back home. Mimmo was serving a family of German tourists with cappuccinos and orange juices when Paul entered, and had to wait while the mother carefully counted out a handful of small change, before turning to his regular customer. As he started reloading the machine to make Paul's coffee, he said, 'I've had a message for you since yesterday afternoon – I'll get it for you in a second.'

Paul shook his head, 'I took the notices down about private lessons ages ago – maybe someone made a note of the number just in case they needed it later.'

'I don't think it was about a lesson, it seemed more likely to be someone offering you another job. The woman said she was from some Institute or other.'

Mimmo served the next customer, which involved preparing a *panino* with *prosciutto* and *mozzarella*, as well as a drink, before he was able to retrieve the message. 'Here you are – a Professoressa Viviani.'

He noted with surprise that the *professoressa* was from the Institute of Resistance in Tuscany in Via Carducci; it had been almost a month since he'd been there and he'd more or less forgotten about it. Maybe he'd been a bit quick to write them off, he thought, after all it was run by volunteers and there was no reason why his enquiry should have been prioritised. He looked at his watch: five to twelve on a Saturday morning – probably too late, but worth a try as otherwise he'd have to wait until Monday morning.

He looked over towards the phone to see if it was free and Mimmo, anticipating his request pushed a *gettone* across the counter. He tapped the numbers in, fully expecting his *gettone* to be returned when there was no answer but, to his surprise, as he was just about to give up, the tone changed and the *gettone* dropped.

'*Pronto, Istituto Storico della Resistenza Toscana,*'

'Ah – *buongiorno*. My name is Paul Caddick, I'm returning a call from Professoressa Viviani.'

'You're in luck, Mr Caddick. I'm Anna-Maria Viviani. I was just in the process of locking up before leaving for the weekend.'

'I can ring back on Monday morning if that's more convenient.'

'No need to ring, Mr Caddick. If you have half an hour free on Monday morning we could meet in my office. I gather from your telephone number that you live not far from here.'

'I'm free up until half past twelve on Monday, and you're right, I'm only five minutes away, so whatever time suits you best.'

He heard a rustle of paper as if pages were being turned, then, 'Shall we say nine-fifteen or would ten-thirty suit you better.'

'I think I'd prefer the later time if that's OK, I'm teaching up until ten-thirty in the evening.'

'Alright, that's settled then. I'll see you on Monday,' and he heard a click as the phone was put down. Maybe there was something to be discovered about his grandmother's family. He assumed that the *professoressa* was not just a receptionist and that suggested that whatever the institute had to communicate was of some importance. Hopefully, she wasn't just going to inform him that there was still one of the family living in Viuzzo delle Corti.

Just after twenty five past ten on the Monday morning Paul stood with his finger on the doorbell of the Institute. As before, the door clicked open almost immediately after he rang and he made his way in to the reception. The desk was still piled high with paper and folders but the receptionist had changed; the earnest looking receptionist had been replaced by a teenager with flared jeans, the classic red Che Guevara tee-shirt, John Lennon glasses and hair tied back in a pony-tail.

'Morning,' he said, 'You the geezer here to see the boss?' he said, in an English that betrayed an over-exposure to nineteen sixties gangster films.

'If the boss is Professoressa Viviani, then I am,' answered Paul and then with a smile, 'Your English is very good, if a little cinematographic.'

It was the young man's turn to smile, 'That's good. I'm going to be an actor. I've already worked as an extra on Zeffirelli's latest film: *Othello:* you'll be able to see it in the cinema early next year.'

'I'm impressed. Is the *Professoressa* free?'

'Oh, she'll be through to get you in a minute: she's very keen on punctuality so she won't keep you waiting.'

'Do you work here often?'

'I do a bit whenever I can. My grandfather was a partisan, so I like to help whenever I can.' Paul would have liked to find out more, but at that moment a casually elegant woman, probably in her late sixties, came into the reception area from the door opposite the one which Paul knew led to the study area.

'Mr Caddick, I hope I haven't kept you waiting long,'

'No not at all. I was a couple of minutes early, and your very efficient receptionist has been looking after me since I arrived.'

'Giacomo, I hope you haven't been boring the *Signore* with your fanciful notions.'

'No, *Nonna.*' So the boy on reception was the *professoressa*'s grandson, thought Paul; nepotism was alive and well in Italy and he also now knew that the *professoressa*'s husband had been a partisan.

'His conversation has been very interesting, and his English is very good.'

'Alright. Would you like to come through? … Coffee, or would you prefer tea?'

'Coffee would be fine, thank you, 'Giacomo.' The boy nodded to show he understood and got up to go and make the drinks.

Professoressa Viviani's office was simply but comfortably furnished: unusually the desk was curved which made it seem less threatening than standard rectangular ones, as did the soft leather chairs that faced it.

She offered him a cigarette from an inlaid wooden box, and he declined. 'Firstly, Mr Caddick, may I apologise for the length of time it takes us to deal with enquiries: I'm afraid that we don't have many members of staff. Luckily, one of my researchers was looking through the forms to prioritise them and the name Campolargo caught his eye – knowing that I have a particular interest in the Campolargo's, she passed it on to me straight away.'

He leaned back in his chair and looked puzzled.

'May I ask you, Mr Caddick, how much you know about your grandmother's family?'

It did not take Paul long to summarise the very limited knowledge that he had started with, and the limited amount of information he had discovered since his arrival.

'And, can I ask, what you think about the family based on what you have discovered so far.'

He felt a penetrating gaze on him as he pondered the question. 'I don't think, I'd really thought about it like that – I mean, I hadn't really thought about them as people – I suppose that I've just really been wanting to find out something about my grandmother. Because she died only two days after my father was born, nobody has really been able to tell me anything about her in England and since I've been here, the only things I've managed to discover about other family members have all been bad – I suppose that really, I'd now like someone not just to tell me a little bit about her, but also that she wasn't like the rest of her family... maybe even that she went to England to get away from them,' he looked at her, 'I'm sorry, I'm trying to work it out as I answer – did that make any sort of sense?'

'I think so. I'm sorry to have put you on the spot but, I'm sure you will appreciate, this Institute was originally set up to help former partisans and their families along with families of victims of fascism. Our role in documenting the events of the *ventennio* and collecting information on the protagonists was one which came later and which has always been secondary to our original purpose although obviously, as time goes by, and there are less and less survivors for us to help, creating a record for posterity is becoming more important.' She paused, 'What we do not do, and what we will never knowingly do, is to provide fascists with the means to re-establish links.'

'And you are worried that I may support the ideas that my grandmother's family held.'

She laughed, 'Not any more, Mr Caddick, but it was obviously something that needed to be clarified.'

'If it's any help, I've been an active member of the Anti-Nazi League in England since I was fourteen and have been on plenty of demonstrations.'

She held her hands up, 'It's alright Mr Carrick. I believe you. Now, let me tell you what I know about your family; I think it's probably best that I begin at the beginning rather than just focussing on your grandmother.' He nodded. 'OK. The Campolargo family originated in the Mugello, to the north of Florence and probably came down to the city to work for one of the Medici family during the fifteenth century. There are various mentions of the family in the city records, but they first became important towards the end of the reign of Ferdinando 1 at the beginning of the seventeenth century. The head of the family, one Alfonso Campolargo, spent some time as Governor of Livorno, imposing the authority of the Medici, and seems to have been rewarded for this by the granting of a large area of land to the south of San Casciano. This area seems to have been developed into a prosperous agricultural estate over the next two or three generations, and the family's properties within the city itself were either used by minor branches of the family or rented out to produce additional income. Whether it was just a lucky chance, or whether it was the result of a very astute political calculation, Gastone Campolargo married a first cousin of Francis lll of Lorraine, the year before Francis was nominated by the European Powers who met together to carve up Europe at the end of the Polish war of Succession, as the new Grand Duke of Tuscany. Are you still with me?'

'Yes. I think I've got it all so far, although I may need to to check through my notes after I've written it all down afterwards. I had no idea that that the family would have so much history.'

'That's probably the only benefit of our *campanilismo* here in Italy; we don't like to move out of range of the sound of our own bell-towers, so our history is easier to trace. Anyway, your family seems to have done very well as courtiers until 1848 when...' she consulted a folder she had pulled out of a desk drawer, '... Arrigo Campolargo jumped the gun a little. He clearly realised that unification was on its way and threw his support behind the leaders of the popular insurrection which temporarily deposed Duke Leopold II in 1849. On Leopold's return, Arrigo was effectively exiled to his estate at Bargino, just south of San Casciano, but did not suffer any economic penalty, and was able to become a prominent member of the provisional government when Leopoldo abdicated ten years later, and then maintained his influence under the new Italian state.

'So far, your family had just acted how many other wealthy families behaved; they were very good at looking after their own interests, and quite astute in choosing their allegiances, without ever demonstrating any deep held convictions. They were fairly harsh landlords, but so were many others.' She hesitated, 'Things really start to get interesting, at least from my point of view, with Domenico Campolargo, Arrigo's grandson. That would be your great-grandfather. He was born in 1869 and became heir to the family estates at the beginning of 1885 when his father was one of the few Italian officers killed during the invasion of Massawa, part of what is now known as Sudan. As Arrigo spent most of his time in Rome, Domenico studied Law at the University in Rome, and then studied further in Paris at the Sorbonne when Arrigo managed to get him attached to the Italian Embassy. While he was at the Sorbonne, it appears that he struck up a friendship with Filippo Marinetti...'

'Marinetti the futurist?'

'Yes. Marinetti did his baccalauréat there before completing his studies in Pavia. Now, how much do you know about Marinetti and his politics?'

'Not very much. I know that he was the inspiration for the futurist movement and that because of the futurist philosophy that violent change and mechanisation were necessary in all areas, many of the futurists became active supporters of the fascists, but that's about it I'm afraid.'

'Then you already know more than most. But, what most people aren't aware of is that Marinetti's belief in the value of violence grew out of his contact with the French philosopher Georges Sorel, and it was Domenico Campolargo who introduced Marinetti to Sorel's circle in Paris. In 1918 Marinetti formed the Futurist Political Party and in 1919, encouraged by Campolargo this merged with Mussolini's *Fasci Italiani di Combattimento* to form the Italian Fascist Party. Now, some of this is conjecture, but I believe that large parts of the Fascist Manifesto that was officially co-written by Marinetti and Alceste de Ambris, were actually written by Campolargo. As with many of your more distant ancestors, Domenico Campolargo had the ability to operate in the shadows; he continued to wield influence with the existing government until the March on Rome, when he was able to seamlessly transfer his support to the new regime.' She paused again and looked calmly at Paul.

'Let me get this straight. You're saying that I am descended from someone who was responsible for Italy becoming a fascist country!'

'I think that that is probably overstating his influence somewhat. Mussolini would almost certainly have come to power even if your family had never existed, but Domenico Campolargo did help provide a gloss of intellectual credence to the movement.'

'Phew! I think I'm starting to understand why the surviving daughter wants to have no contact with anyone to do with the family.'

'Ah,' she said taking a deep breath, 'I'm afraid that you haven't heard everything yet, and in some ways, it gets worse... Are you sure that you want to know any more?'

'I think that at this point, I need to know everything – unless you're going to tell me that I'm related to Hitler as well, I doubt that it can be any worse.'

She half smiled, 'No,. You don't have to worry about Hitler, but you do have connections to Alessandro Pavolini and to the *Banda Carità*.'

'I've been reading a bit about Pavolini, and know that Aristide Campolargo, who I assume was a son of Domenico, was closely associated with him, but I've never heard of the *Banda Carità*.' said Paul.

'I'll explain, but it's probably best if I go through things in order. As you will be aware, if you've been reading about Pavolini, he was a brilliant student, and as such, he was talent spotted and his career was nurtured by Domenico Campolargo from very early on. Depending which book you have read, it may well say that Pavolini just happened to be in Rome at the time of the march, so he was able to join its latter stages and be recognised by the new regime as one its most prominent figures,' she looked at Paul, who nodded to signify that that was pretty much what he had read.

'It wasn't quite like that. At the time the march began, it wasn't clear whether or not the military would be called in to suppress it. Domenico Campolargo advised Pavolini to keep out of the way until it was clear that the march would succeed. Pavolini and Aristide Campolargo were then advised to join the march in time for the last few kilometres and the triumphant entry into the capital, assuring Pavolini was seen in the right place at the right time. From then on, Domenico kept more in the background while Aristide established himself as Pavolini's most loyal lieutenant. Domenico and Pavolini were, despite their political failings, both very cultured men and some of the things that they did to encourage the masses by linking culture and history with the fascist regime had a lasting effect on the florentine cultural scene. They were both, however, also ruthless practical men: Domenico invested in arms manufacture, being guaranteed lucrative government contracts, and Pavolini 'persuaded' investors to construct the Firenze-Mare Autostrada, which was only the second motorway to be built in Italy. Once built, of course, it was priced out of reach of most people but assured Pavolini of rapid access to his lover in Forte dei Marmi.

'Aristide, as far as I've been able to ascertain, had no cultural sensitivities; he was more interested in practical matters. If Pavolini's projects, in Florence and beyond, encountered any difficulties, Aristide would arrange for the *squadristi* to apply however much persuasion was necessary to remove the difficulty. In 1943, when the Italian fascists needed to prove their loyalty to their German friends, it was Aristide, who identified Mario Caritā as the ideal person to head up a new department, the DSS or Department for Special Services, which was given carte blanche to track down and extract confessions from 'enemies of the regime. He recruited ex-prisoners who had been considered too dangerous to transfer from prisons into the regular forces, as well as some others who he hand-picked from the Montelupo Asylum. They were probably the most ruthless of any of the groups of Fascist enforcers under Mussolini's Republic of Salō. Very few people who were arrested by them and taken to the basement of their headquarters on Via Bolognese, which was generally known as Villa Triste, survived to tell the tale.'

Paul was shocked; he hoped that that was it, that there were no more revelations to come about his family. He had been looking forward to telling the rest of the family back in England about their Florentine background, maybe with a few little salacious details that he had discovered to make it more interesting – but this – how could you tell your parents and your brother and sister that this was their family background? It wouldn't have been so bad if it had all been hundreds of years ago – but this was only about forty years ago, well within many people's living memories.

'There is a bit more. Domenico Campolargo's youngest daughter married a cousin of Pavolini. It appears that

Campolargo saw Pavolini as a likely future leader and was keen to link the two families together.'

Paul tried to make sense of what he was hearing; this must be the woman who now lived in Viuzzo delle Corti but if she was not only a Campolargo but also a Pavolini, why the refusal to have anything to do with him? He couldn't think of any logical explanation – it was something he would have to try and think through calmly. 'Do you know what happened to the rest of the family – after the war?'

She nodded and pulled a sheet of A4 paper from the back of her file. 'Domenico Campolargo saw what was coming and was "on business" in Switzerland at the time Badoglio signed the armistice in 1943. A significant part of his investments in arms manufacturing had been routed through Swiss based companies, and he lived very comfortably in a large house overlooking Lac Leman, until his death at the age of eighty-three in 1950.' She consulted her notes before continuing, 'His wife, Elvira Alessandra dei Cionci a distant relative of the Savoia – the Italian royal family - who he had married in 1898 when she was only seventeen, had a series of nervous breakdowns and had been "convalescing" since the birth of her seventh child in 1918, had died the previous year. The second son, Filippo, was caught up in the Kefalonia débâcle in forty-three and died at the hands of the Germans; his widow, I believe, you have already met. The eldest daughter, Margarita, was married to a Sienese lawyer, Alfonso Guerrini and...'

Paul interrupted her, 'is that Guerrini of "Guerrini and Becalossi"?

'That was Guerrini of "Guerrini and Becalossi". He died in the 1960s and the current Guerrini is his son. I believe that the firm still does a lot of work for influential people on the right of politics. The next son, Umberto, for a long time ran the family estates while Domenico and Aristide occupied themselves with politics, however, after the armistice in forty-three he became very closely associated with Caritā. Unfortunately, while Caritā himself was shot and killed by the Americans while resisting arrest, Umberto, with his contacts, served a few months in prison and then was able to get out of the country before the true extent of his crimes were uncovered. He and his family first joined his father in Switzerland but, when people started to ask questions and extradition was mentioned, they disappeared. I believe, but have no proof, that they ended up in the United States. A fourth son died in childhood and the second daughter, who presumably was your grandmother disappeared without trace in 1934. As you can imagine, there were lots of rumours about what had happened to her, but until you filled in our enquiry form a few weeks ago, there was no definite news.'

'That still leaves the youngest daughter, doesn't it? The one who still lives in Florence.'

'Although you would think that as she still lives here, we would have plenty of information, we actually know very little about her. She married Pavolini's cousin, Gian Giacomo Melluso in 1940 and was seen regularly at social events for the next year or so. In July 1944 when the streets of Florence were very unsafe, Melluso appears to have been killed by a stray bullet, leaving Maddalena as a widow – his body was found just outside his house. Maddalena gave birth to a daughter eight and a half months later and has lived as a virtual recluse since then. She sold Melluso's house in Piazza dei Donati and moved into a much smaller one in San Frediano until selling up again and moving in with her daughter and son-in-law after her daughter's marriage to a Professor of Classics in one of the *Liceos*. In the past, we tried to contact Maddalena Campolargo to interview her about her family, but our requests were always refused. It's quite a few years now since we last made any attempt to speak to her.' She smiled and, after a pause, said 'I think, Mr Caddick, you said that you had a teaching commitment, and we seem to have taken far longer than the half an hour that you anticipated.'

He looked at his watch and saw with surprise that it had somehow got to ten past twelve. He thanked her effusively for all the information with which she had provided him but she waved aside his thanks. She stood up a fraction before him and held out her hand which he took. As was about to open the door, a thought struck him and he turned back towards her. 'Could I just ask – do you hold such in depth information on all those who were involved with the fascists?'

She shook her head, 'No, Mr Caddick, usually we just have the bare details on file so that we can cross reference them with accounts given to us by the survivors...'

'So how is it that...'

'I have a particular interest in your family, Mr Caddick, particularly Umberto Campolargo, and, if he is still alive, and is unwise enough ever to set foot in Italy again, I want to make sure that there is enough evidence to make sure that he pays for his crimes. Now, Mr Caddick, I'm afraid that you will have to excuse me. If you do find out any further information about your family, I would be very grateful if you could share it with me.'

When Paul got back to his bedsit that evening, he couldn't remember anything that he'd taught in either of the schools or in his private lesson with Chiara, the university student who needed to improve her conversational skills. He hoped that he hadn't said anything stupid, but his thoughts had been miles away. He was just an ordinary young man from a fairly ordinary family, to whom nothing really interesting ever really happened; the most interesting event he remembered was his grandmother winning just over three hundred pounds on the football pools. Now, all of a sudden, his family seemed to have played a significant part in the major events in twentieth century European history – it was mind blowing. What was he supposed to say to his father – ring him when he finished his nine to five job as Clerk to Glossop Council – 'Hi Dad. Guess what – your grandfather was responsible for Mussolini coming to power Oh, and by the way, your dad was a spy!' No. Most of what he had found out, he would need to keep to himself.

As he finished teaching relatively early on Tuesday, he bought a flask of wine and some prosciutto, and invited himself round to Simon and Lucio's where he felt able to discuss most of what he'd been told the previous day. Lucio, who as an archaeology student also had a good grasp of Italian history, helped him contextualise some of the information that the professoressa had given him about the earlier historical periods.

According to Lucio, finding out any more about the more recent period would be very difficult. With the exception of a few die-hard fascists who were harmless because they were easily identified and so easily ignored, to talk to most people in Italy, you would get the impression that there had not really been many true fascists and that everyone had really supported the opposition. It wasn't true of course; the majority of people had been very happy with Mussolini when he appeared to be successful. What had happened was that after an initial period of recriminations and witch-hunts, people had accepted the more comfortable narrative in which most of them became victims at least to some extent. The next generation, Lucio's generation, had grown up with that narrative and it had become the accepted one. In Lucio's view, the only way that Paul could find out more about things that his relatives had done was to talk to a lot of old people and painstakingly cross-reference the information they provided. Obviously, the daughter of Domenico Campolargo who lived on Viuzzo delle Corti would be a useful source – if he could get to her.

To that end, Lucio told him that he was going to go along to a lecture with Gabriela on the following day and that, hopefully, Rosa Conte would be there. If she were, then he would try and convince her to meet Paul.

Paul asked if Lucio knew anything more about her, but he shook his head. Gabriela had said that she was friendly but quite reserved, although that could be because she was still a very recent addition to the group of archaeology students. Lucio agreed that it was best not to mention any of the things that Paul had discovered so far. With Simon, they spent an hour or so indulging in fruitless speculation about how Rosa's grandmother fit into the overall scheme of things, and why she was so determined not to have anything to do with Paul or any other Campolargos. By the time the flask of wine was finished, their speculations had started to become so bizarre and improbable that they were no longer able to take the subject seriously. Paul felt far more relaxed by the time he left their flat, glad that he'd been able to share his story with friends and that they had helped him to put it in perspective; yes, people to whom he was related – even if he'd never known them – had done terrible things, but he was in no way responsible for their actions and had no reason to feel any guilt.

Chapter 10

Wednesday was another day when he was teaching until late, but when he called in the bar on the Thursday morning Mimmo had a message for him from Lucio. He was to meet Lucio, Gabriela and Rosa at seven-thirty on the Friday evening at Enoteca Fuori Porta in the San Niccolò area.

Mimmo also handed him a note from Signora Vaccherini, letting him know how much he needed to leave for the electricity bill. He asked if she had said when she would collect it, but Mimmo said that she had just said that all her tenants should leave the amounts they owed with Mimmo. Some disappointment must have shown on Paul's face for Mimmo looked serious and leaned forwards towards him. 'Paul. May I give you a word of advice?' and then, without waiting for an answer, 'Don't waste any time thinking about the *Signora*... She allows herself occasional diversions, but she's absolutely devoted to her husband and never allows the diversions to become any more than that – I hope you don't mind me saying this, and I don't want you to take it the wrong way.'

Paul thought for a moment as Mimmo watched, then he smiled and squeezed Mimmo's hand. 'Thanks,' he said, and Mimmo's smile showed relief. To Paul's surprise, he too found that he felt relief as he made his way into the centre, and he realised that, now he knew exactly where he stood with the *Signora* – nowhere – it was as if a weight had been lifted from him, all the better because he hadn't realised that the weight had been there.

He felt that it was important to make a good impression on Rosa and, after buying himself some shoe cleaning equipment in the Standa store in Via Pietrapiana, he made his way to the San Lorenzo market where, after making it clear that he was not a tourist and had no intention of paying tourist prices, he managed to get fifty percent knocked off the ticket price of a beige Wrangler cowboy style shirt which had black patterned shoulders and cuffs. The shirt had been on display on a mannequin, which was very convenient as he didn't have an iron with which to take out any creases. When he left his bedsit again at seven o'clock, he was wearing his new shirt under a brown leather bomber-jacket that had been a twenty-first birthday present from David, his elder brother. The black jeans he wore were fashionably flared, and overall, he felt very pleased with his appearance.

Leaving home at seven meant that he was there in good time which gave him the dilemma of whether to grab a table inside or outside. If he had been on his own, or with a group of Anglo-Saxon friends, he wouldn't have hesitated to grab one of the two free tables outside but, as he was meeting three Italians, and it was late October, he doubted very much that they would want to sit outside amongst the Dutch, German and Australian tourists who occupied the other tables. The problem with going inside immediately, however, was that he wouldn't be able to see the others arrive. He decided to pretend to study the menu that was pinned up outside to fill the time in until the others arrived.

While he was waiting he was pleasantly distracted by the sight of a pretty girl with a mass of dark hair which she tossed back over her right shoulder as she sat down at one of the free tables outside. The top she wore was a fairly baggy one, gathered in by a large belt at the waist. Below she had on a pleated denim skirt which rode up momentarily above her knee as she crossed her legs revealing very shapely sun-tanned calves. She was clearly waiting for someone – probably her boyfriend – and Paul was just thinking what a lucky person the boyfriend must be, when Gabriela and Lucio arrived.

As Gabriela and Lucio turned the corner, the girl with the sun-tanned calves stood up and waved, and Paul realised who she must be – he felt gladder than ever that he had made the effort with his appearance before coming out.

'Ciao, Rosa.'

'Ciao, Gabbi – Ciao, Lucio,' and there were double air-kisses all round before Paul was introduced.

'Rosa,' said Gabbi, 'this is Paul, who must be your second cousin, or your first cousin once removed, or something like that.'

'Hello,' said Paul, suddenly feeling unsure of himself and not really knowing what to say, 'I noticed you arrive, but hadn't realised who you were. I wasn't expecting...' He stopped, aware that he couldn't say what he hadn't been expecting without having to overload her with compliments that were certainly inappropriate at that stage of their acquaintance.

'I think I'm probably a little bit unusual amongst my friends by always being early for appointments – I'm sure you weren't expecting a Florentine girl to be early,' she said with a smile, helping him out of his difficulty.

'Let's go inside,' said Lucio, 'it starts to get chilly quite quickly here when the sun goes down. They moved inside and were directed to a table on the opposite side of the room to the windows, where they were soon brought menus.

'The cold-meat platters and the cheese platters are very good here,' said Gabriela, who appeared to be taking charge of the group, 'if everyone's OK with it, we could order a couple of those to share,' No-one had any objections. Lucio suggested that it would work out far cheaper to buy a litre of the house-wine rather than separate glasses. He pointed out that as the Fuori Porta advertised itself as a wine-bar, their house-wine would have to be good to avoid damaging their reputation. Everyone saw the logic of this and Gabriela called over the waitress to order the two platters, the wine and a jug of tap water. While Gabriela and Lucio made suggestions and sorted out the order, Paul took the opportunity to study Rosa more closely, and he was aware that he too was under scrutiny.

'We did speak, very briefly, a few weeks ago... but then you passed me on to your mother.'

She sighed and shook her head, 'I'm really sorry about that. I've absolutely no idea what all that was about. Apart from a cousin on my father's side, who lives in Bologna and who we hardly ever see, we don't have any other relatives, so I would have expected them to be delighted when you appeared out of the blue.'

'There's no need for you to apologise – it was hardly your fault, and until we know what your mother's reason was, we can't really judge.'

She smiled, 'That sounds very reasonable. But tell me, why do you think that you're related to my grandmother? I've never heard anything about any English relatives. Are you sure that you've got it right and there isn't some mistake?'

'I'm sure I'm right, but it's quite a long story, so I think we'd better leave it until after we've eaten these,' he said, leaning back to make it easier for the approaching waitress to place the two large wooden platters on the table.'

Once they had finished the platters and each had consumed three balls of different flavoured ice-creams, Lucio prompted him to tell his story to Rosa. He explained how, just as she had not known that she had any English relatives, he had also been unaware that he had any Italian connections until it had come out after his grandmother's death. Without going into any of the negative information he had discovered about the family, he explained how he had found the reference linking the family to San Casciano and then how he had got more information by talking to old men in bars in that town. He glossed over the less than legal way in which he had discovered where they lived, not wishing to get Mimmo's friend's wife into trouble, but explained that he had had confirmation of the relationship between their grandmothers from the *professoressa* at the *Istituto Storico della Resistenza Toscana*.

'So we really are related - and I always thought that apart from my father's older brother, his wife, and my cousin in Bologna, I had no other relatives.' She shook her head.

'It's worse than that, actually – or better than that – depends how you look at it really. You're not the first relative I've met while I've been in Italy, and I know there are more.' She seemed stunned but when, after a few seconds, she was about to say something, she was prevented by the waitress.

'*Desiderate altro?*'

'No, thank you. Just the bill please,' said Lucio.

Rosa gave a little gasp, 'Oh, it's quarter past nine. I need to be home for half past.'

'I'll walk you up the hill,' said Paul, and then, seeing the look she gave him, explained, 'Before I rang, a few weeks ago, I decided it would be a good idea to find out where my relatives lived, in case I was invited round.' He pushed some money over to Lucio and then held the denim jacket that had been hung through the strap of Rosa's handbag, so that she could slip into it easily. 'Thanks, Gabbi – I may catch up with you later, Lucio.'

'Probably not tonight. I'll see you over the weekend sometime. Ciao.'

As they began to walk up the steep Via Monte alle Croci and then turned onto the even steeper steps leading up towards San Salvatore al Monte, Paul explained how he had tracked down Carmela di Lollo and described the condition in which he found her. Rosa said little as they ascended, just occasionally asking him to expand on parts of his description. In the dark, Paul couldn't see her face well and found it difficult to gauge how she was taking the news.

At the top of the steps, he made to step across the pavement ready to cross the *Viale* towards the final part of the steps, but Rosa restrained him by placing a hand gently on his forearm.

'Have you got a *gettone?*'

He pulled his wallet out and then, having removed the handful of change from the bottom of his back pocket, replaced it and held up his hand so that a streetlight fell on the change that now lay in his palm. She leaned towards his hand and with the well-manicured index finger of her right hand moved some of the coins about to reveal a *gettone* underneath.

'May I?'

'Of course.'

There was a payphone at the corner of the bar where the steps joined the *Viale* and she inserted the *gettone* and dialled.

'Ciao, Papa. It's me.'.... 'No, nothing's wrong – we've only just finished studying and I hadn't realised how late it was'.... 'No. I don't need a lift – I could do with some fresh air to clear my head after all that studying'.... 'Probably about half an hour – maybe forty minutes,' ... 'Yes, I'll be quiet and make sure I don't wake mum up.'.... 'I will – don't worry.'.... 'Ciao, ciao!'

She replaced the hand-piece and took Paul's arm to steer him to the left towards Piazzale Michelangelo, instead of crossing the road.

Paul was used to seeing the Piazzale crowded with tourists but now, at half past nine on a weeknight in late October, there were only about twenty cars still parked there; the permanent stalls had been shuttered for the night, the smaller stalls had been folded up and wheeled away into storage and very few people remained. Paul noticed three dogwalkers, a small group of young people sitting on the base of Michelangelo's statue of David, laughing and talking loudly in one of the germanic languages in between swigs of beer, three young couples embracing at various points in the piazza, and a handful of other people looking at the classic view over the city. Rosa led him to a section of the balustrade which was a fair distance away from the nearest people and leaned on it with both hands, looking over the city.

'I think I prefer this view at this time, when it's dark,' she said. He followed her gaze over the calm dark surface of the river down below which reflected the illuminated bridges perfectly creating the illusion that each reflection was a perfect structure in its own right. Beyond the river, the Duomo, Palazzo Vecchio, Santa Croce, and San Lorenzo with their strong illumination seemed to have been deliberately placed with the overall composition of the view in mind. 'So much that's beautiful; so much to admire, and so much hidden beneath the surface – I think that subconsciously, that might have been one of the things that made me choose architecture – to find out what lies underneath .' She turned and looked at him, 'There's more, isn't there? More things that I haven't been told?'

He looked her in the eyes,' I've managed to find out a fair bit about the family's history – not all of it good – but I still know very little about either of our grandmothers and how they fit in with the others.'

'Apart from Carmela di Lollo, are there any other relatives that I don't know about?'

He nodded, 'I haven't met any of them but I know that your mother has at least one cousin in Siena, the son of our grandmothers' oldest sister, and Carmela and her husband, Filippo had three daughters; apparently one is in Milan, one in Geneva and one in New York. There may also be other relatives in the United States as one of the brothers and his family went to the States at the end of the war.'

'I think I need a bit of time to process the things you've told me already, then we need to see each other again, don't we?'

'We do; there's still a lot more to find out and I'd love you to be able to help me. Although...' he paused, trying to find the right way of saying it, 'I think that I would very much like to see you again even if we already knew everything there is to know.'

'She smiled shyly, and taking his arm again said, 'Come on. You can walk me almost home.' They walked in silence, but she kept her arm through his all the way and the silence didn't feel awkward. When they were just within sight of the doorway to her house she stopped and turned towards him. 'I'm really glad we managed to meet... you're a lot nicer than I thought you would be... Thank you,' she said and, after quickly giving him a light kiss on the cheek, turned and ran to her door. She didn't look round again and the door closed behind her.

It was only when Paul was half way down the steps leading back to San Niccolo that he realised that he hadn't told Rosa how to contact him, and he couldn't really ring her at home where his Campolargo heritage made him *persona non grata*.

In the hope that he might find Simon, he made his way to the *Birreria Centrale*. He was out of luck. He looked in through the door and scanned the tables; at first the only person he saw who he recognised was Baz, the cocky language assistant who he had met on his first night in Florence. He was about to step outside again before Baz noticed him, when a girl further down Baz's table half turned, waved and called, 'Hi, Paul. Come and join us.' His heart sank, he had no objection to Claire but he really didn't fancy spending any more time than he had to in Baz's company. He sighed, nodded agreement and indicated that he would get himself a beer and then join them.

With a *birra piccola* in his hand, he squeezed past two others, who he assumed were also language assistants, and wriggled in to the small space that Claire had created for him by her side. 'Hi, Claire. Good to see you again. How are you liking Florence now you've settled in?' Claire opened her mouth to reply but before she could get a word out, Baz's voice came from across the table.

'Claire's doing fine, she just needs to let her hair down a bit more, get out more often in the evenings instead of sitting around moping because her latin-lover's a long way away, she needs to enjoy herself more.'

Paul could see that Baz had clearly had too much to drink and that this was accentuating his already overbearing nature, He knew that he should really just smile and wait for Baz to get bored, but he couldn't resist having a little dig.

'Hello, Baz. I didn't realise that your ambitions extended as far as being Claire's spokesperson. Do you get to carry her handbag as well?' He watched Baz struggling to process what he'd just said, ready to react, should Baz decide to escalate matters. He felt Claire's hand on his forearm.

'Come on you two. Lighten up. I'm honoured that you both take such an interest in my welfare.'

At that moment, someone at the other end of the table called out.' Hey, Baz. It's your round – come on, get some beers in.' Baz glared at Paul for a moment then got unsteadily to his feet and made his way over to the bar.

'Hey. What was all that about?'

Paul shook his head, 'What a prick! Sorry, but he's really smug and irritating. I almost didn't come in when I saw him holding court here, but then you spotted me and called me over.'

She laughed. 'Sorry, I caught sight of your reflection in the window and thought I'd much rather talk to you than listen to Baz. I didn't realise that you two would hit it off so well!'

He joined in with her laugh. 'I only really called in because I was hoping to find Simon, I needed to ask him a favour but it will have to wait – I'll track him down over the weekend some time.'

'I wouldn't look for him too soon; he's busy at the moment.' She waited for him to ask the obligatory question before expanding, 'At my *liceo*, there's also a very pretty Spanish assistant. She was feeling a bit homesick and lonely, so I insisted that she came out here with me tonight. She and Simon seemed to hit it off straight away and it wasn't long before they disappeared to look at his etchings!'

He laughed. 'There's nothing like a good linguistic exchange! ... I'm surprised to see you this late; I thought you'd have been at the station by now.'

She pursed her lips, 'Fraid not. Gennaro's got an exam tomorrow morning, but he's coming up afterwards and staying for four days.'

'That's good – hope you have a good time.'

'Oh, we will. Don't worry about that.'

They chatted for a bit longer then, as he finished his beer, he excused himself, explaining that he hadn't intended to stay long. Claire said that she was ready to go too and asked if he'd mind walking her the first part of the way.

It turned out that Claire had a room overlooking Piazza Vettori, which was in almost exactly the opposite direction to his own room but he decided that he'd walk her all the way, and then make his way back along the Lungarno. When he said that he's walk her all the way she looked momentarily alarmed, 'Paul, I don't...' He stopped her by putting a finger on her lips.

'I know you don't. I just don't feel like sleeping yet, and a walk will do me good.'

Once they had got round the first corner and were out of sight of the *Birreria*, she slipped her arm through his and kept it there while they walked across Piazza della Signoria, under the Uffizi and over the Ponte Vecchio before releasing him as they turned into Borgo San Frediano. He was initially surprised when she took his arm but once he had seen the looks she got and heard some of the ribald comments that were made as they made their way across the areas that were now almost entirely populated by wine sodden young men and a few clusters of bored policemen, he understood why she had felt it desirable to have an escort for the first part of the journey.

'Is it always as bad as that?' he asked.

'As bad as what?' she replied appearing genuinely puzzled.

'You know, the looks and the wolf-whistles and the suggestive comments.'

'Oh, that,' she said, dismissively, 'You get used to it.'

'But that's terrible, and why have I never noticed it before.'

'That's because, if you've ever been around at this time of night and a girl has walked past, you've probably been too busy looking at her yourself to notice what other men are doing.'

'I haven't – I mean, I don't.'

'Hah! So what do you do then if you're out and a pretty girl walks past on her own?' He opened his mouth to speak, but she cut him off, 'You look at her, don't you?'

'I may have a discreet look but.'

'Aah! No "buts". How many men have we just passed? Two hundred and fifty? Three hundred? More? What do you think three hundred "discreet" looks look like? ... Now, do you see?'

He inclined his head, 'OK You win. I'm ashamed of my sex.'

She laughed, 'Don't worry too much. I'm afraid we're just as bad if we see a good looking lad – it's just that we get less opportunity. And when we do, unless there's safety in numbers, we have to be really discreet, because if a lad looks at a girl, that's a positive thing, but if a girl looks at a lad then she's a slag.'

'And how does the boyfriend from Bari handle the gender politics - I'd always heard that attitudes in the South were a bit more ... traditional?'

She laughed. 'Oh Gennaro knows what's best for him, although I think his parents were a bit shocked the first time they met me.'

'When they got to Piazza Vettori she thanked him and moved her face towards his to be kissed on both cheeks in the Italian way. 'When in Rome..' he said and then waved as he turned down towards the Arno and Ponte della Vittoria.

After spending parts of the evening arm in arm with first one pretty girl and then another, he found himself half hoping that Mimmo had been wrong and that Signora Vaccherini would drive past again while was walking home and offer him another ride – but it was not to be.

As he knew that both Simon and Lucio had other things on their minds that weekend, he modified his plan slightly, and when, on the Wednesday morning, he finally bumped into Lucio, instead of giving him a verbal message to pass on to Rosa, he gave him a note in an envelope. It had been useful, probably essential, he thought, to have Lucio and Gabriela with him when he first met Rosa, but for some reason, he felt that he wanted them to be alone for their next meeting. The note inside the envelope simply said, "Hi Rosa, It was really good to meet you last Friday. Can you make one evening this weekend for a Pizza? If you can, I'll see you by the monument in Piazza Demidoff at seven o'clock. I'll wait there on Friday, then if you can't make Friday, I'll be there on Saturday and if necessary, Sunday. I don't have a phone but if you ring the Ciacco Bar on Borgo La Croce, the message will get to me sooner or later. Paul p.s. I'd love to see a photograph of your grandmother, if you have one." He had hesitated for quite a while before signing the letter; should he put "love from" or "kisses" or "regards"? "Regards", he rejected straight away as it sounded far too formal, "love from" he felt tended to be used too often, and because of that, he felt it was a bit too bland. He would have liked to have put *"baci"* or "kisses" but when he thought of the word he couldn't help also thinking of the little hollows by her collar bone and how he would like to place real kisses there. The thought unsettled him somewhat as she was also a sort of cousin and he wasn't sure how appropriate it was to be thinking that kind of thing. In the end he decided that just his name alone was the safest option.

On the Friday morning, when he called into the bar for his coffee and doughnut, he was surprised to be given a letter by Mimmo. 'Somebody's popular. A very pretty young lady left this for you about an hour ago. I told her that if she waited long enough you'd appear, but she said she had to get to a lecture.'

The handwriting on the envelope was neat and feminine but with an extravagant flourish at the end of his surname. He glanced at the back of the envelope to see if there was a return address, although he didn't expect to see one as he was already ninety percent sure who it was from, before he opened it. He smiled as he saw that she had written it in her best school English, but then his smile gradually disappeared as he read through the letter – " Dear Paul, Thank you very much for your nice letter. I am very pleased to receive it. I enjoy very much to meet you Friday last but, I am sorry, this weekend I am not in Florence. I will contact you. I hope that you have a pleasant weekend. Your friend Rosa," So, her family have found out that we met and have put a stop to it, he thought. Maybe it would have been better if they had never met – he'd just got used to the idea that his research into his grandmother's family was a waste of time. Now, he'd allowed himself to get caught up in it again, only to be disappointed again. He screwed up the note and was about to throw it in the bin, but then thought better of it and pushed it into his pocket.

On the following Thursday, he and Claire were both invited round to Simon and Lucio's to eat and to play a game of Risk. Knowing that the game could go on for hours, he took the Midget and was very careful about the amount he drank – even though the police in Italy were far more relaxed about drinking and driving than in England, he wanted to be absolutely sure he didn't hit anything on the way home. Having a clearer head than the others meant that, once they started playing, his strategy seemed to be working more effectively than his opponents, until Lucio said, 'Oh sorry, I should have mentioned before, Rosa said that she can meet you on Saturday evening if that's OK with you.'

'Did she say where?'

'She said, you'd know.'

Paul felt a surge of happiness. He'd be able to find out more about the family history - then he realised that the happiness wasn't because he'd be able to find out more about the family history, it was because he really wanted to get to know Rosa better. He was kidding himself by pretending that he was pleased because of the family history – that was just a convenient excuse. After that, he made mistake after mistake in his strategy and only luck prevented him from being the first to be knocked out of the game, and even then it was only a brief respite.

'So,' said Claire, leaning back in the seat of the Midget, stretching her legs out and placing her hands behind her head, 'who is she then?'

'Please don't sit like that when I'm driving, it's very distracting – in fact, please don't sit like that at all,'

She laughed, 'You're trying to change the subject,' but she lowered her arms and pulled the hem of her skirt down a couple of inches. Paul said nothing and for a few seconds the only noise was the noise of the Midget's engine as he negotiated Piazza Dalmazia before entering Via Corridoni to head towards the *Viali*.

'Well?'

'Well what?'

'Who is Rosa and why haven't I met her?'

'I'm sure there are millions of people who you haven't met – including one or two in Florence.'

'Don't be evasive. I saw the look on your face, and I saw how you didn't concentrate on the game afterwards. ... Somebody's in love.'

'It's complicated. I'm not quite sure what's happening at the moment, and until I know, I certainly can't explain it to anyone else.'

'Maybe if it's so confusing, you need someone else to help explain it to you – someone who's not involved.' They were both silent for the rest of the way to Piazza Vettori.

There was a space free towards the middle of the square and he pulled the Midget into it. He looked at her, 'Can I come up?'

Her eyebrows raised, 'Sorry?'

'I think you might be right. Maybe someone who's not involved can help me to get my mind straight over this.'

She relaxed, 'I've got a ridiculously expensive tin of Twinings English Breakfast Tea. You can replace it, if you drink it all – I'm not making coffee at this time of night.'

'Thankyou – you may have a glittering career ahead of you as an agony-aunt?'

Claire's bedsit was a little smaller than his, but with a bigger bed which left little free space in the room. The room had clearly been created by subdividing a much larger one as the ceiling was high and contained part of a fresco. Claire indicated that he should sit on the edge of the bed and took the kettle into the tiny bathroom to fill it with water.

'Only one sink, in here – makes life a bit difficult sometimes.'

'I bet it does.'

When the tea was ready, she sat down at the other end of the bed and leaned back against the wall, 'Now, tell Auntie Claire all about it.' And he did.

'So you see, I'm not sure what to do next. She seems really nice and I liked her when I met her – but she's my cousin – and I don't even know if it's legal to fall in love with your cousin. Do I just treat her as if she were my sister and try and find someone else to take my mind off other things? If it is wrong, will she just be disgusted if I make any sort of advance and never want to speak to me again? Is it just something that will pass quickly?'

'OK, OK – I'll do my best – but I think we need another cup of tea first. You make it this time – You saw where everything was.'

'Alright. Legal stuff first. Unless you're thinking of living in South East Asia, there is absolutely no problem with Rosa being your cousin, even though she isn't – she's your second cousin, I think. That's the easy bit; all your other questions were about love and feelings, and they involve two people. In general, if you fall in love, you fall in love – I don't think that it's something you can decide to do or decide not to do – if it happens it happens. If it's just one way then you'll be unhappy for a bit but you'll get over it in the end – everyone does – or nearly everyone; a few people kill themselves but you're probably too sensible to do that.'

He smiled, 'I'll try not to.'

'Good. Now, I'm going to say something you won't like.'

'OK I can take it.'

'You've only met her once. Don't you think that you're jumping the gun a bit? Did you ask her if she's already got a boyfriend?' He shook his head.

'OK. Take it nice and steady. Get to know her. See if she likes you. Make sure she's not already with someone. If she likes you then she won't start going with anyone else just because you don't rush at things like a bull in a china shop, and if she doesn't like you then she probably won't change her mind, especially if you try and pressure her. Oh, and whatever you do – don't treat her as if she were your sister – that would be weird!'

Paul laughed, 'Thank you. That's helped clear my head a lot. I'll go away and let you get some sleep now.' She stood up and he gave her a hug and then left.

He was by the side of the statue in Piazza Demidoff at five to seven, but Rosa was there before him.

'Ciao. Sorry to keep you waiting.'

She laughed, it's only five to seven now, so you're early, it's my own fault for being even earlier.' She kissed him on both cheeks and then put her arm through his, 'Where are we going?'

'I'm open to suggestions. It's your city; I've only been here for a few weeks.'

She thought then said, 'Did you say you'd got a car?'

'Yes. It's over in Piazza d'Azeglio, about a fifteen minute walk.'

'OK. Let's go and get it. There's a nice little pizzeria up in Fiesole where we're not likely to run into any my parents' friends or any of the other people we know.'

'Worried about being seen with me?' he asked, half seriously.

'By my parents' friends, a little bit; I'm not ready to explain you yet. The other people we know don't worry me; I just want to be sure that we can talk without being disturbed.'

When Rosa saw that the car was a convertible, she insisted on him putting the roof down for the journey up to Fiesole. The benefit of this was that as they sat at a table for two on the roof terrace of the pizzeria, the night no longer felt cold. As almost all the other customers were sitting inside they were able to choose the table with the best view over Florence. The clouds there had been during the day had cleared, and not only were most of the main floodlit monuments visible from where they sat, but they could also see the illuminated marble façade of San Miniato and the more austere *Forte di Belvedere* in their positions overlooking the centre from the South.

'Do you know why the Medici had the *Forte di Belvedere* built there?'

Paul shook his head,' Presumably they were expecting to be attacked from the South at the time.'

'No. When it was built. All the cannons were facing northwards, over the city, so that if there was ever any danger of a revolt against the Medici, the people could be bombarded.'

'I thought that the Medici were popular, most of the time.'

'The earlier ones were – most of the time. By the time Ferdinando had the Forte built, however, they had abandoned their original way of keeping in the background and ruling as private citizens, and had become dukes.'

'Power corrupts,' said Paul.

'And absolute power corrupts absolutely,' she finished the quotation.

'Didn't he live somewhere near here?'

She gave him a puzzled look. 'Who?'

'Harold Acton, the art historian; I thought he lived in Florence. Wasn't it one of his ancestors who said that about power?'

'No idea... Ah, here's the waiter with the menus.'

Once they had ordered, they settled down at their table to wait for the crostini they had ordered as antipasti and he casually broached the subject of the previous weekend.

'Thanks for the note you left for me last week. Your English is quite good.'

'Fibber!' she laughed, 'My French is quite good, but my English is rubbish. I can read textbooks because a lot of the technical terms in English are similar to Italian, but I need a phrase book to help me use it.'

'I thought that everyone studied it at school in Italy.'

'We do, but most people only do it to a very basic level, then, if you happen to find yourself in a section at school where the main foreign language is French or German, you don't bother anymore – unless your family pushes you.'

'And yours didn't?'

'No. At one point, I asked if I could do a course at 'The British' because a couple of my friends were going, but Mum and Nonna said that there were far more important things to study. I think Dad would have been happy to let me go but once the others were set against it, he wasn't prepared to back me up.'

'Never mind. You've got your own private tutor now.'

'And how do I pay for my lessons?'

'Now that's a good question. I'll have to think about that... or maybe I could just do it as a kind of missionary work!' They both laughed.

'So, did you have a good time last weekend?'

'It went quite well, but there was quite a lot of time spent travelling.' He gave her a quizzical look.

'Turin. It takes about three hours each way to get to Turin by train.'

'And what were you doing in Turin, have you got a friend studying there?' He realised as soon as he'd asked the question in as casual a voice as he could manage, that he'd used the masculine form of friend rather than the feminine form. He hoped she hadn't noticed although the amused look she gave him, suggested that she had.

'If I had "*un amico*" 'she emphasised the final o, 'in Turin, I think that the last thing my father would be paying for would be a train ticket to go and spend the weekend with him. We may be in the mid-eighties now but I'm afraid a lot of parents still cling to some very traditional ideas about appropriate behaviour for young women... I'm sorry, I meant to put it into my letter, but then it took me so long to write it that I ran out of time and then forgot I hadn't included it.'

'You still haven't told me what "it" is.'

'Gymnastics. I do gymnastics – although I'm getting a bit old for it now – and there was a competition in Turin last weekend.'

'Really! How did it go?'

'Oh, it went alright. I was third in the floor exercise and fourth on the uneven bars but rubbish overall because my beam always lets me down.'

'A third and a fourth sounds great. But I thought female gymnasts were always really scrawny and light as a feather.'

She shook her head and laughed. 'I could pretend to be insulted that you're calling me overweight, but that's probably not a good idea just before we eat. No, I think, like most people who don't follow gymnastics but only see it when it's on television during the Olympics, you've probably got an image of Olga Korbut fixed in your mind, or of Nadia Comaneci, but Olga was very unusual and the pictures they always put in the papers of Nadia are of the Montreal Olympics when she was only fourteen, she's developed a lot since then, even though she was competing regularly until last year.'

'Alright; I stand corrected.'

They continued to chat about gymnastics while they ate the crostini and waited for their pizzas to arrive. Paul was impressed by the number of hours training that were required to do the sport at a high level.

'So you don't have much free time, with your training, competitions and studying at the University.'

She shrugged, 'It's not too bad. The good thing is that everything I do, I enjoy, and because I've accepted that I'm not quite good enough to really get to the top, that's taken the pressure off the gymnastics. If I stop enjoying it, or if it starts to get in the way of other things I'd rather do, then I can back away from it.'

When they had finished their pizza, Rosa said. 'I've been enjoying the evening so much that I'd forgotten that you didn't ask me here to ask about me, did you? We're supposed to be delving into our family history, aren't we?'

'I suppose so, although you seem to be far more interesting than any other member of our family.'

She smiled but said nothing.

'Alright,' he sighed, and took a sip of his wine. 'I got a lot of background information from the woman who runs the *Istituto Storico della Resistenza Toscana...*'

'Why have I never heard of them?' Paul turned his palms upwards and shrugged his shoulders to indicate that he had no idea, and then continued, 'I made some notes after I spoke to her, because there's a lot of information, and it's complicated – or at least it is for me, as I don't really know that much about Florentine history.' He took his notes out of his jacket pocket and placed them on the table in front of him.

As he went through the earlier parts of their family history, she would occasionally stop him and comment on how things fitted into other aspects of Florentine history that she knew of. When he mentioned that the land at Bargino had been given to the family by the Grand Duke Ferdinand, she pointed out that he was the same Duke who had built the *Forte di Belvedere* to make sure that he could protect himself from the ordinary people.

She was incredulous when he recounted how Domenico Campolargo had been well acquainted with both Marinetti and Pavolini, as well as presumably with all the main fascist leaders, people who had been covered, albeit not in any great depth, in history lessons at school.'

'But that's Nonna's father, and she's never said anything at all about any of them, yet she must have met some of them. She's never said much about her father, just that she never really saw much of him and that he was very strict.'

'I'm sure she did meet some of them, although she may not have known who they were when she was younger.'

'But she's sixty-six now, nearly sixty-seven, so she was grown up before the war, in fact she got married more or less when Italy joined the war.'

He nodded, and put his hand over hers on the table, 'What do you know about your grandfather?'

'I know his name was Gian Giacomo Melluso - that he was twelve years older than her – the dates are on his tomb – that he was killed towards the end of the war and...' she paused and frowned, 'I don't really know anything else. Now I think about it, anytime I've ever asked about him, Nonna has always managed to change the subject – I assume it's because she still misses him, even after all these years.'

'It might be... or it could be the opposite. Maybe she never really loved him but was pushed into marrying him by her father and her brothers.'

'But why would they do that?'

'Because of who he was.'

She looked at him with narrowed eyes. 'Go on – tell me the worst – you can't leave me in suspense now.'

'Gian Giacomo Melluso was first cousin to Alessandro Pavolini. Obviously, that doesn't prove anything – even Count Dracula probably had some very nice relatives but, given our family's history of making sure that we're always linked to the right people, I would have thought that being tied to the family of the rising star of fascism, would have been just the sort of thing that our great-grandfather would have been keen on.'

She was silent and, after a couple of minutes when the waiter looked over, obviously keen to clear up and prepare the pizzeria for the following day, Paul asked for the bill.

On the way back to the Midget she didn't take his arm and as he opened the passenger door for her, he saw that there were tears in her eyes. She seemed lost in her thoughts as they drove back down to the city and around the *Viali* up to Piazzale Michelangelo. She only spoke once on the way, and that was addressed to herself rather than to him, 'Poor Nonna.' Paul reached for her hand but she gently withdrew it after a couple of seconds contact.

In the Piazzale, he made to accompany her home, but she shook her head.

'Not tonight,' and she turned to go.

'Hey,' he said gently, 'We have a saying in English – Don't shoot the messenger.'

'I'm sorry. It's not your fault. I've got a lot of thinking to do. Goodnight,' and she gave him the faintest of kisses on the cheek and then turned and fled.

Chapter 11

He neither saw nor heard anything of Rosa over the next two weeks. The dreary autumn weather made everything appear dismal and even the tourists, who could usually be relied on to bring a bit of variety to everyday life, seemed to be either huddled together in little groups under dark umbrellas, or rushing head down in straight lines through the streets, almost totally enveloped in the cheap emergency cagoules they had purchased from the street stalls outside the station. Whenever Paul saw these, it always amazed him that a nation renowned for its fashion sense and artistic heritage, could have come up with a design that was so ugly. Whenever he went out for a run, he always found himself taking routes that involved passing along the section of the *Viali* nearest to Rosa's house, both as he he headed out and on his way back. As he ran, he scanned the face of every female he passed hoping to bump in to her, just by chance – but nothing. When the weather brightened up he walked up to Piazzale Michelangelo and sat reading his book on the parapet near to the spot where he had stood with Rosa at the end of the evening on the day they'd met.

On the Saturday afternoon at the end of the second week he decided that he would walk up to San Miniato and, after refreshing his memory of the frescoes in the church, sit on one of the benches between San Miniato and San Salvatore to read the paper. Half way up the steps, however, by the entrance to the *Giardino delle Rose*, which as usual bore the legend 'Closed for Restoration', he stopped. He realised that he was behaving in a ridiculous way; he remembered how, as a twelve year old, he'd spent ages at school, following around a girl in the year above, who he was sure was destined to be the love of his life when she once noticed him. Unfortunately, when she had noticed him, after being amused the first time – which was a bit hurtful, but he knew that you had to suffer for love – the second time she'd noticed him it had been a slap around the face and, "Piss off creep. Go and find someone your own size to perv over". Probably just hanging around waiting for Rosa was the worst thing he could do; he turned round, went back down the steps and headed into the centre for an ice-cream.

Whenever he saw Gabriela, he asked casually about Rosa, not because he expected to receive any interesting information in return, but because, if by any chance she asked about him, it would get back to her that he had asked about her and she wouldn't think that he wasn't bothered. In the meantime, he was determined not to let the situation get him down.

He had struck up a casual friendship with two Russian Language Readers from the university who he had met in Mimmo's and discovered that they were sharing a room just three doors further along Borgo La Croce.

Both Natasha and Korki had boyfriends back in Russia who they were quite sure that they were going to marry after their return to St. Petersburg, but both of them were quite clear that as their fiancés had made clear that they couldn't possibly be expected to remain celibate for a whole year while their future wives were away, what was sauce for the goose was sauce for the gander. Paul found Natasha somewhat intimidating, but he got on well with Korki who, although she was quieter, spoke the better Italian. They had laughed and joked about the liberated lifestyle they enjoyed outside Russia and on a couple of occasions Paul had sat chatting with Korki while Natasha "entertained" a guest in their room. That evening, after his retreat from Via Monte alle Croci, Korki was in Mimmo's when he called in and, after getting himself a latte macchiato he went over to join her. They chatted for about a quarter of an hour by which time both their cups were empty.

'I'm getting another black tea. Would you like anything?'

'No, thank you.' Then as she started to rise, 'Wait... I can make you one upstairs... if you like.'

She looked at him, 'That's what you'd like.'

He wasn't sure whether it was a statement or a question, so he just nodded his head.

'No complications?'

Now he shook his head, 'No complications – friends now; friends afterwards.'

'You have protection?'

There's a machine in the toilets here.

'OK. Give me your keys and I'll go first. I'll see you in five minutes.'

He slid his keys across the table. 'Don't close the outer door completely, or I won't be able to get in.'

As he ascended the stairs, he could hear water running and, as he opened the door the only visible sign that he had a guest was the pile of neatly folded clothes on his table. The sound of water was coming from the shower and he slid the bathroom door back along its creaky runners.

'Prassiwi,' he said, dredging his memory for an appropriate thing to say.

She laughed, 'That almost sounded like Russian. Have you been practising?'

'No. You occasionally hear Russian words in the background of some of the old spy films, to create atmosphere. I remember someone saying that who was supposed to be looking at a painting in an art gallery. I thought the painting was quite good, so I'm hoping it was complimentary.'

'It will do... but now I need my back soaping.'

She was very energetic and Paul guessed that, while Natasha had been enjoying herself regularly, Korki had been letting the sexual energy build up inside her until it was almost at bursting point. But when it was over, it was over; they had both enjoyed it and that was that. Life would be far less complicated if all relationships could be based solely on mutual physical attraction he thought, as he looked down the length of Korki's naked body stretched languidly alongside him. The street lights shone obliquely through the window and picked out the curves of her languid body in a chiaroscuro worthy of Caravaggio's best.

'You should have been a model,' he said.

'I was – now, didn't you invite me up here for a cup of tea, or did you lure me here under false pretences?'

'How dare you suggest such a thing,' he said, sliding off the bed with a laugh, 'Do they teach you nothing about English gentlemen in Moscow?'

'Saint Petersburg,' she corrected, 'Yes. They teach us that you are all effeminate and that you attend single sex schools where you all sleep together, and you drink lots of tea'

He laughed, 'I'm sorry if I disappointed.'

'You've still got a chance to live up to your national stereotype with your tea.'

'It will have to be English tea from a teapot – I don't have a samovar.'

'English tea will be fine.'

He felt a lot better after she'd gone. With occasional diversions like that, he could afford to give Rosa as much time as she needed to do her thinking. He decided that when he got back from England after Christmas, he would seek her out and find out where he stood – until then he was happy to let things drift.

The weather had brightened up, although the days were still getting shorter and, as it was now December, the whole city seemed to cheer up as Christmas decorations began to appear and people began to bustle around hunting for Christmas presents. He was happy to join the crowds in his free time; fortunately his nephew was still only a baby and he could easily pick up a present for him once he got back to England, but the adults: his parents, his brother, sister and brother-in-law would all expect something that was manifestly Italian. It was a shame in a way that he was flying rather than taking the Midget, as the car would have made taking presents much easier, however, it wasn't really practical to drive the little car over the Alps in the middle of winter and going round them by cutting across the South of France would add too much distance on to the journey. As he had plenty of free time, he looked around carefully for the presents being determined not to just buy the first things he saw and then regret it when he saw other more suitable things later. Eventually he bought a twenty centimetre high replica of

Cellini's *Perseus* for his parents, paying three times as much in a small shop near Palazzo Pitti as he could have got one for on one of the many street stalls, but being confident that the one he had bought was made of quality material and he would not get home to find that the head had broken off on the way. For his sister he bought a gold charm of Michelangelo's *David* to go on the charm bracelet that she had been steadily adding to since receiving it as a present on her eleventh birthday. Buying for David and Al was easier, as he knew that if he found things that he wouldn't mind receiving himself, then they would be fine for them too. In the end he bought them each a sweat-shirt; the one for David was white with what appeared to be twenty wine stains on the front, each labelled with the name of an Italian wine; the shirt for Al was blue with a classic picture of a *Lambretta* scooter on the front. He also bought a *Pinocchio* glove puppet for Luke; even if he wasn't old enough to play with it yet, it could be put away somewhere and given to him later.

Chapter 12

On Thursday the twelfth, there was a bitterly cold wind blowing as he made his way back from the *Academia*, and he was looking forward to a glass of hot *Vov* when he got to Mimmo's, before going upstairs and settling down with a book. She was sitting at one of the tables to the side of the bar and not directly in his line of sight as he went through the door, and it was only when Mimmo inclined his head to the left that he turned and saw her.

'Rosa!' He stopped, not sure how to continue.

'Ciao, Paul. How are you?'

He noticed that there was a tremor in her voice and a pleading look in her eyes, and realised that she was worried about the meeting. He smiled, said, '*Due Vov,*' to Mimmo, and went over to join her at the table. 'You can't imagine how pleased I am to see you again – I've really missed you.'

'You probably won't believe it, but I think I can imagine it.'

Without any conscious decision on his part he felt his facial muscles pull his face in to a smile and he took her hand and looked into her eyes, which he now noticed were moist with tears. 'You said that you had a lot of thinking to do,' he looked at her enquiringly.

There was a discreet cough behind Paul, and in front of him Rosa looked up and smiled as Mimmo brought the two glasses of *Vov* to the table. Paul thanked him and passed him a two thousand lire note.

'I didn't realise at the time, just how much thinking I'd have to do. The trouble is that when you're nineteen you think you know everything and then things happen and you realise that you don't know anything useful yet – when does it start to get better?'

'I hope that's a rhetorical question and that you don't see me as middle-aged at twenty-three! You know, I really am pleased to see you again; I was worried that you might have decided you didn't want to again.'

'I'm sorry, Paul. At first, seeing you would have just confused me and stopped me working things out, and then I was worried that you'd have forgotten about me and.. I don't know... I think I was a bit scared by what I felt... so then I felt miserable and didn't know what to do... and then Gabbi said that you're going away at the end of next week.' She paused for breath and Paul took both her hands in his.

'I'm only going away for ten days. I promised my family that I'd be home to see them over Christmas, and they've even bought me the ticket as a present ... but I'm coming back – unless you tell me to stay away!'

She shook her head,' If I've learnt anything over the last month, it's that I definitely do not want you to stay away.'

He felt a warm feeling spreading across his chest and shoulders and was fairly sure that it wasn't the Vov. 'What are you doing tomorrow?'

'I have a lecture at ten thirty in Via degli Alfani, but after that I'm free. I've got plenty of studying to do, but nothing that can't wait.'

'I could come to the lecture with you. I only teach from Monday to Thursday so I'm free all day.'

She smiled and shook her head, 'No. I think that if you came to the lecture, there wouldn't be much point in me being there – concentration would be a bit of a problem.'

'OK. I'll meet you in the bar opposite the entrance to the lecture rooms in Via degli Alfani. What time does your lecture finish?'

'It should be over by eleven thirty, although occasionally the prof gets a bit carried away, especially if anyone asks what he considers to be an intelligent question.'

'Let's hope everyone's in a hurry to get away and no-one asks any questions.'

After a while, he offered to get the car and give her a lift home, but that she said that she felt so full of energy that she wouldn't be able to be calm at home unless she worked off some of the energy by walking up the hill first. That suited him well as it meant that he got to spend more time with her and didn't have to concentrate on driving while he was with her. Although he was aware that the way Rosa took him was not the quickest way, it still seemed to take no time at all to reach the road behind San Miniato. This time when he moved his head forward, tilting it slightly to one side to facilitate the kiss on the first cheek, Rosa did not turn her head and her lips sought his with an urgency that surprised him. When they finally separated, she smiled and with an, 'eleven thirty', turned and made her way to the house. Paul felt like whooping with joy, but just managed to restrain himself.

In the morning, he left twenty minutes earlier than he needed to and instead of heading straight for the bar where they were due to meet he took a slight deviation and passed along Via dell'Oriuolo where he had noticed a small jewellers when he had been looking for presents for his family. He wanted something that was pleasant but not too showy, that could be seen as carrying a message but that did not go over the top; the last thing he wanted was to make Rosa feel that he was being presumptuous. In the end he chose a small silver heart encrusted with tiny semi-precious stones and hanging on a silver chain. The shop assistant did suggest that he might consider one with two entwined hearts instead, but he declined with a smile; he felt that they weren't quite ready for the two entwined hearts, even if he hoped that it wouldn't be long before they were.

It was nearly twenty to twelve by the time Rosa emerged from the lecture theatre and managed to disentangle herself from her fellow students. Paul watched from the bar as the elaborate ceremonies involving air kisses, hugs and waves took place on the other side of the road before she was finally able to toss her scarf back over her shoulder and make her way across.

'*Caffé?*'

'Ciao – No, just a glass of water, thanks. They've turned the heating on far too high in there.'

He studied the delicate movements of her throat as she drank the water, then, as she put the glass down on the counter and turned towards him, her head dipped slightly and her throat disappeared beneath her scarf. Every movement she made seemed to him to flow gracefully and he imagined she must be a natural at gymnastics.

'I'd like to see you compete.'

'What?' she said, her mind evidently following a completely different train of thought.

'Gymnastics. I'd really like to watch you doing it.'

'OK,' she laughed. 'Watching a training session should be no problem but there are no more competitions now until the end of January, and even then, it's a fairly low level one.'

'You're on. Just let me know where and when.'

'If you want to see some training, then you need to come along to the gym in Borgo Pinti between seven and eight in the morning on Mondays, Wednesdays or Fridays.'

'It will have to be Monday or Wednesday, as my flight back to England is next Friday.'

'Make it Wednesday; I occasionally don't make it out of bed on time on a Monday.'

'I'll be there. Now, let's go for a walk while the weather's fine.'

'I didn't forget about the photograph... of my grandmother... I had a look through the drawer where most of our photos are kept, but there was nothing there... so I asked Nonna, if she'd got any photographs of when she was my age or even younger, but she said that any there had been had all been destroyed during the war. It's a shame really... not just because you wanted to see one, but I'd like to see what she was like ... Mum says that I look like very like Nonna, but I can't see it. She has very intense dark eyes – a bit like yours really except ...'

Paul looked at her, 'Go on. Except what?'

She frowned,'I'm not quite sure how to explain it. Your eyes are very alive – they always make you look as if you're interested.... but Nonna's eyes, even though they're the same colour, and the same shape ... it's as if... it's as if there's some kind of pain there... I don't mean physical pain; her eyes don't hurt her... it's as if she's been mentally hurt at some time and uses her eyes as a barrier to keep people out.'

'Even you?'

Rosa hesitated for a few seconds before replying. 'It's not something I've ever thought about before now. She's just been Nonna: always there when I needed her, if I was upset about something, or if I needed some help with homework, or someone to play with in the garden when I was little – but she's never told me anything about herself; if ever I've asked she's always changed the subject or told me about when my mum was growing up.'

'Does she see many people apart from the family?'

'No. She hardly ever goes out and, if any of Dad's work colleagues come round at all, if she meets them at all, it's usually only briefly, and then she excuses herself and goes to her room to read.'

'What about holidays?'

'When we were little: Franci and I, we used to go to Forte dei Marmi for a month every summer. Nonna used to come with us so that she could look after the two of us in the evenings if mum and dad were going out, and she'd cook at mid-day for when we got back from the beach, but she never came down to the beach with us.'

'Maybe she just doesn't like the beach – not everyone does.'

'Oh, but she does. Every morning when the rest of us were still in bed – or at least Franci and I were – she'd go down to the beach very early and have a swim. I only know because I saw her swimming costume hanging out to dry every day. Once Franci got to about five years old, she never came with us to the sea again; she insisted that she was just in the way but, if ever we went to the mountains, it was as if she were a completely different person.'

'In what way?'

'She seemed younger, much more energetic. She always wanted to take us out for walks and if we met anyone else out walking or in the shops, she'd stop and chat and laugh. We used to moan, at the time, because we would have much preferred to be at the seaside or somewhere where there was "something to do"' 'Rosa gave a soft self-deprecating laugh, 'Silly little girls. I really like going out walking now, and I can't stand sitting for hours and hours on a deckchair or swimming in water that's been churned up by ten thousand other people.'

'I'd probably have got frostbite if I'd tried sitting in a deckchair for several hours in Blackpool,' joked Paul.

'Blackpool?'

'It's where lots of people in the North West of England traditionally go to on holiday. It's very different to Forte dei Marmi but, to be fair, you could have a lot of fun there as a kid.'

Paul then described a typical Blackpool holiday to Rosa: the beach with the donkeys, the pleasure beach and the arcades, the piers with their variety theatres, Madame Tussaud's, the tower and the trams. Rosa thought it sounded wonderful, like Rimini with more waves and without the rows and rows of umbrellas where everything was regimented.

'It was wonderful, as a kid; there was always something to do and something to see, but now, a lot of the people who used to go there can go on cheap package holidays to custom built resorts in Spain where the only thing they want is guaranteed sunshine during their holidays. Thousands of people go and come back with sunburn and complaining about the poor quality of Spanish food.'

Rosa looked surprised,' Don't you like Spanish food?'

'I enjoy food everywhere, and on the rare occasions I've eaten Spanish food, cooked by Spaniards, it's been really good. The problem is that the tourists stay in hotels that are full of other English people and, because of that, the hotels think that they need to cook "English" meals, and they don't do it very well. It's part of our English stubbornness: we don't trust foreign food, we expect all foreigners to speak English and generally look down on everything that's not British.'

'But you're not like that!'

'Aah. That's the nicest compliment anyone has ever given me.'

She looked at him, initially puzzled and then laughed and punched him lightly on the arm, 'Idiot. You're making fun of me!'

When they parted, in Piazzale Michelangelo, they agreed to meet up again the following evening. Rosa really needed to get some studying done and her parents would begin to object if she were out three evenings in a row. Although Paul would have liked to have seen her at every possible opportunity, he was aware that both reasons were good ones and determined not to put any pressure on her, which also had the advantage of leaving him free for a last Friday evening in the *Birreria Centrale* before going home for Christmas.

Simon was there with his Spanish conquest, Claire was also there with a slightly uneasy looking young man with feather cut dark hair and a muscular neck, Lucio and Gabbi called in for half an hour and most of the other people who Paul had come across over the past three months were also there.

Claire introduced Paul to Gennaro and asked him where Rosa was; Paul smiled as he realised that the question was entirely for Gennaro's benefit, to reassure him that the single man who had just come in and sat next to his girlfriend was not a potential rival. He explained that as he'd kept Rosa busy for the previous evening and much of today, as well as having arranged to meet again the following day, she needed to get some studying done. He asked Gennaro how long he was staying and learnt that he would be there all week and that then he was taking Claire down to meet his parents, and she would be staying for Christmas. Apparently they had met Claire twice before, in Florence, so it wasn't quite as nerve wracking an experience as it could have been, but it still represented quite a big step for her to come and stay at his parents' house. Paul asked how his parents felt about him having a foreign *'fidanzata'* and Gennaro told him that his parents were quite comfortable with it, although he thought they would have been less comfortable if one of his sisters had turned up at home with a foreign boyfriend. 'But I think that here in the North, people in general are a bit more open minded,' he added, showing that he had understood why Paul might be interested in the subject. Paul hoped that he was right, although in his particular case he suspected that the normal rules might not apply.

The following evening, Paul managed to find a space for the Midget on the Lungarno close to Piazza Demidoff, and when Rosa appeared just before seven, he led her to the car and opened the door for her.

'Where are you taking me?'

'I thought that seeing as Ferdinando the first granted our family lots of land around Bargino, that we'd go and see if we could find somewhere to eat there.'

'Do you think we'll be treated as members of the local gentry?'

'Given what we know so far about our ancestors, I think it's probably not a good idea to mention anything about our family tonight – we might end up hanging upside down from a lamp-post.'

They had a little walk round Bargino for five minutes but couldn't find anywhere to eat that looked affordable and so retraced their route for a couple of kilometres back towards Florence where they had noticed a small hotel and restaurant by the side of the road, in an even smaller village called Calzaiolo. Here, the prices were low and the portions ample and, as at no point was the restaurant full, they were able to enjoy a comfortable meal without being rushed. Paul was going to have the *tagliatelle ai funghi* as his first course but instead followed Rosa's advice and chose *tagliatelle al ragu di cinghiale* instead.

'Mmmm. Fantastic. And I bet you can make a lot of *ragu* out of a wild boar. I don't think I've ever had a sauce so full of flavour.'

'I thought you'd like it. My uncle in Bologna goes out every autumn with a hunting party and when they divide everything up at the end and he comes home with a big piece of boar, my aunt uses some of it to make *ragu* and then splits it into portions to freeze. If ever we go to visit in winter, it's always the first first-course that we're given.'

For their main course, Paul had chosen *rosticciana* and was brought a big plate of roasted ribs, while Rosa had chosen *cioncia*, a traditional rustic dish made out of a pig's muzzle which had an unusual, but not unpleasant, gelatinous texture. Rosa grinned as Paul tasted it, 'It's an acquired taste. I know a lot of people who can't stand it and others who really love it. You don't often see it on the menu in this part of Tuscany, so I couldn't resist getting it.'

'It's... interesting... I think it's a taste I could acquire... but it's a bit of a shock when you're not expecting it.'

'We could have always asked if they could do any English food for you,' she said with a twinkle in her eye.

'Ah, but when I eat, my Italian heritage gets the upper hand – especially when I'm near to my ancestral home.'

'I'd like to see Bargino again in the daylight; it would be interesting to see where the land was, and what's happened to it now.'

'We need to be very careful,' and Paul described how his enquiries about the Campolargo family had gone down in the Butcher's and the Bar in San Casciano.'

'There must still be plenty of people around who were alive at the time. If you think, it's only forty years since the end of the war – anyone over fifty would remember it well.'

'They'd need to be a bit older than that. My grandmother died at the end of 1935 and she must have left here at least seven months before then, because she got married in Gibraltar in the May of that year, and your grandmother married in 1940 so she probably wasn't here after that. They'd need to be fifty-five to have any real memories of your grandmother and over sixty to have a chance of remembering mine, probably older than that.'

'So what can we do?'

He thought for a while, swirling his wine round in his glass, then finally, 'I can think of four things we can do, although some of them might turn out to be dead ends.'

'Go on.'

'The first thing, which has a slight chance of helping, is for me to go back to Barberino and talk to Carmela di Lollo's carer. There's just a chance that there may be some old family photographs there that we could borrow and copy. She may also be able to give us the addresses of Carmela and Filippo's daughters, although, having said that, the daughters may not be helpful; I got the impression that they weren't that bothered about their own mother, let alone more distant members of the family.'

'If you do go back, could I come with you? I know that it'll be sad to see her but I've never seen any relative on Nonna's side of the family and, if I do look a bit like Nonna, it might just trigger something.'

'I'm certainly not going to turn down your company,' he said, placing a hand over hers on the table. 'The second thing we can do, which may be better if I do alone, is to try and talk to

Guerrini, the lawyer in Siena. He must be your mother's cousin but, as there doesn't seem to be any contact between the Guerrini and your nonna and mum then there must be some reason for that, and they would probably lump you in with your nonna. Neither I, nor even my father have had any contact with my grandmother, so whatever the family disagreement is, they may see me as being outside it.'

She nodded, 'I'll think about that... again, I'm curious to see these relatives but... Keep going.'

'Option number three is probably the easiest option. Did you notice that bar at the crossroads in Bargino?' She nodded. 'There must be people who go in there who remember the Campolargo family. Although people seem to clam up as soon as I ask any questions, I'm sure that someone will be prepared to talk; even if they only talk to complain about us, at least that will tell us something more about the family, and hopefully, we'll get more than that.'

'And the fourth option,' said Rosa, looking Paul in the eye, 'is for me to confront Nonna – because we know that she knows all the answers.'

'But we also know that she's not going to give you the answers and, as it sounds to me as if you've always got on well with your nonna, then I don't want you to ask her, and certainly not to put any pressure on her. Your good relationship with her is more important than anything else – I'd rather give up looking rather than this... obsession of mine, be the cause of you falling out with your nonna.'

'So what's going to happen when she finds out about us? I'm going to fall out with her sooner or later anyway.'

Paul caught his breath. Although he knew they had been growing closer together, he had tried to tell himself that she might just see him as a very friendly relative and have no intention of things going further, but that "us" showed him that she wanted what he wanted.

He smiled and placed his other hand on the table palm upwards for her to place her free hand onto. 'You don't know just how happy that "us" makes me feel, but are you sure? You don't mind about us being cousins? And what about the rest of your family – it won't just be your nonna who won't be happy about it?'

'Why do you think it took so long for me to think through things after that evening up in Fiesole? It wasn't just because you'd told me things that I might have wished weren't true – I knew you were right about those – it was falling in love that scared me, with all the complications that that involves. I wasn't sure if I was mature enough to handle it all, but the benefit of having done all that thinking is that now I know exactly what I want, even if I'll probably have to wait to get it. As for being cousins – so what? Apart from the fact that we're only second cousins anyway, all the royal families around Europe have been doing it for centuries, and there are lots of normal people as well, they just don't go around shouting about it.

The table was too wide for him to reach across and kiss her, so he raised her left hand to his lips instead.

The seats in MG Midgets are not conducive to kissing so, after he had parked on Via delle Porte Sante in front of the gates leading up to the entrance of San Miniato al Monte, they walked slowly towards Rosa's house, each with an arm around the other's back. Just before they came into view of the house, they stopped and sat down on one of the benches. 'I got distracted before; I don't want you to confront your nonna about the family. Hopefully, if we can find the information we need elsewhere, it will help us understand why she's so negative about me and we might be able to work out how to change her mind. OK?'

'OK. I'm not going to confront her, but I can't promise not to ask her anything at all.'

He kissed her then moved his head away, 'You've chosen me, so your judgement must be impeccable. I trust you absolutely.'

She stuck her tongue out at him, gave him a last quick kiss and then turned to walk quickly towards the door of the house calling, 'Tomorrow morning at ten – usual place.'

The following morning they walked and they talked and they hugged and they laughed, not minding the bitterly cold wind that carried some very fine flakes of snow in it. By tacit agreement, they kept off the subject of the Campolargo family as both were aware that there was nothing they could do at the moment. Instead Rosa wanted to know all about England and what the English were like. Paul told her about cities like York and Lincoln, Gloucester and Bath and about areas of natural beauty such as the Lake District and the northern Northumbrian coastline. He laughed at Rosa's lack of knowledge of Geography as, like most Italians, she assumed that the only thing north of London was Scotland. One day he would take her to see all of them – and more – but she had to promise to come in the sea with him – whatever the weather. She agreed that she would go in the sea if he would also take her up the tower he'd mentioned previously in the town where he used to go to the sea as a child.

After wandering through the centre and along the bank of the Arno they stopped for a hot chocolate with a swirl of mounted cream on top, at the cafeteria in the Boboli Gardens, and she licked a blob of cream off the end of his nose for him. After the hot chocolate, they made their way up through the gardens to exit on the *Viale* and head back towards Rosa's house. As they neared the top of the gardens, where the walls of the *Forte da Belvedere* protected them from the wind, a middle-aged man, well wrapped up with a thick jacket, a scarf, a Davy Crockett hat and a pair of leather gloves, came in the opposite direction. Paul felt Rosa stiffen slightly and saw the smile on her face become less mobile.

'*Buongiorno*, Rosa.'

'*Buongiorno, Signor Antino*. How are you?'

'Fine, thank you. Aren't you going to introduce me to your friend?'

'Oh, sorry. This is Paolo. Paolo, this is Signor Antino who lives next door to my family.'

'*Piacere,*' said Paul, extending a hand.

'*Piacere.*'

'If you'll excuse us, Signor Antino, I have to get going or I'll be late for lunch. Enjoy your walk.'

'Shit!' said Rosa, as soon as they were out of earshot. 'Of all the people to meet, it had to be him.'

'Surely, even if he mentions having seen you to your parents, all he saw was you holding hands with a young man. Your parents can't seriously object to that at your age.

'Oh my parents won't have a problem with that, the only thing that will annoy them will be my having been seen by him. His only argument of conversation is the way moral standards are slipping and how young people today have no sense of shame. He'll exaggerate what he's seen when he tells his wife and she'll add a bit more on when she tells the rest of the neighbours. Mum and dad know what they're like so they'll believe me, so long as I mention having been seen by him before he starts spreading rumours.'

'In court, in England, witnesses have to swear to tell, "the truth, the whole truth, and nothing but the truth," I think that your best bet is probably to tell "the truth" and "nothing but the truth." Yes, you were walking with someone, holding hands, but you're not ready for them to meet him yet.'

She smiled, 'Good idea; I feel better about it now. But I'm also going to tell them that they will get to meet "him" sometime over the next few months.'

On the Monday and Tuesday their timetables made it impossible for them to meet other than for a quick sandwich at lunchtime, but on the Wednesday morning Paul was outside the Gym in Borgo Pinti when Rosa arrived at ten to seven. Paul recognised the car that dropped her off as being that of her father and so kept his distance until the car had disappeared round the corner, then he went over and gave her a hug.

'How can your body possibly function at this time in the morning, and in this cold?'

She laughed, 'Years of practice. I just focus on what I'm doing and try and shut everything else out.'

'OK. I'll just be sitting at the back, although I can't promise to stay awake at this time.'

'It was you who wanted to come,' she reminded him with a laugh, now you've got to look enthusiastic.

He was enthusiastic. Watching her go through her warm-up routine in her tracksuit was exciting enough, but when she slipped the tracksuit off and sidled onto the floor exercise area with the grace and sinuosity of a cougar stalking a kill, he was entranced. He watched as she pointed her feet like a ballet dancer and then, without apparently exerting any force, launched herself in to the air and came down into the splits position before raising herself up on the palms of her hands that were placed flat in front of her and pivoting into a handstand. The rest of the routine was equally impressive and, at least to Paul's eyes, appeared to be executed flawlessly; he was amazed to see how strong and flexible she was, as he studied the changing profiles of the muscles and tendons in her legs, arms and neck. At the end he felt like applauding but wisely stayed quiet at the back of the gym, outwardly calm and composed but inwardly bubbling like a volcano.

'Incredible,' he said after she had showered and changed. 'Let me buy you breakfast.'

'OK. I've got half an hour.'

They were both aware that the following day would be the last chance they had to meet before he left for England, and they decided that something special, although not too expensive, was called for. After some debate they decided that a little restaurant in a back street not far from Vivoli, the self-proclaimed best ice-cream maker in the world, would be the ideal place. They could eat well, drink a bottle of *spumante* and then round it off with a really good ice-cream. Before they opened the *spumante*, Paul took out the box with the silver heart and chain inside, which he had carefully wrapped in Christmas paper.

'You can open it now, or you can wait until next Wednesday, I don't mind.'

'Usually, I prefer to leave presents until Christmas Day but I'm worried about what my reaction might be if I open it in front of the others – so I'm going to open it now.'

'She gasped as she opened the box and saw the heart inside.'

'It's beautiful. Thank you so much. Now I've got a little something for you as well. It's not much, but it's all I could manage without asking Dad for an advance of next month's money,' and she gave him a decoratively wrapped parcel about thirty centimetres long by ten wide and two deep. He was about to open it but she said, 'Save it until Christmas Day. I'll call you from the SIP late in the afternoon.'

Chapter 13

Christmas in England was pretty much how he'd expected it to be; his mother fussed over him for the first hour or so, while his brother and father rolled their eyes and shook their heads when they were sure that she wouldn't see them. Once the first hour was over, it was as if he'd never been away, which he much preferred. They were mildly curious about his time in Italy, but as none of them had ever been, he soon realised that the things he was trying to describe didn't really matter much to them and that it was better to keep descriptions short. He told his father everything he'd found out about his grandfather, and his father said that if Paul stayed there for long and they came out to see him, that he would like to visit the grave. Paul had hoped that he would be curious about the period when his grandfather seemed to have operated as a spy, as there wasn't much he could do to further his enquiries over the holiday period, and he had hoped that his father would look into it for him after he had gone back. Unfortunately, however, John showed no enthusiasm for the task, and Paul knew that anything he needed to find out, he would need to find out for himself the following summer.

The one thing that he was able to do while he was there was to borrow his brother David's car on the Monday before

Christmas and drive over to Nottingham to take a picture of his grandmother's grave in Beeston Cemetery. Fortunately, John had been taken there fairly regularly by his Auntie Ethel to place flowers on his mother's grave, so he was able to tell Paul which cemetery it was in and more or less how to find it. It had struck Paul while he was on the plane flying back over, that being able to see the grave, even if only in a photograph, may have made some of his Italian relatives more willing to speak to him. Fortunately, he had thought to take a pan-scrub with him to clean the gravestone up a bit before photographing it because, as he suspected, it had been completely neglected since the last time his "grandmother", or as he now tried to think of her, his great-aunt Ethel, had been well enough to visit, which must have been at least six years ago, possibly slightly longer. As he was about to take the photograph, a thought struck him and he lowered the camera. There was no florist open anywhere near the cemetery but he knew that it was wasn't too far to the Queen's Medical Centre, where his sister had trained, and he was sure he'd be able to get some flowers there. As it turned out, he saw a sign to a small garden centre before he got to the hospital and was able to have a pot made up with plants that were resistant, and that should guarantee some colour all the year round.

When he got back to the cemetery, he placed the pot carefully on the grave, using his heel to scrape off the grass and moss underneath it, and only then did he take his photograph. Although he wasn't religious in any way and had no belief in any sort of afterlife, having placed the flowers and bestowed some care on the grave, somehow made him feel that it made her more of a real person with a real connection to him. Third of June 1914 to twenty-fifth of December 1935 – younger than me and only a year and a half older than Rosa he thought, and in two days' time she would have been dead for exactly fifty years; he shuddered.

His father had never liked to make much of a fuss about his birthday, but when Paul got back home he saw that his sister and brother-in-law's car was outside and realised that they were there because it was his birthday. John wasn't home from work yet and Paul assumed that if any of his colleagues had discovered that it was his birthday they would have insisted on going for a drink after work, particularly as many of them would be taking the next day off as it was Christmas Eve. Julie had made sure that she got there early to make sure that their mother didn't start cooking anything, insisting that she and Al were taking everyone out for a meal to celebrate John's fiftieth. Their mum said that John would prefer a quiet evening in and that she'd bought some nice rump steak specially for his birthday, but Paul backed Julie up, insisting that the steak be placed in the freezer to be used another day.

'He gets away with it every other year, but he's not getting away with it on his fiftieth. You know what he's like; once he's finished moaning about us making a fuss, he'll forget and really enjoy himself.'

Julie and Al were back again the following evening, this time with baby Luke, and this time to stay over until the weekend. As Julie was only eleven months older than Paul, they'd always been fairly close and he was looking forward to getting the chance to talk to her properly. He felt that he needed to share the things he'd discovered with someone, and he knew that Julie would listen to what he had to say more than the others; he also wanted to know what she thought about him and Rosa, before any of the others knew about it.

He got his chance on Christmas Eve. He used the fact that he'd been away from his parents for several months as an excuse to return home after the first couple of pints, leaving David and Al to make the most of the Christmas spirit. John and Hazel went up to bed shortly after eleven leaving Paul and Julie in front of the television which, after a glance at Julie to seek approval, Paul turned off and put a Genesis tape on instead.

'Good,' she said, 'We'll see quite enough TV tomorrow. Now, little brother, tell me all your news.'

He started by telling her about Florence, about his students – including some humorous anecdotes about some of them, and about one old lady who turned up every time, even though she was in her eighties– he told her about Signora Vaccherini in a way which had her laughing out loud, and then he told her about how he'd tried to find out about their grandparents. He didn't say anything about himself and Rosa but Julie understood, as he'd hoped she would.

'You really like Rosa, don't you?' He nodded, although it was a statement rather than a question.

'What do you think? I'd really like your opinion.'

She took his hand, 'No, you wouldn't. You'd like my approval, which isn't quite the same thing – although I'm sure you won't take any notice of either if you don't like them.'

He leaned back on the settee. 'You're partially right. I probably won't take any notice if you don't approve, although I'd rather have your approval than not have it. Where you're wrong is about your opinion, because I do value that as well.'

'Alright. From your description, she sounds really nice, so in terms of approval, I approve. Now, in terms of opinion, whose opinion do you want: your sister's, or that of Staff Nurse Julie Garvey of The Royal Oldham Hospital?'

Paul hesitated, 'I want my sister's, but now that you've reminded me of your medical expertise, I think I also need that of Staff Nurse Garvey.'

'OK. Well as your sister, it doesn't bother me at all that you are distant relatives, especially because you've only just met more or less like any... I don't want to say "normal" but can't think of another term, any normal couple. I might have felt a bit different about it if it had been cousin Jane, who we've known all our lives, but I'd have got over it.'

'Cousin Jane! You might have got over it, but I don't think I would.'

'As a Staff Nurse, I'm trying to think back to the genetics I studied, and to remember some relevant statistics. I'd need to check for the exact figures but I think that statistically, the chances of serious birth defects are twice as high for the children of cousins than for the children of non-cousins but...' and she held a finger up to stop him interrupting, ' two things: firstly the possibility is only about three percent for non-cousins so that only takes it up to six, which is still low – and secondly, that's without screening; the majority of that increased risk can be screened out. I seem to remember having read somewhere recently that, throughout the world, about ten per cent of marriages are between first cousins, and in some countries or cultures it can be as high as fifty percent. Did you know, by the way, that Darwin was married to his first cousin, and if there was any problem, he would have been aware of it.... So, as a Staff Nurse, I'd say, to be on the safe side, you ought both to have some tests before you think about having children ... but then I'd say that you are only second cousins so the risks are minimal anyway! Does that help?'

Paul leaned over and gave her a hug. 'Thankyou.'

As soon as he woke up on Christmas morning, he opened the drawer of the bedside cabinet and took out the packet that Rosa had given him; he wanted to open this one while he was on his own. He undid the ornately tied ribbon that held the thick Christmas paper together and dropped both ribbon and paper on the floor next to his bed. Inside was a cardboard box which, as white lettering on the navy blue lid proclaimed it to contain a set of salad servers, he hoped had been reused. Prising open the lid, he found that whatever was in there had been carefully wrapped in tissue paper for protection. A slip of paper on top of the tissue paper bore the handwritten message, "Don't drop it – it's fragile!" He smiled, and carefully unwrapped the layers of tissue to reveal an oblong shaped plate of glass with rounded corners and slightly bevelled edges. On the plate, a classical Florentine view had been carefully etched, looking out over the city from the Piazzale Michelangelo. In the foreground, a young couple stood by a parked sports-car admiring the view. Dabs of glass paints had been applied carefully to bring different areas of the picture to life: some pale-blue streaks in the sky, hints of orangie-red on the cupolas of the Duomo, San Lorenzo and just the slightest hint to suggest that most of the roofs were made of terracotta, but what really brought a smile to his face was that the male of the two young people had fair hair, while the female's was dark and the sports-car they stood in front of was bright yellow.

The more he looked at it, the more details he noticed and the more pleased he became with his present, until finally he noticed that engraved in the bottom right hand corner was a tiny rose with a 'C' around it. Up until then he had been impressed by her taste, now he was amazed by her talent: she must have done the whole thing, both the engraving and the touches of colour. If she can't make a living as an archaeologist, he thought, she could certainly make a living as an artist.

The rest of Christmas Day was just as he remembered every other Christmas Day to have been except that now there was baby Luke to fuss over, which meant that for the first time ever, he wasn't the youngest member of the family. They opened their presents altogether around the tree after breakfast, and everyone thanked each other effusively, although with varying degrees of sincerity, depending on the particular present, and they all ate far too much turkey, except David, who was clearly feeling a little delicate after the previous evening's excesses.

After their Christmas Dinner, Paul and David did the washing up; Julie wouldn't allow Al, who she said was using it as an excuse to get out of entertaining Luke, and after that they managed to combine games of *Scrabble* and *Trivial Pursuit* with looking after Luke until it was time for the television to go on for the usual festive fare. Starting at five-to-five, *All Creatures Great and Small*, was followed by a brief news summary and then *Hi-de-Hi*, *Only Fools and Horses* and *The Two Ronnies*.

It was at just after seven, half way through *Hi-de-Hi*, by which time Paul was half asleep, when the phone rang out in the hallway. Hazel was nearest the door and also the most awake, as she was the only one who was keen on *Hi-de-Hi*, and she was on her feet and through the door while Paul was still uncrossing his legs.

'Paul!' shouted his mother from the hallway, 'Phone!' And then, two seconds later smiling as she stepped to one side to let him through the doorway first, 'Young lady called Rosa, for you.'

'Thanks.'

'Sounds very nice,' and she closed the door behind her.

'Ciao, Paul.'

'*Buon Natale*. And thanks very much for the present – it's wonderful –almost as good as hearing your voice again. Everything OK?'

'Yes. *Buon Natale* to you as well. I'm glad you like the present; it took me ages, especially the car – I've never done cars before. Anyway, sorry I couldn't get away earlier; I hope it's not too late.'

'No, it's fine. How's your day been?'

She told him how it hadn't been particularly exciting. Her uncle and aunt from Bologna were staying and they tended to be very traditional and had insisted on watching the Pope on television, at which point her grandmother had conveniently developed a headache and retired to her room. Her aunt liked to seem cultured, and had bombarded her with almost entirely pointless questions about her degree course for much of the afternoon. Eventually, when she'd been despairing of ever getting away, her sister had announced that she needed to go down in to the city to return a book to a school-friend who was leaving on a skiing holiday the following day. Her father, obviously taking pity on her had asked her to accompany her sister, which had allowed her to finally get to the SIP. Paul told her a little bit about his day but all too soon they had to bring the conversation to an end, conscious both of the meter ticking over at the SIP, and also of the fact that Rosa needed to rejoin Francesca. They agreed to meet at seven o' clock in Piazzale Michelangelo the following Sunday evening, providing that Paul's plane wasn't delayed. Although he could tell that everyone wanted to ask questions when he returned to the room, no-one did, and he assumed that Julie had told them to leave him alone.

The following afternoon, Paul managed to get out of the house with David and Al and they went to watch Oldham play Bradford City, as Oldham were the only one of the local teams to be at home that day, except for Manchester City where all available tickets for their match against Liverpool had been snapped up weeks ago. As so often happens on Boxing Day matches, a significant number of players gave the impression of having overdosed on Christmas-Pudding and sherry, and Oldham slipped to an unexpected one-nil home defeat in an uninspiring game. That did not deter the three from travelling over to Stockport two days later to watch a rumbustious derby match with Burnley, where there was a lot less skill but at least all the players seemed to care.

When they got back to the house after the match at Stockport, it was time for Julie, Al and Luke to leave and make their way over to Al's brother's house. Al gave Paul a wink and a slap on the back and Julie gave him a long embrace. 'Have a good journey, little brother,' and then, in a lower voice, that only he could hear, 'Give my love to Rosa, and remember my advice.'

Chapter 14

Paul's plane wasn't late; the Monarch airlines flight from Luton managed to arrive fifteen minutes ahead of time and, as a result, instead of having to get a bus into Pisa Central Station, Paul just managed to catch one of the very infrequent direct trains from the airport to central Florence.

Paul used the last two shots on the film in his camera taking portrait shots of Rosa, one sitting on the wall at Piazzale Michelangelo with the city spread out behind her, and the other a soft focus shot with the background deliberately out of focus so as not to distract from the main subject. 'The first one is to send to my sister, and the second one is just for me!' the next day he would take the film into a photographic shop not far from the *Birreria Centrale* and leave it to be developed.

She told him how, when she had told her parents about bumping into Signor Antino, they had at first been amused and limited their response to some good natured teasing, but when she had continued to not tell them anymore, she had received a lecture about the dangers of meeting strange men when nobody else knew where she was. 'I'm sure they're worried that you're slipping me drugs and plan to sell me off into the white-slave trade at the earliest possible opportunity.'

'Now that's an idea. I hadn't thought of that; I'd probably get a lot for you. Maybe we can go away for a weekend in Yemen at some point.' She stuck her tongue out at him and they both laughed.

'Sooner or later, they are going to have to meet you though,' she said, becoming serious. 'I'm sure that once they know you, all the prejudices they've got, whatever they may be, will melt away – they can't know you and not like you. They've always been open minded until now.'

'But don't forget, we still have no idea why my grandmother left Italy and whether or not she and your grandmother had fallen out before hand – that could explain everything.'

Two days later, Paul met one of Rosa's family for the first time. They had agreed to meet at half past nine on New Year's Eve and then wander round the main piazzas of the city looking for the best free entertainment and the liveliest parties. Rosa was more than five minutes late, which was unusual for her, and when she appeared she was with another girl wearing a faux fur coat under which a long blue, sequinned dress led down to a pair of high heeled shoes that must have made walking down the steps extremely awkward, and explained why Rosa was late. The girl had fairer hair than Rosa but apart from that there was a clear facial resemblance, and Paul realised straight away that this must be her sister.

They looked at each other with interest as Rosa introduced them. 'So this is the mystery man you were all over in the

Boboli Gardens – he doesn't look too bad – I don't know why you want to keep him hidden.'

Paul laughed as Rosa glared at her sister. 'Maybe I've got hidden defects that your sister needs to iron out before I'm fully presentable. Love the lipstick by the way.'

'Shall I borrow it, and put some on too?' said Rosa with a half-smile.

'No. I don't think that bright blue would suit you quite as well.'

'It's a special one, just for New Year's Eve.. I don't normally wear this colour.'

They all laughed and started to move towards the *Ponte Vecchio*, where Francesca was sure that she would find some of her school friends.

When they left Francesca, Rosa reminded her that they had promised to be home by two and arranged to meet by the bust of Cosimo 1st in the middle of the bridge at one thirty. Francesca gave them a wave and said, 'See you later. Don't do anything I wouldn't do.'

'That probably doesn't rule out very much... I hope she's OK. It's the first time she's been allowed to come down into the centre on New Year's Eve without our parents. I'm supposed to be looking after her.'

'She'll be fine, now she's with her friends. When I was a teenager, my mates and I were always out having a good time on New Year's Eve, and apart from a few headaches, no-one ever came to any harm.'

'You're right. I know. Come on, let's go and see what's happening in Piazza della Repubblica.'

Before midnight they were in Piazza della Signoria where a large clock had been set up and was counting down the minutes towards the New Year. A stage had been erected and an orchestra was playing lively classical music, although it was impossible to get anywhere near it, as Paul thought that there must be at least twenty thousand people in the piazza. As the clock ticked over the last second, there was an explosion of sound: *spumante* corks popped, people cheered, the church bells rang and the sky behind the Uffizi was transformed by the psychedelic flashes of an enormous firework display. But it was sometime before Paul got to see the fireworks as he was clasped in a tight embrace with Rosa whose tongue was urgently exploring the inside of his mouth.

When they separated, she looked up at him and said in a small, slightly hoarse voice, 'I can come back to your room, if you want.'

'I do want, but it's not the right time. I don't want our first time to be rushed, especially for you.'

She leaned her forehead on his chest, 'Thankyou – I love you so much.'

Later, as he lay in bed, alone, staring at the ceiling, he couldn't help wondering if he'd done the right thing but, as he allowed Rosa's image to blend with those of Signora Vaccherini and Korki as he drifted towards sleep, he knew that it had been the right decision. Rosa was special, and everything he did with her had to be special. He also realised, with just a slight pang of regret that any future diversions with Korki or Signora Vaccherini were now out of the question.

On Friday the third, Paul picked his photographs up; Rosa looked stunning in the last two in the envelope and he was pleased with how the pictures of his grandmother's grave had come out. Before he left the shop he ordered three extra copies of the best picture of the grave, a couple of extra copies of the picture of Rosa that he had taken to send to Julie, and an enlargement of the other picture of her, that he intended to frame and put on his wall.

In the afternoon, he picked Rosa up with the Midget from Piazzale Michelangelo and suggested that they had a drive out to Barberino, ostensibly so that Rosa could see her aunt for the first time but mainly so that he could ask the Filipino *badante* if Carmela had any old family photographs. Before leaving

England he had purchased a few typically English products to use as little presents and one of these, a packet of shortbread, he took along for Cheskka, the Filipino.

She was surprised to see Paul again but also, he thought, pleased to have some company other than their senile great-aunt. After Paul had explained to her that Rosa was another of Carmela's great nieces, he gave her the pack of shortbread, telling her, with only a slight deviation from the truth, that he had brought it specially for her from England, out of gratitude for what she was doing for a member of his family. Rosa asked a lot of questions about Carmela's health showing a, for Paul, surprising familiarity with various aspects of the illness – something he'd have to ask her about afterwards, he thought.

When he judged that there wasn't much further that could be discussed about the illness, he asked casually if Carmela had any photograph albums with old pictures of the family. As Rosa's grandmother had lost all her photographs in the war and, as it was now fifty years since Paul's grandmother had died, there was no longer any trace of any photographs, they would both be very keen to see any photographs that existed, particularly of the pre-war period. Cheskka said that if there were any they would almost certainly be in the room that had once been Filippo Campolargo's study; if they didn't mind waiting a few minutes, she would go and have a look.

While she was away Paul asked Rosa how she knew so much about the disease and she told him that her father's father had suffered from SDAT, or Senile Dementia of the Alzheimer's Type for several years before he died. At the time, she had read up lots about it and aged fourteen was convinced that when she grew up she would become a doctor and find a cure for the disease. Later, however, she had realised that for someone who felt faint if ever she saw a needle, and who was squeamish about blood, medicine was probably not the best degree course to follow. At least in Archaeology, if ever she came across any bodies, they would have been dead for several centuries, maybe even longer.

When Cheskka returned, she was carrying three large albums; two of them were full of colour photographs and were clearly from the post-war period, but one, the slimmest of the three was full of older black and white photographs. By looking first at the later photographs it was easy to work out which was Carmela and also Filippo. From there, they were able to trace Carmela back to the earlier photographs and use that to work out who some of the other figures must be. There were a few photographs of Carmela and Filippo's wedding, but there was no-one there who looked a likely candidate for Maddalena, and neither of them had any idea what Chiara had looked like. They did find a picture of Filippo, together with two other young men standing behind a distinguished looking older man who they assumed to be Domenico Campolargo. Of the younger men, one seemed to be a few years older than the other and they realised that they must be Aristide and Umberto respectively. Tucked into the front of the album was an even older photograph which was clearly a formal studio portrait of the family. A younger Domenico stood with a hand on the shoulder of a strikingly beautiful but fragile looking woman who sat cradling a baby, who Paul guessed to be a bit older than Luke, so probably about a year old. Standing by his mother's knee was a boy, presumably Aristide, while a slightly younger boy and a little girl sat cross legged on the floor in front of their mother.

They were nearing the end of the album and had almost given up all hopes of finding a photograph of either of their grandmothers when Rosa put a hand on Paul's to stop him turning over to the penultimate page.

'Just a minute. I think there were two pages stuck together there.' Paul looked back and saw that she was right. The corner mounts of some of the photographs had somehow become entangled, and he had to be very careful in pulling them apart as he did not want to damage the photographs.

When he finally did get the pages apart, Rosa gave a gasp. She was looking at a photograph of six women ranging in age from about thirty down to mid-teens. 'That's my nonna – I'm sure of it,' said Rosa pointing a finger that trembled slightly at the youngest of the women who could not have been any older than sixteen, at the very most.

'The people who say you look like your nonna, are right I think. She was very beautiful.' Rosa flashed a smile at him. 'No,' he said, shaking his head, 'I wasn't just trying to give you a compliment, I really meant it. She was beautiful, and she does look like you.'

'She also looks very like this other one here,' said Rosa, indicating one of two others who only looked a few years older than Maddalena, 'If we hadn't known that Nonna was the youngest, I wouldn't have known which of the two she was. The other one must be your grandmother – you finally know what she looked like.'

Paul studied the photograph for a minute and then said slowly, 'And if she looked so much like your grandmother when they were young, when I get to meet your grandmother, I'll be able to see what she would have looked like now – if she'd lived... Of these older three, this one here is Carmela, one of the others must be Margarita, and the other one will be Aristide's wife. The other younger woman must be Umberto's wife.'

Rosa picked up the older photograph that they had found tucked into the front of the album and looked several times between the two images. 'This one is Margarita. Look at the noses and the shape of the chins; they're pretty much identical.'

'Brilliant, Sherlock, I don't know how you do it.'

'Elementary my dear Watson,' and despite the presence of Cheskka, she gave him a peck on the cheek.

'Cheskka, would it be possible for me to borrow a few of these photographs to have copies made? I'll bring the originals back as soon as they're done.'

The Filipino shrugged her shoulders, 'You don't need to worry about that. Nobody else will ever want to see them. Just bring them back whenever it's convenient – or not at all.'

'Thank you, Signora, but we will bring them back soon and we'll come and see you and Aunt Carmela again other times as well.' Paul raised an eyebrow but said nothing.

'I didn't realise you'd get so attached to Carmela so quickly.'

'Idiot! Whatever Carmela used to be like, she's hardly a person now. I was thinking about Cheskka; can you imagine how mind bogglingly boring her life must be, stuck out there with a dribbling vegetable who's got nothing left to do except die.' He smiled.

They discussed the photographs on their way back to Florence where they were in time to drop them off at the photography shop before it closed for the night.

'Do you want to sell this one?' asked the man in the shop, looking at the photograph of Domenico Campolargo and his family, 'It's an original.'

'Sorry?' said Paul, puzzled.

'It's an original Alinari portrait photograph – no later than 1910, I'd say.'

'The Alinari brothers were really famous photographers from around the middle of the last century; they were artists almost as much as photographers,' said Rosa to Paul, and then to the man in the shop, 'No, I'm sorry, it's a family heirloom but, just out of interest, what's it worth?'

'A family portrait in good condition like this would probably be worth about twenty thousand lire to a collector but, if anyone in it is well known, then it could be worth a lot more.'

'No,' Said Rosa, smiling sweetly, 'just old family members.'

'Well done... I thought for a minute you were going to tell him that it contained both Domenico and Aristide Campolargo.'

Rosa pulled a face, 'Can you imagine the reaction if my family found out that we'd sold that, which would probably get the photograph, and the Campolargo name all over the front page of La Nazione? That would ruin any chance of them accepting that we're a couple.'

'I wonder if they'll ever accept it.'

'They will. I know they're being odd about this family thing, but they're not normally like this... really.'

'Go on. I'll believe you.'

As Paul walked Rosa home they decided that it was best to leave the second part of their action plan until the following Friday as, with the long weekend for Epiphany, it was unlikely that the extra copies of his photographs that Paul had ordered that morning would be ready much before midweek, and they both had busy days on the Thursday.

It took them some time to find the office of Guerrini and Becalossi, which turned out to be in a relatively recent part of the city, near the Stadium. A very thin receptionist smiled at them as they entered the reception area which had obviously had quite a bit of money spent on it fairly recently, and where a mixture of shiny stainless steel and mahogany had somehow been put together to form a harmonious whole. The practice must be doing very well, if they could afford the sort of interior designer who could create that, thought Paul.

'Good morning. How can I help you?'

'We'd like to see *Avvocato* Guerrini, please.' Paul gave the receptionist what he hoped was his most winning smile.

'Do you have an appointment?'

'I'm afraid not. We're relatives, and we just happened to find ourselves in the area and thought it would be rude not to pay our respects.'

'*Avvocato* Guerrini is with a client at the moment, and he is due in court at eleven, so he's unlikely to be able to see you today.'

Paul smiled again, 'We'll wait, then even if he only has five minutes between appointments, we'll be able to say hello."

'Alright,' said the receptionist doubtfully, 'but he may not get chance to see you, and I wouldn't like you to have wasted your time.'

'Don't worry. It's not a problem. We'll just sit here and have a look at the paper.'

Just before twenty to eleven, a man in his sixties, carrying a briefcase and wearing an immaculately tailored grey three piece suit emerged from a door at the side of the reception accompanied by a nervous looking young lawyer who saw him to the door and shook his hand as he almost bowed him out obsequiously.

'Massimo,' said the stick-like receptionist, 'Could you please tell the *avvocato* that there are two of his relatives here who have been waiting for a quick word with him before he goes in to court. And then to Paul and Rosa, 'What names shall we give?'

Paul had been hoping that she would forget to ask, but gave their names without letting his concern show on his face.

A few seconds later one of the phones on the switchboard buzzed and he saw a red light come on.

'Pronto.' ... 'Yes, a*vvocato*,' ... 'About fifty minutes.' ... 'I did, *avvocato*,' ... 'I'm sorry, *avvocato*,' ... 'No, *avvocato*.' ... 'Straight away, *avvocato*.'

She turned towards them, looking a bit red in the face. 'The *avvocato* will see you now - but he can only give you five minutes.'

As they stood up, the nervous Massimo reappeared and indicated that they should follow him back through the door. The back offices were much more extensive than Paul had expected with a fairly large open-plan area with two offices on either side, separated from the open-plan area by tinted glass. Massimo led them to what appeared to be the largest of the offices where the name Alvaro Guerrini was etched into the dark glass in ornate gold lettering. Massimo knocked on the door and a booming voice came from the other side.

'Avanti.'

Avvocato Guerrini was on his feet and met them half way between the door and his desk. He first gave Rosa a brief handshake and waved her towards one of the chairs facing the desk, and then extended his hand palm upwards to Paul', sliding his hand into Paul's before turning it so that they were interlocked and his thumb pressed against the knuckle of Paul's first finger. Then he ushered him into the other chair facing the desk.

'So, you thought it would be rude of you to be in the area without paying your respects. May I ask, Miss Conte, if this is the first time you have made the trip from Florence to Siena?' Paul saw the colour rise to Rosa's face, but she was clearly not expected to reply as the *avvocato* shifted his penetrating gaze to Paul, 'And may I ask, Mr Caddick, on what grounds you claim to be a relative of mine?' There was no warmth whatsoever in the voice, but Paul tried to smile and appear relaxed as he replied.

'My grandmother and your mother were, I believe, sisters. I believe that that makes us first cousins once removed.'

There was a fleeting frown on the *avvocato's* face, which immediately returned to its original cold distant look as he pulled a file from the side of his desk and glanced at what appeared to be a family tree fixed to the inside off the front cover. 'Chiara Maria Eleonora Campolargo, born in Florence on the 20th of May 1914; disappeared on the 28th of December 1934, declared dead for legal purposes by the Prefecture of Florence on 28th June 1935.' He looked at Paul and raised an eyebrow, 'Do you have anything to add?'

'No... I can confirm that that was my grandmother, although clearly the date of death is incorrect.'

'Is your grandmother still alive now?'

'No, I'm afraid not; she died some time ago.'

'The *avvocato* nodded,' and Paul thought he detected a sense of relief. 'Now, I have very little time. Perhaps the two of you wouldn't mind telling me why you are here.'

'Certainly,' said Paul, determined to meet the *avvocato's* gaze without flinching. 'Neither of us knows very much about the early lives of our grandmothers. We know that at some point there must have been a disagreement between the six siblings and that, as a result, they lost contact with each other. We are curious to know what happened in our family and, as we have recently discovered that you are related to us, and indeed administer the affairs of some other members of the family, we thought that it would be useful to get to know you, and to ask if you could tell us anything about the family.'

Guerrini gave a humourless smile, 'Mr Caddick, as I have already mentioned, your grandmother went missing on the 28th of June 1935. There were rumours that she may have been abducted by an English farm labourer who disappeared at around the same time; I am unable to give you any further information about your grandmother. With regard to yours, Miss Conte, I'm afraid that it was her decision to break off all contact with the rest of the family. Now, unless my information,' he glanced at the file, 'requires updating, your grandmother is still alive and in possession of her faculties. Therefore, I would suggest that the best person to provide you with the information you require is your grandmother herself. Now, if you'll excuse me, I have important work to do.' He closed the file and stood up indicating the door.

Rosa and Paul thanked him for his time and then, just as Paul was about to follow Rosa through the door, a thought struck him. He turned, 'Did you know either of our grandmothers, yourself?'

Guerrini hesitated, clearly in two minds whether to respond or not, then he said, 'My memories of your grandmother are very, very hazy; my memories of Signora Melluso are clearer but not, I'm afraid, positive. Based partly on my own memories, but also on what I have been told, I'm afraid that she was generally argumentative, ungrateful to her family, and deceitful. Good-day.'

'How dare he!' fumed Rosa, as soon as they were outside the main door of Guerrini and Becalossi; 'what does he know about my grandmother?' There were tears in her eyes as Paul put an arm around her and ushered her away. 'If he's a typical example of the Campolargos, I can understand why my family don't want anything to do with them. Nasty, spiteful man!'

'Look on the bright side. When I do eventually get to meet them, I won't need to do much to rise above people like Guerrini. He's enough to give anyone the creeps, right from that weird way of shaking hands he has.'

'What way? He just gave mine a very light shake, a sort of unavoidable thing he had to do, but wanted to get over as quickly as possible.'

'That's odd; he sort of slid his hand into mine then rotated it and gave me a weird squeeze with his thumb. I thought he must have a deformed hand at first, but there was no sign of it after that.'

They decided to have a wander round the centre of the city before going back and soon found themselves in the main Piazza del Campo. Although the cold mid-winter sun was shining brightly and the Torre del Mangia cast a long dramatic shadow across the shell shaped piazza, like the pointer on a sundial, there were very few other people there and they could enjoy the full dramatic effect of the thousands of stones that had been lovingly carved into the correct shapes to complete the jigsaw.

'Have you ever been to the *Palio*? It must be an incredible spectacle with the piazza jam packed with people and all the surrounding windows and balconies full up as well.'

Rosa shuddered, 'I watched it once, on television, years ago. What I remember most is two beautiful horses colliding and falling on one of the tight bends. They were magnificent animals but both had to be put down. I've never watched it since. These stones are beautiful but... Mason!'

'What?' Paul looked at her, completely at a loss to understand what she'd said.'

She laughed, 'Guerrini... the handshake... he's a Freemason, and he was trying to find out if you were too.'

'He can't be. Surely they don't exist anymore. I thought that all that was back in the days of Tolstoy... you know – Pierre Bezukhov in *War and Peace*.'

She shook her head with a smile, 'I haven't read any of Tolstoy's novels, only some of his philosophical writings.'

'You should. *"War and Peace"* is easily the best novel ever written, even if Tolstoy insisted it wasn't a novel. But anyway, tell me what you know about freemasonry.'

'We-ell... I don't know much... but, I think that originally, the Freemasons were set up as a secret society with the intention of doing good deeds but, because they were – or they are – a secret society, doing good deeds started to get mixed up with helping each other. I think that they have lots of different secret handshakes so that they can recognise each other without other people knowing. I've heard people saying at the university that lots of politicians and other influential people are Freemasons. The communist group at university is always complaining that the government is run by Freemasons, and that if you're not a freemason, then you don't get any big government contracts. I've heard my dad complain as well, that the only reason that the Head Teacher at his school got the job is because he's in the same masonic lodge as the *Assessore dell'Istruzione Pubblica.*'

'So you think that Guerrini was trying me out to see if I'm a mason as well?' Paul said incredulously.

'I'm sure he was. If you'd given him the right handshake back, he'd have told you everything you wanted to know. He probably tests out all his clients the first time he meets them, to decide how important it is to get a result for them.'

'And probably a lot of the judges as well! .... I suppose if the Freemasons have been around for a long time, the leading members of the Campolargo families will have been members. Getting influence by networking and manipulating sounds just the way that Domenico Campolargo and others before him went about their business.'

'Did you not hear about the Loggia P2, over in England? That was a masonic lodge that had a lot of very important people as members, it was all tied up with the collapse of a big bank, the Banco Ambrosiano...'

'Roberto Calvi, God's banker!' interjected Paul, 'Yes, now I remember – that was big news in England because they hung him under Blackfriars Bridge and tried to make it look like a suicide. So Guerrini was involved with all that!'

'Maybe – it was never really cleared up. They found a membership list but a lot of people claim it was incomplete and that there are still people out there influencing all the important decisions.'

'No wonder people don't want to talk to us. – Do you think your nonna knows.'

Rosa, looked unhappy, 'I don't know. I just don't know any more.'

'It could be,' said Paul slowly, 'that it's one of the reasons why she won't have anything more to do with the Campolargos and, if most, or all of the male members of the family have been masons, then she might assume that I am as well. It would make sense.'

They decided to put off going to try and talk to people in Bargino until the weather was good enough to put the hood down on the Midget, and for the next few days their meetings were mainly confined to quick lunches as they rushed in various directions between lectures or lessons. When they met in the bar on Via degli Alfani on the Friday, Rosa told him that she would have to do some extra gymnastics training over the weekend as the competition that she'd told him would be towards the end of January would be on the twenty-fifth in the *Palasport* at Montecatini. She would have to travel there in the minibus with the rest of the team but there was no reason why he shouldn't come and watch, and she'd have plenty of free time before her event.

He watched her train on both the Saturday and Sunday, as well as making the effort to drag himself out of bed on the Monday and Friday mornings. He watched, entranced by the fluidity of her movements and was convinced that she would do well. Rosa herself was quietly confident; she was only doing the floor and the uneven bars and knew that she could put on a good performance in front of Paul.

Chapter 15

When he got to Montecatini, the *Palasport* was easy to find and there was plenty of parking available immediately outside.

When he went in, he saw that Rosa was engaged in an animated discussion with the team's trainer and he leaned on the rail at the side until the discussion was over and he saw the trainer walk away. He began to walk around the edge of the arena until she saw him and came to meet him. She was clearly pleased to see him, although he could tell that there was something she wasn't happy about.

'What's up?' he asked, putting his arms around her.

She put her forehead on his shoulder for a few seconds then looked up and smiled. 'Oh, it's nothing. I don't mind anything now that you're here. One of our girls, who usually does the beam, hasn't turned up; she sent a message to Marco, our trainer, last night. Now he wants me to do the beam instead, because I'm the most experienced. I was just a bit upset about it, because I really wanted to do well today, with you watching.'

'I'll tell you what – when you're doing the floor and the bars I'll admire your skill and technical ability, but when you're doing the beam, I'll just concentrate on your beautiful body. How's that?' She laughed and relaxed.

The asymmetric bars was the first of the disciples to be held, and after watching Rosa get though a strenuous warm-up routine, Paul watched, spellbound, as the dozen girls who were competing were each called up in turn. For the first two performances he had to fight the need to look away as the girls rotated round the top bar and wrapped their legs around the lower bar allowing the momentum to spin them round before reaching out again for the higher bar, however, by the time it was Rosa's turn, he was already able to watch without wincing. Rosa was good, there was no doubt about that, but so were the other girls and with the exception of two girls who, even to Paul's untutored eye, went through less ambitious routines, he would have found it impossible to differentiate between the others if he had been called upon to judge. Fortunately, the judges knew better what to look for than Paul did and there were small differences in the sets of marks awarded to each girl.

Rosa was awarded the equal second highest marks amongst the gymnasts on the asymmetric bars which she was reasonably pleased with, assuring Paul that she was most confident about the floor exercises which would end the day. After the bars, Rosa slipped her coat on over her tracksuit and they went out for a walk as she was not involved in the vault.

They wandered up into the centre of the town and had a quick walk round the central park where the most famous and ornate of the thermal baths were sited. A thin winter sunshine shone down on the marble colonnaded buildings and glittered on the pale blue surface of a circular outdoor pool at the heart of the complex. 'You can bring me here to take the waters when I'm old and arthritic,' said Rosa, leaning her head on his shoulder.

'We can come together. With all the running I've done, I think my joints will probably need treating before yours do! Come on. Let's be heading back towards the *Palasport*, we can maybe pick up a sandwich on the way.'

There were several elegant looking bars with large display cabinets full of inviting sandwiches and cakes. Rosa just had a small *tramezzino* as she didn't want to eat much before competing again, just enough to take the edge of her appetite. Paul, on the other hand, chose a large sandwich with a milanese cutlet, two slices of tomato and some lettuce leaves inside. The bar they had chosen was next to a jewellers and they lingered for a minute after leaving the bar. 'That's what I'd like, if I could afford it... I just love sapphires, far more than diamonds on their own.' Paul made a mental note, that at the appropriate time, he was going to get her some jewellery with sapphires set in it.

He took her arm and gently pulled her away from the jeweller's in the direction of the gymnastics. 'You need a very rich boyfriend – or one who's good at jewel heists!'

The next discipline was the beam and Rosa said that she just wanted to get it out of the way so that she could concentrate on her floor exercises. Unfortunately, when the contestants drew lots to decide the order, she was eleventh out of twelve which meant that she had much more time to worry about the beam before taking her turn. When the ninth competitor was called, the team's trainer came over and told Rosa that she needed to go and check in with the officials and rub her hands with chalk dust. 'I haven't seen anyone yet who has done anything that I haven't seen you do in training. If you really push yourself, you could end up winning this one. Go on. Go for it.' Rosa raised her head and gave Paul a light kiss and a watery smile, then made her way over to the officials' table. 'It's all about confidence at this stage,' said the trainer to Paul, ' If she really believes in herself, then she could even win this, but she'll need to reproduce all the best moves she's pulled off in practice... Well, not long to wait now so, fingers crossed.'

Paul watched as Rosa mounted the bar going straight into a handstand, then her legs opened and slowly and gracefully moved downwards until she was doing the splits while still upside down. She held the position for two seconds and then her legs rotated through ninety degrees before one of them came down onto the beam allowing her to right herself and somehow move gracefully into an upright position. She did two forward walkovers punctuated by a somersault. Paul was lost in admiring her beauty and grace, but knew from the trainer's excitement next to him that she must also be doing very well technically. Finally, she did two rapid backwards walkovers before speeding up into a third which was clearly going to provide the launchpad for her dismount.

The third walkover was very slightly misjudged and only the side of the hand which should have pushed her off, came down on the edge of the beam. Paul wasn't sure afterwards if he had really heard a crack or if it was just his imagination going into overdrive. Rosa tried to twist her arm round to recover her position, but her whole weight was coming down on the edge of her hand and the arm couldn't manage it and collapsed under her, bringing the side of her head crashing against the edge of the beam, temporarily stunning her so that she had no control over her body as she fell awkwardly to the ground.

It seemed as though there was a collective gasp and everyone in the hall froze for a moment. Paul was the first to react, calling out her name as he vaulted over the rail in front of the spectator area, but it was only a split second before the others, as others had already started to move by the time his feet landed on the wooden floor of the sports hall. An official and another of the competitors reached her at the same time as he did and they all dropped to their knees or crouched next to her. 'No, wait,' said the official, grabbing Paul's sleeve as he reached out to Rosa, 'We have a doctor on site... he should be here in seconds ... let the doctor decide how she should be moved.' Paul pulled his hand back slightly, but then moved it forward again as Rosa moaned and opened her eyes. Her eyes saw Paul and she tried to smile, but at that moment the numbing effect of the adrenaline was no longer enough to deaden the pain, and her low moan turned to a stifled scream as a spasm of pain coursed through her left arm and shoulder.

Just then, the doctor arrived, an earnest looking young woman with a very new looking medical bag. 'Out of the way please... everybody stand back ... they're ringing for an ambulance now ... OK, where does it hurt?' Rosa was too distressed to answer the questions but fortunately, the official, a calm woman in her mid-forties, who had evidently seen many injuries over the years, was able to give a reasonably accurate description of the accident, suggesting that there was almost certainly significant damage to the hand, wrist and shoulder, and that Rosa had also banged the side of her head on the beam as she fell.

Paul was grateful that, although the doctor appeared very young and probably hadn't had to deal with an incident like this before, she was not too proud to recognise the value of the official's experience, and had a very soothing manner. Talking reassuringly to Rosa all the time, she took a syringe out of her bag, broke the top of a phial of medicine, which Paul later noticed was morphine, and injected it into Rosa's arm; she gently asked Rosa to move her toes and then reassured her that there didn't appear to be any damage to the spine. She gently explored the side of Rosa's head where she had banged it and, despite Rosa wincing with pain, and her fingers coming away coated with blood, she smiled and said that again, there was no serious damage; the head wound appeared to be only superficial, but she would need monitoring for the next forty eight hours as she had been knocked cold for a couple of minutes. She left exploring the arm and shoulder for a while to allow the morphine to begin to take effect and then, very gently, began to explore with her fingertips. 'Who's with her?' asked the doctor, looking round the assembled crowd, which Paul noticed had now grown to about a dozen people.

'I am,' said Paul.

And at the same time, 'I'm the team's coach. I brought her here. I'm responsible.' The trainer looked almost as white as Rosa, and Paul could see that he wasn't going to be much use without direction.

'Get one of the other girls to get her bag out of the changing rooms, and bring her coat or she'll freeze lying there – and then ring her parents.' The young doctor smiled approvingly at Paul.

'I'm afraid that there is a fracture in the clavicle. My guess is that it's a clean break that won't require surgery, but we won't know for certain until a CAT scan has been done; there is also a break in the wrist but there are so many small bones there that I can't tell you anything more specific from a superficial examination. Fortunately, there doesn't appear to be any damage to the nerves or the spine.'

'What does the broken clavicle mean for her gymnastics? Will it heal completely?'

The doctor gave a wry smile. 'Collar bones almost always return to normal. Usually it's about three months before patients can go back to their normal activities but, given the stress that gymnasts' collar bones must be under, I would have thought that she shouldn't do any more gymnastics for at least six months.'

Paul felt the hand of Rosa's uninjured arm in his and he lifted it slightly and bent down to brush her fingers with his lips. 'My wrist?' whispered Rosa, who was calmer now under the effect of the morphine.

The doctor put her hand very gently on Rosa's forehead and reflected before replying. 'I honestly don't know; it all depends on how bad the break is and whether it needs a plate in it or not. It could be stronger than it was previously, but it could also lose three or four percent of its mobility. Now for a normal person that would hardly be noticeable, but for a gymnast... I don't know what it would mean.'

At that point the trainer returned, 'I've spoken to Signora Conte; she and her husband will be here in about fifty minutes.'

'Well you'll have to direct them on to the hospital in Pescia, another ten kilometres, because that's where the ambulance will be going.'

Paul was allowed to travel with Rosa in the ambulance and held her hand all the way. Carlotta, another of the older girls in the team, who had rushed to get changed, also came along. The ambulance was met in Pescia by a senior nurse who told Paul and Carlotta to sit and wait on some fairly uncomfortable black plastic chairs, while Rosa was taken off to be scanned and x-rayed. The conversation between the two was desultory; Carlotta tried to engage him to distract him, but he was too concerned about Rosa to be any sort of company.

After about three quarters of an hour, they were called by a doctor and led down a long corridor to a ward containing eight beds. Two of the beds were unoccupied; in one, an old lady lay sleeping, and four beds were occupied by women of various ages, all of whom were talking to visitors gathered round the beds. Rosa was in the third bed on the right hand side, with the side curtains drawn, so that only the end facing one of the unoccupied beds on the other side of the ward was open. She had obviously been given more painkillers, and a drip had been set up to allow the painkillers to be topped up whenever necessary. She seemed only half awake because of the drugs and was clearly struggling to smile at them. Paul held her good hand again and Carlotta smiled and asked if the doctors had said any more yet.

Just then a doctor appeared, nodded to Paul and Carlotta, attached a clip-board to the end of the bed, adjusted a small tap on the drip and was about to walk off again when Paul stopped him.

'Excuse me.' The doctor turned as if amazed that anyone should would dare to speak to him.

'Yes?' he turned on a wafer thin smile that had maybe been learnt many years before in Medical School. 'Can I help you?'

'I hope so, Doctor. Do you have the results of the CAT scan or the x-rays yet?'

'We do. May I ask if you're the next of kin?'

'I'm her... fiancé,' he said with a glance at Carlotta. 'Her parents are on their way from Florence and should be here fairly soon.'

'Then we'll leave the explanations until everyone's here, shall we? That will save me having to explain everything twice. It is Saturday afternoon, and I do have a lot to do,' and the doctor walked off.

Although it had been Paul who had told the trainer to call Rosa's parents, he had been so busy worrying about Rosa that he hadn't thought of the implications of this. He had imagined numerous scenarios in which he might meet Rosa's parents but this definitely wasn't one of them. Maybe it would be better to slip away and find out the prognosis later on from Carlotta. 'Rosa,' he said, bending down close to her face, 'Rosa. Maybe, I'd better go ... before your parents get here.'

She shook her head and he felt her grip tighten slightly around his hand. 'OK' he said to her with a smile, and then to Carlotta, 'Rosa's parents aren't keen on me for some reason.'

'They won't make a fuss here,' replied Carlotta hopefully.

Fortunately, Carlotta was right. They were led into the ward, looking extremely concerned, by a nurse who, when she saw that the two chairs were already occupied said, 'Sorry, only two visitors at a time – off you go into the waiting room.' Rosa's mother greeted Carlotta but avoided looking at Paul, while her father gave them both a quick nod and sat down in the place that Paul was vacating, and took Rosa's hand.

This time, Paul made a bit more of an effort to be sociable with Carlotta who, it now struck him, must be quite a good friend of Rosa's if she had been prepared to abandon the competition and accompany her to the hospital without being asked. He thanked her for having given up her time in the way she had, and asked how long they'd known each other. She told him that they'd known each other ever since they first started school at the age of five. For the first few years it had been an on-off friendship but they had become proper friends after they had discovered that they both had a love of gymnastics in common and had done a lot of studying together during the five years of the *liceo*.

'How well do you know Rosa's parents?'

'When we used to study together, sometimes it would be at my house and sometimes at Rosa's. Whenever we were at her house her mum and dad were always really nice; it would be a drink and cakes as soon as we got there, then when the *Professore* got home, he'd ask if there was anything we hadn't understood, and if there was he'd go through it really patiently with us until we understood it, and then Rosa's mum, or sometimes Signora Maddalena, her gran, would have cooked a fantastic meal. I always loved studying there because it was great food and everyone was always so happy at the table ... Why don't they like you? Have you done something to upset them?'

'Not that I know of. They've always refused to meet me – back there... in the ward... was the first time we've ever met... if you can call that a meeting.'

After what seemed like an interminable amount of time. Rosa's father came in to the waiting room, rubbed his forehead with his right hand and made his way over to where they were sitting. Paul stood up, not quite sure what was going to happen next, but initially Rosa's father just gave him a glance and addressed himself to Carlotta. With regard to most of the injuries the news was as good as they could have hoped for; the first doctor's opinion on the broken clavicle had been confirmed by the scan, and the doctor in the hospital had confirmed that the bone would be completely mended in three to four months – in the meantime she would have to wear strapping to keep the bone in place for the first month and then be very careful not to bang it, or lift any significant weight for the rest of the healing period. She would have a very sore head for a couple of days and a flap of skin on her scalp had been glued down, but unless she experienced any dizziness over the next forty-eight hours, there would be no long term consequences from the bang on the head. The wrist was more complicated, as there were two small bones broken. The doctor had said that ideally one of them ought to be fixed with a metal plate, but that the location of the second break, even though it was a fairly minor one, made it impossible to screw the plate on at the moment. For now, they were doing their best to set both bones but the doctor had said that there was a higher than even chance that the bone that they would have liked to plate wouldn't take properly and may have to be re-broken and reset, after the other bone had healed.

Carlotta gave Rosa's father a hug and said, 'You must be really pleased that it's not worse and that she'll be alright afterwards. It was horrible when it happened and she just lay there at first.'

'We are. I don't think I can remember ever feeling as worried as when we got Antonio's phone-call. But thank you for staying with her and coming to the hospital, you've always been a good friend to her. Now, have you called your parents to let them know you'll be late?'

Carlotta raised her hand to her mouth as she gave a sharp intake of breath. 'Oh no – I forgot. I've only been thinking about Rosa.'

Rosa's father put his hand in one of his jacket pockets and pulled out a few *gettoni*. 'Take these. There's a phone at the end of that corridor. Tell your parents that we'll bring you home and, unless they've already prepared something, we'll feed you before we drop you off, as well. Go on, now,' and he inclined his head towards the door.

He remained where he was until the door had swung closed and then turned to Paul. 'Now, young man, I need a few words with you before Carlotta comes back. Sit down please,' he gestured to the seats and Paul did as he was bid and then watched as Rosa's father sat down next to him. There were a few seconds silence before he began to speak; to Paul they seemed like an eternity. 'First of all, I really want to thank you for the way you've looked after Rosa today. Not only has Rosa been singing your praises but, the doctor who was on duty at the sports hall also told us how helpful you were. I – and my wife as well – we are really grateful for the support you've given Rosa today ... and that makes what I have to say next all the harder.' Paul waited for him to continue with a sinking feeling in his stomach. 'I'm afraid that because of something that happened in the past, well before you were born, that both my mother-in-law, Rosa's nonna, and my wife are adamant that there should be no on-going relationship between you and Rosa.' Paul noticed that he was looking somewhat shamefaced and was clearly not comfortable with delivering the message. 'Because of that, I must ask you not make contact with Rosa again.'

'May I ask what the reason is that makes me so unsuitable for your daughter, and what, if anything, I have done to deserve being ostracised in this way?' He looked Rosa's father directly in the eyes, but the latter was unable to hold his gaze and dropped his head.

'I'm afraid that I don't know.'

Fortunately, at that moment, half the double door swung open presaging the return of Carlotta who, as she held a small plastic cup of coffee in each hand, had pushed the door open with her hip and was facing the other way as she slid in to the room. This brief respite gave the other two time to compose themselves before she was facing them. 'Mum and dad are fine about it. They said not to bother feeding me, as Mum has been cooking *cinghiale in umido*. If I let them know when we set off, she'll know when to start the *polenta*. Oh, here's a coffee for you Paul. I didn't get one for you, Professore as I wasn't sure when you'd last had one – but I can go and get another if you want.'

He smiled, 'Kind of you to offer, Carlotta, but we had one just before the trainer rang, and then the nurse brought us another one a few minutes ago. I'll let you know when we're ready to leave; it shouldn't be too long now, although Rosa will have to stay in overnight. Goodbye, Paul, and thankyou again for helping Rosa.'

Paul understood that he was being politely asked to leave and, as this was not really the appropriate time or place for the confrontation that he knew would have to come, he held out his hand to Rosa's father, who appeared to undergo an internal struggle but then accepted it and gave Paul's a squeeze. '*Arrivederla, Professore.* Please tell Rosa that I'll be thinking about her.' '*Addio*, Paul.' Paul noticed the different degrees of permanence implied by the choices of salutations and thought, 'we'll see about that,' then he turned to Carlotta and embraced her, 'Ciao.'

He had not thought about how he was going to get back to his car. He asked at the hospital reception what was the easiest way to get to Montecatini and was told that the quickest way was by train but, at that time (and here the receptionist looked up at the clock by the entrance) on a Saturday evening, the trains would be running every two hours. He would probably be better walking the first three kilometres and then hoping to get a bus the rest of the way; the station was nearly two kilometres away from the hospital and not in the same direction as Montecatini. In the circumstances, setting off walking seemed the only sensible solution.

A light drizzle was falling as he set off and orange streetlights reflected off the near deserted road as he trudged along the road signposted Montecatini, feeling cold and trying to work out whether he was now in a stronger position with Rosa's parents after giving some sort of proof of reliability or, as he had no intention of complying with her father's request, if he was in a worse position as whatever he did from now on would be seen as disrespectful. He shrugged his now thoroughly damp shoulders and gave up trying to work it out – *che sarā, sarā.* Instead, he tried to recall images of Rosa going through her routines before the accident, remembering every fluid line of her body as it was accentuated by the leotard.

He had just joined the Lucca-Montecatini road and was wondering whether he should stop at the pizzeria which he could see a sign for in the distance when he was passed by a silver coloured saloon car. He noticed the brake lights of the car flash on and it came to a halt about eighty metres ahead of him. As his thoughts were still almost entirely occupied by images of Rosa and wondering whether or not to stop for a pizza, he was only peripherally aware of the car, until it had reversed half the distance that separated them, and he realised that it was the *Mirafiori* of Rosa's father.

Rosa's father leaned across to the passenger window, past his wife, who looked straight ahead avoiding looking at Paul. 'Get in. I hadn't thought – you must have left your car in Montecatini.'

Paul thanked him and said that he hoped his wet clothes wouldn't damage the car's upholstery and when this was met with a dismissive snort by Rosa's father, slid into the back alongside Carlotta. Fortunately, it took less than ten minutes to get to the *Palasport*, where Paul's Midget was the only car left in the carpark. 'He said goodbye to Carlotta again and thanked Rosa's parents profusely, apologising for the disturbance. Rosa's mother said something that he couldn't quite make out, but her father responded civilly, insisting that it was the least they could do after what he'd done for Rosa that afternoon.

Chapter 16

The problem he was going to have, he thought, as he lay on his bed, staring at the ceiling, was that until Rosa was reasonably mobile again, it was going to be very difficult for him to see her again. One or other of her parents, maybe both, would be with her during all the hospital visiting times and, once she was at home, it would be even worse; at least he could telephone the hospital to ask for news, but when she was convalescing at home, even that chink in the armour that surrounded her would be closed off. No – the only way would be to use Gabriela as an intermediary again. In the morning he would have to ring Simon and Lucio and see if he could get himself an invitation to lunch.

It was Simon who answered the phone and after some general chat where he ribbed Paul for having forgotten his old friends now that he was in love, he insisted that if Paul was free he should go round, '... and isn't it about time you brought the mysterious Rosa round with you?' Paul agreed that it was time but that unfortunately it wasn't going to be possible that day. They could wait for the details until he got there, he thought, otherwise they'd be on the phone for hours.

In one of the bars he passed on the way, he bought a two litre bottle of *Chianti Rufina* so that he didn't arrive empty handed. It was just as well that he'd bought a large bottle as not only was Simon there with his pretty Spaniard, whose name Paul couldn't remember, as well as Lucio and Gabriela, but Claire and Gennaro were there too.

'So where is the mysterious Rosa then?' said Claire. 'I'm dying to meet her.'

Paul smiled, 'She's not mysterious; Gabbi knows her and Lucio's met her – unfortunately, she's in hospital in Pescia today.' There was general consternation and concern and Paul took them through most of the events of the previous day... 'And the only way I can think of finding out what's going on over the next few weeks is if you...' he said, looking at Gabriela, 'can find out for me. Maybe when you've taken notes in a lecture, I can photocopy them and then give you a lift up to near her house.' Gabriela agreed without hesitation saying that she hoped that if she were ever unable to attend lectures that one of her friends would do the same for her. She offered to go round the following day, but Paul said that he thought it would be better to wait until Wednesday as Rosa probably wouldn't even be sent home from hospital until sometime on the Monday afternoon, maybe even the Tuesday morning.

'So what do you intend to do about the family, it sounds as if they're going to make life very difficult unless you decide to back off,' enquired Simon.

'There's not a lot I can do until Rosa's fit enough to get around again. I suppose I could get the younger sister on my side without too much difficulty, but that probably wouldn't achieve very much. Her dad's probably the weakest link; I got the impression that he was really embarrassed about having to tell me not to see Rosa any more without being able to give me a reason for it. The trouble is, at the moment, if I try and make contact, it's just going to piss them off.'

'Roses,' said Gennaro, surprising them all as he spoke for the first time since they had moved onto the subject of Rosa. They all looked at him. He swallowed then continued, 'two weeks on Friday it's Valentine's Day. Send four bunches of roses: a dozen red ones for Rosa, a dozen yellow ones for her sister and a dozen white ones for each of her mother and her grandmother.'

'Semiotics... you might be on to something there... if they understand them.'

Gennaro shrugged, 'Everyone understands a dozen red roses, and the others, even if they don't get the meaning, they make a nice gesture.'

'Hello!' said Claire, 'are you two going to talk in a language that the rest of us understand?'

Gennaro looked at her guiltily, but before either he or Paul could explain, it was Paloma, the pretty little Spaniard, who took up the idea enthusiastically, *Muy bien! Rosso por amor, blanco por humildad y 'Yo soy digno di ti', y amarillo por amistad.'* Then while the others' brains were processing the Spanish, she repeated in English, 'Red for love; white for humility and 'I am worthy of you' and yellow for friendship.'

The rest of the afternoon passed off successfully and Paul managed to put his problems with Rosa's family to the back of his mind; he hoped that Rosa would also find someone she could talk to – maybe her sister; he had never realised until now just how important it was to have friends with whom you could discuss things. Although nothing had changed during the afternoon, he now felt much more positive and optimistic that everything would turn out alright. He had agreed to meet up with Lucio and Gabriella, and anyone else who might be available in the *Birreria Centrale* on the Thursday evening; he would have liked to have made it the Wednesday, but as he didn't finish work until ten thirty that night he knew it would be unfair on Gabriela, who was the one he really wanted to see.

Thursday evening was a very long way away and he couldn't remember a time when the fingers of his watch had moved as slowly as they seemed to do throughout Monday. No matter how long he thought he'd resisted for, every time he glanced down at it, it scarcely seemed to have moved. As Chiara, the most interesting of his private students had had gone to London for her work placement, he now had a five hour gap between the extra-mural course he was running for students and the evening session at the *Academia*. He wandered round the Bargino Museum for an hour; he wandered aimlessly round some of the larger shops in the centre, he stopped a couple of times for coffee, trying to focus on the articles in the newspapers that were always provided in every bar for the use of customers – La Nazione, in the first bar, and Corriere dello Sport in the second, without being able to remember a single word that he had read afterwards; all this and he still had an hour and a half to kill before he could go to the school and begin to set up his lesson.

As he wandered aimlessly, he suddenly became aware that he was passing the school where Rosa's father taught. With the exception of a light just inside the entrance and one illuminated window on the second floor, the school was now in darkness. Paul had a good look through the main entrance and then followed the wall, first one way and then the other from the entrance. After that, he looked round the nearby streets and was pleased to note that the school had no alternative entrance and that, as far as he could see, there was no carpark for the staff – that would mean that all the teaching staff, including Rosa's father would have to enter the grounds through the main entrance each morning. Once he had conducted his survey, he felt slightly less helpless and was able to begin thinking about what skills he was going to teach that evening.

On the Tuesday morning he was near the gates of the school before seven o'clock, rocking on the balls of his feet and regularly banging his gloved hands together to try and keep some circulation going in the sub-zero temperature, while the white clouds formed by his breath crystallised in front of him. 'It must be nice being somewhere warm in winter,' his mother had said when he'd left after Christmas. He had tried several times to explain what a continental climate was, but he hadn't managed to get it to sink in – Florence was a thousand miles to the south, so it must always be warmer – whatever Paul said. As soon as the gates were opened at seven, Paul went in and asked the caretaker what time Professor Conte usually arrived, only to be told that it could be anytime between half past seven and nine – it all depended what time the *Professore's* first lesson was.

Fortunately, he had a lesson first thing, and Paul felt a great sense of relief as he saw the *Mirafiori* park a little further up the street. He watched Rosa's father lock the car-door, pull the collar of his sheepskin coat up high and then slip on a pair of sheepskin gloves before giving a quick glance at the traffic and stepping in the road to cross towards the school. When the other man was almost upon him he stepped out and faced him.

'*Buongiorno, Professore.* I'm sorry to disturb you, but I just have to know how she is.'

The older man stopped, looking slightly put out, then he seemed to think better of it and his look softened. '*Buongiorno.* I didn't expect to see you here. You look frozen.'

Paul shrugged, 'I didn't want to risk missing you so I had to get here early. But if you can tell me that she's doing well, then that will warm me up.'

Rosa's father looked at his watch and then reached out and took hold of Paul's arm, just above the elbow. 'Come on. I'll get you a coffee; you look as if you need one.'

Paul was ushered into a bar fifty metres further along the road where he asked for a latte macchiato and Rosa's father ordered a coffee. 'Now, don't get the wrong idea because I've bought you a drink, the request I made on Saturday hasn't changed, it's just that I feel you deserve this. Rosa was allowed home late yesterday afternoon. We could have insisted on her being transferred to Florence on Sunday, but we decided it would be less traumatic for her to stay in Pescia for the observation period. She's been heavily strapped to support her collar bone, and they've also used strapping on her wrist instead of plastering it. According to the doctor, if she can avoid banging it or rolling onto it during the night, there's a good chance that both breaks will heal without their needing to be plated.'

'That's going to be very difficult during the night.'

'Difficult, but not impossible. For the next ten days, the other four of us in the house are going to take it in turns to sit with her after she goes to bed. If we each do two hours, then we can manage it.'

'Thank you for telling me this Professore. I feel a lot better now – especially now I know what good care she's going to get. May I get further updates from you? – And I'll get the coffee next time.'

'Paul, I like you, and I'm sorry that a continuing relationship between you and Rosa is not possible. I'm worried that your ... continuing to ...' He paused, clearly struggled for the right way to phrase what he wanted to say, 'to follow her progress, is just going to make it more difficult for you to let go.' As at the hospital on the Saturday, the *professore* again looked extremely uncomfortable as he said this.

'I'm sorry, Professore. I want to be completely honest with you. Unless Rosa indicates that she wishes me to do so, I cannot envisage any circumstance under which I will,' and he deliberately repeated the words that her father had struggled to find, 'cease to follow her progress.'

He looked a little put out by what Paul said, and Paul wondered if it had been a mistake to be honest, but then the *professore* sighed and shook his head. 'Alright. Rosa has another scan on her wrist next Monday and then we'll know if the bones have started to knit together correctly. Meet me here at twenty to eight next Tuesday then, if the news is good, we won't need to meet again after that.'

'Thank you, Professore. I'm very grateful to you.'

As he had not yet got round to looking for new students to replace Chiara and Giulio, the only lesson he had on Thursday was the one and half hour lesson in the evening at the Academia. The lesson was with an Intermediate group which, when the course had begun back in October, had numbered seventeen students. Three students had since left the course; one before the end of the first month, and two more had just not returned after Christmas. He had been concerned to have lost three students but Signor Malesano had assured him that at this stage, to still have fourteen out of seventeen was a very good retention rate. The first student to leave had been entitled to a refund of fifty percent of the course fees but the other two, having left after the end of the first full month, had forfeited their right to a refund. 'With a bit of luck,' said Malesano with a half-smile, 'they'll realise that they do need to learn English after all and pay us another course fee when the next round of courses start at the end of the month.'

This particular group was one which Paul enjoyed teaching; unusually, all the students were fully committed and often asked interesting questions which gave him an excuse to stray away from the somewhat rigid method prescribed by the school. Two of the students particularly came to mind when he thought of this group: one, and he knew he should be ashamed to admit it, was a shop assistant from the ladies-wear section in a very upmarket department store in Piazza della Repubblica, who always wore very striking sheer flesh coloured stockings with extravagant black patterns. At times, when the students were working at exercises in their books he found it hard to tear his eyes away from the tights, a task which was complicated by the long shapely legs that they enclosed. The girl, who sat directly in front of his teacher's desk had a very disconcerting habit of crossing and uncrossing her legs as she worked – movements which always dragged his eyes back, even if he'd managed to previously look elsewhere.

The other student who came to mind when he thought of this group was a complete contrast to the other; at eighty-four years old she was by far the oldest student he'd ever taught and was also, to his great surprise, the best. After the first week of the course he had decided that, at the end of the next lesson, he would suggest to her that she switch to the Higher course, but then noticed that, over the weekend, she seemed to have forgotten much of what she had learned the previous week. He had spoken to her after one lesson when the same pattern had been repeated for the following two weeks. He had asked her if there was anything extra he could do to help her build on her knowledge between lessons and she had told him, quite candidly, that she was aware that she was gradually losing her short term memory. She had passed much of her early life in Algeria and spoke fluent French and Arabic. She was sure that learning another language would help to keep the part of her brain controlling language skills functioning as long as possible, and that was why she had decided to learn English, however, it was the lessons that mattered, not what she did in between when her days were full of grandchildren and great-grandchildren.

She was always the first student to arrive, and her daughter-in-law, who Paul had spoken too once when she dropped her off, told Paul that she was surprised by how much her mother-in-law looked forward to the lessons. Apparently, she insisted that, for some reason, the lessons reminded her of being young again; because of this, Paul always met her with a smile and tried to give her as much encouragement as possible.

That evening the lesson involved listening to a story on a tape, going through the story again while following a transcript, answering some comprehension questions in English, and then discussing the answers. While the students were writing down their answers to the questions, Paul's mind wandered to Rosa, although influenced by the usual distraction, and he wondered what Rosa's parents would think if he made her a present of a pair of striking, almost Gothic, stockings like those infront of him. He was jerked back to reality by a question from the old lady, 'Excuse me... Should we try to use all the different tenses in our answers?'

He smiled at her, 'You don't have to. But if you would like to, to reinforce your understanding of tenses, then I think that's a very good idea.'

'Thank you, Maxi,' she said, and continued writing.

It didn't register immediately as his mind was still engaged with Rosa, silk stockings and shapely legs, then he realised what she had called him. Could he have misheard? Could it just be a slip of the tongue? ...Or... had she known his grandfather? He thought – eighty four years old – it was the beginning of nineteen eighty six – so she'd probably been born in nineteen o one – when had his grandfather been born? He thought back to the military cemetery – nineteen twelve – so his grandfather was ten years younger than Signora Frei – it was possible – but how? and when?

At the end of the lesson most of the younger students were always much quicker to leave than the old lady, and it was the same tonight, each wishing Paul a cheery good evening as they filed out, heading homewards for their evening meals. As usual, Paul stood by the door as they left with a cheery word for each of them: 'Goodnight... Have a good evening... Well done today... Goodnight... Keep practising those pronouns... Enjoy the skiing... - ... Signora Frei, could I have a quick word before you go?'

'Of course, but I haven't got long; my son is picking me up from the bar next door at twenty to.'

'Let me walk down with you. We can talk on the way, or over a coffee.'

'Willingly, but it will have to be decaf for me at this time of day.'

The traffic looked horrific so, as he bought the drinks, he was fairly sure that they would have a few minutes before she had to go.

He slid into the chair facing her and smiled. 'Signora Frei. During the lesson, you called me Max.'

'Did I really? How silly of me. I do apologise – you're Paul, not Maxi.'

'There's no need to apologise. My grandfather was called Max and he came to Florence, a long time ago – during the nineteen thirties and then probably during the war.'

'Oh that would explain it. I'm very relieved.'

'About what, Signora?' he asked, confused.

'My memory. You see it's often playing little tricks on me and everytime I see you, I seem to be seeing someone I knew a long time ago. You look very alike, you know... except for the eyes... Maxi had gentle, sad, hazel coloured eyes.'

'I'd be very grateful if you could tell me more about my grandfather. You're the first person I've ever met who knew him.'

'Really! Well of course...'

'*Mamma. Sei pronta?*'

'*Si, Fabio. Un minuto.* This is Paul, my English teacher. It seems that I knew his grandfather. You must come round for tea, Paul, and I'll tell you all I can remember about him. Come for tea tomorrow – at five o'clock... Fabio, give him one of those business card things of yours with the address on.'

'Thank you very much, Signora. I'm looking forward to it.'

He stood and helped her ease her chair back, so she could stand.

Gabriela and Lucio were waiting to be served in the *Birreria Centrale* when he arrived and he insisted on paying for a bottle of wine for the three of them to share. He didn't have to ask; Gabriela started to tell him about her visit to Rosa as soon as they sat down. Being aware of what Paul needed to know more than anything else, she told him that so far, everything was going as well as could have been hoped and that there had been no setbacks. That helped Paul to relax and then she was able to fill him in with the details. They had mainly talked about the injuries and about the lectures that Rosa had missed so far, as most of the time her mother had been in the room with them,

'Not because she really wanted to know what we were talking about; I think she's just feeling very protective at the moment. Fortunately, after a bit, Rosa asked her if she could make us some coffee, so we got five minutes to talk about other things. She said that sometime over the next week or so, before the sympathy vote disappears, she's going to try and talk to her grandmother – she said that you'd know what that was about. She also said that she wants to see you on Valentine's Day ... but I'm not sure she'll be up to it. Anyway, I'm going back again next Wednesday – her mother insists on coming to pick me up – she seems really nice.' Gabriela smiled and looked at him quizzically.

Paul shook his head ruefully, 'Hopefully, I'll get chance to find out for myself sometime.' Then he brightened up, 'But you'll never believe what's just happened..' and he told them about Signora Frei and how he would hopefully know a lot more about his grandfather by the end of the following day.

The Frei family lived in a three storey stuccoed house on the Via Brisighellese a couple of kilometres north of the city at the foot of the steep slopes leading down from Fiesole towards Pian di Mugnone. A paved strip about three metres wide separated the front of the house from the road, and a woman in her fifties wearing a housecoat, who was standing on the first floor balcony, indicated that he should park there, and then disappeared into the house. By the time Paul had got out of the car and locked the door, she had reappeared at the main house door, on the ground floor just behind Paul's car. The woman held out her hand and introduced herself as Rita, a friend of Signora Frei who popped round for a couple of hours most days to help around the house and keep her company. She then led Paul up two flights of stairs to a south-facing sitting room on the second floor. Signora Frei was sitting at an angle to the large french-windows so that she could see down the valley towards the city. She was sitting with a rug over her legs, but wore an elegant, if slightly old-fashioned, white blouse with a lace collar above it. 'Hello, Paul. Thank you for coming,' she said in English.

'It's my pleasure,' he replied in the same language and held out a bunch of yellow and orange gerberas for her. Her face lit up and all of sudden he could imagine what she must have looked like forty or fifty years before.

'You shouldn't have,' but the look on her face made him glad he had. 'Rita will find a vase for them; she and my son and daughter-in-law really look after me – I'm not sure what I've done to deserve it. Now, young man, tell me what happened to my old friend, Maxi. What did he do after he left Florence?'

Paul shook his head, 'I'm afraid he never really left Florence, or rather, he did, but he didn't get very far. He was killed at Santa Croce sull'Arno in August forty-four. He's buried in the military cemetery in Compiobbi. I never knew him, and even my father only has very vague memories of him.'

'Oh I'm so sorry. I didn't realise. You poor thing.'

He smiled to reassure her, 'Don't be sorry for me. It's all so long before I was born that I'd never really thought about him until I came to Florence and discovered that he was buried here... But now, I'm curious and would like to know as much about him as I can.'

'You look very like him, except for your eyes – and I don't just mean the colour – your eyes are full of life; they look as if you always want to get the most out of life and as if you could laugh easily. Maxi's eyes were dead, no... that's not the right word – it gives the wrong idea.... they were sad. He had very sad eyes, even when he smiled, he looked as if he'd forgotten how to be happy.... But he was handsome... Oh yes, he was handsome.' Despite the wrinkles, Paul was sure he saw the ghost of a smile play around the corners of her mouth, and for a moment he wondered. 'Almost as if reading his thoughts, Signora Frei continued, 'My sister Giovanna, who was six years younger than me was desperate for the opportunity to make him happy – and she didn't hide it – but he wasn't having any of it. He was always nice to her, paid her compliments, but never any more than that.' She paused, and with a malicious little smile that took Paul completely by surprise said, 'If I hadn't already got my poor Giorgio, I might even have tried to seduce him myself.' She laughed at the expression on Paul's face. 'Don't look so shocked. I wasn't always old – the only advantage of old age is that you can finally tell the truth about everything, and not care what people think.' Paul laughed.

'So how did you first meet my grandfather?'

She leaned her head back on the chair and closed her eyes for a moment, then, when she opened them and looked at him again, it was as if there was a dreamy far away quality in them. 'You know that your grandfather was a spy, don't you?' Paul nodded as he didn't want to interrupt her. 'My Giorgio was a partisan, even before they called themselves partisans. After the armistice we didn't see much of him as he was with a group on Monte Morello, but occasionally, after they'd watched the house for an hour or so, to make sure it was safe, he'd come to visit me. He'd spend about half an hour bringing us up to date with what was happening and then we'd ... but you don't need to know that bit. The first time he brought Max with him was in mid-November of forty-three, and after that they usually came together. He'd sit in the kitchen and chat with my mother and my two sisters while we were in the other room. He never talked about himself, and it was only after the war that Giorgio told us how important he'd been; apparently his job was to try and co-ordinate some of the partisan groups and recruit new cells wherever he could. Even with Giorgio, he only spoke about himself once and that was when they'd drunk a whole bottle of home-made grappa that Giorgio had told him wasn't very strong, when infact, it must have been at least seventy percent proof. He told Giorgio that he'd lost a woman who he'd really loved and said he didn't think he could ever get close to any other woman.'

She paused, lost in her own thoughts, remembering people, places and sensations from long ago. Paul watched her as she gazed through the window, wishing that, just for a moment, he could see what she was seeing. He didn't interrupt her thoughts, but tried to imagine for himself, his grandfather sitting in the family's kitchen with Signora Frei's younger sister desperately trying to impress him, with her mother looking on resignedly in the strange wartime circumstances.

'I'm glad I've been able to talk to you about Max,' said Signora Frei, returning to the present, 'We always think about all the bad things from that period and that means that we forget the good things and the good people who got caught up in it. It was a terrible time, when you could never be sure whether you, or someone you loved, would be killed or dragged off to Villa Triste, which came to pretty much the same things but... but those evenings when Giorgio and Max appeared without warning, as if by magic, were some of the most intense and happy of my life.'

Paul took both the old lady's hands, which had been folded on her lap, in his, 'And I'm really grateful to you for sharing your memories with me. I can understand why my grandfather used to come here with your husband – the atmosphere and the company must have given him some happiness too.'

She smiled, 'You've got a silver tongue on you young man. You're very like him in a lot of ways.'

'Can you remember the last time you saw him?'

She thought for a moment. It must have been towards the middle of July. We could hear the big guns in the distance but it was before the Oltrarno was in the hands of the allies. They didn't stay long because they knew that things were getting critical. Giorgio told me much later that they shouldn't have risked coming down here at all that night, but he thought he might be killed and he wanted to see me for what might be the last time. Afterwards he went back up onto Monte Morello with his men.'

'And my grandfather went with him?'

She shook her head, 'No. He was going back into the city. The way he said goodbye to us all was very restrained, but at the same time very intense. It was almost as if he knew he'd never see us again.'

When he got back into Florence he felt he wanted to talk about his grandfather, but not just to anyone – it had to be to someone who really cared. He would have liked to talk to Rosa, but obviously that wasn't possible; Julie was the other person who he knew would be interested and he contemplated a trip to the SIP, but then realised how long the phone call would be, and how much it would cost. He would give a potted version to Gabriela as he had mentioned the appointment the previous evening and she would want to know, so that she had something to tell Rosa the following Wednesday. Eventually, he decided that rather than talking, he would make do with writing a long letter to Julie and, after cooking and eating a pan full of calf's liver with thinly sliced and lightly seared red onions, dressed with a dash of balsamic vinegar, that is what he did.

Later, after finishing the letter, the writing of which he had found therapeutic, he wandered into the centre to see if Lucio and Gabriela were there. They weren't, but Simon and several of his other acquaintances were, and he gave a brief summary of his visit which he knew would be passed on to Gabriela; he would hopefully get the chance to talk through it in detail with Rosa in the not too distant future.

After a little more than an hour with the others, he made an excuse and left, feeling that that evening he preferred to be alone with his thoughts rather than chatting about unimportant things with his friends. Instead of making his way straight home he walked down to the Lungarno and leaned on the parapet below the *Corridoio Vasariano*. He could see that, as usual, the *Ponte Vecchio* to his right was covered by a mixture of tourists and street vendors, but after a brief look towards the bridge, his gaze settled on the lights of Piazzale Michelangelo and the illuminated marble façade of San Miniato on top of the hill up above. Less than two hundred metres from the church, and not much further from the Piazzale, he knew that Rosa was sitting, trussed up like an oven-ready turkey. He wondered what she was thinking about; was she thinking about him, wondering where he was and what he was doing, or did the pain make it impossible to think about anything other than her injuries?

The following Tuesday morning, Paul was in the bar close to the school where Rosa's father worked, a quarter of an hour before the appointment, impatient to hear the latest news. As he saw the *professore* approach, he ordered a second cappuccino for himself and a coffee for Rosa's father.

The barista was just placing the coffee on the counter as he walked in and Paul pushed it along towards him. He nodded his thanks and drank the coffee in one go before beginning to speak. 'You'll be very pleased to know that we won't need to meet again.'

'You mean that the results of the scan were positive?' said Paul excitedly.

'I do,' said Professore Melluso with a smile, 'the results couldn't have been better. The orthopedician said he was amazed at how well she was doing. He said that he hadn't really expected Rosa to be able to get through the week without the bones moving – but she has – and now they've been able to put a light cast on it. They're going to have another look in three weeks, but they were very positive.'

Paul couldn't stop a huge grin spreading across his face. 'That's fantastic. I don't know how to thank you. I know that all the effort you and your family have put in must have played a massive part. Thankyou.'

'I think, Paul, that if you have children of your own one day, that you'll realise that parents will do anything to make sure that their children are healthy... and thanks are not necessary.'

Paul shrugged a shoulder and smiled, 'Well, I feel grateful anyway.'

The expression on Rosa's father's face became serious, 'Don't forget, Paul, that this doesn't change anything; we still don't want your relationship with Rosa to continue,' he raised a hand to stop Paul as he saw he was about to speak. 'I don't know the reason but, I've known my mother-in-law for nearly thirty years, since I was fifteen, and in all those years, I've never known her judgement to be wrong about anything important. I'm sorry.'

'Rosa's been talking to her grandmother.' Said Gabriela when they met up on the Thursday evening. 'She said that the discussion got pretty heated but that her grandmother still refuses to tell her why she disapproves of you. Rosa is really upset about having upset her grandmother, but she insists she's not going to back down. Since their discussion, the grandmother has spent most of the time in her room. She only comes out for meals and even then she doesn't say very much to anyone, and nothing at all to Rosa. Her mother says she's got to apologise, but she won't because she says she's done nothing wrong – that if there's a reason why she shouldn't see you, she has a right to know what it is.'

'I wish she'd waited. I'd feel happier if everyone was being nice to her while she's recovering. Still, I suppose there's no use crying over spilt milk – how was she physically?'

'A lot better now that she doesn't need to think about protecting her arm all the time, and the cast she's wearing is much less cumbersome than all the strapping she had on last week. I also got the impression that she's not feeling as much pain now as she was before.'

The following Thursday, Gabriela had even better news for him. Although the atmosphere in the house was still tense, especially when Rosa and her grandmother couldn't avoid being in the same room, Rosa was much happier. This was mainly because she had started to go for short walks, at first with her mother, but after the first couple of days, when her mother was satisfied that the walking did not cause her a problem, she had started to go out on her own. 'I went out with her and she showed me the path where she usually goes. There's a footpath that leads through the woods behind, and round the far side of, San Miniato, before coming out again on Via delle Porte Sante. When she's been out so far, she's deliberately walked slowly so that if you can meet her there, you can have a few minutes together without her parents worrying and coming out to look for her...' Gabriela anticipated what Paul was about to ask, 'Half

past three tomorrow afternoon, is the answer to your question.'
Paul couldn't resist giving her a big hug.
'Sorry, Lucio ... I couldn't help it.'
'*Figurati.*' Laughed the Italian.

On the Saturday afternoon, which was bright but bitterly cold, he was in place, sitting on a bench pretending to look at a newspaper, ten minutes early, so eager was he to see her again – a precipitousness that he regretted, as the cold wind seemed to find its way through every layer of material that covered him. After what his impatience made seem like an age, she finally appeared at three thirty-three accompanied by her sister. He stood up as they came towards him and grinned as she waved her good hand at him. He gave Francesca a smile and then stood somewhat uneasily, arms extended but not sure where it was safe to get hold of her. She had obviously anticipated the difficulty as she laid her right forearm along his left and holding his arm just below the bicep so that, as she leaned in with upturned face to kiss him, their bodies were kept slightly apart.

After a few seconds, as their tongues began to rapidly probe each other, there was a little cough and Francesca cleared her throat. 'Don't forget about me. Remember I'm only fifteen and there are certain sights I should be protected from... unless you're really desperate for an audience.'

Paul blushed but Rosa laughed. 'Sorry, Franci. Here's two thousand lire; go and have a wander round the Piazzale and get yourself a coffee or something. I'll see you in about half an hour on the corner.' She kissed her sister on both cheeks and gave her the banknote and Francesca went off laughing to herself. 'I told them at home that I wanted to go slightly further today, and I brought Francesca along so that they wouldn't worry.'

'And were they right to worry?'

She looked up at him with wide open eyes and a half smile, 'That depends on what your intentions are, doesn't it?'

He blushed again, 'I didn't mean... I meant...'

She interrupted him with a kiss and laughed, 'I know that wasn't what you meant. You meant does it hurt when I walk.'

He nodded. 'Well the answer is that it does, but it doesn't really hurt anymore than sitting in a chair, trying to keep my back straight and shoulders pushed back all the time... so as long as I don't fall over, or try swinging my arm around, then it doesn't really make any difference.'

'I tackled Nonna, but she wasn't giving anything away, other than what we already knew – that the Campolargos were not very nice people and it was best to have nothing to do with them. I pointed out that you are no more a Campolargo than I am... less really, because I've always lived with a Campolargo and my mother is half Campolargo as well, whereas even your father never knew your *nonna*. She said I didn't understand, and I said that what she was saying was illogical and that she was the one who didn't understand... I think I might have suggested that she couldn't be expected to understand young people in love, at her age, which was probably a bit cruel... but she deserved it.'

Paul moved to hug her, but pulled back in time, remembering the injuries she was carrying, and instead stroked her cheek with his hand. 'Somehow, it will all work out alright in the end. I know it will.'

'I hope you're right. I don't like this atmosphere at home.'

'I think that your dad would really like to be on our side. I've seen him a couple of times to find out how you were going on, and both times he's been friendly – even though he still insists that I shouldn't see you.'

Rosa stopped, her eyes opened wide with surprise, 'He didn't tell me he'd seen you. When was this?' Paul told her all about his meetings with her father, including the original conversation in the hospital in Pescia. At first she was annoyed that her father hadn't said anything, even though Paul had asked him to pass on his best wishes, but Paul shrugged and said that, in the circumstances, it wasn't really surprising, and that, if anything, she needed to make sure to be extra-nice to him, as he was the closest they had to an ally.

For a while they walked slowly, arm in arm through the wood, where the low winter sun cast stark shadows on the frozen leaves that had remained on the ground since autumn. Part way round the path they came across what appeared to be a war memorial, but with no explanatory plaque. Seeing the memorial reminded Paul that he needed to give Rosa the details about his meeting with Signora Frei and the revelations about his grandfather. She listened attentively, occasionally asking him to repeat something that wasn't clear, but not commenting until he had finished. When he had finished he looked at her and was surprised to see that she was crying. He stopped and turned so that he was facing her full on and she did not have to twist to look at him. Placing his hands where he judged her hips to be under her long coat, and being careful not to press against her upper body, he leaned in and gently licked away the tears with the tip of his tongue. 'What's wrong?'

'Can you imagine loving someone so much, that even after nearly ten years, you still can't look at anyone else? He must have been so sad, and it sounds as if he knew he was going to die and didn't really care.'

He gently slid his hands upwards, remembering not to exert any pressure, and then took her face in them and looked her unblinkingly in the eye. 'Yes... I don't think I could have done three months ago, but now... Yes, I can.'

They were able to meet several times over the next few days. Rosa had not yet returned to the university so it was just a case of fitting in meetings between Paul's lessons. On the Thursday, Rosa said that as the following day was Valentine's Day, that they should meet in the evening and eat together. In Paul's view, it was not a good idea as it would be clear to all her family, exactly why she was going out that evening and could turn out to be comparable to waving a red rag at a bull. However, Rosa was so keen on the idea that, despite his misgivings, he couldn't say "no",' and they agreed that they would meet and eat at *Enoteca Fuori Porta* which was where they had first met. As Paul walked back down into the centre after their walk, he called in and booked a table for two for eight o'clock. He also remembered Gennaro's advice and, before getting to the

Academia, called into a florists and, at great expense, ordered four dozen roses to be delivered the following morning.

Chapter 17

The following morning, he went down to Mimmo's to have breakfast just after ten, and was surprised when Mimmo said he had a message for him. Something about the way Mimmo said it, caught Paul's attention. He quite often got messages cancelling lessons, or asking if he was available to do other lessons, but Mimmo's tone of voice said that this was different. 'What was it, then?' he asked, and took a sip of his latte macchiato.

'A Signora Campolargo wants to meet you in *Rivoire* at five-fifteen this afternoon.' Paul spluttered and some of the froth from the milky coffee went up his nose and made his eyes water. 'I said that I'd let you know but that I wasn't sure if you had any other appointments. I asked for her phone number so that you could ring her back, and she just said, "He'll be there", and hung up.'

'When was this? When did she ring? And she said her name was Signora Campolargo?'

'About a quarter of an hour ago, and when I asked her name she just said "Campolargo", thinking about it, she didn't say "Signora". Do you know her?'

Paul gave a slight shake of the head, 'No. But I think I know who she is... and she's right, I'll be there.' Mimmo looked at him curiously, but knew better than to ask any more questions.

Paul had walked past *Rivoire* in Piazza della Signoria many times but had never considered going in. It claimed to be the oldest and best chocolaterie in Florence, and certainly had the air of being the most expensive. The clients he was used to seeing as he walked past were either extremely well-heeled Italians, who obviously considered it one of the places where one needed to be seen, or wealthy tourists who had it on their tick list of things to do while in Italy, along with *Harry's Bar* in Venice, the *Gambrinus* in Naples and *Bar Necci* in Rome. This afternoon was no different and he felt slightly self-conscious as he walked through the door and looked around. However, before he had time to try and work out which of the customers was the woman he'd come to see, a navy-jacketed, black-trousered, white-shirted waiter wearing a sober maroon tie and with *Rivoire* embroidered in red thread over the breast pocket, came up to him and gave a slight bow of the head. 'Signor Caddick?' It wasn't really a question; the waiter seemed to know exactly who he was, but Paul politely confirmed his identity anyway. 'Would you care to follow me,' this time, a command rather than a question. The waiter led Paul to a table, discretely tucked away behind one of the large plants that were strategically placed around the interior, to give those guests who were not there to be seen, as much privacy as possible.'

The lady at the table had her back to Paul and the rest of the salon, so all he could see as the waiter helped him slip off his coat was a mass of elegantly coiffured white hair, held up with a mother of pearl hair-slide. As he slid into the chair which a second waiter had pulled back for him, he was able to get a proper look at the woman. She had striking wide-set dark eyes and a well-balanced face, set off by an aquiline nose. Paul could see that make up had been applied to the attractive face with a very light touch as if the woman was aware that the lines around her eyes and mouth made her more interesting and shouldn't be hidden. From her neck and wrists, Paul judged that she was well into her sixties, but otherwise, her face and figure would not have been out of place on a woman ten years her junior. She smiled at Paul, although Paul noticed that it was only her mouth that smiled and that the dark eyes remained expressionless.

'Hello, Paul. Thank you very much for the roses; they were beautiful. Will you take chocolate or would you prefer a cocktail?'

'A chocolate please, Signora. I hear that this place is famous for its chocolate – and I'm glad that you liked the flowers.' He was determined that he would wait for her to let him know why he had been summoned before showing any curiosity.

'Yes, they are. Enrico Rivoire was master chocolatier to the Savoias and came with them when Florence was the capital of Italy in the late eighteen-sixties. They've been making the best chocolate in the city, possibly in Italy, ever since.' She made a slight movement of her hand and immediately one of the waiters was by her side. 'Two of your luxury hot chocolates and a selection of your *pasticceria*, please.'

While they waited for the order to arrive, she asked him about his work in Florence, about what he thought of various Florentine attractions and other subjects which he knew were not the reason why he was there.

Finally, after they had drunk, or perhaps thought Paul, given its richness, eaten would be a more appropriate verb to describe how the hot chocolate had been consumed, she came to the point.

'I want you to know, Paul, that the reason why it is impossible for you to continue seeing my grand-daughter, is not that I have anything against you personally. In fact, I like what I've seen for myself, and my son-in-law speaks very highly of you.'

'Then why..?'

'I'm sorry, Paul. But there are other matters that make this impossible. Matters that I am unable to go in to with either you or Rosa... or even my daughter. I'm afraid that you'll just have to trust me on this, and believe me when I say I want what's best for everyone.'

Paul noted that there was a slight edge of pleading in the otherwise calm voice, but he felt angry now; did this woman really think that an expensive cup of hot chocolate and a few little cakes would make him give up the woman he loved?

'You met Rosa because you wanted to find out about your grandmother, my sister Chiara. If you'll agree not to see Rosa again, I'll tell you everything you want to know about Chiara.'

He rose, 'Thank you very much for the hospitality, Signora. Maybe one day, when I'm married to Rosa, I'll be able to return it. Until then, I don't think we have anything more to say to each other.' He looked round for a waiter to bring him his coat, and as he did so, he felt her hand close round his wrist with a much firmer grip than he would have expected.

'Sit down, Paul.' He started to pull away but paused as she added with a note of desperation, 'Please!' and he saw that there was a tear in her eye. He wavered.

'I'm sorry. That was beneath me and insulting to you – I'm afraid that there's a bit of Campolargo heritage in all of us.' She smiled through the tears that were now running freely down her cheeks. 'You deserve to know everything about your *nonna*, with no conditions attached.' He sat down, and for the next hour he sat spellbound as she told him about how his grandfather had arrived on the Campolargo estate as a temporary labourer and how her sister had fallen in love with him. She told him how the affair had had to be hidden from the rest of the family who would have used strong measures to put an end to it, indeed how these strong measures had extended as far as almost killing Max when they had been discovered. She told him how Chiara had run away during the night, and how they had arranged for her to be away in Siena at the time, so that she couldn't be accused of complicity, and how she had never seen Chiara again. She had had a couple of secret messages during the first year after her sister left and after that, nothing. She had only found out about Chiara's death several years later.

At the end of her story, he told her about his visit to her lawyer nephew in Siena and what he had said about her. To his surprise she laughed, 'Margarita never believed that my being with them when Chiara left was a coincidence, and she never forgave me for it. So I suppose that in-a-way, I deserved that description. Luckily, none of my brothers was as intelligent as Margarita, so they didn't believe her.'

He now thanked her for her hospitality with much more sincerity than he had previously, and couldn't thank her enough for the information she had given him about his grandmother. It was amazing, he thought, in the last week he'd found out just about everything there was to know about both his grandparents, after months of getting nowhere.

'I'm sorry I can't give up Rosa, as you wish. I do hope that sometime, when everything is... sorted, that we can be friends.'

'I would like that too, Paul, but I don't think that it's going to be possible.'

Paul was glad that he'd dressed well for the appointment as he would have been somewhat pushed for time to get back to his room, change and then make his way over to the enoteca. When he got there, the table he had booked was ready and he took his place and waited for Rosa, hoping that she had not been dissuaded or impeded by her family. Just after half past seven she slipped through the door, looking, he thought, a little stiff. As soon as her eyes adapted to the interior light, however, she gave a broad smile and moved towards him with a reinvigorated step. Paul rose, kissed her, pulled her chair out for her and helped her slip her coat off. 'How's the collar bone coming on, it looked a bit uncomfortable as you came in?'

'Oh, it's fine; I think it's got so used to being cushioned all the time that walking down all those steps was a bit of a surprise for it.' She smiled and raised his hand and rested it lightly on her collar bone. 'See, there's not even a bump over the break any more.'

The silky-soft touch of her flesh under his fingers had distracted Paul from thinking about her bone and he let his fingers open wide and gently caress her until they reached her sternum when he withdrew them and managed to refocus on her injuries. 'My very own bionic woman;' he said with a smile, 'did they show that programme here in Italy?'

She laughed, 'with all our private TV channels, it's been on again and again and again, like most of the American TV shows... If I remember right, the bionic woman had to give up her sports career, didn't she?'

He shook his head, 'I can't remember... Anyway, I've got a lot to tell you. I was invited for a drink at *Rivoire*, this afternoon... by a lady who put a proposition to me.'

Her eyes opened wider, 'And did you accept... the invite, I mean?'

'Of course... I was always taught that it was ungentlemanly to refuse a lady.'

Rosa looked at him with mock seriousness, aware that she was being teased and doing her best to frown. 'So do I have a rival for your affections; I know it's Valentine's Day but I didn't expect you to receive other propositions; perhaps it's just as well I've come out so I can keep an eye on you.'

'The lady's proposition involved giving you up,' he looked at her with a little smile and then took hold of both her hands as her pretend frown became a real one, 'A proposition which I refused out of hand.'

'But who...?'

'You're going to be at least as surprised as I was when I realised who she was. It was your *nonna*.'

'No!' Rosa gasped. He raised her hand and kissed it, then leant back as the waitress brought a bottle of *spumante* to the table, poured two glasses and left the rest of the bottle in an ice-bucket next to the table.

As the waitress moved away, he took Rosa's hand again and gave it another kiss. 'It's not quite as bad as it first sounds, so wait till you've heard everything before you make any judgements. At first, the proposition was that she would tell me everything I wanted to know about my grandmother, if I would agree to give you up.'

'But how could...' He stopped her by placing the index finger of his free hand on her lips.

'I thanked her for the drink and stood up to go but then she backed down. She told me about my grandmother without linking it to us. She still doesn't want us to see each other, but she said that my grandmother was a completely separate matter and that I deserved to know.'

'But I don't understand.'

'Neither do I. She seems sure that things won't work out between us, but in general she seemed really nice – just like you'd described her. I tried to get her to tell me why she thought there was a problem, but she just insisted that there were things that she couldn't tell either us, or your mother about.'

'Maybe she's starting to lose it... like Carmela.' Offered Rosa, struggling to think of any rational explanation; or maybe she doesn't think you're our social equal,' she said, almost smiling.

'That was the main reason why my grandfather was considered unsuitable in the thirties, and why they had to run away... but your *nonna* was very definitely on their side, so it would be a bit hypocritical of her to change her mind now... so, I don't think it's that.'

They sat silently for a couple of minutes sipping their *spumante*, each trying to solve the conundrum, until Rosa sighed and managed to redirect her thoughts, 'So tell me all about your grandmother. Was it all very exciting?'

He nodded, 'all very *Romeo and Juliet*, although the Capulets heavily outnumber the Montagues... You know the story, don't you?'

'Of course, but I can't remember which family was which.'

'Juliet was a Capulet, so she would be Chiara, and Tybalt would represent one or more of her brothers.'

'And they both end up dead because of a breakdown in communication, but because of that, the two families make up their quarrel and peace is restored.'

'Very impressive, I hadn't thought through the analogy in that much detail – I was thinking more in terms of drama and tragedy, but let's hope that Shakespeare was right about the consequences.' He topped up their glasses and they clinked them together. 'To a successful combined future for both the Capulets and the Montagues.'

She looked at him and smiled, 'There will be..now, tell me about your grandmother and stop distracting me by showing off how cultured you are.'

Over the next half an hour he did so and she listened, enthralled, occasionally closing her eyes to try and imagine the scenes that Paul was describing. 'So we don't need to go out to Bargino any more,' she said when he had finished.

He shook his head, 'I think that now that I know where everything happened, I'd like to look at the actual places and, you never know, now that I have some information to start with, people might be more willing to talk to me. The people who helped them escape, or who worked for the Campolargos at that time, may still be alive. It would be really good if your *nonna* would come with us, but I don't think that that's going to happen any time soon!'

For the next three weeks they were able to see little of each other: Rosa had to prepare for an exam and because of the time she had missed was concerned that she wouldn't do well enough and would need to retake in a future session, so she was spending as much time as possible studying, either on her own or with other archaeology students; Paul, as part of his efforts to replace the income he had been receiving from his two students who had only needed lessons until Christmas, had agreed to translate a long medical article from Italian into English; this was proving more difficult than anticipated as he found he needed to spend a considerable amount of time in the library of the medical faculty to ensure that he was using the correct English medical terms. By the middle of March, however, the worst was behind them. Rosa had given her exam, which was conducted orally; the examining professor had offered a mark of twenty-eight out of thirty and, despite thinking that maybe she ought to have done better, she had accepted the mark. Paul had handed his translation over to the Assistant professor of endocrinology who had commissioned it, and received a handsome payment in return.

Paul and Rosa had met up briefly on the Thursday evening and decided that she would come to the *Birreria Centrale* the following evening, so that her curiosity about Paul's other friends, and their curiosity about her, could finally be mutually satisfied. Her parents were aware that she was meeting Paul, and expressed their disappointment, but did not stop her. Before she arrived, Paul had made sure that there would be space for her between himself and Gabriela, so that she would feel as comfortable as possible, having found it difficult to picture her in the environment of the *birreria*. He watched her slide past Gabriela into the empty seat and introduced her to Simon, Paloma, Claire, Gennaro and a couple of others who had turned out that evening, and then said he'd go to the bar and get a glass of wine, or a coke. 'Which do you prefer?'

'A big beer – like that,' she said, using her limited English and pointing to Claire's half litre of *birra scura*.

'Are you sure?'

'*Si fueris Romae, Romano vivit morae,*' she smiled sweetly.

'Eh?', Paul looked perplexed but Simon laughed.

'*Brava!*' and then to Paul. 'Uneducated plebeian. Do they teach you nothing on the wrong side of the Severn Bridge? When in Rome. Call yourself a linguist.'

Paul laughed with everyone else. 'OK. Do any of you patricians need a top-up while I'm going?'

When he finally got back from the bar he was pleased to find that Rosa was chatting away with his friends, it helped, of course, that she already knew Gabbi and Lucio, but she seemed to have been quickly accepted by the others too. Claire gave Paul a little smile and a discreet thumbs up sign as he sat down.

'Don't let me drink too much,' Rosa whispered in his ear when she was momentarily freed from the general conversation, 'there's something important I need to tell you.'

He raised an eyebrow slightly, and tilted his head in a 'tell-me' gesture, but she shook her head and said, 'Later, when we're alone,' and he had to be satisfied with that for the moment.

Rosa fitted in with his friends so well, and the conversation was so animated that by the time they left, just before eleven, he had almost forgotten what Rosa had said and was surprised when she dragged him into another bar before they crossed the river. She ordered two coffees, paying a small supplement so that they could drink them sitting down.

Paul drank his coffee straight away but she left hers untouched in front of her as she was anxious to begin talking. 'You need to come round to house tomorrow evening at seven.'

'What? Your house?'

'Yes. Of course, my house.'

'But...'

'Listen. Nonna's started acting very strangely. Yesterday, she went to see a priest.' She paused and looked at Paul.

'I'm sorry. I'm still not with you. I don't see what's strange about that. This is Italy; that's what people do, isn't it?'

Rosa sighed, like a teacher having to explain something that she considered obvious, to a particularly dull child. 'Nonna's an atheist. I don't remember her ever going to church, or ever having a good word to say about the church. Franci and I haven't done the First Communion and I don't think that Mum did it either. Nonna's always said that we should think for ourselves, and not let other people tell us what to think.'

'So why is she going now? Death bed conversion?'

'I haven't seen her looking as alive for ages as she did this afternoon. Yesterday she asked Mum where a priest who used to play with Mum when they were children has his church, and this morning she called a taxi and went there. I was down at the university earlier, so I didn't see her again until I got back about half past four. As you know, we've hardly spoken since I told her she was too old to understand love any more,' she gave him a guilty smile before continuing, 'but this afternoon, as soon I came in, she shouted for me to go to her before I'd even got my coat off. When I got to her sitting room, she was as friendly as she used to be. She said she was sure I'd be seeing you and that I should tell you to come round tomorrow at seven.'

'Why? I mean, that's great but, why the sudden change of mind? Did she give a reason?'

Rosa raised her shoulders and held her hands out, palms upwards, in an eloquent gesture indicating that she had no answer to the central question. 'I asked her... several different ways, but she just smiled sweetly and told me to run along and do some studying.'

Chapter 18

Paul went for a long run in the morning, trying, with only limited success to try and understand what was happening. Afterwards he stood, still thinking, under the shower until the water had turned tepid and then ate a few slices of *prosciutto* and some *pecorino* dipped in honey as a light lunch. He tried to read afterwards but found that he couldn't concentrate and, each time he turned a page, he had to look back because he couldn't remember what he had just read. Eventually, he gave up and went out for a walk into the centre. He couldn't believe how slowly time was passing; he tried to think how he usually filled his Saturdays but couldn't think of anything useful. At the market around San Lorenzo, he bought himself a new royal blue shirt with thin yellow stripes and piping, he then took this home and ironed it, putting a damp cloth over it to try and get the creases out where it had been folded in the packet. He looked at his watch again, and groaned – still only five past five. He tried reading again, and somehow his watch finally managed to reach twenty past six. It wouldn't take him forty minutes to walk up there, but he didn't want to rush and arrive there sweaty. As a result he had ten minutes wandering around the stalls in Piazzale Michelangelo before completing the final four hundred meters, when his legs suddenly felt like lead.

'Conte Melluso,' said the engraved brass plaque under the doorbell – no mention of Campolargo – he noticed. He raised his right hand and with extended index finger moved to within an inch of the bell-push. He noticed that his finger was trembling and took a deep breath as he concentrated on steadying his hand. Then he pressed. 'Drinnng,' he heard faintly coming from inside the house. He heard, or thought he heard, footsteps on the other side of the door and, for a moment, he wanted to turn and run as if he were a child again playing with his friends at ringing people's doorbells and then running and hiding. Fortunately, the feeling passed just before the door opened and Rosa threw her arms around him. She rested her head on his chest for a moment and then looked up and smiled out of a paler than usual face. He kissed the face lightly. 'Come on,' he said, 'throw me to the lions.' She smiled, took his hand firmly, and led him along a corridor which began with coat racks and was then decorated with brightly coloured abstract paintings.

The corridor ended with an arched doorway with a doorful of stained glass, but Rosa stopped at a door on the right hand side, just before the end. She tapped on the door, and a voice that Paul recognised from *Rivoire* said 'Avanti!'

Rosa's grandmother was standing to one side of the French windows that led onto a terrace, where he could see that some garden furniture had been covered up for the winter. Paul guessed from her position in the room that she too had felt nervous about this meeting and had preferred to walk about rather than sit still.

'Hello again, Paul,' she said, stretching out a hand, which he took and shook gently. 'Please sit down – you too, Rosa.'

The room was comfortably furnished with a two seater cream coloured leather sofa and two small matching chairs grouped around a glass-topped oval coffee table, supported on a sculpted central plinth that appeared to be made up of three or four contorted human figures, looking a little bit like a Rodin sculpture. There was a large mirror framed in, what Paul thought was beech, on the wall facing the French windows, while a long, low bookcase ran along the whole of the wall facing the sofa. There was an oil painting of a mountain scene, again in a simple beech frame in the middle of the wall above the bookcase, but no other decoration on the three walls he could see without turning away from Rosa's grandmother. He felt a light pressure on his arm and allowed himself to be guided to the sofa by Rosa, who sat down very close to him, maintaining hold of his hand.

'I'm afraid that I haven't made your lives very easy over the last few months, and I really am sorry for that but..' and she raised her right hand so that she was almost pointing at them, 'I did have – or perhaps I should say, do have – a very good reason. Part of the reason why I haven't given you an explanation is because you might find it hurtful to know, but I've come to realise that the real reason, and the one that I've lied to myself about, is because I'm frightened about the consequences for me – cowardice, I suppose you could say.'

'But, Nonna...' began Rosa as her grandmother paused.

'No, Rosa. Be patient, until I've finished,' she gave a strained smile. 'Now that I've finally worked up the courage to confess, I need to just go through with it.' She paused again and then gathered herself to continue. 'Not long before my sister Chiara eloped with your grandfather, my family introduced her to a very dashing young man called Gian Giacomo Melluso – Yes, Rosa, the same one – the Campolargo family was always very good at being in the right place at the right time or 'backing the right horse', as I think you say in England. Well, Gian Giacomo was not only rich, handsome and intelligent, but what was far more important to my family, particularly my father and my eldest brother, was that he was a cousin of Alessandro Pavolini and they were very close.' She shot a glance at Paul, 'You know about Pavolini?'

He confirmed this with a nod and she continued. 'Well, it appeared that Pavolini was destined for the very top, so my father was keen that there should be a marriage between the two families, and Pavolini, being no fool himself, and aware that my father was very influential, was also keen to make the alliance. I think that probably, the collapse of their plan infuriated them more than the fact that Chiara had gone, but all it really meant was that their plan was delayed. Gian Giacomo was given what he described to me later as "a reprieve", and told that in due course I would be his bride – it didn't really make any difference to him – in fact, I think he was probably grateful for the delay. He was told that I was hot-headed and opinionated and that he needed to use all his charm until we were married – and the one thing that he did better than anyone else was charm.'

'How do you know that he was told how to behave with you?

She gave a little snort and a bitter smile, 'Oh, once we were married, he told me quite openly that as far he was concerned the marriage was just a business arrangement, that he expected me to be nice to him but that he would do whatever he wanted, whenever he wanted and it was very clear that it would also be with whoever he wanted. I was a fool. He could spend hours talking about literature and the arts and the things he wanted to do to improve people's lives. He said how he hoped that he could influence his cousin to do good things in the future and, if ever I, living my cocooned life beyond San Casciano happened to hear of something bad that the Fascists in Florence had done, then it was always something that he had been arguing against, or would have argued against if he'd been certain of having the right person at home to believe in him.... It was all lies, of course, but I was too naive to see it; I had so much self-confidence that it was obvious that I was the sort of woman who would be able to give him the strength and support he needed to turn Italy into a good country.... Yes, I know, I was a fool, but you have to remember that I was only just sixteen when Chiara left, and after that there was no-one to advise me about what was right and what was wrong. I was always the clever one, but Chiara was the one with all the common-sense...'

Paul passed her a tissue out of the box on the coffee-table as he saw that there were tears in her eyes. She gave a little smile of thanks and then continued. 'As soon as it was clear that Italy was going to get involved in the war, the marriage was arranged and then everything changed; I never knew whether he would be coming home or not, and if he did, what time it would be – occasionally he even brought other women home with him.'

'Nonna!' Paul disengaged his hand from Rosa's and put his arm round her.

'Shhh... Go on, Signora.'

'You don't need the details of what my life was like as Signora Melluso – but you can probably understand why I don't use the name – even saying it makes me feel unclean... Everything changed in July of forty-four. Everything was chaos in the centre of the city and people only left their houses if they absolutely had to; it was best to keep the doors locked and the shutters firmly closed.... Bans of fascist thugs were roaming the streets and quite a lot of people were shot. It was July the twentieth when I heard lots of shouting and whistles from the streets around Piazza Donati where we lived – I say "we" but I hadn't seen him for three or four days. He was working as a liaison officer with the Germans and usually slept at headquarters, or with one of his mistresses – I didn't really care. Well, I was looking through the slats on the shutters when a desperate looking man ran into the Piazza and moved towards one of the other two streets leading off, but then checked, moved towards the other, then stopped again and started to move towards the shadow on the far side of the Piazza. He might have been able to kill a few of those who were chasing him as he would have the element of surprise, but he wouldn't have lasted more than a few seconds. I don't know why, but without thinking I rushed to the door, opened it a crack, and called out "Here". I got the door closed behind him just as the first of his pursuers came into the piazza and luckily they didn't see where he'd gone. As the man came in I pushed him against the wall with my hand over his mouth to keep him quiet while I looked at the door, terrified of what might happen next...' She stopped and looked out of the windows, tears flowing freely down her face.

'And what did happen next, Nonna?' said Rosa gently, reaching across to take her hand.

'I looked round, straight into his eyes, and realised that it was him.'

'Who?' said Rosa, confused, thinking that it had to be Gian Giacomo Melluso, but not understanding why that would be a surprise.

'It was Max, wasn't it?' said Paul.

I think he was more shocked than I was; Chiara and I looked very similar, and the light in the hallway wasn't bright. He just put his arms round me, said "Chiara" and started to cry. Then the Germans started hammering on the doors of every house in the piazza. Max moved back from me and pointed his gun at the door – I'd completely forgotten about his gun, I was so surprised to see him. I almost pushed him back into the living room and then went and opened the door a crack. There were two of them, a German soldier and an Italian who must have been one of Carità's men. I think it was the only time since my wedding day that I'd been glad I was married to Gian Giacomo. The Italian recognised me and told me that they were searching all the houses looking for a dangerous escaped prisoner – fortunately, they accepted my word that they would only be wasting their time if they searched my house, and they moved on to another... Paul, when I told you that I didn't hear about Chiara's death until several years after it had happened, what I didn't tell you was that it was your grandfather who told me all about it; I can tell you what he told me about their journey back to England and about how she died, but not now – that's another story.'

'But, Nonna, how does this make it inappropriate for Paul and I to be together? I still don't understand.'

She shook her head sadly. Paul, who had begun to have an idea what this was leading up to, said a little shakily, Go on, Signora.'

Rosa's grandmother stood up and went over to the French doors so she was standing with her back to them. 'When he first turned up, to work on the estate near Bargino, with his big green eyes, that always seemed to be about to laugh, it was wonderful; he was so different to the other workers and to our brothers – and then he had a way of looking at you – especially at Chiara – that made you catch your breath. I think both of us fell in love with him although, because Chiara was the person I loved most in the world, I managed to convince myself that what I wanted more than anything else was for them to be happy. It was probably just as well that they escaped together, as I'm not sure how long I could have kept on pretending to myself that I was happy for him to be Chiara's... Anyway, in forty-four, I was so unhappy that I couldn't hide it any longer.... He didn't have a chance.... Max stayed for four days – probably the happiest four days of my life.... Halfway through the third night, the bedroom door opening woke me up and Gian Giacomo was there with a gun in his hand, taking aim. He was taking his time over it because it was dark and his eyes obviously weren't used to it yet.'

'So Paul's grandfather killed mine. Is that all! I don't blame Paul for that – it's nothing to do with him.'

There was a slight shaking of the head from the old lady and then she said steadily, 'No, Max didn't kill Gian Giacomo – I did. He was going to kill Max, but he didn't think about me – I suppose he didn't think I was capable of doing anything – but Max's gun was on the floor by the side of the bed. I just grabbed it, lifted it and pulled the trigger. The bullet could have gone anywhere – I think I closed my eyes as I pulled the trigger – but we were lucky – if I was aiming for anything, I suppose it was the middle of his body, but the bullet got him just below his left ear.'

Rosa's hand was over her mouth and her eyes opened wide, but Paul's mind and thoughts were working rapidly – he had understood. He stood up and moved behind the old lady and placed a hand gently on each shoulder and said softly, 'But Gian Giacomo wasn't Rosa's grandfather was he?' He felt her shoulders sag and placing an arm round her guided her back to her chair, worried that if he didn't she might collapse. He poured a glass of water from the jug on the table, placed it in her hand and guided her hand towards her mouth. Then, turning to Rosa, who was watching fascinatedly, 'Does it make any difference to you if I'm your first cousin rather than your second cousin?'

With an effort, she managed to pull herself together, 'Of course not,' then giving him a brief kiss, she got up and went to kneel on the polished terracotta tiles in front of her grandmother who she embraced. 'It's alright, Nonna. It makes no difference but... thank you, thank you so much for telling us. It must have been terrible keeping this bottled up for all these years... Mum knows?'

Maddalena shook her head, 'When she was little, it was easiest for her to think that her father had been killed in the war, like plenty of other fathers and then... once you start living a lie, it's not easy to change it. By the time she was old enough to have understood if I'd told her that her father wasn't who she thought he was, I didn't have the courage to tell her that I'd lied to her all her life – and I couldn't have told her that her mother was a murderess, could I?'

'Oh I don't know, Nonna. Having an exotic mother has its attractions.' Paul was glad to see that they were both smiling now. 'So you've never told anyone?'

'Not until the day before yesterday... I'm afraid I exploited an old playmate of your mother. Lorisse Foresta was a nice boy, always very earnest. He lived just across the road from us when we lived in San Frediano and he absolutely adored your mother who was just a few months older than he was. She, of course, had her eyes on older, more glamorous boys, so she broke his heart and he became a priest – she denies it, of course. Anyway, even though I've had nothing to do with the Church or priests for years, I know that whatever is revealed to them in the confessional goes no further – so I confessed. I had to talk to someone because I wanted to know what could happen if I told you everything.'

'And what did he say?'

'Well, apparently I've got a few hundred years to do in Purgatory, and I should be spending most of the rest of my life saying prayers and lighting candles.' She smiled mischievously.

'No, Nonna. That's not what I meant, and you know it.'

Maddalena caressed Rosa's hair fondly. 'Well, if you decide to denounce me to the police, there'll be a bit of a fuss in the newspapers and the Campolargo and Pavolini names will be back in the news again; but the authorities are very wary about reopening old wounds and legally everything will be brushed under the carpet: Statute of limitations; self-defence, old age, senility... More importantly, there is apparently no legal obstacle to cousins marrying; I thought it had been banned, but apparently not.'

Paul interposed, 'It's something I'd already asked about – my sister is a nurse – we were only talking about second cousins at the time but she said that even for first cousins there's no problem.. it's just advisable to have a medical check-up first.'

At that point there was a knock on the door of the room and a voice called, 'May I?'

'Come in, Franci.' The door opened and Rosa's sister stuck her head around, taking in the sight of the little group clustered together, with poorly disguised curiosity.

'Mamma wants to know if you'll be eating with us, or if she should put something on one side for you and Rosa.'

'We've almost finished now, I think. Tell your mother that Paul will be staying and that he'll be a regular visitor from now on.' And to Paul, 'We have lots more to talk about, but nothing else that can't wait.' Even the poor attempt to disguise her curiosity had now slipped from Francesca's face. 'Oh, and Franci,' she called as the head began to withdraw, 'ask your father to put his best bottle of *spumante* to chill. We'll be through in ten minutes.'

When Francesca had closed the door again she said, 'There's is just one more thing that you probably should know... My husband had a document case with him when I killed him. Inside it were detailed plans of all the defensive installations on the Gothic Line. I wanted Max to stay here where I could have kept him safe, but he said that if he could get the plans through to the Allies it could save thousands of lives. He promised me that he would do everything he could to get back to me but... after he left just before dawn... I never saw or heard from him again. I thought that he'd just abandoned me like everyone else... it wasn't until Rosa told me how cruel I was a few weeks ago that I started to realise that he hadn't been able to come back.... I'm so sorry.'

Rosa stepped up to her grandmother and spoke firmly and clearly. 'Paul's here now, and it's as if your Max had come back. We'll do our best to live your life for you – like a sort of memorial to yours and Max's love.'

Maddalena put her arms round her granddaughter. 'Thank you Rosa, that's really sweet of you, but it's not what I want. I want you and Paul to live your own love, not to try and recreate mine, or even Chiara's.... Now, let's go and drink this *spumante.*'

Epilogue

Although Paul, was now welcome in Rosa's house at any time, they still continued to meet elsewhere sometimes, as they were never really alone in the house. One evening, a couple of weeks later, when Rosa sat down opposite him at a table in the *Enoteca Fuori Porta*, he could see that she was bursting to tell him something.

'Do you remember Antonio – from the gymnastics team? Well, he rang earlier – it's the Italian National Championships on the fifth and sixth of April and he wants me to go with them.'

'But... you...'

'No. Not to compete. He wants me to go and help the team out during the competition – giving advice and reassuring some of the younger girls.'

'That's good,' said Paul, genuinely pleased for her, even if it meant being without her for a whole weekend, 'where is it being held?'

'Lissone... just north of Monza,' she added as he looked blankly, then she smiled and took his hand. 'I only need to be with the team while they're in the hall. There is a bed available for me in the hostel where they'll be staying.' She watched as a broad grin spread across his face.

'But if you got a better offer, you might consider it.'

'Mmmm. Just think – there'll be all those agile male gymnasts around, not to mention the Lissonesi.'

'I think you're probably better looking for a long distance runner. Stamina could turn out to be very important.' She leaned forwards and kissed him, only breaking away when a waitress gave a discreet little cough alongside them.

The hotel that Paul had managed to book after several phone calls was a medium sized hotel on the outskirts of Monza, built above a Restaurant and Pizzeria and with its own private car-park. A friendly looking man in his late thirties with hair that was just beginning to recede was on reception when they arrived. He took Paul's passport and Rosa's ID card, promising to return them later that evening and showed them up to their room. The room was spacious and brightly decorated with two red walls and red bed linen contrasting with white woodwork and red and white flock wallpaper on the remaining wall. The en-suite bathroom, however, appeared to have been decorated by someone who hadn't communicated with the main decorator, as the dominant colour was royal blue with white trim and a champagne coloured suite.

As soon as they had viewed the room, Rosa allowed herself to fall backwards onto the bed, being careful, Paul noticed, to make sure the weight was taken by her right side where the collar bone hadn't been broken. 'I'm completely at your mercy,' she said with a smile.

Paul sat down beside her, leaned over and kissed her lips while sliding his right hand up her top. He stopped when he encountered her breast and his thumb circled her nipple before he moved his hand round so that it was behind her back where he could gently raise her up.

'Come on. Food first. We need to get your energy levels up. I don't want you passing out on me, you wanton!' She laughed, got up, and headed for the garish bathroom.

'Just give me a minute.'

'When they got back to the room and closed the door behind them, he pulled Rosa towards him and kissed her hungrily, excited to feel her tongue feeling its way around his. When he felt her easing his shirt out of the top of his trousers, he withdrew from her mouth and let his lips slide over her cheek and down onto her neck. Then she tilted her head back exposing the full beauty of her throat and he carried on exploring with his lips and tongue. As his shirt came free and she started adroitly to undo his buttons, he moved his mouth away from her and started to ease her top up, until she had to momentarily leave his buttons and raise her hands over her head so that he could slip the silky turtle-necked garment right off and drop it on the floor behind her. He breathed in and held his breath for a moment, admiring the perfection of her braless form. She smiled and allowed him to gaze for a moment before moving in again and quickly undoing the last two buttons and moving onto his belt. As she did so, he gently cupped a breast in each hand and then moved in with his tongue making little circular movements as he felt his trousers being pushed down over his hips. Moving his own hands behind her he managed to open the clip on her waistband and then pull down the zip that was keeping her skirt up. Before the skirt had reached the ground he had eased his fingers inside the top of a pair of scarlet pants and slid them down over sinuous hips honed by years of gymnastics.

As he slid the pants down, he allowed his lips to run down over her body, between her breasts and over her flat stomach, lingering a moment on her Mount of Venus, before coming to a halt on her upper thigh as his hands reached the floor and she was able to step out of her pants. He then moved her back so she was at arms-length so he could take in the full extent of her beauty. Her instinctive reaction was to cover herself with her hands. 'We can wait, if you want... you don't have to do anything before you're ready.'

In reply, she moved her hands and put them behind her head for a moment so she looked like a Bernini statue, then she moved her hands forward again and, placing them behind his head, pulled him towards her. 'Now,' she said, and then with a desperate ragged edge to her voice, that he found irresistible, 'I'm ready now – please!'

###

Discover other titles by Phil Whitney

- Off the Beaten Track in Italy (Travel Guide)

- The Visitor's Guide to Florence and Tuscany (Travel Guide)

- Affairs of State (Available in 2016)

Keep up to date at www.facebook.com/Phil.Whitney.Author